"You're ... provocative woman at this ball."

She breathed a sigh. "You really think so? I'm not aware of this."

"You're certainly a temptress, luring to your side every man here."

"And what of you, kind sir? Are you aware of how devastatingly handsome and mysterious you are?"

"No, my attention has been focused on one woman in particular, and I'm dancing with her now."

She tilted her head, keeping her gaze on him. "Are you always this forward?"

"*Oui*." He chuckled. "Are you?"

"It's for you to find out."

His dark eyebrows lifted. "Am I to believe you are this way because you're tempted to taste the forbidden fruit?"

His charm hypnotized all of her senses, weakening her limbs. To keep from falling under his spell, she changed the subject. "What is your costume, kind sir?"

"What do you want me to be, *Chère*?"

Her heart knocked against her ribs. "That's not a fair answer to my question."

"The truth is, my She-Devil," he replied, huskiness filling his voice as his fingers stroked her hand, "this costume was a last minute decision. So please, tell me what you think I might be, and it shall be so."

Praise for BELONG TO ME

"I really enjoyed the pace of this book, it flowed really fast with no wasted details. There is a really good plot in the story as well. The touches of humor easily raise a smile and...her characters are passionate creatures who are attracted to each other in spite of themselves....Full marks to Phyllis Campbell for a very entertaining read and some very memorable characters."

~Mary, A Romance Review (5 Roses)

"Ms. Campbell does not disappoint the reader in her story....The reader is brought back in time, as the historical setting is realistic and well written without too many frills or over-explanations. Ms. Campbell has written an historical worthy of any well-known mainstream author, and has proven that this genre suits her very well. After a long time of not reading in this genre, this reviewer was happy to discover an author like Ms. Campbell in the e-book industry. Her writing career merits close watching as this reviewer foresees more to come from this very talented author."

~Val, Love Romances (5-Stars)

"A delightful romance with well-done mystery interwoven amidst the love story. Phyllis Campbell's criminals add a brilliant blend of the sinister and comical in their actions. There are just enough twists and turns in solving the crime that the reader will continue to be surprised. This is a fun read that anyone who enjoys a good historical romance will want in their collection."

~Gina, Love Romances (5 Stars)

Belong to Me

by

Phyllis Campbell

This is a work of fiction. Names, characters, places, and incidents either are the product of the author's imagination or are used fictitiously, and any resemblance to actual persons living or dead, business establishments, events, or locales, is entirely coincidental.

Belong to Me

Contact Information: info@thewildrosepress.com

Cover Art by Nicola Martinez

The Wild Rose Press
PO Box 708
Adams Basin, NY 14410-0706
Visit us at www.thewildrosepress.com

Publishing History
First American Rose Edition, 2009
Print ISBN 1-60154-626-2

Published in the United States of America

Dedication

I want to thank my good friend
Lisa Dawn MacDonald,
because without her encouragement
this book would have just been a memory.
Thanks, Lisa, for your words of wisdom!

Chapter One

New York 1852

The masked man in black glanced her way. Charlotte Hamilton held her breath as her heartbeat started a frantic rhythm. This was him...the very person she had come to seduce tonight.

Charlotte's palms moistened inside blood-red-gloves as she took deep breaths in hopes of calming her nerves. Amongst the couples crowding the ballroom, the mysterious man wearing black weaved around them, his cape flipping out from behind until he stood with a group of aristocrats.

The way he moved and tilted his head reminded Charlotte of yesteryear. Now after two years, she'd be able to confront her absentee husband.

She'd been in a foul disposition since arriving in New York three days ago because the rotten lout she'd married couldn't be found. Finally, her friend, Ian Fauxley, discovered her husband would be at this very ball tonight, looking for a woman dressed as the She-Devil.

Charlotte grinned. Her plan was unfolding perfectly. Her truant husband would think she was his informant for his current investigation, but instead, he'd meet *her*...the wife he hasn't seen for two years.

Dressed in midnight from the silk scarf covering his hair to the tips of his polished knee-boots, Neil Hamilton exuded confidence and charisma. When he had rescued her from kidnappers years ago, she'd fallen in love with him. And now, from across the room, those memories she'd stashed away assailed her.

His lips curved into a grin while he moved away from the influential people he'd been conversing with and kept his focus on her. The crowd around her seemed to disappear, leaving her staring only at him.

The shape of his chiseled jaw and the structure of his muscular frame emphasized his build. His cape had been tossed over one shoulder, displaying his loose-fitting raven colored shirt and tight trousers. Was his costume a pirate? But the long cape suggested he was not. When she met his eyes through the mask, his intent stare made her heart's rhythm increase triple-fold.

Had she forgotten to breathe? Insecurity spread through her, a feeling not experienced since she'd been a bookish girl. She whipped around and grasped her friend's arm.

Charlotte breathed slower, trying to regulate her quick heartbeat. "I don't think I can go through with this."

Mrs. Allison Archibald patted Charlotte's hand. "Do not fear. Simply remain the She-Devil you've portrayed for the last half hour. Your husband will be swept away by your charm." Allison pulled away and eyed Charlotte's costume. "And he'll definitely be enthralled by your seductive attire."

The tight-fitting, blood red gown squeezed Charlotte's chest, threatening to cut off her breath. She ran a shaky hand down the silk waist. The material molded to her curves like a wet cloth. A low-cut bodice showed more cleavage than she'd ever displayed, and she moved her hand to cover the exposed skin. Red gossamer sleeves hung straight on her arms, gathering at her elbows, and the skirt flattened against her body. Her attire was indecent compared to the others here tonight. Although her friend's Egyptian gown was alluring, it didn't come close to being as seductive as Charlotte's costume.

"How can I seduce a man when I've not done this sort of thing before?" Charlotte's voice squeaked as panic gripped her throat.

"Nonsense." Allison flipped her hand through the air. "You were the belle of the ball back home. Men from all over want you. You have a way of seducing them with your smile and your words. Albeit, this time you'll be going a touch farther, but I'm confident you will turn out a great performance." Allison grinned. "After all, you've had me as your teacher for two years."

Charlotte chuckled stiffly. "Indeed, but now the time is at hand, and I fear I may turn into a coward."

"Think of it like this; you are both in mask, and he doesn't know who you are."

"Not yet, he doesn't." Charlotte arched an eyebrow.

"Oh, my dear friend. Where is your sense of adventure? Where is the bold woman who only a month ago suggested traveling to New York to find that good-for-nothing Mr. Hamilton so she could exact revenge?"

Charlotte breathed deeper, steadying her heart. "You are correct. I shall put aside my worries for now and become the She-Devil I'm dressed to be." Before her doubts took control, heavy footsteps vibrated on the floor behind her. A mixture of spice and leather wafted around her, stirring unknown quivers in her stomach.

He was here! The time was at hand.

"Bonjour, Mademoiselle."

His deep French accent sent heated tremors spiraling down her spine, and Charlotte shivered. She should hate him, but now, the only revenge she sought was to seduce him and make him desire her, just as she had longed for him all that time. She would dangle her charms within reach but would not let him follow through with his desires. The final blow would be presenting him with the annulment papers.

Served him right for breaking her heart!

Straightening her shoulders, she turned to face him. He stood dangerously close, and a soft gasp sprang from her lips. His tall frame and wide chest made her throat grow dry. The top of her head barely reached his chin.

Collecting her wits, she smiled. "Ye—" She cleared her throat. "Yes?"

His sculptured lips curved into a grin. "May I have the privilege of escorting you for the next dance?"

"Of course, but only because my partner has yet to claim me." She laid her unsteady hand on top his and he led the way.

Heat from his powerful body radiated from his skin. He spoke not a word as he slid his arm around her waist and took her in the dance hold. When their feet stepped in time with the string quartet's waltz, he pulled her body scandalously closer.

Under her hand, the smooth material of his shirt slid beneath her fingers. Flesh and sinew flexed under her palms. Tightening her lips, she held back the moan that wanted to escape, reminding herself that this was revenge and nothing more.

"Are you aware of the spectacle you've made tonight, *Chère*?"

Shock trembled through her body at the blunt sensuality of his words. Did he know who she was? Of course not. He wouldn't know her true identity until she removed her mask. And even then she wondered if he'd recognize her.

"I don't care what people think of me," she admitted.

"You're certainly the most provocative woman at

this ball."

She breathed a sigh. "You really think so? I'm not aware of this."

"You're certainly a temptress, luring to your side every man here."

"And what of you, kind sir? Are you aware of how devastatingly handsome and mysterious you are?"

"No, my attention has been focused on one woman in particular, and I'm dancing with her now."

She tilted her head, keeping her gaze on him. "Are you always this forward?"

"*Oui.*" He chuckled. "Are you?"

"It's for you to find out."

His dark eyebrows lifted. "Am I to believe you are this way because you're tempted to taste the forbidden fruit?"

His charm hypnotized all of her senses, weakening her limbs. To keep from falling under his spell, she changed the subject. "What is your costume, kind sir?"

"What do you want me to be, *Chère*?"

Her heart knocked against her ribs. "That's not a fair answer to my question."

"The truth is, my She-Devil," he replied, huskiness filling his voice as his fingers stroked her hand, "this costume was a last minute decision. So please, tell me what you think I might be, and it shall be so."

She looked away from the shadow of his eyes peering through the mask, and scanned his body. Perfectly he fit in his dark and mystifying attire, so flawless it made her heart skip a beat. Too bad he didn't want her as a wife two years ago. Perhaps she wouldn't have thought she had wasted the last twenty-four months of her life.

"I don't rightly know." She shrugged. "Are you a night rider?"

"I have a better idea. Since you are the Devil, I shall be Hell."

Lost in a dream, she gazed into his masked face. "If you are Hell, then I'd gladly become wicked just to be with you."

He tightened his hold on her, and her breasts brushed his chest. They danced entirely too close, but she didn't protest. It was as if a warm blanket of comfort had wrapped around her. All humor disappeared as desire crept into her body, weakening her limbs. The foreign flutter in her chest excited her. Silently, she cursed her body's weakness. This was not the way she wanted to react. She had to be in control—not him.

"Mademoiselle She-Devil? May I ask you a personal question?"

"What is that?"

"Are you by chance taken?"

Afraid to make a sound, she held her breath. Should she lie to him? Yet it was too soon to tell him the truth. With a firm decision, she buried her secret deep inside her, and would not give a hint to her true self. "No, I'm not taken."

"Who is the man that was with you and your friend?"

Her heart flipped with the knowledge he'd been watching her. "Which man?"

"The one dressed as an ancient God."

"He's my friend's escort."

The music came to an end and she leaned into him, not wanting to leave his arms. Warm, peppermint breath breezed across her cheek and tickled her.

"I'd like it very much if you belonged to me tonight." His words came out as a request, but his tone held more of a command.

Charlotte's heart soared. Never in her life had a man's voice or touch affected her like this, and although it scared her, the new sensation stirred something from within. She wanted more—wanted him to feel the same urgency flowing through her right now. The three days after she'd married him, her body had never reacted with such a need like it was doing now.

"I think, sir, you are indeed the devil and not I, for your words are tempting me far greater than I expected."

His face moved forward and she thought he meant to place a kiss on her cheek, which she'd gladly accept. Instead, his lips brushed her earlobe, sending chills down her spine.

"I'll show you sin if you'll let me," he whispered in her ear. "Give me the word, *Chère*, and I'll take you to a most pleasurable place."

Without waiting for her to answer, he withdrew and escorted her back to Allison. Charlotte's heart pounded with every step, yet desire shot through her. She'd never experienced this passionate longing, and God help her, she wanted it with her husband, this devilish, seductive man. She wanted him to love her, wanted him to be the father of her children...the way it should have been.

Chiding her thoughts, she quickly pushed them from her mind. That would never happen. She didn't want a man in her life that had trampled her heart.

"Until we meet up again, my sweet She-Devil." He bowed over her hand and gallantly kissed her knuckles, then leaned into her ear. "We have much to discuss...later." He pulled away then turned and left.

She glanced at the spot his lips had made on her gloved hand. Her mouth turned cotton dry.

Allison clutched onto her arm. "Good God, Charlotte. Is he not absolutely wicked?"

Charlotte's gaze followed her husband through the crowd. "You cannot fathom how close that is to the truth."

"What happened?"

Charlotte smiled. "He made me feel things I've never felt before."

"Did you seduce him?"

"I highly doubt I could accomplish such a feat with a man like Neil, but his words touched deep within my soul and awakened my desires. He was certainly seducing me. I may not have to work too hard tonight to get him where I want him." She met her friend's stare. "Which reminds me...did you secure a room for me?"

"Up the stairs and the third door on your left. The room will be vacant and nobody will disturb you."

She breathed a little easier. "Splendid. Thank God for your connections. Everything seems to be falling into place now."

"Then I shall not worry about you for the remainder of the evening." Allison winked, then left Charlotte's side and wandered to Ian Fauxley who stood with a group of men.

Charlotte waited anxiously as the next hour slipped by. While she turned suitors away who'd come to ask for a dance, her attention remained drawn to her husband. As Neil swept from person to person in conversation, his lithe movements held her captivated. His deep laughter filled the air and sent her heart into an erratic rhythm. People seemed to like Neil. Since leaving her side, he hadn't danced with anyone, and she smiled from the knowledge.

Earlier, Allison had assured her that Charlotte could seduce Neil. She'd had doubts, but no more. He couldn't keep his eyes off her and she couldn't stop watching him. Closer than she realized, her goal was in sight.

The night wore on and he periodically looked her way. Even though the mask shadowed his eyes, she suspected his thoughts were indecent. The prickly sensations racing up her spine made her ever so conscious of the lustful desires pulsing through her.

Why had she waited so long to experience this? Her widowed young friend, Allison, had led the wild life, moving from one lover to the next, which Charlotte had thought she'd wanted once upon a time. But the more she watched her lonely companion who had never found true love, the more Charlotte wanted a family. She yearned for Neil to see the woman she'd become, and damn it, she wanted him to suffer as she had suffered.

As if examining a painting, she studied her wayward husband. He carried himself like a gentleman and his genuine smile charmed many. Holding his drink, his lean fingers caressed the stem of the champagne glass. When she imagined his skilled fingers skimming her body, she grew warm with anticipation.

He turned and captured her stare—and held it. Time stood still. The tinkling of laughter dimmed, and she felt as if she were floating. She couldn't stop herself from remembering his scent, his voice, and especially his touch.

Without breaking their stare, he placed the glass on the tray as the butler passed, then moved in her direction. With each step he took toward her, her heart pounded until he stood in front of her yet again.

He mocked a small bow. "Bonjour again, Mademoiselle She-Devil."

"Greetings, Sir Hell."

A deep laugh escaped his throat, sending another round of sexual tremors shooting through her. This feeling rejuvenated her, assuring her that she could accomplish her seduction...and enjoy doing it.

"I thought you might like to take a stroll outside

for some fresh air," he boldly suggested.

Her heart skipped in a quick beat. The very thing she wanted was within reach. Her mind told her this was wrong, that she needed to reveal her identity first, but her heart argued, telling her not to pass the chance for passion.

"You're a mind reader?" she asked.

"No, but your thoughts are sinful, I cannot help but know what you're thinking."

Time to take the lead. Her plan would not work if she didn't act now. "I fear outside might be too chilly. May I suggest a room upstairs, instead?"

His brows lifted and his grin widened. "A room?"

"Yes. The hostess has provided me a room for the evening."

He took her hand, hooked it around his elbow, and led her toward the grand staircase. As they made their way toward their destination, the dim hallway threw discreet shadows everywhere, shadows made for lovers. Anticipation made her palms moist and she clenched her hands into fists.

He didn't speak. Nobody would recognize her, she was certain, but would they know Neil? Thankfully, he'd followed her into the room even as indecent and improper as it was. Once inside, he closed the door. One small lantern had been lit, shadows dancing on the walls. A bed sat against the far wall, and a loveseat and coffee table placed nearer to her.

He faced her. In the flickering light, his piercing look set her heart to a wild patter. "So, my darling She-Devil, would you entrance me by telling me something about the woman behind the mask?"

Charlotte tilted her head to the side. "You cannot wait for the unveiling? It's a little more than an hour away."

"I cannot."

She smiled. "I don't think I shall tell you.

However, I'm not from New York. I'm here with friends."

"I assumed as much. I'd have remembered seeing a woman so beautiful." His fingers trailed softly across her cheek.

"How long have you lived in New York?" she asked, trying to keep her voice from trembling.

"For quite a while." His fingers moved from her cheek down to her neck. The tingling sensations caused her breath to catch in her throat.

She swallowed hard. "I must admit, I feel awkward being alone with a stranger."

"But we're here due to your suggestion."

"I know...I just..." She swallowed hard. "I'm very nervous."

He gestured toward the door with a nod. "Then shall we leave?"

She smiled wider. "Alas, I cannot. I fear you have drawn me inside your web of temptation, a place I'd rather be than downstairs with the others."

"Nay, *Chère*, it's you who has lured me." He took a step closer, his fingers trailing further down her neck. "But there's an urgent need to discuss why I wanted to meet you tonight."

Her heart stilled. Since he thought she was his informant, how could she seduce him before he discovered she was not who he thought? She couldn't let him ask questions.

"I fear I cannot wait." She moved to the lantern and turned it lower. "You have pulled me into your power, and I find myself wanting more."

He shifted in his stance. Could he be uncomfortable because of her forwardness? But she refused to stop. Not yet.

"I must confess you are not the person I was led to believe you were." The tone of his voice was uneasy. "You've also trapped me with your charm, my wicked woman, but I really need to ask you some questions pertinent to my investigation."

She stepped next to him and laid her hands on his black silk shirt. Under her palms, his heartbeat pounded in an erratic rhythm. "You'd rather discuss something as mundane as that when you have me alone? I'm offering you something much more entertaining than talking."

His Adam's apple jumped and his body stilled. What if he didn't take her up on the offer? How could she seduce him if he wasn't willing?

He licked his lips. "I suppose we could postpone our conversation just a little while longer."

A thrill shot through her chest, stirring a volcanic fire within her bosom. He brought his fingers to her neck again, and this time there was a slight shake to his hand. She wanted to bask in her victory, but it was too soon.

His tender caress closed her mind as his fingers inched their way toward her breasts. She wouldn't stop him. Even if her life depended on it, she couldn't.

She moistened her dry lips with her tongue. "What would you like me to do with you, sir?"

He chuckled, sliding his free arm around her waist. When he pulled her against his body, she gasped. Pressed against her hips, his thick arousal caused her breathing to quicken and made her throat dry.

"You can do anything you'd like, my temptress, because I'm certain whatever you do will bring me sinful pleasure."

Tingles ignited and coursed through her body, yet she didn't want to stop the passion spiraling through her. This was not going the way she'd expected, this flirtation was spinning out of control, and she needed to be in control.

"You're making me feel things I've never experienced before," she admitted in a whisper.

His fingers trailed between her breasts, practically burning her exposed skin. A sexual shiver passed through her. She couldn't decide which was better, his tender caress or his sensual words.

"Can this be true, *Chère*? I fail to believe you're innocent."

As his stare daringly assessed her, Charlotte filled with wanting. She yearned to be close to him, to kiss him, to touch him—the husband she had wanted—here in this magical, private setting. A surge of excitement stirred between her legs.

"There's only one way to find out," she replied in a voice too husky to be her own.

A deep growl escaped his throat moments before he leaned in to kiss her. When their lips met, sparks sliced through the air and shocked her system into a fevered frenzy.

Moaning, she urgently circled her hands around his neck and crushed her mouth to his. His large palms cupped her face as his tongue slipped between her lips. Lust overrode everything except passion, desire, and the need to be accepted by the husband who had so cruelly rejected her on their wedding night.

Long, masculine fingers threaded through her hair and found the tie to her mask, then released it. He broke the kiss just long enough to gaze upon her features. Would the low glow of the lantern show him enough of her face to remember who she was?

His gaze narrowed as his forehead creased. She held her breath. Could he see her at all? And would he recognize her?

Within seconds, he shook his head and his mouth turned upward, pearly white teeth gleaming in the moonlight. "You're absolutely beautiful, just as I'd imagined," he whispered.

What did he look like? Could he be as handsome as he'd been two years ago?

Charlotte pulled on the ties of his mask, but he brought his lips back down to hers before she could see. The mask slid through her fingers as she concentrated on finding the opening to the scarf hiding his hair. The knot came apart and the material floated to the floor. She pushed her fingers through his silken waves, bringing forth his sigh.

Breaking the kiss, he pulled her to the loveseat. He gathered her in his arms as they sat. Urgently, his mouth met hers again in a wild kiss, and his hands moved over her body, enflaming her skin.

Gentle, yet determined lips wandered down her neck, toward the valley of her low-cut bodice. "You're certainly a She-Devil."

Before unfastening her gown, he kissed the mounds of her breasts. Her head spun and lifted her hopes as if she floated on a cloud. She couldn't stop him, or even herself, especially when he expertly pulled open her bodice. It didn't take him long to undo her corset and chemise. With bared breasts, the air tickled her skin.

Charlotte's mind screamed for her to stop him. This was wrong—morally wrong. She had come to New York to throw the annulment papers in his face. Yet, her heart argued this was exactly what she needed. Didn't she deserve one night of pleasure after being deserted by her husband following their wedding night? Besides, she wouldn't go much further. She'd allow him enough to get a taste of her passion before she'd take it away.

When he latched his mouth to one of her nipples, she gasped. His hot, velvety tongue swirled around the tip, making her moan. She held his head to her bosom, threading her fingers through his soft, thick hair.

All negative thoughts dissolved quickly. Nothing mattered except the heady sensations drowning her. He moved his mouth from one breast to the other while his hands held them in place. He devoured her, and she released a pleasurable sigh. Nothing in her life had felt this good—so sensational and fulfilling. Yet, even while her passion was being sated, the throbbing between her legs let her know what other things she yearned for.

He lifted his head, and with wide eyes gazed into her face. She held her breath. Hopefully, he didn't want to stop so soon.

Sliding his palm down her body toward her legs, he let his hand speak for him. He pulled up her dress, inch by incredible slow inch until he touched her stocking leg.

Her heartbeat hammered with excitement...and fear.

Neil's hand moved up to her bare thigh. She grabbed hold of him, stopping his progress. As much as she wanted his skilled touch between her legs, she knew she couldn't. That would only make her want more.

A grin touched his mouth before he covered her lips with his gentle kiss. She let out another moan and returned his kiss. Soon she relaxed, as did her thighs, letting his hands travel further up her legs. As his mouth made love to hers, he unsnapped her stays before delving his fingers into her moist body.

Pleasure surrounded her and the urge to part her legs overwhelmed her. With his help, she allowed him to touch her. There. One by one, he drove his fingers into her wetness. She raised her hips to meet his thrusts. His lips and tongue consumed her mouth, and she copied the way his tongue slid and caressed hers. Gripping the hardened muscles on his shoulders, she held on tight, keeping rhythm with his mouth and hands.

The tingling sensations spiraling through her body grew to an explosive peak, igniting and spreading between her legs. A deep groan tore from his throat as his fingers quickened. A shudder ran through her body, making her want to scream out in pleasure. Instead, she released a deep sigh while cascades of trickles rushed over her body.

As the incredible sensations faded, she panted. Trailing kisses down her neck to her chest, he left lightning paths of wetness in its wake.

Shameful desire washed over her, causing her heart to ache, and at the same time, panic suffocated her. How would this affect her future? After experiencing a taste of what this man could do to her body, could she let him go so easily?

But of course. All she had to do was remember how he'd broken her heart.

All too soon, he straightened and adjusted himself next to her. She pushed down her skirt, covering her lower half. He gazed upon her as his knuckles brushed softly across her cheek.

"Did I hurt you, my darling She-Devil?"

She chuckled, keeping her attention on everything but him. "Not at all."

"Then what troubles you?" His knuckles tenderly traced her face.

"The moment was perfect, but I can't believe I let things go this far."

"*Merci*. It was a most pleasurable experience." He leaned over and briefly kissed her lips.

"I'm relieved you do not think poorly of me."

"All I can think about is how passionate and desirable you are." He pecked her on her lips as his hand fondled her bare breast.

Charlotte's heart soared.

He'd said the words she had waited to hear for a long time. Trying to study him was impossible since the shadows were too deep and only showed the outline of his striking face.

A small light from the lantern touched his eyes. They were magnificent. He was every bit as handsome as he'd been when she'd first met him.

"Should we introduce ourselves now?" she asked. "I think it's only proper considering what we've done."

"I suppose we can meet formally." The French accent suddenly disappeared, just as she knew it would. "I'm from South Carolina, although I've spent the past two years in New York." He gave her a mock bow. "Mr. Hamilton at your service."

The name struck her again, like she'd heard it for the first time.

Anger welled within her, reminding her of his abandonment.

She wanted to hate him, but found herself trying to forgive him, the passionate moment too fresh in her mind.

She peered at him, the rugged jaw, the sculptured lips, and the seductive eyes. Oh, those eyes.

He touched his finger to her lips in a soft caress. "Now it's your turn. What intoxicating woman did I have the pleasure of kissing, touching, and hearing moan just now?"

A deep pain gripped her chest, yet at the same time, the hilarity of the moment struck her. She gave a throaty laugh. "Are you certain you want to know?" She laughed even harder.

His forehead creased in puzzlement. "Of course."

"Oh, Neil, you may not believe this." She pushed him away and righted herself on the sofa. After retying her underclothes and fixing the bodice, she arranged the skirts around her legs before facing him. Her hesitant chuckle emoted into hysterical laughter.

"Madam? What ails you, and why are you using my Christian name?" He put a hand on her forearm. "I never told you my name."

She narrowed her eyes. "I'm the last woman on

earth you ever expected sharing intimacies with."

His forehead creased. "Explain yourself."

"Mr. Hamilton, you have just been seduced by Charlotte Ashton Hamilton—your wife."

Chapter Two

Have I awakened from a nightmare?

Astonished, Neil stared at the sensual woman on the sofa beside him, his mind whirling crazily in dazed confusion. Wasn't she the woman who'd sent him the missive this afternoon about having information on his case?

No. Obviously this was some kind of joke. This magnificent woman who made his body burn with passion was his child bride? This incredible woman couldn't be the scrawny girl with a boy's figure he'd married two years ago—the same girl whose father blackmailed him into marrying her, Neil reminded himself.

He shook his head. What kind of game was she playing? He gritted his teeth, anger boiling inside his body like a volcano ready to explode.

She stared at him as fire brimmed in her eyes. But there were also tears. Perhaps her tears would extinguish the anger obviously raging inside her.

He leapt to his feet and shot her a glare. "The hell you say! Do you not think I would recognize my own wife? You, Madame, are not my wife."

She brushed the wrinkles from her gown. "Yes, Neil. I am. Unfortunately, I am Charlotte Hamilton, like it or not."

Through the shadowed room, he gazed over her body and face. She looked nothing like the child bride he'd remembered. "But...but...this cannot be," he stammered.

"It's true, Neil."

"My wife is in South Carolina."

She let out an impatient sigh. "I was in Charleston, until I decided to come looking for you. I am tired of being alone. I want a real marriage. I want a husband who loves me and wants heirs."

Panic consumed him. No! This could not be happening. He'd been at the height of his career for months. He couldn't let anything take him down, not even a seductive woman with kisses that melted his resistance. Especially not from a woman who proclaimed to be his wife.

"I'm sorry, but I cannot accommodate your wishes. Not today, and certainly not next month. Maybe not even next year." He breathed heavily, anger pumping through him faster.

Her face hardened and the tears in her eyes suddenly vanished. "Fine then, I want an annulment. I have brought the papers for you to sign. Yes, I know the church frowns upon annulments, but it also frowns upon abandonment." She rested her hands firmly on her hips.

He couldn't keep his gaze from roaming over her. Denying all possibility of her accusations, he shook his head. Nobody in New York knew he was married, so they would not likely play this game with him. And he had not told the She-Devil his first name. So how did she know unless…

"If you are really Charlotte, then tell me how we met."

Her lips stretched in irritation and she narrowed her eyes. "Two men kidnapped me and held me for ransom. My father hired you to rescue me. You disguised yourself as an old man to gain their trust. You delivered the ransom money from my father and saved me from being killed." She shook her head. "I had lost my head and thought myself in love, damn you, and when you wouldn't marry me, my father paid off your debtors as a bribe. Then three days after our wedding, you left."

His chest constricted and his world came crashing down around him. He knew she had been infatuated with him back then, but by the looks of her hardened gaze, he doubted that now. If she had a blade now, she'd likely run him through.

Neil balled his hands into fists at his side. "You conniving little hussy."

A bark of laughter escaped her. "What? Me, conniving? How did you come to that conclusion?"

"Because...because...look at you." His hand swept through the air, gesturing her length. "You knew how much you had changed. You knew I would be seduced by your beauty."

She tilted her head and tapped her foot. "Of course I'm conniving. I'd planned to show you what you've missed out on these past two years. Tell me, dear husband. Do you finally regret leaving me?"

Her remark came too close to the truth, but he still wasn't going to let this brazen little thing know it. He also didn't like her air of haughtiness. The stubborn lift to her chin and the fire sparking from her eyes sent chills of trepidation up his spine. Had he been the subject of a cruel hoax?

Besides, she did mention something about annulment papers.

A calming breath helped him gain back control. "Charlotte, tell me about this annulment you seek."

She heaved a sigh. "I have the papers at my hotel."

It still didn't settle well with him that she had this all planned out. Neil tilted his head. "Tell me, do you have a lover and that's why you're in a hurry to dissolve our marriage?"

"What in God's name are you talking about? The reason I want to end our marriage is because I don't want a husband who is repulsed by me."

"Repulsed?"

She lifted her chin. "Yes, Neil. I don't want a

husband who doesn't love me. I'm still a virgin. Do you know how humiliating that is considering how long I've been married?"

"What about now?" he asked. He swept his hand through the air. "You're now a goddess. You cannot tell me men are not sniffing your heels waiting to climb into bed with you."

He clenched his teeth. He'd be in line, too, damn it!

"Well..." She wrung her hands against her middle. "If you must know, there is a man who is interested in me."

He arched a brow. "Indeed?"

"Yes. Ummm...Ian Fauxley."

The name was like a slap in the face. Neil inhaled before forcing a laugh. "You must be mistaken, my dear. Ian is one of my closest friends."

"Think again, sir. He's my escort. He was the one who convinced me to seek an annulment. He was also the one who arranged our little meeting. It was me all along, not a woman who had matters to discuss your case."

Heat rushed to his face and he balled his hands. "I'd think Ian would have the intelligence to keep away from a married woman."

"And I assure you that you don't know him as well as I." She arched a brow.

"That's neither here nor there."

Tears sprang to her eyes and she wiped them away. She planted her hands on her hips and glared. "As it is, I still want an annulment. What time tomorrow shall I come to your office with the papers?"

"I don't know when I'll be in. Give me the name of your hotel and I shall come to you when I have the time."

She stepped closer and pointed her finger in his face. "You'd better not put me off. I will not leave until the papers are signed. Grant me an appointment, Mr. Hamilton. I'd like to get this finished."

"Let me check my schedule tomorrow, then I shall send you a note with the time of our meeting."

"Thank you." She brushed her hands down her dress once more. "Until then." She turned to leave, but he took hold of her upper arm and stopped her.

"Before you return to the party, we'd better fix your hair."

He stepped behind her and helped stuff the pins holding her auburn curls in place. Silky hair glided through his fingers and he was reminded how coarse it used to be. Now satin waves caressed his skin. Closing his eyes, he imagined her naked as her glorious locks stroked his bare chest. The scent of roses wafted from her body and floated through his head, stirring life into his body once again. Silently, he cursed himself and withdrew.

"There, you're now presentable," he said awkwardly.

She jerked away from him, then lifted her skirts above her ankles as she rushed out of the room.

He shook his head. Unbelievable. That beautiful woman was his wife? In the two years they'd been separated, he hadn't dallied with any other woman. Not that he hadn't been tempted, but his career came first. Strange how she had been able to melt him into submission and made him anxious for her kiss and touch.

Had his carefree life come to an end? He couldn't step into the role as husband as she'd wanted. Impossible. Not with his busy career.

Especially since he was working on an important case. A few of his clients had accused him of stealing from them. He convinced them to give him time to prove his innocence. The reason he came here tonight looking for the She-Devil was because he thought he had a lead. Granted, it surprised him when the woman started seducing him, but he needed to get answers.

And to think his conniving wife had this all planned. Very different from the gawky girl he'd known.

He exhaled a heavy sigh. Did Charlotte want to control him now as she tried to before?

Certainly, she wasn't this charming and seductive when he'd rescued her from kidnappers two years ago. His blood soured with the haunted memories. Back then, her boyish frame led him to believe she was in her twelfth or thirteenth year, so he'd coddled the poor, frightened child while they waited for her father. She must have decided then she wanted him for her husband. When her father promised Neil her hand in marriage as his reward, he tried to discourage the man from the disastrous match. That was when her father paid off Neil's debtors, and suggested that he'd take the money back if Neil didn't marry Charlotte. There'd been no choice. Marry Charlotte or go to debtor's prison.

Now he did have a choice.

At the time of his marriage, his investigation business wasn't a thriving career. Today things were different. He didn't need a wife, and he certainly didn't need any heirs. They would only hinder his future plans.

Neil raked his fingers through his hair and groaned.

How could he ignore her now? Her beauty had literally taken his breath away, and just thinking about making love to her made his trousers tighten from his growing arousal.

Damn, why was this happening?

****

Charlotte halted in front of a mirror before entering the ballroom. She swiped her fingers across her brow. Did she look like she'd experienced a man's passionate touch? Was it obvious? She glanced at the wrinkles in her bodice and smoothed them before continuing down her dress, flattening out any reminders of what had just occurred not too long ago.

Others might be able to tell what she'd done upstairs. She placed her cold hands on her hot cheeks, wondering if pleasure was still affecting her expression. Gingerly, she ran the tip of her finger across her mouth and over her swollen lips. Did her expression glow, or were lines of anger creased on her forehead that would betray her?

Grasping what pride she had left, she held herself erect and marched into the ballroom in search of Ian and Allison. She dared not tell them how everything turned out. But then, what had she expected? Did she think Neil would rush into her arms in joyous reunion once she showed him her passionate side? Although she despised what he'd done to her after they were married, she still longed for the man who could love her. Apparently her fantasy of how it would be was not reality.

She hoped she wouldn't look as flustered as she felt.

Her friends stood in the corner of the ballroom, staring into each other's eyes like they were the only two people in the room. Their love pulled at Charlotte's heart and made tears spring forth once again. Why couldn't love be that simple for her?

She groaned. Why had she lied to Neil about Ian? What possessed her to hint that Ian would be her lover? She supposed because he and Neil were friends, she lied out of embarrassment and humiliation. Hopefully, Ian would play along in this game of deceit.

Giving a polite nod to the men coming her way, she stepped past them and hurried to her friends. As

Ian glanced at her, his mouth hung open. Dark brown eyes stared at her, his eyes narrowing as she approached. His gaze swept over her disheveled appearance, and inwardly she cringed.

He knows. Oh, God, do they all know? She tried blinking away the tears threatening to spill from her eyes.

"What in the hell happened to you?" His voice rose as his gaze raked over her.

She put a hand up to his mouth. "Shhh, Ian. Lower your voice."

Allison grabbed her arm. "Charlotte! You've been crying. That's not what we'd planned."

"Allison, it's all right," Charlotte assured her friend. "I had not been thinking correctly. I thought once I showed him how much I'd changed, he'd want me." She shook her head. "But he doesn't. He wants the annulment." Tears brimmed in her eyes and she blinked to keep them from falling.

"Oh, Charlotte." Allison took both her hands and squeezed. "Tell me what I can do."

Charlotte pulled away and pressed her shaking hands to her stomach. "I wish to return to the hotel. I don't think I can stand to be here another moment."

"I shall call out the bastard," Ian snapped. "Where is he? What did he say to you?" He grasped her shoulders, his fingers digging into her skin. "Answer me, Charlotte." He scanned the crowded room, eyes blazing with fire.

A small laugh escaped her throat and she touched his arm. "Ian, thank you for being so protective, but considering who I was with, what he did wouldn't be considered ruining my reputation." She sniffed. "Besides, I was a fool for thinking he'd be ecstatic to see me and to notice how much I've changed."

Allison stroked Charlotte's hair. "You're talking

nonsense. Given the shock the poor man went through, I think if we gave him a couple more days..."

"No. My mind is made up. I will serve him the papers tomorrow." She sighed. "But for now, I would like to return to my room. I have a fearsome headache, and...and I would rather not think of the lie I told Neil."

Allison tilted her head. "What lie?"

"Please don't be upset," Charlotte fretted. "But the lie slipped out. I didn't want him to think I've been sulking for two years in his absence. He humiliated me, and I wanted revenge."

"What was the lie?" Ian asked warily.

She took a deep breath for courage and stared at him. "I told him you were vying for my attention, and I hinted I was considering making you my next conquest." She shrugged. "No other name came to mind. Please forgive me."

Instead of the angry eyes she expected to see from Allison, her friend threw back her head and laughed. "Oh, Charlotte. This is the most enjoyment I've had for a long time."

Charlotte scowled. "This isn't a laughing matter."

"I disagree. It'll be so exciting to watch your husband squirm in front of his friend."

Ian's face stretched in a smile. "I must admit, it'll be the first time in my life I'll be able to make him jealous. I'll rather enjoy our ruse."

"So, do you still plan on going through with the annulment?" Allison asked.

"Of course. I haven't lost leave of my senses just because of the passion we shared." *And passion it was!* She quickly ushered out the thought.

Charlotte scanned the ballroom. Unmasked people crowded the floor, but one lone figure captured her attention. She inhaled sharply. Neil stood against the wall, his gaze fastened directly on her. She tried to tear her eyes away, but now she could actually see him in the light.

So very handsome. More so, even when she first met him. Her chest ached with sadness. Why did this charming, seductive man have to be her heartless rogue of a husband?

From behind, Ian leaned to her ear. “Do you want me to speak with him?”

“Don’t look now,” she replied softly, glancing over her shoulder at Ian, “but he’s watching us. I don’t want him to think we’re talking about him.”

Ian moved closer and slid his arm around her waist. “Tell me when you want me to take him out back for a quick lesson in manners.”

His unexpected humor made her chuckle. Ian’s brown eyes softened and she smiled. “Thank you for easing my burden. I want Neil to believe his presence has no impact on me.”

“Do you want me to give you a kiss?”

“No.”

“Tell me what you want and this servant will obey.” He lifted her hand and brushed his lips on her knuckles.

She dropped her smile. “Just take me back to the hotel, please.”

He nodded. “Yes. Allison is also ready to leave.”

She stole one last look at Neil. His blank expression made her heart drop. Obviously, he didn’t care if she was in another man’s arms. Gritting her teeth, she hoped to revive her anger, but sorrow pierced her heart. The scar from his abandonment ran deep, and she feared she’d never be able to forgive him now.

****

Neil leaned against the wall, his arms folded across his chest as he studied the quaint scene with Charlotte and his friend. Damn, his wife. He couldn’t believe it, but she had succeeded in making him jealous. Ian cooed over her and kissed her hand, and Neil longed to be in his friend's place.

Itching for a moment alone with his so-called childhood friend, Neil balled his hands into fists. Never in his life had he been jealous of anyone, and he certainly wasn't going to start now.

When Ian left to fetch the cloaks, Neil pulled away from the wall. He strode to his friend as Ian waited for the butler to bring the garments. Ian must have sensed him standing behind him because he spun around.

Ian's eyes widened, then as quickly, he smiled. "Good evening. What brings you here tonight?"

Neil linked his hands behind him just to keep from strangling his friend. Ian was supposed to be his best friend, and yet he was the very man who wanted Charlotte as his mistress.

"I've come to the ball, just as you." Neil paused and rubbed his chin. "But why are you in New York?"

"I'm here with friends." Fauxley's back seemed to straighten more.

"I know you're here with my wife."

Ian hadn't reacted the way Neil expected. In fact, his friend's smile grew. "So, you've seen her?"

"Yes, and I cannot believe she's the same snake I married." Neil swiped his fingers through his hair.

"Snake, indeed." Ian chuckled. "Come now, you are over exaggerating. She's certainly not the girl you married, but she's no snake."

"You don't know her like I do."

"That was two years ago. Are you still blaming her for her father's actions?"

"When I turned down his offer, the bastard bribed me, knowing I had debts to pay. I know Charlotte was behind everything. So yes, I still blame her, damn it."

Ian shrugged. “As I said before, that was two years ago. I’m telling you, she’s changed.” He glanced in Charlotte’s direction. “What do you think of her now?”

Neil scowled. “What makes you assume I think anything about her?”

“Perhaps because of the way you’re acting.” Ian shrugged. “Did you not speak to her?”

“A little while ago.”

“Ah.” Ian nodded. “That would explain why she’s in a hurry to get back to the hotel. You must have disturbed her.”

“Yes, it was quite a shock for me, too.”

The butler returned with the cloaks and handed them to Ian. “I had better take these to the ladies.” Ian took a step back.

Neil touched his shoulder. “Wait. I was just wondering...umm, well, Charlotte mentioned you’re with her...that you are pursuing her.”

“Yes.”

Ian’s nonchalant attitude grated on Neil’s nerves. The way his friend stood so casually, so smug, as if he didn’t have a care in the world. The bastard!

Neil narrowed his eyes. “Forgive me for being blunt, but I must know—” He paused, choosing his next words carefully. “Are you planning on making Charlotte your mistress?”

Ian remained indifferent, standing so fearless. Neil’s rage boiled deep within, and it became difficult to control the urge to drive his fist through Ian’s face.

“As a matter of fact, I am. If she will have me,” Ian answered. “Did she not tell you she wants an annulment?”

“She mentioned it.”

“Are you going to give her one?”

Neil nodded. “You know I never wanted to

marry her in the first place."

"I'm relieved you haven't changed your mind. I was worried when you saw how beautiful she was, you'd want to reclaim your rights." Ian scratched his chin.

Neil laughed, although fury was the underlying emotion. "Beauty is only skin deep, and I know Charlotte's ugliness comes right from the bone."

Ian gave a self-assured smile. "I'm relieved you don't know her, because you'd feel differently. To me, she is a very beautiful woman inside and out."

Neil bit the inside of his cheek. His friend walked away, toward Charlotte and her lady friend. Ian took special care to put Charlotte's cloak around her shoulders, then he whispered something near her ear, which caused her to grin.

In the light, she did bear a slight resemblance to the girl he married. Her eyes sparkled when she smiled; her lips still heart shaped. But that was as far as the similarities went. Her body certainly didn't portray the figure she had as a girl of eighteen. Tonight he realized she had blossomed. A full bosom and small waist flattered her form. Curved hips, and shapely limbs belied the boyish frame he'd remembered.

Her beauty captured his heart, but he stamped down these lustful thoughts. Her vindictiveness and how she had manipulated him was hard to forget. People didn't change that drastically in a few short years. Because of her loveliness, she most likely used her beauty to influence men and charm them into her web of deception.

Charlotte walked out of the room on Ian's arm, but before going through the doors, she turned and looked at him. God, she was lovely.

He held her gaze for a brief moment before she turned up her nose and sauntered away.

Damn! What was wrong with him? He still felt

the imprint of her body against his. His fingers tingled with the memory of the smoothness of her skin. He cursed his wandering thoughts. He wanted to experience the softness of her body once more and hear her passionate moans of delight. She was the most sensual woman he'd ever known.

He growled. He'd either have to jump into a cold lake to get rid of these feelings and his lust-filled thoughts of the one woman he detested so much, yet desired so badly. Indeed, he was in trouble!

Chapter Three

The morning sun blazed through the polished windows of the dining room, heating Charlotte's face. She circled the spoon in her cup of tea as she stared outside. The city had come to life earlier than expected. Peddlers announced their wares, their voices ringing through the streets. The rhythm of horse's hooves on the cobbled street thundered in her ears, making the pain in her head throb with tension.

Ian had come to the hotel room this morning and called upon Allison. Together, they left to take in the sights in New York. They'd invited her, but she declined. Neil was bringing her a note today to confirm their meeting, so she must wait.

Charlotte frowned. It was hard to watch Ian and Allison together. When would her life be romantic? When would she find the man who would make her smile with a love-struck expression and smolder with emotion like Ian had for her friend?

Last night she'd actually let herself fantasize that life with Neil. The attraction between them had been mutual. His touch and sensual words had stirred a spontaneous fluttering in her chest, and when he'd kissed her, he'd woven a spell over her limbs, causing them to weaken. His skillful hands had stroked life into her body, and his tongue left her quivering for more.

She closed her eyes. She shouldn't have spoken so audaciously...and she shouldn't have lied to him about Ian. Why had she told Neil such an outlandish story? He would certainly expect Ian to act like the doting suitor now. Would Neil discover the truth before he signed the annulment papers?

With her head in her hands, she slumped in her chair. What if he didn't sign them at all?

No. She couldn't think that way.

Her restless night had made her irritable. Doubts filled her head and created tightness in her chest. Would their passionate moment of splendor last night change his mind about the annulment? Everything had been magical, but she couldn't bear to be with a man who didn't want her. Why had she entertained the thought of changing his mind after seducing him?

Ridiculous!

She growled, pushed away from the table, and marched to the window. The lovely summer morning beckoned her to come out and partake of its beauty. If she stayed on the main walkway in front of the hotel, she wouldn't get lost. Perhaps she might run into Neil on his way to see her. But then she didn't have a proper escort. How could she wander the streets by herself?

Yet as she studied the people, she realized there were several ladies taking a stroll by themselves. Charlotte shrugged. After all, she was still a stranger in this town. Once Neil signed the papers, she'd be gone.

Anticipation quickened her heartbeat. She hurried to collect her parasol then left the hotel room. Outside, a soft breeze teased the wispy tendrils around her face. She brushed away her hair and patted her knotted coiffure on top of her head. The parasol shaded the sun from her face as she wandered down the street.

Vendors held out their wares, trying to persuade her to buy their fruits, poultry, and even blankets. She passed, smiled and shook her head. The items they had didn't interest her. But when she passed the window exhibits, she slowed her walk to a leisurely stroll. The display of lavish dishes caught her eye. Next, it was the candlesticks that caused her to pause. When she moved by a window with the latest style of gowns, she came to a complete halt.

New York was much more civilized than South Carolina and the fashions were better on the eyes. Her dressmaker back home always designed Charlotte's frocks to match the newest styles.

In this particular window, she stared in awe at a shimmering blue evening gown with a daringly low-cut bodice. Fringe decorated the thin shoulders, and a tapered skirt appeared to fit snugly against a woman's legs. Charlotte closed her eyes, imagining how the silken material would caress her own legs as she walked.

She fought the temptation to go inside. If she did, she'd certainly buy the dress. Where would she wear such a gown? If she wore it back home, she'd set everyone's tongues a wagging. But here in New York, this evening dress was probably very popular.

"Thinking about your next seduction?"

The man's deep voice boomed from behind, startling her. She snapped her attention to his reflection in the glass window before swinging around to face him. Her heart leapt.

Coffee-colored trousers molded well to Neil's muscular legs, and his cream-colored shirt stretched taut underneath his matching waistcoat. Scolding her wandering eye, she looked back to his face and lifted her chin.

"What seduction are you referring to, Mr. Hamilton?"

An assured smile touched his lips and his eyes twinkled. "The next man you plan to seduce."

She was tempted to slap his handsome face. Instead, she kept one balled fist out of view in the folds of her skirt while the other tightened around the handle of her parasol.

"You're wrong again. Although I was admiring the dress, I knew I wouldn't be able to wear something so daring in public."

He turned his attention to the display window and cocked his head. "Why not? The bold dress you wore last night was just as stimulating."

She huffed. "Last night I was in costume. Last night I portrayed someone I could never be again."

He took a step closer as his fingers breezed up her cheek. "I wouldn't mind seeing that woman one more time."

Warm tingles ran rapid through her body, so she pushed his hand away. Her heart raced, but she concentrated on her anger. "Fortunately, I won't be staying in New York much longer, so purchasing the dress is out of the question." She waited for him to reply, but he remained impassive, so she turned toward the window. "Were you, by any chance, on your way to see me?"

"No."

She glanced over her shoulder and lifted an eyebrow. "No? And why not?"

"Because, I don't have any time for you today." He folded his arms and rocked back on his heels. "I'm working on a case that needs to be solved immediately."

She scowled. "If you are so busy, then what are you doing here?"

"If you must know, I was asking questions about my case in the shop across the street."

His gaze swept down her gown, and the color of his eyes darkened with desire. A thrill rushed inside her. Although she still disliked him, satisfaction filled her, knowing he found her alluring. She quickly cursed her body's response to his heated stare.

"Where is Ian?" he asked.

She lifted her chin and faced him. "Ian is with my friend, Mrs. Archibald."

"Why is he not with you?"

She let out a bitter laugh. "Why should it matter? You aren't concerned with my life."

"Last evening you gave the impression he came here with you, and you were going to be lovers, yet where is the overeager young swain now? Then, when I asked you if the man dressed as a God was your beau, you told me he belonged to your friend." He paused briefly and scratched his chin. "So, what other conclusion should I have drawn when he's not with you now?"

She stomped her foot. "You have an over-active mind, Neil Hamilton. Do you know that? But of course you do." She inadvertently flipped her hand. "You wouldn't be in your line of business otherwise. But to answer all of your meddlesome questions—I told you Ian belonged to my friend last night because I didn't want you thinking I was taken. I was very attracted to your mysterious character and I didn't want to frighten you away, you... jackanape!"

He threw back his head and loudly chuckled. "Oh, such language for a lady of high society."

Ignoring his comment, she took another deep breath. "The reason Ian Fauxley isn't with me now is because I asked to be alone. I expected you to send me a note, verifying our meeting. Ian has taken Mrs. Archibald out to show her some sights." She straightened her shoulders. "Have I answered all of your questions?"

His lips turned up into a mocking smile. "Yes."

His gaze moved over her attire again. His expression was not entirely unpleasant. When his blue eyes softened, butterflies danced in her stomach.

In defiance, Charlotte lifted her chin. "I'll be continuing my stroll since you're obviously out of sorts this morning. So, if you'll please excuse me."

Even as she scooted past him, he stayed in step beside her. His quiet presence annoyed her. She held her jaw tight, her lips stretching in irritation. "Now what do you want? More questions? I thought you had a case to solve?"

"Actually, I do have more questions."

She kept her angry march just slightly ahead of his. "Then please ask so you can soon be on your way. I know how very busy you are today. Too busy, in fact, to make time to sign a few papers."

He chuckled. "Fine. I'll make time. But you'll have to take the afternoon meal with me because that's the only free time I can spare."

She halted and turned her wide-eyed gaze at him. "Are you jesting?" Her hand flew to her chest as she laid the dramatics on thick. "The renowned Neil Hamilton, the investigator, actually has a moment during his meal to spare for his wife?"

"Do not mock me, woman."

She tilted her head. "What makes you think I want to dine with you? Have you forgotten you cannot stand to be in my presence?"

"Do you want to eat with me or not? Like I've mentioned, that's the only time I can spare."

"And where will our outing be?"

"Anywhere your scheming heart desires, my dear wife."

She scrunched her eyebrows together. "I'm not familiar with this city as you well know, so you choose the restaurant."

"I think you might want a private setting in case you are tempted to cut my throat." He smiled wickedly.

Unable to stop it, a grin tugged her lips. "You read me well."

"That's my business." He stepped closer and brushed his fingers along her hair. "And because I have the talent for reading people's thoughts, I know you still want me. Last night was merely a repartee for you. I can see it in your eyes. You ache for my touch, and you pray I'll ravish you with kisses. Admit it, Charlotte."

Gasping, she slapped his hand away and hoped he didn't feel her scalded cheeks. "You're sorely mistaken." She gathered her skirt and quickly stepped past him, calling over her shoulder, "You really are a cad!"

"My dear, Mrs. Hamilton?" His voice rose. "Are you going to meet me or not?"

Without turning, she shouted, "When pigs fly and hell freezes over!"

He laughed loudly. "All right, my dear. I will pick you up at your hotel on the noon hour."

She clenched her jaw and kept her feet stomping all the way down the street. His deep laughter rang through the street and made her cringe. Heat poured through her body from embarrassment, or was it from his touch?

Red, hot anger pulsed through Charlotte as she moved from shop to shop; purchasing items she wouldn't normally buy. It didn't matter how indecent the dresses were or how costly the jewelry. This was Neil's money, the little he'd sent her during the past two years. She'd never wanted to use it before, but now she couldn't wait to spend it all. Yet the excitement of spending money wasn't with her today. She worried he would follow her, and peering over her shoulder got tiresome.

While she loathed the very ground her uncaring husband slithered across, at the same time her body tingled in remembrance of his touch. And to make things worse, he'd known it and commented on her weakness.

Her feet ached from her tight shoes, bought only for looks and not comfort. She returned to the hotel sooner than she'd wanted. Unfortunately, it was just in time for the luncheon with Neil.

The man she met at the masquerade seemed so different from the man who'd left her after their wedding. Instead of cold and mean, he bore a close resemblance to the caring stranger who'd rescued her from kidnappers. Could she have been wrong about him all along?

No. Pain from his abandonment still held a fresh scar in her heart. When he'd rescued her, he'd shown her a kind and giving man; one she wanted with her always. It didn't take long for her to give her heart to him, but when he'd refused her father the first time, her stubborn pride had taken over. She couldn't let him slip through her fingers; she wouldn't allow that to happen. She'd been young and innocent, and her father had spoiled her beyond reason. And, when she'd set her sights on something, he gave it to her. That is why he had paid off Neil's debtors and bribed him to marry her.

Wearily, she moved to the full-length mirror in the bedroom and pulled out the pins that held her bun together. She brushed out the kinks then pulled back the sides with some new combs that glittered with diamonds.

The green day dress was discarded before her maid helped Charlotte change into a fresh gown. Light violet adorned the material and brought out the auburn tones in her hair. As she stared at her reflection in the mirror, worry creased her brow. Had she made a shambles of her life by her hasty decision last night? After all, he was the one supposed to be miserable. Not her.

The loud knock on her hotel room door sent her heart thumping. Her traitorous body experienced a healthy dose of sexual anticipation, and she cursed her weakness. She had to keep her mind on the annulment.

Squaring her shoulders, she walked to the front door, stopping her maid before the servant responded first. "I'll answer it."

The maid nodded and left the room. With a shaky hand, Charlotte opened the door. Neil had not bothered to change, and he still looked incredibly handsome. With his over-coat draped casually across his arm, he appeared very relaxed. She tore her gaze away from his physique and looked into his eyes. They were a soft blue and dreamy, testifying of his calm state.

She was far from relaxed.

"Good afternoon," she greeted without a smile.

"Good afternoon to you, my dear." His gaze boldly slid over her and she tried to ignore the chills running down her spine. She had to remember the annulment papers lying on the desk.

"Are you ready?" he asked.

She lifted her chin. "No, I'm not. I specifically remember saying I wasn't going with you, so if you will excuse me, I have more important matters to see to." She tried to close the door, but he blocked it with his arm.

"And I, my dear, will not be toyed with." He brazenly stepped inside and firmly shut the door behind him. "Let me see the papers."

Charlotte didn't hesitate in dashing unladylike to her bedroom and grabbing the documents. She hurried back to the sitting room. It was up to her to get this over quickly and painlessly.

Neil had made himself comfortable on one of the sofas, his arm outstretched across the top, ankles crossed, a vision of total relaxation.

She handed him the papers. "Sign it now, please."

His gaze skimmed the writing briefly and he leaned forward. "I'll read it later. I want my solicitor to go over it to make certain everything is in order."

She gasped. "Are you jesting? The solicitor I hired is very capable, and has a good reputation. I cannot believe you're doubting his abilities."

"I'm not going to trust the man, especially when he sympathizes with you."

She huffed. "You are extremely bullheaded."

Neil neatly folded the papers and placed them inside his satchel. He slapped his knee as he lifted himself off the sofa. "Now, do you want to dine with me or not? It'll be your loss if you decide not to join me."

She didn't want to, but her hungry stomach grumbled the decision for her. Besides, she needed to convince him to sign the document. "What could we possibly have to talk about? We can't stand each other, and we constantly disagree."

He took her hands in a loose hold. "Then we shall just have to find a subject we can both settle on."

"And what would that be?"

"We will find one, I assure you." His mouth stretched from ear to ear.

Oh, she wanted to hit him, spit in his face...or better yet, be held in his strong arms while he kissed her passionately. Silently, she cursed.

Without another word, he placed her hand in the crook of his arm and escorted her out of the room.

The restaurant he'd chosen was immaculate. It was the most extravagant eating establishment she'd ever seen. She studied Neil's expression and he watched her in return.

Was this restaurant one of his ways of seduction? Crazily, her heart prayed it would be, and then once again, she criticized her thoughts. This was just a game for him, something from which only he could benefit.

He rested his hands on the table. "Does my

choice please you?"

Her gaze darted around the room taking in the low hanging chandeliers and crystal goblets on the waiter's tray as he walked past their table. "It's very lovely."

"I remember when I first laid eyes on this place," Neil said. "I was certain they created it for royalty. Ian's cousin lives here in New York and introduced me to fine dining."

She raised her brows in curiosity. "Ian's cousin?"

"Yes, he was my first employer after I moved here. Didn't I tell you about him when I wrote? Remember, right after I arrived?"

She remembered, and the bitter taste of abandonment still lingered in her mouth. After reading the letter, she'd thrown it in the fireplace.

Charlotte quickly lost her pleasantness. Her heart clenched and she glared at him. Straightening her back, she refolded her napkin. "Are you still close friends with Ian's cousin?"

"We still keep in contact, but I wouldn't say we are close personal friends."

The waiter arrived and the conversation stopped. Neil ordered for both of them without consulting her to see what she wanted to eat. Anger boiled in her blood. Obviously, he wasn't the least bit concerned with her thoughts or desires. So typical. This dashed any ideas she had about any further dalliances with this selfish rogue. Even if he had ordered her favorite dish.

"So, Charlotte, tell me what you've been up to lately. Were you aware that I received a letter from your father about a year ago?"

She gasped. "Father wrote you before he died?"

"Yes. He begged me to return to South Carolina and stop you from ruining my good name. He said you were creating a scandal. Is this true?"

She laughed harshly. "No, it's not true. In fact, I

mourned your abandonment for nearly six months before realizing you didn't deserve my tears. That was when I met Allison. She wasn't a child like most of my friends, and Father didn't like the idea of my befriending a more sophisticated woman, especially one with a bolder lifestyle." She adjusted the napkin on her lap. "Allison took me to soirées held by socially promiscuous groups. It appalled Father, but what I think bothered him more than anything was he couldn't govern me any longer."

Neil nodded. "I believe your father wanted to keep you a child forever."

"And he would have if you hadn't married me," she clipped.

His brows lifted in puzzlement. "I must correct you, my dear. He would have kept you a child if he hadn't bribed me into marrying you. Remember?"

She sighed. "Yes, of course I do, but you don't know anything about me, or about my heart, do you? Of course not. You didn't stay around long enough to find out."

Neil sipped his wine while silence surrounded them. He tried hard to think of something to say that wouldn't upset her. Reluctantly, he admitted he liked her smile. She should smile more often. Yet so far this afternoon, all he'd accomplished was to make fire shoot from her eyes. Perhaps it didn't matter. Her cold heart wouldn't forget or forgive anyway.

He gulped down his drink. "What are your plans once the annulment goes through? Do you plan on becoming Ian's mistress?"

"I really haven't decided," she coolly replied. "To be perfectly honest, I'm looking for a man who can show me the love and respect I've missed having so far in my life."

It was his turn to gasp, although he swallowed it with his wine. "Are you telling me Ian doesn't show you those things?"

"Ian doesn't love me. He sees me as a prize. That's the only reason most of the scoundrels are after me. That, and of course, because of my inheritance."

He sat back in his chair and folded his arms. "Oh, I think not, Charlotte. You're very lovely. The men back home would be insane if they didn't try to win your affection."

"I'm surprised you'd say that, when only two years ago you thought of me as a homely child," she bitterly pointed out.

He scrambled to put his words together. He didn't want her to know the truth, although that was very close to how he'd felt. "I didn't think you were homely, but you were not the kind of woman I wanted for a wife. I wasn't ready to marry, but most of all, I hated being forced into an unwanted marriage."

The subject was temporarily postponed when the waiter brought their food. Charlotte's eyes widened at the steamed seafood and mushroom rice. When pleasure highlighted her face, his heart skipped a beat.

"Oh, this looks absolutely delicious." She glanced up at him. "Thank you for ordering for me. How could you have possibly known this was my favorite?"

He lifted his eyebrows. The truth was, he didn't know. This particular dish also happened to be his favorite. "I just thought you might like it. It pleases me to see I selected well."

A smile lit her face and nearly melted his resistance.

She heartily dove into her meal like a starved person. He enjoyed seeing a woman who ate instead of picked at her food like some bird.

After a couple of bites, she cleared her throat. "Tell me about some of the cases you have solved."

He wiped his mouth with a linen napkin and grinned. Because this just happened to be one of his favorite subjects, he told her about some of his hair-raising experiences. When he relaxed, the bitter side of him disappeared and he found he could talk with ease. She listened, and even laughed a few times.

"Your cases sound very exciting," she told him. "As a child, I used to fantasize about sneaking around and spying on people."

He arched an eyebrow. "Did you now?"

Her soft laugh sounded like heavenly bells. "Many times my governess found me in a tree or somewhere I shouldn't have been."

"I cannot imagine that." He grinned. "Actually, I cannot imagine your father allowing you to have such boisterous activities."

"I spent most of my adolescence with him angry at me."

"So, did you solve any mysteries?"

"Oh, yes." She laughed.

Forgetting his manners, he leaned forward with his elbows on the table. "Do tell."

"I discovered who had been taking my fancy slippers."

He arched an eyebrow. "The kitchen maid, perhaps?"

She shook her head.

"The butler?"

Her laughter grew. "Wrong again."

"Then who?"

"My puppy."

He tilted his head back and roared with laughter. When he looked back in her eyes, her golden specks glittered like stars. So lovely. So desirable, he wanted to take her in his arms and shower her with affection.

"Those vexing animals always get in some kind of trouble," he replied.

He kept the conversation flowing, and when he finished, he realized that they were not arguing. In fact, it was nice to talk with her. Almost too nice.

He paid for their meal and left with her on his arm. A surge of pride burst in his chest to be escorting the most beautiful woman in New York. He took her down the streets and enjoyed her delightful sense of humor. As long as they stayed on neutral subjects, she didn't argue or bring up the past.

Regretfully, it was time to walk her back to her hotel. He stopped at the door to her room and stared into her intoxicating eyes. She didn't look away, but the color in her cheeks darkened beneath his close scrutiny.

"Would you like to come in for a drink?" she asked.

If he agreed, they'd be alone together. A new energy sparked within his body. He really wanted to, but knew if he stayed any longer, he'd try to ignite the heated passion they shared last night. He certainly couldn't do that now that he knew her true identity. Yet, he couldn't deny the ember of excitement at that prospect.

"No, Charlotte. I really better go. I've spent too long with you as it is. I still have a lot to do before finishing the case I'm working on."

"Then I should let you go." She turned and opened her door, but didn't walk inside.

He looked past her and scanned the empty room. "When is Ian expected back?"

"I'm not certain. He didn't give me a time. I'm not his mother, you know." Her voice turned bitter.

Silently, he cursed. It was really none of his business, but he had to know how she and Ian spent their time together. "Charlotte, if you and Ian aren't doing anything this evening for supper, you're both welcome to come to my townhouse and dine with me."

"Thank you, but if you remember, my friend, Allison, is staying with me as well."

Her hypnotic eyes kept him spellbound, and he held tightly to his control to keep from falling under her magical charm. "Bring her along. I'd like to meet the friend who made your father so upset."

The corner of her lips twitched into a grin. "I'll ask Ian when he returns."

"If you decide to come, Ian knows where I live. Dinner is at eight."

As he stood in the doorway, he tried to think of something that would keep him with her a little longer, keep him staring into her eyes, but he couldn't think of a single thing. "Well..."

She sighed heavily. "Yes, well..."

He moved next to her and ran his fingers across her cheek. An invisible pull tugged him toward her and all he wanted to do was take her in his arms and smother her with his kisses. He breathed deeply, trying to fight the sensations the best he could. "Thank you for sharing the afternoon with me. I had an enjoyable time."

"As did I," she answered softly. "Surprisingly enough, we didn't argue much."

"Indeed, it was quite astonishing. Most of the afternoon I could see the beautiful She-Devil I met last night, instead of the woman I thought I'd married."

She laughed lightly. "Do you know I had the same thoughts? The man you portrayed this afternoon was the mysterious man at the masquerade instead of the horrible creature I'd married." The tone of her voice lowered when she mentioned the night before.

Automatically, his gaze moved to her mouth; the same pair of lips he'd enjoyed devouring less than twenty-four hours ago. Those lips that had moved beneath his in a mixture of heaven and hell when he touched his tongue to hers.

Burning sensations roared through his body, convincing him to act upon his impulses. He stepped back before something happened and he was completely under her control.

Charlotte tugged on her ear as she lowered her eyes. "I'll let Ian know of your invitation. If he doesn't have other plans, I'm confident he'll accept."

He too another step back. "I hope to see you tonight." He bowed slightly. "Until then."

The urge to take her in his arms consumed his very being, so he turned and hurried down the hallway.

Why couldn't he get over the lustful memories floating through his head? He wanted to feel her touch all over again, and taste her mouth beneath his. He must be addled. What other reason could there be for the inferno burning in his loins?

Chapter Four

Charlotte paced the floor of the hotel room, wringing her hands against her stomach. Why did she act so love-struck?

She clenched her jaw. Wasn't it bad enough she'd melted under Neil's touch last night? But today in broad daylight, she nearly swooned from his nearness. Remembering the hell he'd put her through after he'd left her two years ago was essential. She needed to recall the insecurities she'd had because of his treatment. He'd made her feel as if she wasn't good—not only for him but for any man. And what about the humiliation he put her through last night?

She'd be a fool to think he'd transformed into the caring, kind-hearted man she thought she'd fallen in love with. That, too, was part of his disguise. This was the very reason she'd hardened her heart against him. And this was the very reason she could not accept his invitation for dinner tonight. He must have hypnotized her to agree, curse his hide!

The door to her suite opened and in walked Ian and Allison. Charlotte forced a smile. "How was your outing?"

Allison's eyes sparkled with life. "Splendid. And how was your afternoon?"

Charlotte rubbed her temples. "Not as exciting as yours, I'm afraid."

Allison hurried to her side and took her hands. "Did Mr. Hamilton come?"

"He happened by during my morning walk."

Her friend's eyes widened. "And?"

"And I gave him the annulment papers. He hasn't signed them. He says he's going to have his solicitor look them over."

Allison huffed and folded her arms across her chest. "That man. How I would enjoy strangling him."

Charlotte chuckled. "Stand in line."

Ian handed his hat and over-jacket to the maid. "Charlotte, you do not seem too upset over seeing your husband." He turned and faced her with a raised eyebrow. "Can I assume the meeting went well?"

Charlotte scowled. "No, you cannot assume anything of the sort. The meeting didn't go as I had planned. He didn't sign the papers. In fact, the arrogant man had the audacity to ask us to dine at his townhouse tonight."

Ian's eyes widened. "And what was your answer?"

Charlotte turned toward the window, afraid her heated cheeks would give away what had really transpired between her and Neil. "I didn't really give him an answer, but said I'd suggest it to you, first."

Ian barked with laughter. She swung around in surprise. He walked to her and grasped her hands. "I think we should go. It'll be most enjoyable."

She scowled. "Enjoyable for whom? Have you forgotten what he did to me two years ago, not to mention what happened last night? Has it slipped your mind how much he loathes my very presence?"

"No, I haven't forgotten, but I think if we go tonight, we might be able to convince him to sign the papers."

She narrowed her eyes. "How so?"

His smile stretched. "Because of what you told him about us. If he sees how much we care for each other, I believe he'll sign."

Allison laughed as she accepted a glass of brandy from the maid. "My dear Ian, I beg to differ."

"And why is that?"

"Because I don't think I'll be able to conduct myself in a manner that will help with your plan. You forget, my wonderful man, I'm a very jealous woman."

He chuckled, sauntered to her, and wrapped her in his arms. "My sweet, Allison, you have no need to doubt where my loyalties lie. My heart is with you, always."

Allison tilted her head and grinned. "And what if Mr. Hamilton doesn't react the way you hope? What if he abhors the site of his wife being pawed at by his best friend? What will you do then?"

"If I know Neil, he'll give in and sign the papers because of his arrogance. The matter will be concluded quickly, and we may all return back home where you and I will continue our secret affair." His brows wagged above twinkling eyes.

Allison grinned. "Why do I not believe you?"

Charlotte sank into the nearby sofa, ignoring her friends in their comfortable embrace. Confusion clouded her thoughts and left her feeling torn. She really didn't want to see Neil again, especially if she had to act as if she were in love with another man. Then again, it might be rather enjoyable to see if she could make him jealous.

Her heart lifted slightly. Neil really didn't love her; he had just experienced a healthy dose of lust last evening. With this knowledge, there were endless possibilities she could do to disrupt his night.

She straightened on the sofa and grinned. "Ian? Allison? I've decided it will be a brilliant idea to go to Neil's for dinner tonight."

Ian and Allison exchanged smiles. Ian focused his attention back to Charlotte. "What made you change your mind, my dear?"

She studied her fingernails. "Oh, let's just say, I'm in the mood for a little revenge."

Allison laughed. "What's that supposed to mean?"

Charlotte lifted her gaze. "I feel like giving my husband a dose of his own medicine. I want to make someone jealous tonight."

"Just as long as it's not me," Allison warned.

Charlotte rose from the sofa and walked to her friend. She took Allison's hands and squeezed. "I need your help, though. The only way I can make Neil jealous is by using Ian."

"You're right, of course. How else will we be able to get your husband to come up to scratch?"

Charlotte shook her head. "I don't want him to come up to scratch, just make him see what he's lost."

"Splendid idea." Ian clapped his hands. "The gown you wear tonight must be very revealing."

Charlotte glanced at Allison and arched her brows. "Is it all right? Will you allow Ian to help me?"

Allison nodded. "It'll be amusing to see your husband squirm. Now, what about that gown?"

The picture of a dress pierced her thoughts; the scandalous frock she'd seen in the shop's window this afternoon. The same one she thought would be too daring to wear any place but New York. But then, they were still here.

"Ian, you need to take me shopping."

His eyes widened. "Right now?"

She clamped her hands tightly to his arm. "Yes, now, because I know the perfect dress. I saw one this afternoon during my walk. It's extremely daring. The bodice is very low cut, and the fringe on the sleeves won't hide my arms at all."

"It sounds most becoming. Besides, we'll just be

at Neil's for dinner, and you won't have to cause a scene in public. Wear a cape and reveal it at the house."

"That will work perfectly."

Hopefully, all would fall into place the way she wanted. She'd show that cad of a husband exactly what he'd missed out on since he left her.

"Ian, do me a favor, though," Charlotte added.

"What's that?"

"Don't make him too irate."

Ian threw back his head and laughed. "If I don't, Neil will think I'm not sincere. We grew up together, he knows me well. Trust me, what I do tonight will be for his own good."

Her heart dropped. What was Ian going to do now?

****

Neil paced the hardwood floor of his bedroom while the valet chased around him, readying him for the evening. Charlotte was coming!

He stopped in front of the full-length mirror as his valet brushed his deep blue waistcoat for the tenth time. Neil adjusted the collar of his white silk shirt and tugged down the midnight blue cravat tightened around his neck.

George, the valet, stepped back and looked over Neil's attire. His servant nodded. "I think you look especially refined tonight, sir." George's gaze met Neil's in the mirror. "By chance, are you out to impress a certain lady?"

Neil chuckled. "No, George. I'm just going to entertain some old friends."

"Is it certain they're coming?"

"They haven't confirmed my invitation, but that doesn't mean they aren't coming. If I know Fauxley, he'll enjoy catching me off guard."

George retrieved the black over-coat and slipped it onto Neil's arms. "Well, you are going to make an impression tonight whether you desire to or not."

Neil's smile stretched, but held back the laugh lodged in his throat. Yes, he did want to impress Charlotte, but for the life of him, he couldn't figure out why.

The chime from the front door startled him. They were here! But more importantly, *she* was here. His gaze switched to the bedroom door, his palms moistened with excitement. What was wrong with him? His adolescent years had passed. Why did he act like an over-eager schoolboy now?

He waited until the voices of his guests drifted up the wide staircase and into his room before he left to greet them. Taking a deep breath, he walked down the hallway to the top of the stairs.

As he looked down to his guests, his heart filled with pride over his acquired wealth. One large chandelier hung point-center on the ceiling, making everything below sparkle like champagne, especially Charlotte. The light touched her hair and enhanced the auburn color. When her tongue darted out and moistened her tempting lips, he wanted to taste her sweetness again.

Neil's butler, a graying, stooped old man with a cheerful disposition, greeted the guests and took their wraps. When the butler retrieved the last garment, Neil began his descent of the grand staircase.

"Good evening," he welcomed, causing all eyes to turn his way. "I'm so very delighted that you all could—" When Charlotte turned to face him, her beauty took his breath away. Neil's train of thought came to an abrupt stop. His mind completely stopped working. Nothing else mattered but the seductive woman in his hall.

Hungrily, he devoured her with his gaze as he took careful steps toward his wife. When he stood in front of her, he lifted one of her hands covered by an elbow length, silver-blue glove, and brushed a soft kiss across her knuckles. The urge to take her in his arms overwhelmed him. His hands burned to caress the bare skin on her chest that the exposed bodice provided for his view. He wanted to stroke forth the passion he'd made her feel before.

A presence drew him out of his hypnotic state when Ian stepped away from the other woman and to Charlotte. Ian took her hand away and tucked it protectively under his own.

Fauxley cleared his throat. "Hamilton, I'm certain Charlotte is grateful for your warm greeting, but she's with me tonight."

Neil hardened his jaw, glaring at his so-called friend.

Fauxley lifted his chin in a challenge. "But I don't believe you've met Charlotte's charming companion, Mrs. Allison Archibald." Ian took her elbow and drew her forward. "Mrs. Archibald, this is Neil Hamilton."

Putting aside his anger, Neil grasped Mrs. Archibald's outstretched hand. He'd detach his friend's head later when the two of them were alone.

Neil smiled. "It's a pleasure to make your acquaintance."

The woman nodded. "The pleasure is all mine, Mr. Hamilton."

He placed a proper kiss on her knuckles, but wanted it to be Charlotte's delicate hand instead. The other lady's beauty didn't compare to Charlotte's breathtaking loveliness. As Mrs. Archibald stepped away, his gaze moved to his wife. He pushed past the angry thoughts aimed toward Ian and concentrated on Charlotte's heart-warming smile.

"Your place is very lovely." Her voice sang like harps from heaven.

"I'm happy you approve."

He glanced over her attire once more, and his

loins tightened. Her silver-blue dress with the fringed shoulder straps was provocative. She wore no jewelry around her neck to distract from the lovely sight of her bosom. Diamond ear-bobs hung from her finely shaped ears and made him want to nibble on her.

He couldn't stop staring. She was exquisite, and the smallest glance from her torched his blood. And that dress! Stunned, he couldn't believe she would wear a gown designed to arouse men and cause duels.

He replayed the scene with her this morning in front of the store's window. Was that the same gown he accused her of using to plan a man's seduction? Was he going to be that man? His hopes escalated but were quickly dashed. Ian was the man she intended to entice.

Ian cleared his throat again. "So, Hamilton? Are you going to offer us a pre-dinner drink like a good host or ogle Charlotte's body all night?"

Embarrassment washed over Neil, but instead of going with his first instinct to throw his fist into Ian's face, he decided to be honest. "Well, considering she's legally my wife, I think I have the right to admire her beauty."

A deep blush colored Charlotte's cheeks, but she remained silent.

"But you're correct, Fauxley," Neil continued. "I haven't been a very attentive host. Would you like some sherry?"

"That would be refreshing." Ian led Charlotte into the sitting room.

Neil offered Mrs. Archibald his arm and followed behind.

Charlotte walked into the room on stiff legs, her heart pounding so hard it threatened to leap from her chest. She wasn't aware that her hand was squeezing Ian's arm until he slowly pried her fingers loose.

"Keep up the good performance," Ian whispered in her ear.

She really had no idea what he meant. Ian was the one performing, not her. She couldn't mumble a coherent word without being tongue-tied. My, but she did enjoy seeing Neil squirm. A powerful feeling swept over her, and she liked the effect. At least she wasn't the only person acting like a perplexed adolescent.

Although lines of anger marred Neil's expression, he politely carried on a conversation. Every time she added her opinion, it brought her his attention. His hungry gaze skimmed over her as she sipped her sherry, making her heart skip.

The butler announced dinner, and Neil hurried to offered his arm. "May I escort you to the dining room?"

Before accepting his offer, she glanced at Ian for his approval, hoping it would infuriate her husband. Ian merely nodded. When she looked back at Neil, his jaw hardened. She secretly hoped her ploy worked.

She took Neil's arm and walked beside him into the dining room as gracefully as she could with quivering legs. Her mind constantly fought the delight sweeping through her body from his nearness. She welcomed Neil's attentiveness, but his shallowness bothered her. She knew he acted this way only because of his jealousy over Ian.

Her physical appearance had nothing to do with the person she'd become. Although she'd changed outwardly, she hadn't on the inside. Neil hadn't bothered to get to know her then, so why would he now?

They sat around the table and the butler served a fancy seafood dish. By the way Neil smiled at her, she knew he had this menu prepared especially for her tonight. He'd remembered her favorite dish from this afternoon's meal.

Neil inquired about their plans for their time remaining time in New York, and he made some suggestions for places they might want to visit. He offered to be their tour guide. She didn't readily agree, but Ian acted as if this would be acceptable.

Neil wiped his mouth with a linen napkin then placed it on his lap. "I know it's sudden, but would you be interested in going to the opera tonight? One of my favorites is playing, and tonight is the last night."

She shrugged, but before she could answer, Ian cleared his throat. "I don't know. Charlotte, my love?" She met his eyes. "Does an opera interest you?"

"I don't have anything else planned." She glanced at Allison. "How about you?"

Her friend nodded. "I think the opera sounds lovely."

Unease washed over Charlotte and tightened in her chest. When she left the table and walked into the parlor with the others, she took hold of Allison's elbow and whispered, "I cannot go out in public looking like this."

"I don't think you have any other choice."

After Neil excused himself to retrieve his cape and hat, she turned and clasped her hands together. She paused to catch her breath. Her corset felt too tight. "But I cannot wear this. It's indecent." Her voice trembled slightly.

Allison patted her hand. "Just keep the cloak around your shoulders. If Neil tries to take it off, tell him you're chilly."

Charlotte laughed softly. "What possessed me to wear this?" Heaven forbid if Neil discovered she had worn this dress for him. She didn't want him to know of her insecurities.

Ian moved beside her and slipped his arm around her waist. "Wearing this gown was the best thing you could have done. Can't you see how it's affecting him? He's so jealous it's hard for him to see straight." He grinned wickedly.

"Jealous? That's utter nonsense, Ian."

"Just keep up the good work. We almost have him where we want him."

She scrunched her brow. What was he saying? Where did she want him? She opened her mouth to voice her confusion, but Ian turned and walked away with a knowing grin.

Suddenly an uneasy thought occurred to her. Was she just a pawn in the game her friends were playing?

****

Charlotte sat rigid in her seat at the opera. Beside her, Ian made a spectacle of himself, fawning over her every time she moved. She clenched her jaw, trying to keep from screaming. Below their box, the performers sang, but she didn't hear a word. Instead, she tried listening to what was happening behind her, where Neil and Allison sat. Charlotte busied her hands, toying with the fringe on her shawl.

Ian's gaze constantly dipped to her bosom whenever her shawl fell away, and his fingers softly caressed her arm. His attentiveness drove her insane, and to make it worse, she couldn't see if his display had any affect on her husband.

Then again, what was her wayward husband doing with Allison? Charlotte fisted her hands, stifling the urge to peek over her shoulder.

When the curtains closed for intermission, she sighed heavily. Ian stood and touched her shoulder.

"My dear, would you please excuse me? I see some friends across the room, and I must speak with them."

She drew her brows together, silently turning down his request.

Ignoring her, he smiled. “I'll only be a moment.” He kissed her on the cheek and hurried out of their box.

She glanced at Neil. His eyebrow rose. She silently cursed Ian for choosing this moment to flee.

Allison stood and smoothed out her skirt. Neil quickly rose beside her. “Mr. Hamilton,” her friend began. “If you'll excuse me, I must go visit the powder room.”

He took a slight bow. “But of course, Mrs. Archibald.”

Charlotte jumped up. “Allison, could you hold up a moment and I'll join you?”

Allison nodded, but just as Charlotte stepped toward her friend, Neil clasped her arm and stopped her.

“Could I have a word, please?”

She glanced at Allison who gave her a dismissal wave. Charlotte cast a scornful glance at her husband's fingers around her arm. He withdrew his touch.

“There's still thirty minutes left of the intermission. Would you like to take a little stroll outside with me?” he asked.

The evening's shadows would make their walk tempting and might bring back sensations she didn't want to recall. Refusing his offer was essential. There was no way she could be alone with him—especially outside.

Charlotte shook her head, but he didn't give her a chance to voice her answer. His hand slid around her elbow as he led her out the nearest door. Clenching her jaw, she forced her feet to follow him. Although she didn't want them to be alone, she also didn't want to create a scene.

They walked around many couples who had

come out to partake of the crisp cool air. The walkway was well lit—unlike the place they had been last night.

Had it really only been last night when she kissed him so passionately?

He took her farther away from the others until they were nearly secluded and stopped. "You're probably wondering why I wanted to speak to you."

She clutched the shawl tightly around her neck. "Yes, actually."

He turned toward her and folded his arms across his broad chest. "I've noticed the way Ian acts around you, and I must say, I don't approve."

She arched an eyebrow. "You don't?"

"Yes. Although he made it quite clear he wants to make you his mistress, the fact still remains, you're a married woman."

Her lips twitched as she tried to hold back a laugh. "That didn't seem to bother you yesterday."

"Well, things have changed," he quickly continued. "It's not appropriate to allow Ian such pleasures out in public, and especially in front of your own husband."

"We're getting our marriage annulled, so why should it matter? Besides, I'm quite certain you haven't remained true to your marriage vows these past two years. In fact, you thought I was a different person last night."

"That's untrue. I have not bedded another woman since we married. And last evening was...different." His jaw hardened, and a nerve jumped in his cheek. "The fact remains we're still married and your behavior with Ian is scandalous."

She released a bitter laugh. "Oh, Neil, I cannot believe you. You don't make any sense." She flipped her hand in the air, which caused the shawl to slip down one of her shoulders. The air against her skin caused cool tingles against her rising body temperature. "First you were reluctant to admit you even had a wife, and now you're dictating what I can and cannot do? What gives you the right? *You* were the one who abandoned the marriage."

His gaze roamed over her shoulders and across her bosom before his jaw relaxed. The small amount of light from the moon let her see a spark of hunger in his eyes. Her heart hammered. Dare she admit she enjoyed the way he looked at her?

"I have every right to dictate to you." His tone was husky.

"No, Neil." Her voice shook. "You relinquished that right when you left me."

"Then, by damn, I'm taking my rights back."

Clamping his hands over her shoulders, he pulled her to him. His head bent and captured her lips. She pushed her hands against his chest, but he was much stronger. His fingers bit into her shoulders and she fought harder, but his persistent kiss burned like a fire on her lips. His mouth eventually wore her resistance down, and she relaxed and gave in.

His lips softened against hers and she sighed. This was what she'd wanted all night. Since the moment he descended the stairs in his townhouse looking so handsome, she'd thought of his arms around her and his mouth moving across hers in passion.

She circled her arms up his chest, hooking them around his neck. The out of control rhythm of her heart sent warmth careening through her body—just as strong as last night.

He withdrew his mouth and rested his lips against her cheek. "Charlotte, you're so very beautiful tonight. I was afraid this was going to happen when I saw you walk through my door."

Sensations erupted in every nerve of her body and she dared admit she enjoyed the way he kissed her, the way her body fit against him. But her mind argued, reminding her of how much he'd hurt her.

"No, Neil." She breathed deeply. "The only reason you want me is because I don't want you. And the only reason you think I'm beautiful is because of the alluring dress I'm wearing."

"You're incorrect, my dear." His arms tightened around her waist and he kissed her lips again. His tongue dove inside her mouth and she moaned. He caressed her bare back, which the dress provided for him.

A deep sigh tore through his throat. She loved the thrill, wanted more of it, but not right here. This was improper.

Pushing her hands against his chest, she quickly withdrew from his embrace. "Neil, the only reason you want me is because another man wants me. You don't love me. Lust is the only emotion you're feeling right now."

She wrapped the shawl around her shoulders, keeping her bosom hidden. "This body you ogle is only a tiny part of who Charlotte Ashton Hamilton really is, and you're not willing to get to know the real me. All you want to do is take your pleasures out on my body, and I won't be used."

With a heavy heart, she turned and ran back into the building, leaving him standing alone.

****

Neil stared at the performers on the stage but didn't see a thing. Confusion clouded his mind from Charlotte's words. He didn't fully understand women, Charlotte in particular. Didn't women want men to notice them? Wasn't that why Charlotte wore that particular dress? And now that he had noticed her, she still wasn't satisfied.

Charlotte had wanted his attention during the three days after their marriage, and now as he practically drooled over her luscious body, it appalled her. She accused him of trying to use her for sexual pleasures—yet wasn't that the very thing Ian claimed to be after? Ian didn't want a wife, just a mistress.

A movement from Charlotte pulled him to his senses. She kept her gaze locked to the stage, but it seemed all he could do was look upon her as he sat beside Mrs. Archibald in their assigned chairs.

What did his wife really want? She'd mentioned there was more to her than just her body. What did he want out of this relationship? Did he even want a relationship? These endless questions plagued him, making his head throb.

He'd ignored his wife for two years, and now she was back and more beautiful and passionate than he'd ever thought possible. But she sought an annulment, and she expected him to stand back and watch Ian paw at her person in public. That he would not do. So maybe he was jealous, but damn it, this was not fair. He ached to touch her and claim his husbandly rights.

His thoughts were still in turmoil during the carriage ride home. On impulse, he invited everyone inside his house. They retired to the drawing room where the ladies were offered sherry while the men had a whisky. Ian's attention remained on Charlotte. The longer she allowed it, Neil's temper lifted. He bunched his fists at his side. After what seemed like eternity of torture, he couldn't take it anymore.

As Ian and Charlotte stood to leave, Neil quickly met them at the door. "Before you go, there's something I wish to say." He paused a second to finish his drink, then placed the empty glass on the nearby tray the butler held. "I've made a decision tonight that will affect both of you."

Charlotte's eyes widened, but Ian's were just passively curious. "Ian," Neil continued, "I know you plan on taking my wife as your lover, but I don't think that's a good idea. She's still my wife, and I wish to fulfill my rights as her husband."

His gaze switched to Charlotte. Color drained from her face and her mouth dropped open.

She gasped. "No, Neil. You cannot." Her voice rose. "You told me you would sign the annulment papers."

"I've had second thoughts, my dear." He took hold of her trembling hands. "It would please me if you would stay." He pulled her out of Ian's reach. "In fact, I insist you stay." He looked to his friend. "Ian, would you see to it that my wife's trunks are packed and sent here posthaste? I'm certain she'll want to get settled as soon as possible."

Charlotte met Ian's wide stare and shook her head. "Ian, please don't."

Neil's heart wrenched, but he wouldn't give in.

When Ian didn't answer right away, Charlotte turned to Neil and scowled. "I don't accept your offer, sir. I detest you with every fiber of my being and I still want to dissolve our marriage."

His heart clenched. Guilt caused his gut to sink, but he remained contained, determined to get his way.

Ian stepped forward and patted her shoulder. "Charlotte, there's nothing I can do. You are, after all, still married."

"No." Tears filled her eyes. She looked at Mrs. Archibald. "Please don't make me stay."

A lump formed in Neil's throat. Had he made the correct decision? Silently, he cursed. He wanted her for himself, and damn it, he would not share.

"Charlotte, sweetheart?" His voice softened. "What if I made you a deal?"

Her deep gray eyes glared back at him. "What kind of deal?" she snapped. "The kind where I sell my soul to the Devil?"

His fingers brushed a tear from her cheek. "No,

nothing like that. I'm just suggesting a simple bargain. Stay with me for one month, and then if you still don't wish to be married, I'll sign the papers. But we have to live as husband and wife that whole time."

She shook her head. "That's too long. Make it two weeks and I'll agree."

"No." He tried not to grin at her temperament. "I want a month. That gives us enough time to get to know each other again..." He paused, then asked, "Are you afraid you might like me after a month's time?"

She pursed her lips. "I'm not afraid of anything."

"Then will you make the deal with me? We owe it to ourselves to discover if the passion we felt last night can last."

Her gaze switched between him and her friends, and Neil secretly thanked Mrs. Archibald and Ian for not siding with Charlotte this time. When she finally met his stare, a look of defeat rested on her lovely face.

"All right. A month's time, and no longer."

He leaned over and kissed her cheek. "It's sealed then."

Chapter Five

Something soft brushed across Charlotte's cheek and she stirred in her sleep. The soothing caress smelled of roses, the sweet fragrance teasing her senses to awareness. The bed beneath her moved as someone sat beside her, and her dreamlike state changed to reality. A man's scent of spice and leather brought her sharply awake.

She blinked and focused on the room. The surroundings were not familiar. The wood frame bed and matching dressers were too masculine. Her gaze slid to the man looming over her, a red rose dangled between his fingers as he stroked it across her cheek. Her heart sank.

Seeing Neil's handsome face brought back last night's pandemonium, things that happened at the opera, and especially the horrible deal he had forced her to make.

He grinned. "Good morning, my sweet."

He moved the rose down her cheek to her mouth, then softly across her lips. His eyes rested where the rose stopped, and she feared a kiss would soon come. Before she could protest, he dropped his mouth to hers for a brief kiss. When he pulled away, the warm glow from his gaze sent shivers over her body.

"Do you know how beautiful you look in the morning?" he asked softly.

Reality came crashing around her. She had to live as his wife for a whole month. Last night hadn't been a nightmare, after all.

She pushed her hands against his solid chest

and moved him upright, then quickly sat up. When his eyes dropped to her chest, she looked down and noticed how the satin camisole molded to her bosom. She reached for the sheet and tugged it up, but his hip blocked any movement.

Last night, she'd gone straight to the room he'd assigned her before her trunks had arrived. She quickly stripped down into her camisole and drawers and climbed into bed. The stress throughout the day had worn her frazzled nerves, and when her head hit the pillow, she slept like the dead. Now she wondered if he had tried to crawl into bed with her sometime during the night.

"How long have you been here?" she snapped.

He touched the rose to her chin. "I've been watching you for about ten minutes. Do you know how lovely you are when you're asleep?"

"No. I don't recall ever seeing myself sleep."

He chuckled and slid his gaze over her bosom once more. "You look very tempting this morning."

"Then I suggest you stop looking at me."

He didn't appear the least affected by her words. A smile still graced his mouth as if she'd said nothing.

"So, are you ready for breakfast? Cook has prepared something delicious. Your maid told him what you like to eat, and it's waiting whenever you snap your fingers."

Her mood lightened a fraction of an inch. "My maid's here?"

He nodded. "Ian brought her by early this morning with all of your things." He tilted his head. "Do you feel safer now?"

"I'd feel safer if you'd moved to another city."

"Good to see you haven't lost your spunk, my dear." He touched her chin, but she slapped his hand away. "As soon as you're ready, you can have breakfast."

"Have you already eaten?"

"Yes. I've been awake for a while now. I'll be going to the office shortly. Unfortunately, I've got a case that really needs to be solved. With any luck, I'll finish it today."

Her spirits lifted a little higher. "So you won't be constantly by my side?"

"Don't look so excited, or I just might decide to stay home and entertain you."

"That's not necessary. I'll be able to keep myself busy."

He shrugged. "If you get bored today, come into the office. I'd like to introduce you around."

"I have no desire to meet your friends," she hissed. "Isn't it enough you've kept our marriage a secret? It would really start tongues wagging if they found out the truth now. I wonder, though. Would the truth cause you embarrassment?"

His lips quirked into a crooked grin. "It wasn't common knowledge when I first moved here. Besides, I told you when I'd agreed to marry you it was in name only."

She lifted her chin and looked away.

He sighed. "Well, if you change your mind, my driver will take you to my office."

He moved to stand, but stopped and leaned over her, pressing his lips to hers for a kiss. She gasped and pushed the heel of her hands against his chest, but his arms circled around her shoulders and pulled her closer. Although she resisted, he didn't break the kiss.

Memories of the night at the mask ball rushed upon her, causing her body to melt. Her mental struggle for control lost and his mouth moved across hers, urging her lips open. He dipped his tongue inside for a quick sweep, and she held back the moan ready to escape.

When he pulled away, disappointment washed

over her, but soon reality hit her like a bucket of cold water. The rogue! How dare he take advantage of her? She lifted her hand and slapped his cheek. His eyes widened in shock, then a smile crept across his mouth.

He chuckled. "I'll see you later, *Cheré*." He winked, stood, and left the room.

Anger multiplied with every step he took, and she hated him that much more. And she hated herself, too, for her ridiculous weakness. She picked up an empty basin from the bed stand and threw it at the closed door. The porcelain shattered, the pieces scattering across the floor.

Neil must know what kind of power he had over her, and she wished her body would shield his tempting effect. There had to be a way to stop herself from melting every time he kissed her.

Within minutes, the door opened and her maid hurried in with her breakfast, pausing when she noticed the mess on the floor.

The older woman's eyes widened. "What happened?"

Charlotte sighed heavily. "I missed."

"You missed?" asked Clara.

"Yes. I was aiming for Neil's head."

Charlotte flipped off the covers and climbed out of bed. Hastily, she dressed as Clara chased around behind. While the older woman finished touching up Charlotte's hair, she chomped on a fresh pear and a scone with honey butter. As soon as she left her room, she ordered the buggy brought around for her day's excursion, instructing the driver to take her to Allison's hotel.

When she arrived, she rapped hard on Allison's door until her friend answered. Allison wore a nightgown and a matching wrapper. Her blonde hair tumbled wildly around her shoulders. Puffy eyes gave evidence that she'd still been in bed.

"Allison!" Charlotte moved into the room without waiting for an invitation. "We have to figure out a way to get me out of this insane bargain."

Allison yawned and stretched her arms above her head. "Why are you about this early in the morning?"

"Wake up and pay attention."

"I'm awake." Allison nodded, rubbing her eyes.

"I need your help to get myself away from my husband."

Allison's eyes widened, and then suddenly laughter erupted from her throat. "Do you hear yourself, Charlotte?"

Charlotte scowled. "Of course, I hear what I'm saying. I'm talking, aren't I?"

Allison walked to the sofa, plopped down unladylike, then folded her legs underneath her. Charlotte joined her.

Allison's grin widened. "You've been wanting your husband to pay attention to you for over two years, and now that Neil is finally attentive, all you can think about is getting away?" Allison tilted her head sideways, giving a smile filled with empathy. "Isn't this what you've dreamed about since he left?"

Charlotte slumped back on the sofa. "Oh, Allison, I don't know what my heart desires anymore. I used to think everything would be dandy if Neil would act like a husband, but now I'm so confused. I know he's attracted to me. The night of the masquerade proves that. But I feel my appearance is the only reason he's acting this way, and I don't want him to like me just because he thinks I'm beautiful or some kind of temptress."

Allison nodded. "I know how you feel, but remember, physical attraction tempts the man, then after he's hooked, he'll get to know your personality." Allison swept her untamable hair off her shoulder. "I, too, am tired of having men fall at my feet and offer me the world because they think I'm beautiful and wealthy. But, I know that when I find the man I want, I'll already have him because of my looks. We have the rest of our lives to get to know each other."

"But Allison?" Charlotte leaned forward. "What if after a month I don't like his personality? What if he wants me, but I don't want him?"

Allison laughed. "Then your marriage will be based on great sex."

The corners of Charlotte's mouth tugged upward, and she shook her head. "You're incorrigible."

"Yes, but that's why you like me."

Charlotte frowned. "Neil hurt me so much. How do I know he won't get tired of married life and break my heart again? I don't know if I can make him fall in love with me forever. I suppose he was right when he asked me last night if I was scared. I am. I'm petrified."

"Do you want Neil back in your life, or are you doing all this to get him out?" Allison patted Charlotte's hands. "You must decide."

Charlotte stared at her hands resting comfortably in her lap during the few minutes of silence. So much to ponder—so much to decide, and she didn't know where to start. "I'm so afraid I'll fall in love with him and he'll not return my love. Then I'll be as miserable as I was two years ago."

Allison cleared her throat. "What are your plans for today?"

Charlotte lifted her head and shrugged. "I was going to plan my escape, but since you'll not help me—"

Allison laughed. "You're right, I won't help."

"Then maybe Ian will help me."

Allison shook her head. "I rather doubt that. Not today, anyway. He had a very exhausting night." Allison stifled another yawn behind her hand.

Charlotte crinkled her forehead. A deep blush swept across her friend's face, and embarrassment washed over Charlotte. "Oh, dear heavens." She straightened. "Is Ian still here?"

Allison nodded as a sly smile touched her lips.

"Then I'd better leave."

Allison shrugged. "He's not awake, but I'm certain once he is, he'll want some privacy."

"Oh, Allison." Charlotte stood and made her way to the front door. "I cannot believe I've been going on about my problems and all this time you've been wishing I'd leave so that you could get back to Ian."

Allison followed her to the door. "I didn't want to seem impolite."

Charlotte turned and playfully swatted Allison's shoulder. "Now, I'm the one who is embarrassed."

Allison didn't reply as Charlotte left.

All the way back to Neil's townhouse, Charlotte thought about Allison and Ian. There was a relationship that seemed to have spontaneous romance, and her friend didn't have a care in the world.

Then again, Charlotte knew her friend, and Allison didn't keep her lovers for very long. Once upon a time, Charlotte had wanted that kind of life. Now she looked forward to having children and growing old with the man of her dreams.

She rolled her eyes. That would never happen now. Not while she was still married to Neil. He'd been the man of her dreams before he broke her heart.

The driver stopped in front of Neil's place and a footman opened the door. Taking a deep sigh, Charlotte gave her hand to the groom as he helped her from the carriage. She looked up and scanned the two-story building. This place wasn't home, and it never would be. But if she planned right, it wouldn't have to be her permanent place of occupancy.

Charlotte dragged herself up the stairs, looking for some activity to keep from becoming bored. She wandered through the rooms, trying to familiarize his things. They were all clean kept and in order, but the dark colors added dreariness to Neil's life.

After a few minutes of searching, she found his room, which incidentally, adjoined hers. She wiggled the door handle between the two doors, and thankfully, it was locked.

Moving slowly to the center of the bedroom, she eyed the expensive decor. Touches of forest green, burnt red, and coffee brown decorated his rugs and curtains. The room's furnishings piqued her curiosity, and the first thing she noticed was the cleanliness. Obviously, he paid his servants well.

Her attention shifted to the enormous bed, and her throat turned dry. His blue bedspread was a mite darker than his eyes, and the color reminded her of the lustful look she'd witnessed this morning when his gaze swept over her bosom.

Last night he'd mentioned living as husband and wife for the next month. Did it mean actually sleeping with him as part of the arrangement? If that were the case, she'd certainly rethink the whole deal. But if she didn't sleep with him, would he count the days that passed that she didn't share his bed? Perhaps she'd better. She still wanted a child, and making love to him was the only way.

Leaving his room presented a problem when his intoxicating, manly scent of spice surrounded her and made her comfortable. The longer she stood breathing in his scent, the more her body became hypnotized with the memory of his heated touches and wild kisses. Images of their passionate moments together at the masquerade ball propelled through her mind.

She wandered to his large closet, slid open the

doors and beheld the numerous outfits he'd acquired. As she looked closer, she noticed that the first two closets were of his everyday attire, but the other two looked like costumes.

On closer inspection, she could see that they were indeed disguises. He had a change of clothes for each character he'd become, when sneaking around and fooling people into getting what he wanted. She recognized the old man's clothing that he'd worn that first time they met when he rescued her from kidnapers. It hung neatly beside the Hell's seduction costume.

She remembered that day as though it were yesterday; being the curious young girl she had been two years ago. Two men who had loathed her father kidnapped her for ransom. Neil had disguised himself as an old beggar man to gain the trust of Benji and Henry—the imbeciles who had taken her. It had been Neil's soft eyes and long, lean fingers that led her to believe he was somebody else under those ragged and filthy clothes. If not for Neil, she could have been killed, for Benji and Henry were mean and cold-hearted as the devil.

Neil had been the most perfect man she'd ever laid eyes on. In her tender eighteen years, she hadn't fully developed, and so he thought her to be younger. Why hadn't she seen back then how forcing someone to marry her would eventually ruin her life?

On instinct, she reached into the closet and took hold of the black cape he'd worn at the masquerade ball and brought it to her nose. Remarkably, it still held her rose scent from that night. She closed her eyes and sank against the cedar closet door.

Was it really only two nights ago when she'd experienced passion so wonderful with a man who heated her body like never before? Sexual tingles roamed throughout her body, so she quickly fled from his room, slamming the door behind her. She had to keep her mind on other subjects.

When the noon hour arrived, it relieved her to at least have something to do. The cook asked her what she wanted to eat, but Charlotte didn't feel hungry. Neil's suggestion kept plaguing her thoughts, and only out of boredom did she decide to go to his office.

The slight bounce in her step and smile tugging on her lips surprised her as she readied for her outings. She tried to tell herself she wasn't excited, but her joyful attitude suggested differently.

She rushed into the kitchen to find the cook. "Would you make me a picnic basket? I'm going to surprise Neil at work."

When Charlotte arrived at Neil's office, she took a deep breath for courage then entered the building. The lobby was empty, so she moved to the adjoining room, thinking that someone might be there, but once again, nobody occupied the space. Another room off to the side caught her attention, but was hidden behind a closed door.

She knocked, but didn't get a reply. Pressing her ear against the hard wood, she listened, and when no sound came, she walked in. Once inside she detected her husband's spice scent. Cautiously, she wandered through his office, touching each book, paper; anything her fingers could caress as her mind told her that he had also touched these.

She cursed her sappy emotions. She needed to stay strong.

Many framed letters were displayed on the wall on one side of the room. On closer inspection, Charlotte realized they were thank you notes and letters of appreciation from Neil's clients.

It was rather strange to see how well-liked her husband was in New York. Her heart sank. If they worked out their marriage problems, then surely his popularity would keep him here instead of back home in South Carolina where she wanted to be.

She scooted around his desk and sat in his high back leather chair. How long would she wait for him to return? She sighed. Somebody would be here soon or they would have locked up the office.

Across the cluttered desk, a piece of paper grabbed her attention. The neat scrawling invited her to read it. As she skimmed the handwriting, she realized that this may indeed be the case he was presently working on.

September 4, 1852

I haven't quite realized the mystery surrounding this man, but it intrigues me more every time I see him. No matter how hard I look for a flaw, I just can't find one. Due to his hideous scarred face, he's not perfect, but he's definitely making me believe in purity. There isn't a thing this man cannot do. I try to talk with him, but he refuses. I must be more inconspicuous when I spy on him. I also need to discover the mystery that surrounds his castle near the Hudson. Is he hiding something in that spacious castle, or is it the man he doesn't want people to discover?

Charlotte's enthusiasm sprang to life. Ideas floated through her mind, and curiosity made her want to help, but knowing her husband's arrogant attitude the way she did, Neil wouldn't allow it. He wouldn't understand that this mysterious man just might speak freely to a woman rather than another man.

With a satisfied sigh, she sank back in the chair and grinned. She'd have to sneak behind her husband's back, but that thought only intrigued her. Checking out a mysterious man and an old castle might put a spark to her boredom and help the next month to pass quickly.

Chapter Six

Neil smiled at his beautiful wife as he seated her behind the large oak dining table. A large chandelier hung above the center of the table. Flickering candles created a romantic mood. Before leaving her side, he stroked her neck, his gaze wandering down the bodice of her gown. Although it presented not a hint of flesh, it molded nicely to her fine curves.

He withdrew his attention from her bosom and walked around the table. "I missed you at lunch today." He pulled out his chair then sat. "I had hoped you would come."

She took the linen napkin and placed it across her lap. "I did come, but you weren't there."

He arched his brow. "Indeed?"

"Yes. Your cook even prepared a picnic, but since I couldn't find you, I returned and ate alone."

He placed his elbow on the table, resting his chin in his hands as he stared into her intoxicating gray eyes. "I wonder why Mr. Stout didn't tell me?"

"Who is Mr. Stout?"

"My secretary."

"He wasn't there, either." She dipped her spoon in the bowl of soup and brought it to her lips. "Your office wasn't even locked."

"That's odd."

She lifted her gaze to his. "So, what kind of case are you working on? Is it dangerous?"

He chuckled. "Not exactly."

"Are you trying to capture a thief?"

He grinned at her curiosity. "Perhaps."

"Find a cheating spouse?"

He tilted back his head and roared with laughter. "Charlotte? Where are you getting these insane notions?"

"I've read a lot of novels."

"Well, unfortunately, the case I'm working on now is not that exciting. In fact, it's so boring I don't even want to discuss it."

He brought his wineglass to his mouth and took a swallow. "So, what kept you busy today, my dear?"

She tightened her fingers around her fork. "If the truth be known, I had an extremely uneventful day. I couldn't find enough to do."

He grinned. "Perhaps I should have stayed home and kept you entertained after all."

She shot him a glare. "So bored was I, in fact," she continued, not even looking at the rise and fall of his eyebrows as he hinted the sexual meaning, "that I went to Allison's hotel room and tried to enlist her help for an escape."

Neil remained silent for a few moments, trying to decide whether anger or hurt ruled his emotions. He knew he'd have to break her down slowly because she'd not forgiven him, but doubt crept into his mind, making him wary. Would he come home from work one day and find her gone?

"What did Mrs. Archibald say?"

Charlotte laughed lightly, dabbing the corner of the linen to her mouth. "She flatly refused to help." She eyed him harshly. "If I didn't know better, I'd think my friends are conspiring against me."

He let out a relieved breath and smiled. "Perhaps they think we are right for each other."

She rolled her eyes heavenward. "You are very humorous. I thought I'd convinced them I deserved better than a husband who'd abandoned me right after our wedding."

Holding his tongue from biting back in defense,

he stroked the lower half of his face. Her words hurt, and although it took courage to admit, he really deserved her anger.

"Let me rephrase that," he said softly. "Perhaps Mrs. Archibald and Ian think you are the woman for me."

"You deserve nothing less than a piranha," she hissed, quickly lifting the wineglass to her lips again.

He chuckled at her temper. "Well, then I suppose I'll just have to prove to you how loving and attentive I can be, won't I?" He set his napkin on his empty plate and leaned back in his chair. "Which brings me to our next subject." His fingers drummed on the tabletop. "I've been invited to a ball tonight, and I'd really like to show off my beautiful wife."

Her hands twisted the napkin on the table, while a frown marred her face. "Are you asking or commanding?"

He shrugged. "I'm informing, but if you don't want to go, I'll understand."

She sighed and her rigid expression eased a bit. "Does that mean I can remain at home?"

"No, but at least I'll understand your frame of mind when your fangs sink into my neck at oft times during our evening."

"Oh!" She threw her napkin on her plate and jmped away from the table. "I'm just as much a prisoner as I was two years ago when you rescued me from those kidnapers." She turned and shot out of the room.

Neil leapt, reaching for her, but wasn't quick enough. The loud slamming of the door echoed through the house, and left a pain of sadness in his chest. He'd have to work really hard at softening her heart, or the next month would be unbearable.

****

Charlotte held her chin erect and pasted on a

smile as her surprisingly attentive husband grasped her elbow and introduced her to his friends and associates at the ball. She caught a few raised eyebrows and thought she might have heard whispers behind her back, but she knew how to ignore gossip. As he pulled her from one couple to the next, she studied his sinfully handsome face and admitted that he seemed proud of her.

He certainly knew the art of deceiving.

Neil had these people wrapped around his little finger. His flowery words charmed and enticed the women, and the stories of his investigations lured the men to hang on his every word.

As her gaze skimmed the length of his body, her heart skipped a beat. He looked masculine and refined in his black coat tails and trousers. The white silk shirt ruffled at his neck and wrists, and the silver necktie accented his bronzed skin perfectly.

Her silver-blue evening gown coordinated perfectly with his attire, making them an exceptionally looking pair. The long elbow-length black gloves accented her black gold necklace and earbobs. She patted the tight twist bun her maid had fixed and her fingers swept along the diamond studs sprinkled throughout her hair.

When Neil whisked her around on the dance floor, his precise steps and rhythm let her know how expertly he'd been taught. He fit right in with this crowd.

The moment came when Neil gave permission for other men to take her out on the dance floor, and she inwardly sighed with relief to be away from his overpowering presence. His masculine spice scent hung in the air around her, and fortunately, most of the men she danced with didn't come close to his alluring sexuality.

Time away from her husband gave her leave to

ask about the mysterious castle and the lord who presided there. It surprised her to think not many people knew about the castle, but of course, the castle was sitting in what they considered farm country.

Finally, a charming older gentleman, Mr. Marcum, told her the castle had been empty for many years, until about four months ago. The occupant of the castle hadn't come into town to make his presence known, so not many people knew about him. There was plenty of gossip, but nothing factual.

Her overactive imagination kicked into high gear, and she decided tomorrow she'd do a little investigating…without Neil's help.

The dance ended and her weary legs carried her to the wall as she waited for the butler to bring around a tray of champagne. She scanned the room for her husband, but couldn't find him in this crowd. Suddenly, his intoxicating scent touched her senses.

"Aren't you enjoying yourself, Mrs. Hamilton?"

Her head swung toward Neil and a breath caught in her throat from his closeness. "Whatever gave you that idea?"

His finger stroked her bottom lip. "The frown upon your tempting mouth."

She shrugged. "I'm just tired, that's all."

"Before we call it a night, will you dance one waltz with me? I'd like to feel you in my arms one more time before we depart."

His tender words made her heart leap, yet she cursed him. She found it harder and harder to fight her own battle of personal restraint. She placed her hand in his and he escorted her to the dance floor. His unmoving stare held her attention.

"I heard you've been asking about the castle," he began.

She gasped softly. "Um...yes. I overheard mention of an old castle that's located near Hudson

Bay, and my curious mind couldn't help but wonder." She paused. "Do you know anything about it?"

He grinned. "What sort of things do you want to know, my sweet lady?"

Excitement made her breathing accelerate. "Well, I've heard it's been empty for many years and that nobody has seen the owner."

"That's correct."

"Do you know who lives there?"

One of his eyebrows rose. "Why the sudden interest?"

She laughed lightly. "You certainly don't know me very well. I just love a good mystery."

He laughed as his arm tightened around her waist. "A man lives there. I've talked with him on a few occasions, but he's very reclusive. I think it's because of his deformity."

"Is he an old man?"

"No. Probably middle age or around in there."

"I wonder why he has chosen to live alone?"

"Like I said, I think it's because of his deformity."

"What does he look like? Is he an ogre?"

He chuckled. "I would tell you, my dear, but I don't want to frighten you. I'm aware of a woman's sensitive nature."

She rolled her eyes. "Oh, posh, Neil. You can tell me."

He shrugged. "He's not a monster, if that's what you mean. He's a normal man. Brown hair, a beard and mustache, normal physique. You know, an ordinary man if you ask me, except of course, for his face."

"What's wrong with it?"

"He has some kind of a scar or burn on the left side. It's somewhat of an oddity because it practically covers up his eye and most of his face."

A shiver ran through her. "I wonder how he

could receive such a mark?"

"I don't have that knowledge."

"And the castle, is it really old?"

"Yes. I think it's one of the oldest standing buildings in New York. I could be wrong, but it's what I've heard."

She sighed heavily. "That's amazing."

"Yes. Maybe someday when this man comes out of seclusion, I'll take you there."

"That would be wonderful."

Charlotte smiled. This bit of information would get her through the rest of the evening and pump her full of energy for the morrow when she'd get to work on her own investigation.

It made her curious why this man interested Neil. Her husband really didn't give her any indication of why he was investigating him, but there had to be a reason. Neil even mentioned on the paper she'd read that he thought this mysterious man was perfect. It seemed impossible the only reason Neil would be interested was to find fault with the man.

As her mind began working, she routed out her plans. She'd visit Neil's office tomorrow, but wait until he left. Snooping was her only way to get information, and his office and the study at home were the only two places that would hold anything of value.

One way or another, she was going to discover important information about the mysterious man who lived in the castle. She gritted her teeth. *Men!* She'd prove to Neil she was more than just a decoration.

The next morning, Charlotte pulled herself awake, and through her groggy state, she smelled the fragrance of a rose as it caressed her cheek. Neil loomed over her on the bed, just as he'd done the morning before. Because of their late night, she wasn't ready to rise, so turned away and rolled toward the wall.

"Charlotte, my dear, wake up."

She groaned with resistance and pulled the blanket up to her chin.

He chuckled, then the bed moved as he leaned over and kissed her cheek. "Sweetheart, I've got to go to work."

She let out a few more grumbles of protest. His fingers moved her chin toward him, and his lips nestled hers. He'd kissed her just as he'd done yesterday morning.

"Charlotte, I'm going out of town this afternoon and I won't be back until late tonight. If you need anything, let my butler know."

Although she kept her eyes closed, this information brought her mind alert. She waited until Neil left the room, then sat up and listened for him to leave the house. When the clip clop of the horse's hooves echoed down the street, she swung her legs off the bed. She grabbed her robe and wrapped it around her body as she snuck into his bedroom.

His scent lingered in the air and made places on her body grow warm. She pushed away the feeling and moved to his closets, searching through pockets on his trousers and jackets. When she came up empty, she looked through dresser drawers, trying to find any papers with his handwriting, but once again, discovered nothing.

She left the room and padded down the stairs, hoping the servants wouldn't hear. She didn't want to explain why she was sneaking around.

Entering his study was easier than she thought, and she closed the door softly behind her. She searched through the files on the desk first, reading each paper or receipt that she could find. After about an hour of going through his desk, Charlotte sighed with disappointment. She'd come up empty. The last place to go was his office, but she'd have to wait until he and his secretary were gone.

She returned upstairs to her room and dressed in one of her more modest dresses. The yellow cream-colored frock clung nicely to her curves, and the short waist jacket accented her slender hips. The high neck collar didn't show any hint of skin, and the long straight sleeves hugged her arms down to her wrists. The straight skirt dragged behind a small train. A matching bonnet completed her ensemble. By the stares and glances from the people on the streets as she rode the buggy into town, she knew she'd dressed well today.

When she entered her husband's office, a mousy looking man sat at the first desk. He quickly scrambled to rise. This must be Neil's secretary. What did he call him...Mr. Stout? She didn't have time to think up an excuse for being there before the man took off his hat and bowed.

"Good morning."

"Hello. I'm Mr. Hamilton's wife."

He nodded. "Mr. Hamilton spoke of you. It's a pleasure to meet you. I'm Ewan Stout."

When he reached a hand out in greeting, she shook it once before releasing him. "Nice to meet you, also."

"I'm sorry, Mrs. Hamilton, but your husband has traveled to the next town over to get some supplies. He won't be back in his office at all today."

"Thank you. I suppose I'll just have to go shopping without him."

"Do you need money?"

"Oh, no." She smiled. "As I've discovered before, all I need to do is say my husband's name and most of the shop's clerks fall at my feet."

The man laughed. "Yes. Hamilton is certainly a well-respected man around here."

"Well, I'll be going. Have a pleasant day, and I hope to see you soon."

She exited the building and made her way through the crowd to her vehicle parked across the street. Hopefully, she wouldn't have to wait too long before Mr. Stout left. This morning's warm sun beat down upon her, making her uncomfortable at times.

An hour later, the man finally walked out of the office, closing the door behind him. She glanced down at her pocket timepiece. It was the same time of day as yesterday when she been there.

As proper as she could, she hurried across the street to his office and tested the door. When the door opened, relief poured through her. Quickly she entered and rushed to her husband's office. The first place she looked was on his desk. Most of the papers she'd seen yesterday were here, except for the lone article that had captured her curiosity.

Where could it be? Her gaze skimmed through the papers again, but it wasn't there. Irritated, she slumped in Neil's chair and exhaled deeply. She moved her gaze around the room and noticed a small filing drawer she hadn't seen yesterday.

Her hopes lifted as she crouched and pulled out the drawers. There were files with some of Neil's clients, so she scanned through the names in hopes of finding something about the castle. Luck was on her side again, and the file was named plain and simple—Castle.

She opened the file and found another paper. It was dated yesterday.

I've found fault with Lord Thatcher. It's rather comical, yet I shouldn't be the one to point out the bad in people. But the man knows something that's vital to this mystery, yet he won't relent. He knows of my interest, but he says nothing. He's like a dark closet with many ghosts.

A smile touched her lips as refreshing energy

soared through her body, and the mystery was more than she could stand. So many questions ran rapid through her mind. What kind of ghosts did this man have in his closet? Is that what her husband was searching for? And why would Neil want to know? What was the connection between Neil Hamilton and Lord Thatcher?

She put away the file and left the office before the secretary came back. She decided to go to the castle and do a little snooping. It was time she met the mystery man as Neil's wife. Neil gave the impression he knew this man well, so the deformed lord would indeed accept her into his house, she just knew it.

Chapter Seven

Lord Thatcher shielded his eyes with his hand as he glanced up at the sun, calculating the time. He hadn't even been outside for two hours and already he was eager to return indoors. Today's heat practically seared his clothes to his body.

Looking upon the acres of unkempt land, he sighed and swiped his fingers through his hair. What was he going to do about this hellhole? How was he going to keep it up? Servants were definitely necessary, but right now, he didn't know if he had the funds to provide for them. It was bad enough he'd been slaving away for months already trying to make the rooms halfway livable.

He kicked his boot in the dirt. He definitely needed to hire grounds men, but his primary concern was to purchase some tall iron gates to keep out all of the curious onlookers who came to peek at the castle and its new lord. Rumors had been circling the city about a new lord occupying Hudson's haunted house, and although he wanted to put a stop to it, he didn't think going into town would do it.

For fifty years, he'd been the only person sane enough to live in this castle. That was too long to go without servants, no matter how ridiculous the notion of ghosts. In fact, the only good thing about this castle was the inspiration the atmosphere gave him to write a mystery novel. Ghosts and old castles ignited his creative mind.

He rubbed the back of his neck and sighed. Patience wasn't one of his virtues, but if his investments paid off, he'd be one of the richest men in New York in a couple of months. If not...well, he didn't want to think about it.

He picked out a few yard tools from the utility shed needed to get the front yard in order. There were other things to be done also, but at least this would get him started on making his home presentable.

After about an hour, the hot sun nearly baked his clothes on his body and suffocated him. He put aside the hoe, yanked off his shirt and set it aside. He surveyed the premises for inquisitive peepers, but thankfully, nobody was about. With a chuckle, he thought about the ghosts that kept most people away. Hell, he could probably work out here naked and not be noticed.

He grasped the hoe in his gloved hands and pounded it into the dry earth, preparing the ground for seed. Time seemed to pass remarkably fast as his labored breathing and birds in the trees kept him company. Then another sound pulled his attention away from the dirt.

Wheels from a buggy crunched on the gravel nearby and he snapped his head toward the sound to his unwelcome visitor. The sun blared in his eyes, but as the buggy grew closer, it blocked the sun's brightness. When he focused on the intruder in the vehicle, he blinked, certain his eyes were deceiving him. A woman was driving the buggy?

He rubbed the sweat away from his eyes, but when he focused again, there sat a vision in gold staring at him. He waited for her to scream at his deformity, to turn her horse and head back the way she came. But she didn't. Brave woman.

For the sake of propriety, he quickly spun around and grabbed his shirt to hide his naked chest. When he turned, she stopped the vehicle and smiled. It struck him funny to see such a reaction when he was used to women fainting when they first looked upon him. But the lady didn't even flinch. Certainly out of the ordinary.

"Good afternoon," she spoke with a heart-warming voice.

What were her true intentions?

"I hope you don't mind my intrusion," she continued, "but I thought I'd be neighborly and come to make your acquaintance."

A grin tugged at his mouth, and he wanted to laugh. Neighborly? His nearest neighbors were miles away, and he knew she wasn't one of them.

"You live close by?" he asked, trying to hide the scratchiness in his voice.

"Well, not really, I live inside the city, but my husband is an acquaintance of yours. That is the reason I decided to come."

He drew his brows together. Putting his weight on his good leg, he limped closer to the buggy and gazed up at her. "I know your husband?"

"Yes. Mr. Neil Hamilton."

"Ah, yes. I know your husband," he mumbled in irritation.

Her gaze wavered slightly and her hands gripped the reins. Quickly, he put the pleasantness back on his face before he caused her scream and faint dead away.

"You don't look too pleased," she said.

He shrugged and hobbled to his small pile of dirt, his awkward steps slowing him. "Perhaps it's not your fault for your husband's mistakes. It's true I don't care for the man, but," he said glancing back at her, "I'll try and be polite for your sake."

"Pray, what has my husband done to make you this way?"

He laughed harshly. "What hasn't he done?" He shook his head and held up his hand. "No, I won't say more. I shan't degrade the man in front of his wife when he's not here to defend himself."

She fidgeted in her seat. “Would you mind very much if I introduce myself?”

He smiled. “I wouldn’t mind at all.”

She made a move to climb down from the buggy, so he limped over and assisted her. Hesitantly, she placed her hand in his gloved hand until she was on the ground, then he stepped back. But still, she didn’t scream in horror. This brave woman interested him.

“Thank you,” she said. “My name is Mrs. Charlotte Hamilton.” She held out her hand in greeting.

He took it, bowed slightly then placed a small kiss on her knuckles. “Adam Newton, the Earl of Thatcher at your service.”

“It’s certainly a pleasure to finally meet you, Lord Thatcher. My husband speaks of you often.”

He chuckled and shook his head. “I wonder if anyone has told your husband it’s not polite to speak ill of people behind their backs.”

“Oh, no. He hasn’t spoken ill of you at all. In fact, he claims you as a friend.”

He lifted his eyebrows. “Indeed? That’s strikes me funny because I don’t think I could do the same.”

She lowered her gaze for a brief moment, wringing her hands against her stomach. “Well, will you claim me as your friend?”

He laughed. “But alas, how can I? You are married to that scoundrel, Mr. Neil Hamilton.”

She cocked her head. “Tsk, tsk. You’re speaking badly of him again in front of his wife. I thought you said you weren’t going to do that.”

He grinned. “I’m sorry. It’s so hard to keep the words from my lips, but I’ll try harder.”

His gaze raked over her and he liked the pretty picture she presented. Very much a lady. He admired that. But what was her real purpose for being here?

She glanced around the yard at what he'd been doing. "My lord? May I ask why you're out here and not your servants?"

"To be quite honest, I don't have any servants at present. But after working today in this bloody hot sun, I'm beginning to think a trip into town is very much needed."

"I should say so." She grinned. "This is very hard work for a lord like yourself. The least you should do is have somebody help you."

He chuckled. "Tell me, Madame, how did a beautiful and charming woman end up married to a rogue like Neil Hamilton?"

She held her smile and wagged her finger. "Oh, there you go again, Lord Thatcher, degrading my husband."

"Once again, I'm truly sorry. But it seems you don't mind overly much. Could it be you know him as well as I?"

She shrugged. "I couldn't say. I don't know of your relationship to my husband."

"That, my dear, I will never tell."

When her gaze skimmed over his attire once more, he shifted, suddenly uncomfortable with her close scrutiny. He still waited for some signs his appearance repulsed her, but a teasing grin remained on her mouth, which eased his nerves.

"I think, Lord Thatcher, you are not so blind."

He lifted his brows. "Are you divulging your secrets?"

"Not right after meeting you. Besides, if I did I'd be afraid of losing your friendship."

He couldn't help it. She made him laugh. Heartily. Was she genuine? "Oh, but I think I'll still be your friend, especially if your secrets make your husband appear less than manly."

She didn't laugh, just continued to smile.

"I think I'd better leave you to get back to your

work." She stepped toward her buggy. "If you'd like, I'd be more than happy to post a job notice for you in the city's center."

He rubbed his chin, not thinking about anything except the lovely woman in front of him. "That's very kind of you. I'd greatly appreciate it. Going into town is most discouraging for me, and your efforts will be of great help."

"Then consider it done." She turned to climb back into the buggy. He hurried to her side, took her elbow and helped her up.

She fluffed her skirt around her legs then held the reins. "Lord Thatcher? Would you mind terribly if I called on you again?"

He grinned. "Only if you leave your husband behind."

"But what would people think?"

He chuckled and glanced around his lands. "What people? There's not another person for miles, and I'd like to keep it that way."

"Well, all right, but would it be all right if I brought a friend with me next time? I know she'd love to see your castle. We are from South Carolina and have never seen anything so grand."

He hesitated, creasing his forehead in thought. "I am really not the hospitable type, you understand." He fluttered his hand over the scar covering half of his face.

"I understand," she quickly replied.

"But, I'll meet your friend if you agree not to stay very long. And if I can tell she's uncomfortable in my presence, I will ask you to leave."

She nodded. "That is a perfect plan. Thank you for a pleasant visit."

He placed his gloved hands on the reins to stop her from going just yet. He couldn't let her go. Not until he got some answers. "Mrs. Hamilton?"

"Yes."

"Why is it you're not frightened by my face? Not once have I noticed you cringe when you look upon me, and you meet my eyes, whereas most people do not."

Her cheerful smile didn't waver. "Why would I be frightened of you, my lord?"

"Because of my deformities."

She finally moved her gaze to look upon the ugly mark that took up most of the left side of his face and his chin. "That little thing?" She let out a sweet laugh that made his heart sing. "Why would I be frightened of a little scar?"

He chuckled softly and shook his head. "You're either an excellent actress or blind as a bat, Mrs. Hamilton. But thank you, nonetheless. You've cheered me up immensely."

"I'm glad." She gathered the reins tighter in her grasp. "Good day, my lord."

"Until next time." As he waved, he watched her drive away.

He'd better be on his best behavior and not be overly friendly with her. It'd been quite a while since a woman had looked at him like she did, and he liked it.

****

The hands on the grandfather clock slowly ticked by as Charlotte sat in her husband's leather chair, waiting for his return. Dinner had been long past, and try as she might, she couldn't find a single thing to keep her entertained. She drummed her fingernails on the wooden armrest as she stared out the window into the darkened night.

The clatter of horses' hooves on the road out front announced a visitor, and she jerked her attention to the butler who scurried to the door. Sitting straight and proper, she waited for him to inform her who was calling. Instead of seeing her husband coming into the room, it was the servant.

"Mistress, a messenger delivered this letter for you."

She stood and took it from the older man. "Thank you, O'Toole."

Taking a deep breath, she steadied her hands before ripping open the sealed paper. Right away, she recognized Neil's handwriting.

"My dearest Charlotte, I apologize for not being home with you now, but business has held me up for at least another day. I count the hours until I'm back in your charming presence. When I return, I'll stay home from work and take you anywhere your heart desires."

"Ha!" She crumbled the paper in her hands and snickered. "I can't help but think you're lying, my wayward husband. But it's one more day scratched off the beastly agreement you forced me into."

She walked to her chair and sank into the seat. Although she wondered if Neil was deceiving her, at least one good thing came out of this. She'd be able to visit Lord Thatcher tomorrow and not worry about being caught. A smile spread across her face when she thought about the mystery she'd soon discover.

The next morning, she dressed carefully. Her appearance had to be impressive, not alluring certainly, but just a touch sensual. Lord Thatcher must be hungry for a woman's company, and although she didn't want him to misinterpret her visit, she should still look her best.

The puffy sleeves of the deep gray dress tapered down her arms, ending at a point on her knuckles. White lace decorated the high collar on the square neck, almost as if its purpose was to hide the small amount of skin on her neck. The full skirt was pinched into a small bustle in the back.

She had her maid wrap her hair loosely in a bun and cover it with black netting, leaving a few tendrils around her ears. After adding a touch of perfume to her neck and wrists, she was ready to leave.

Allison looked equally as sophisticated, and Charlotte was happy to see the two of them were thinking alike. It relieved her when Ian didn't accompany them.

Allison climbed in the buggy next to Charlotte and fixed her bonnet. "I must admit this is very exciting. When you sent me the note yesterday about our outing, I couldn't wait."

Charlotte nodded. "I'm very happy you are joining me." She urged the horses forward into a fast trot, and then asked, "So tell me, how are things between you and Ian? Do you think he'll ask you to marry him?"

"I don't think he will, but even if he did, I'd have to turn him down."

Charlotte's brows drew together when she glanced at her friend. "But why?"

Allison stared on the road. "Because I was married to an older man for a couple of years, and now that he's gone, I've realized just how much I enjoy my freedom. I'm not ready to give it up."

"Does Ian know?"

"Yes."

"And he doesn't mind?"

Allison shrugged. "He knows I'm not ready to marry, so he stays away from the subject."

The ride to the castle seemed to fly by. The excitement was so much that Charlotte didn't enjoy the green trees, the lush hills covered with wildflowers, and the freshly bloomed daisies that Allison kept pointing out to her. Charlotte's enthusiasm grew when she entered Lord Thatcher's property. The land appeared as desolate as it had yesterday. It made her happy that she'd sent the footman to post the notice for help earlier this morning.

She pulled the buggy to a stop in the front of the castle and she and Allison climbed out. Her attention caught on a set of hardwood double doors, and especially a carved lion's head looming over the entrance.

Charlotte's jaw dropped in awe, and a small gasp escaped her lips. "Can you believe this? Isn't it absolutely Medieval?"

"I can't wait to see the inside," Allison whispered.

"Now remember," Charlotte said in a whisper, "his face is hideously scarred, but you can't be frightened or he'll turn us away. He really is a gentle, kind man."

Allison nodded and licked her lips. "I'm ready."

Charlotte rapped the knocker on the door.

"Did you hear how it echoes?" Allison whispered.

"Yes, it sounds eerie."

They waited a few minutes before Charlotte raised the knocker and let it drop again. This time, the knob turned. As the door swung open, a piercing squeal filled the small foyer. At first all she saw was darkness, and then as her eyes adjusted to the light, a body emerged through the shadows and into the sun's rays. Lord Thatcher wore a black over-jacket and trousers, suited to fit his station.

Her heart beat erratically. "Good morning, Lord Thatcher."

When his eyes rested on her, he smiled. "I rather figured you'd be back."

Her cheeks burned. "Yes, well, my father did tell me I was too curious as a child."

"And are you still curious as an adult?"

She nodded. "Can I help it that your castle has me intrigued?"

Lord Thatcher's gaze moved to Allison. "Mrs. Hamilton, aren't you going to introduce me to your lovely friend?"

Today he wore a dark, thick scarf around his head that tried to hide the scares on his face. He must have done this for Allison's sake. Thank heavens his scarf didn't hide his groomed black mustache and beard, which she thought made him look sophisticated.

"Oh, Lord Thatcher," she exclaimed, "please forgive me. This is Mrs. Allison Archibald."

Allison's unsteady hand stretched out. Lord Thatcher took it tenderly in his grasp and placed a small kiss on her knuckles. Allison's face paled slightly. Charlotte held her breath, praying her friend wouldn't swoon. Allison straightened and lifted her chin, finally gaining control. Charlotte slowly released her breath.

He smiled. "It's a pleasure to meet the friend of Mrs. Hamilton."

"The privilege is all mine, my lord." Allison bowed slightly.

He stepped away from the door and motioned with his hand. "Would you please come in? I'm certain you would like to see inside."

Allison chuckled. "Yes, I have to admit I'm very curious."

Charlotte stepped into the hallway first, and darkness surrounded her. The only light was the shimmering flame of a candle sitting on a large side table by the door.

"You'll have to forgive me, but I don't have an oil lamp on this floor just yet." He retrieved the candle. "This is all I have right now, but after we get into the castle further, I'll be able to retrieve my oil lamp. You don't mind, do you?"

"Oh, no," Charlotte replied as her eyes darted around the floor, praying no mice were scurrying about. "We'll just stay close by you."

Charlotte remained directly on Lord Thatcher's heels, and on a few occasions grabbed anxiously onto the sleeve of his coat. The walls were of stone, and a musky scent hung in the air. Their footsteps reverberated down the cold hallway. A chill ran through her, and she felt a cold aura to the place that a million fires couldn't dissolve. He led them from one room to the next, and in the semi-darkness, his limp echoed through the corridors, accenting his deformed leg.

Each room they passed, she peered into the emptiness. Surprisingly, they were larger than most dining rooms of the wealthy nobility. They held no furniture and reminded her of great dance halls. It was hard to see if the rooms held paintings or decorations because of poor lighting.

"Lord Thatcher? Are there any windows in this castle?"

"Oh, yes, Mrs. Hamilton, but they're all boarded. In my housecleaning, I haven't tackled that chore."

"Lord Thatcher?" Allison's voice echoed through the empty halls. "Are you in need of help to fix up this place?"

"Why, Mrs. Archibald?" He glanced over his shoulder at her, holding up the flame to see her facial expression. "Are you offering your services?"

Although Allison may have been weak-kneed at the door, she seemed to have gathered herself together. "Well, yes, I suppose I am. It just occurred to me that while Mrs. Hamilton and I are here, we might assist you."

"I'm afraid the work is far greater than two gentle bred ladies are accustomed to."

Allison chuckled. "Hard work has never bothered me, what about you Charlotte?"

Charlotte hesitated before answering. The truth was, she'd never worked a day in her life nor lifted a finger to do the work of a servant. Her father had seen to that. She fidgeted with the folds of her skirt. "Well, I don't know what kind of help I'd be, but if you'll show me what to do, I'd be happy to give it a try."

He laughed. "I couldn't possibly allow you ladies to work. You'd ruin those delicate hands of yours."

Relief poured through Charlotte and she sighed.

Ahead of them, a bright rectangle of sunlight lay on the stone floor. Charlotte was drawn to it. She stood agape in the doorway of a most amazing room. Many oil lamps sat on the tables in the large area. Three enormous windows helped to welcome in the sun, uncontained in the late morning light. The sun's heat gave the room a wonderful homey atmosphere, relaxing Charlotte's nerves. In the corner of the room, built into the wall, was a huge stone fireplace with a fire inside.

Charlotte gasped. They were in the library. The tall shelves were higher than she could reach, but long ladders were placed along the bookshelves, helping to reach the elevated locations. Each shelf supported very old novels, their covers dusty and worn.

"I don't believe I've ever seen so many books in one place," she exclaimed.

Allison walked to a shelf and removed a book. "Were all these here when you moved in?"

"Yes. I've replaced a few because they fell apart when I opened them."

"Amazing," Charlotte replied, enthusiastically.

There was a gentle lift to Lord Thatcher's mouth. "Do you like to read, Mrs. Hamilton?"

"Oh, yes."

"What sort of books do you like?"

"Mysteries."

He smirked. "Strange, but I didn't think you'd be the type."

"Why?

He shrugged as he walked to the soft brown leather sofa. "I don't know. I just can't imagine your interest to lie in that area." He paused and grinned. "Would you like to look around?"

"Oh, yes," Charlotte and Allison women chimed in unison.

Charlotte moved from book to book, trying to decide which one to read first. The castle was more exciting than she'd thought possible, and Lord Thatcher intrigued her by the minute. She hoped she could develop a lasting friendship with the man. But then, Lord Thatcher didn't like Neil. This would certainly become a problem in the near future.

****

Adam relaxed against his leather couch as Charlotte scanned the bookshelves, her hand moving along each book as she went. Those two women were different as night and day. Each had their own special beauty, but Mrs. Archibald seemed to be more aggressive after she got over the initial shock of seeing his face. Charlotte presented a sweet demure of politeness in a shy sort of manner. Their tastes in books were even different. Whereas Charlotte looked for the mysteries, Mrs. Archibald settled more for the non-fiction or biographies. He even noticed she picked up a few sonnets.

After the women made their selections, they sat on the sofas huddling around the fireplace. They discussed the books they'd previously read. It surprised him to hear Charlotte was indeed the mystery type woman. The more he knew about this lovely woman, the more intrigued he became.

Mrs. Archibald poured tea as they visited for two more hours. Unfortunately, he couldn't visit with them much longer. Too many things needed to be done around the castle.

He cleared his throat, getting both women's attention. "I hate to put a damper on our lovely afternoon, but I must get back to work."

Charlotte frowned, which made Adam grin. It

was good to know she enjoyed his company as much as he enjoyed hers.

She nodded. "Perfectly understandable, Lord Thatcher. Both Mrs. Archibald and I think it's a pleasure to have spent the afternoon with you."

"Then our feelings are mutual."

He led them back through the castle to the front doors. "I'm sorry I didn't give you an adequate tour, but after I fix up the place, I promise to invite you back for a grand excursion."

Charlotte gently laid her hand on his arm. "Thank you for a wonderful afternoon. Is there anything I can bring you from town?"

His heart sped. It's been far too long since a woman touched him so personally. "Not at this time. You did, I presume, get the job notice posted?"

"But of course."

"Splendid. I hope to hear something soon."

He walked the ladies to their carriage and assisted them inside. Galloping horses coming up his drive made him turn in that direction. When he saw the uninvited visitors, he frowned.

He stepped back away from the carriage to greet them. Three of the sheriff's men rode up and stopped. They passed him rude stares through their squeamish expressions.

"Are you Lord Thatcher?" the first man asked with gruffness in his voice.

Adam folded his arms across his chest. "I am. May I be of any assistance?"

"Yes. We were told Mrs. Hamilton is here."

Confusion rooted itself in his mind as he glanced over at the buggy. "Yes. She's preparing to leave."

"We need to speak with her."

Adam's heart sank as he studied their faces. Something was not right. He hobbled to the buggy and helped Charlotte down. She faced the sheriff's men wearing a worried brow.

"I'm Mrs. Hamilton."

"We need to know the whereabouts of your husband."

A knot formed in Adam's throat as Charlotte's gaze darted back and forth between him and Mrs. Archibald. Why were the sheriff's men asking these questions?

Charlotte raised her chin. "He's out of town, but what business is that of yours?"

The man in the middle, wearing the biggest scowl, stepped forward. "Because Madame, your husband is in trouble with the law."

Charlotte gasped. "What? Are you certain?"

"Yes."

"But why? What has he done?"

"We expect him of thievery."

Charlotte gasped again, and tossed him a harsh laugh. "Neil Hamilton? A thief? I think not. You must be mistaken."

"No, Madame. Several people have come forth and accused him."

Charlotte's brows drew together in irritation. "Like whom?"

"Most of his clients."

"What proof do you have?"

The man shifted in his stance. "Your husband's business is the only thing these fine people have in common. Your husband has done some investigative work for them in the past few months."

She laughed ignorantly. "That's all? That's the only proof you have of his thievery?"

Her question made the lead man in charge blush. "Yes, so far. We're just looking to question him in regards to some improprieties."

"Improprieties? Indeed," Charlotte snapped.

Adam shook his head. Nothing made sense. And poor Charlotte. He wanted to comfort her, but that was not proper.

Charlotte held a straight expression. "Forgive me, but I can't help you. I know he left yesterday morning and that he'll be home tonight, but I can't tell you what time."

"Thank you, Mrs. Hamilton. We'll have a man on watch at your house for when he returns." The man nodded, then mounted and left with the other two following close behind.

Mrs. Archibald placed her hand on Charlotte's shoulder, but Charlotte stared after the sheriff's men as they rode away.

"Charlotte?" Allison asked softly. "What are you going to do?"

"I...I...don't know." She glanced back at Lord Thatcher. "Neil wouldn't do something so despicable, would he?"

He shrugged. "I wouldn't wish anything bad to happen to your husband, but there is the fact that..." he trailed off.

Should I tell her?

"What?" Charlotte grabbed hold of his black-gloved hand. "What's wrong?"

"Well, it's a known fact to most of New York that your husband's finances are not in great condition. His work has been suffering and he hasn't been making payments to his creditors."

"No," she gasped as her hand flew to her mouth.

"Which draws me to the conclusion that his so-called friends have turned on him for some insane reason. Just because he's had a bit of bad luck doesn't mean he's a thief. Your husband wouldn't lower himself to steal."

Tears welled in Charlotte's eyes as she shook her head.

"Mrs. Hamilton, the best thing for your husband right now is to stay away from the sheriff until he can discover who has laid claim to these false crimes."

Charlotte breathed slowly as the confusing thoughts swam in her head. She wanted to cry and scream all at the same time. She wanted everyone to disappear so she could cry in private. It wasn't good to show her emotions now. The shock was too great for her to bear in front of company.

She turned to her host. "Lord Thatcher, thank you for the lovely afternoon, but we shan't burden you a moment longer."

When she moved to climb into the carriage, Lord Thatcher assisted her.

"Mrs. Hamilton?" Lord Thatcher's voice brought her attention around. "If you need anything, please don't hesitate to ask."

She nodded, and then Allison urged the horses forward.

Silence hung thick in the buggy for the first part of the ride back until Charlotte couldn't hold back her doubts. "I think Neil wants me to stay with him for a month not only to rectify our marriage, but because I have the money to help him out of his problems. I'm certain once he gets the money from me, he'll leave me again."

Allison touched her hand. "You can't know that."

Charlotte shrugged. "It's how I feel." Her gaze remained on the road. "What am I supposed to think, Allison?" She didn't look at her friend, but continued. "The note he sent last night said he wasn't going to make it home until this evening. Now I wonder if he's out stealing from another client. Does he expect me to lie for him?"

Allison released a heavy sigh. "Oh, Charlotte, I think your imagination is getting the best of you. Why don't you give Neil a chance to explain before you condemn him?"

Charlotte rolled it over in her head then nodded. "I'll try my hardest to understand his explanation." She seriously hoped her confusion wouldn't control her thoughts when she finally listened.

After Charlotte left Allison at the hotel, she returned to Neil's townhouse. As the horse clip-clopped up the drive, she sighed in frustration. Three different men with deputy badges stood by the gate waiting to pounce on her like wolves on sheep. By their superior know-it-all stance, they were lying in wait for her husband.

Lifting her chin a notch higher and keeping a straight back, she descended from the buggy and made her way toward the house. The men swarmed around her, demanding entrance into her home to search the premises. Their snippish attitudes made her want to drive her fist through their turned-up noses, but Charlotte simmered her anger and let them in. They pushed past her in haste when she opened the door, nearly knocking her down in the process. Their boots clomped on the hard wooden floors, making her stomach twist.

A small crowd gathered outside her home to watch the spectacle, and embarrassment washed over her again. She turned to hurry back to the buggy, but a haggardly old woman stepped in her path and stopped her by grabbing her elbow.

"Excuse me, dearie?" the woman's high-pitched voice squeaked. "Are ye all right? Are those men bothering ye?"

Charlotte yanked her arm away. "I'm fine, and no, those men are not bothering me. Not yet, anyway." Once again, Charlotte tried to leave, but the old lady stopped her.

"Do ye needs me to stay wit ye?"

She gave the tall but portly woman a crossed look. "No, I'll be quite all right."

The lady wrapped her fingers tighter to Charlotte's elbow, her eyes darting around the small gathering. The crowd pushed closer to the house, and the older woman pulled Charlotte away from the onlookers.

Charlotte tried to pry the miscreant's fingers off her arm. "I don't know who you think you are, but you will unhand me or I'll scream," Charlotte snapped.

"Charlotte, it's me."

When she recognized her husband's voice, her eyes widened and a small gasp escaped her throat. She swept her gaze over the old lady once again and noticed a slight resemblance to her husband, but the full bosom and rounded hips were that of a woman.

"I'm in disguise so the sheriff's men won't notice me," he said softer.

She scanned his attire again, still not believing what she saw. "What are you doing here?" Her voice rose. "And why in heaven's name are the sheriff's men here?"

"I don't have time to explain, but you have to help me."

"I will not!"

"Shhh." He tugged on her arm. "Please lower your voice. Charlotte, you have to hear me out, but I can't explain right now. There are too many people around."

"No, I do not have to hear an explanation from you," she snapped.

He released her arm, his face sobering. "No, I suppose you don't, but will you anyway?"

She really should send him on his way, but the gentleness of his voice tore at her heart. She relented. "Where and when?"

He gave her a soft smile. "I'll wait until the men leave. I'll remain as an old woman, so when I come to the door, please let me in."

Chapter Eight

Charlotte's impatient footsteps marked up Neil's expensive gold and red Persian rug as she paced in the parlor, waiting for the sheriff's men to finish their business. She glanced at the pendulum against the far wall as the minutes slowly crept by, each tick making her want to scream.

Another hour passed with her holding her tongue, but she finally had enough. She let her temper explode at the first man who crossed her path. "I do believe your time is up!"

He lifted his chin a notch higher. "But the sheriff—"

"I don't give a hoot what the sheriff says." She anchored her hands on her hips. "Unless he has a handwritten note from the mayor himself, I'll not let you into my house again. Is that clear?"

Neil's servant, O'Toole, quickly took his place by her side, his chest puffed and ready for battle. It relieved her to see he and the other servants ushering the lawmen outside with brooms and sharp utensils in their possession. It was her privilege to slam the door, but when the sheriff's men lurked in the yard, her heart sank.

The butler moved beside her. "Don't believe a word those men say. The master would never do anything as despicable as what they're accusing."

"Thank you, O'Toole, but I'm anxious to hear Neil defend these accusations."

"Can I get you a snifter of brandy? Perhaps that might help calm your nerves."

She nodded as she rested her stressed body in

the softness of the parlor's sofa. "That would be delightful."

O'Toole stepped out of the room, gently closing the door. The ring from the pull-string outside echoed through the house, making her headache pound.

"O'Toole, please send whoever it is away. I don't feel up to company this evening," she called out to him, laying the palm of her hand on her forehead.

"Yes, Mistress."

Sighing, she relaxed her head against the softness of the heavily cushioned sofa. As she took a deep breath, she tried to calm her pounding head, but suddenly, loud arguing voices disturbed her peacefulness. *Neil!*

With her heart in a quick rhythm, she jumped up and hurried to the door. O'Toole stood next to the haggardly lady, physically attempting to prevent her from coming through the door.

"O'Toole?" Charlotte cried out. "It's all right. I'd forgotten she was coming for tea this evening."

Confusion creased O'Toole's brow as he stared dumbstruck at her, but he nodded and stepped away from the door. He opened it wider and let the older woman in.

"I told ye!" The old woman hit the butler over the head with her handbag. "Yer nothin' but a bunch of twitterin' fools."

Charlotte hid her grin behind her hand. Neil did such a good job acting the part of an old woman it was really quite comical. It pleased her to know the butler was so protective.

She grasped control and erased the humor from her face. "Please, come into the parlor with me."

"Ye had better give that butler of yers a good talk'n to, Miz Hamilton," the old woman snapped, glaring harshly at the servant.

"I will." Charlotte assured. "O'Toole? Will you

kindly inform the cook make us up some cakes to go with our tea?"

"Yes, Mistress." He gave a quick scowl to the old woman, then turned sharply and left.

After Charlotte closed the doors, the deep rumble of laughter echoed through the room as Neil's chest shook. She, too, cracked a smile.

"Did you see his face?" Neil chuckled. "O'Toole will never forgive me when he finds out it was really me."

Laughter left her. "I may never forgive you," she softly replied.

Neil sighed as he walked to the sofa. Gingerly, he sat and patted the place beside him. "I want to first start off by saying I didn't do the crimes which have been slandered against me. You cannot believe one word the sheriff's men have said."

She gave him a blank stare.

"Charlotte, you have to believe me, I didn't steal from my clients. I'm not the thief they're after. I believe the sheriff has put words into their mouths."

Glancing over his attire, she asked, "Then why do you hide? Why don't you come forth and proclaim your innocence?"

"You don't know the way of things here in New York. Everything is out of control, especially the government because there is no government. The richer you are the more power you have, and the more power you have, the more in control you are."

"Are you planning on hiding for the rest of your life as an old woman?"

"No, my dear. I plan on finding who is doing these crimes so I can clear my good name."

As he stared at her, confusion swam in her head. It was hard to think right now, and her throbbing skull had nothing to do with it. "What am I supposed to do in the meantime?"

His gaze dropped to his folded hands in his lap.

"I don't know."

"I suppose you want me to stay in New York?"

His head snapped up and his gaze met hers. "Of course. Where else will you stay?"

"I considered returning home."

O'Toole came back in the room holding a tray of tea and cakes. Charlotte kept silent, as did Neil as the butler placed the tray down on the small table in front of them, then left the room.

"Would you like some tea?" Charlotte asked as she leaned forward on the sofa and began pouring.

"Yes."

She handed him his cup. "Well?"

"Well, what?"

"What are your comments to what I've said?"

"I wish you'd change your mind."

Charlotte sipped her tea. "Why? Because of our agreement?"

"Yes, mainly."

"But how are we supposed to play out the month if you're on the run and dressed as an old woman?"

He shrugged. "I'm not certain. I haven't thought it out enough to decide what's going to happen. All of this was rather sudden for me."

After finishing her tea, she placed the saucer back on the tray. She stood and walked to the fireplace. "I'll stay another couple of days. If you haven't straightened this mess out, I'm leaving. Do you understand?"

"Yes."

When she glanced at him, his piercing blue eyes remained on her. Sadness showed through his disguised face. "I don't suppose you'd like to come back home with me?"

Chuckling, he shook his head. "As much as the idea is tempting, my dear, I think my first priority is to stay and discover who is doing this terrible thing to me and why."

"You're right, of course." Although, she'd figured him the kind of man to run off if life dealt him the wrong hand, she supposed he thought this was much more important than when he left her two years ago.

He moved to her side. "I should leave so I don't make any of the sheriff's men curious."

Gently, she laid her hand on his arm. Strange it would feel like a woman's arm, instead of a man underneath all of this padding.

"Neil? Please be careful. Although I'm still quite confused right now, I'm worried about your welfare."

He grinned. "Thank heavens for that. I was beginning to think you were enjoying this."

"No, Neil."

Softly, he stroked her cheek with his knuckles. "I suppose it would be out of the question to kiss you right now?"

She chuckled. "I don't think O'Toole would be able to handle seeing another woman kiss the lady of the house."

"Then I'll save it for later when I'm back to being a man."

She shook her head slowly. "I'm worried about your sense of humor, Neil Hamilton."

"I'll keep in contact with you." He moved to the door. After opening it, she noticed O'Toole had remained close by. How much of their conversation had the butler overheard? Could O'Toole be trusted?

Neil glared at his faithful servant. "Next time I'd be expect'n some kinder treatment from the likes of ye," he snapped.

Charlotte hid her smile behind her hand.

Without a word, O'Toole opened the door and stood back for the woman to pass. "I'll treat you better when you start showing a little more respect for those who are better class of people."

"Bah," Neil spat before leaving the house.

Charlotte moved to the window and peeked

through the curtains. When the old woman passed by, the sheriff's men didn't bat an eye. Silently, she prayed her husband could put his talents to work and find who'd been playing him for a fool.

As the sun rose higher in the sky the following day, a cool western wind swept through the city. It blew the leaves off the trees, preparing the earth for an early winter. Charlotte curled on the sofa, pulling an afghan across her legs. She watched out the window as Neil's neighbors scurried from their homes swathed up in warm coats. She'd chosen not to venture outside, but to stay by the fire. Her vibrant spirit had taken a beating and she sat in the parlor weighing her problems.

During the morning, a few people had dared to disturb her solitude, but she instructed O'Toole to send the neighbors away. She simply wasn't in the mood for visitors. Besides, she suspected they were merely attempting to find out why the sheriff and his men were hanging around the property. Of course, it was difficult to believe Neil could do what they accused, but the fact remained, she really didn't know Neil Hamilton.

She leaned her head against the cushion and closed her eyes. Just before she could relax, the clip clop of horses' hooves pounded on the drive. She parted the curtains, then cursed. The sheriff's men were back.

She stood and smoothed out the few wrinkles on her lavender day dress, then met the obstinate men at the door with a scowl. "What do you want now?" she hissed.

"Good morning, Mrs. Hamilton. I'm Sheriff Jeffrey Franklin." He tipped his hat to her and gave her an artificial smile. "We would like a moment of your time, if you don't mind."

"Of course I mind. Your men have asked me so many questions that my head is empty. I have nothing further to say, and I'd kindly appreciate it if you left me in peace."

The sheriff slowly shook his head. "I'm sorry to bother you, Mrs. Hamilton. We're only doing our jobs, but unfortunately, we cannot leave. I'm posting a few of my men in front of your house in case your husband decides to return."

"I'd have appreciated knowing this last night."

"Then forgive me for my tardiness, Mrs. Hamilton."

Huffing, she slammed the door in his face. During the next hour, the lawmen lurked in front of the townhouse. As each minute passed, her temper lifted a notch higher.

She wandered aimlessly through the house, but it only made her more depressed. Thoughts of home plagued her mind and she seriously considered making the long trip back home. There was no reason for her to stay here now. She doubted Neil would give her an annulment, but staying wasn't going to finish their bargain, either.

The afternoon passed as she stared out the window, and soon weariness consumed her. She stepped out of the parlor and ascended the stairs to her room. Just as she reached to top floor, a loud knock sounded at the door. Without a backward glance, she left O'Toole to answer it. However, she couldn't ignore the familiar male voice that spoke to the butler. She swung around and raced down the stairs to the door before O'Toole closed it.

"O'Toole," she shouted. "Let him in."

Confusion touched the older servant's face, but he did as was told. O'Toole escorted a tall figure into the parlor. The man wore a black hooded cape and leaned heavily on his cane as he limped into the room.

She smiled at her unexpected visitor. "Lord Thatcher. It's a pleasant surprise to see you in town."

"I usually don't come to town, but I just had to know how you were faring."

She shrugged. "As well as can be expected."

Lowering his hood, he curiously glanced around the room. "Why, Mrs. Hamilton, your husband shouldn't be accused of stealing when it's quite obvious he hasn't the need."

She laughed lightly. "Well said, Lord Thatcher. I wish the sheriff would think the same. Unfortunately, that man believes Neil sells what he steals and then purchases these nice things." She waved her hand around the room, indicating the expensive paintings, vases, and statues. "O'Toole? Please take our visitor's cloak."

Handing the cape to the butler, she excused the servant who lingered in the doorway then closed the door behind him. "Please have a seat, Lord Thatcher. I truly appreciate your visit." She sat on the sofa beside him and sighed. "Something is terribly wrong. Those men have been through this house from top to bottom and haven't found a clue, yet they still think my husband is their thief. Neil will not come forth to prove his innocence because he says he knows the way the government is run and they won't give him a chance to prove himself before they hang him."

His eyes widened in surprise. "You spoke to your husband already?"

"Yes, he was here last night, in disguise."

He nodded. "Well, I must say your husband is correct. He's better off in hiding for now."

"Neil is looking for clues to find who has been pointing the sheriff in his direction. I do hope he finds the culprit."

"As do I, but it might take a mite longer than you expect. Sheriff Franklin is a cunning man."

She rubbed her forehead. "I really did not need to hear that. Now I fear all hope is lost. I know not what to do."

"Mrs. Hamilton, please forgive me for being so blunt, but I'm a lonely man living in a huge castle, and I thought you both could come stay with me for awhile."

Her mouth fell open, but she quickly closed it. "Are you serious?"

"Why do you ask?"

"Because of your dislike for my husband."

"You're right, of course. I struggled with myself to even come see you, but I know I'm doing the right thing. Look at it this way—the castle is large enough that Neil might never bother me, or be bothered by me. Also, I'll have the added pleasure of your charming company."

Her cheeks heated. "Why, thank you, my lord."

"So, will you come? My lands are as private as you need right now."

"I should get in touch with Mr. Hamilton somehow to let him know. As long as I can sneak a away without the lawmen following me."

"Do you know how to find your husband?"

She smiled. "Yes. He's masquerading as an old woman." She chuckled over his puzzled expression. "And believe me, he does such a superb job of playing the part that even his servants don't know."

"Well, if there's anything good I can say about your husband is that he has talents beyond imagination."

She laughed lightly. "Exactly." She rose and walked to the window. "I really do hope he can work his way out of this predicament, though."

There was a small knock at the door and O'Toole peeked his head inside. "Mistress? Might you be wanting some tea?"

Lord Thatcher quickly turned his face and Charlotte could sense his unease. "Yes, O'Toole. That would be lovely, thank you."

After the butler left, Lord Thatcher stood. "It's time for me to leave. Speak with your husband and let me know of your decision."

She quickly stepped in front of the door to block him. "Lord Thatcher, I want you to know, you don't have to feel uncomfortable around me."

He gave her a questionable stare. "Are you trying to say that my face doesn't frighten you?"

She swept her gaze over the mark on his face. "The truth is, it doesn't."

One of his bushy dark eyebrows rose.

Hesitantly, she lowered her gaze. "My husband told me what to expect." She looked up at him and smiled. "Now that I know you a little better, I find it's hardly noticeable."

He chuckled, his hand brushing across the scar. "I've been gawked at for so many years. I know the kind of reaction people give me when they meet me for the first time. I shudder when I see young children because I know my appearance will frighten them. I don't mean to cause anyone fear."

She moved closer and touched his arm. "If they knew how kindhearted and thoughtful you really are, they wouldn't be afraid."

He raised his gloved hand and touched her cheek. "No, Mrs. Hamilton. You're the one who is kindhearted." Dropping his hand, he quickly stepped back and took hold of the door handle. "I hope to see you later. Have a good evening."

She followed behind and directed the butler to retrieve Lord Thatcher's cape. When he left, the sheriff's men scrutinized Lord Thatcher curiously, but when their eyes fell upon the scar, they looked away as he passed.

She hurried to her room and ordered her bath drawn. Somehow she must find Neil. But how? New York was too large to search for him, so she must wait for him to come to her.

As she waited for the water to fill the tub, she grinned. Lord Thatcher's castle would give Neil the space and privacy he needed to hide while he searched for the thief. It also would provide her with company when her husband was away, and Lord Thatcher would be wonderful company, she was certain.

Guilt washed over her for thinking of herself. Now was not the time to be selfish, and she should really try to help her husband, even if she didn't trust him. She believed he was really a good man with one evil enemy.

Memories from that night with him at the masquerade ball filled her head. Once again, she experienced the heated sensations that happened when his strong arms circled around her and the thrill as his body pressed against hers. Since that night, he'd been very attentive. He gazed at her with so much tenderness it nearly shattered her defenses. But she had to hold firm to her convictions. She couldn't let him break her heart again.

Charlotte couldn't have a life with Neil Hamilton. His finances were suffering, and he was in hopes of replenishing them with hers.

She shook her head. She wouldn't allow him to use her. Oh, God, but isn't that what she did to him? She used him to escape her father's tyranny.

"Mistress?" her maid interrupted Charlotte's thoughts. "Your bath is ready."

The steam rose from the tub and she sank into the water. The effect from the heat massaged her tired muscles. Clara washed Charlotte's long hair then piled it high on her head.

"Is there anything else you need?" the maid asked.

Relaxing in the tub, Charlotte closed her eyes. "Not now."

Charlotte slid the frothy sponge up and down

her arms and across her bosom, sighing heavily as the water heated her body. In the quiet room, her mind drifted. Neil had been so attentive lately. Why? Was he really angling for her money? Were his finances in poor condition, as Lord Thatcher had mentioned? If they were, would the shops bend over backwards for her? Would people on the streets be so thoughtful and friendly? Charlotte's eyes closed. She lowered herself in the tub so the hot water lapped against her breasts.

"I haven't realized until now, how living as a woman and away from my wife as little as a day is such torture."

The deep voice in the corner of the room startled her and she sat upright, splashing water on the floor as she peered into the dark recesses.

"Where are you? Step out so I might see." She reached for her robe, then remembered it was still on the bed.

He moved out of the shadows, and as he neared, his eyes dipped to her chest and rested on her twin points. Gasping softly, she quickly put her hands across her bosom and lowered herself in the sudsy water until it covered her chest.

He grinned. "Your hands don't seem to be large enough to hide your breasts, my sweet."

She scanned his length. "What are you doing here, and dressed like...like..."

"Like myself?"

"Yes. Why aren't you in disguise?"

The fawn colored shirt hung loosely on his chest, while the coffee trousers fit perfectly to his muscular legs. Dark brown knee boots made him look more like a stable boy than a gentleman. The contrast disturbed her, making her heart pound faster.

He stood above the tub, his gaze roaming seductively. "Outside is dark and cold, and those idiotic men hanging around my house decided to take themselves inside the nearest inn. I found the chance to sneak into my own home, so I took it." His eyes met with hers and his grin widened. "I'm glad I did. If I hadn't, I wouldn't have discovered such pleasures awaiting me."

"Neil," she pleaded, "please hand me my robe from the bed."

He chuckled and moved into the other room to retrieve the article, but when he returned, he dangled the robe inches out of her reach.

"Would you bring it closer?"

His gaze swept over her body and his eyes darkened—hunger evident on his expression. "Would you deprive me of seeing my wife?"

She forced the weakening feelings out of her heart and replaced them with anger. "Yes, considering you haven't wanted to play the part of my husband for two years."

He paused, then nodded and brought the robe to her. "Touché, my sweet."

"Please turn your head," she instructed.

She waited for him to obey, and after a few earth shattering seconds, he turned. Hurriedly, she wrapped the thick terry cloth around her wet body, and because of the moisture, the material molded to her curves like a glove. Although uncomfortable, she couldn't very well take it off to dry herself. Not with him in the same room.

Quickly, she stepped into the bedchamber. "I'm actually happy to see you tonight. I wish to speak with you."

Instead of sitting on one of the chairs in her room, he sat on the edge of the bed. "What about?"

She quickly moved over to the roaring fire, hoping her shaky limbs were due to the cold air on her wet skin. As she pulled her brush sharply through the tangles, she began the process of drying her hair. Glancing over her shoulder, she looked to see if he was watching her. He was.

"I received a visitor this afternoon that greatly surprised me," she said. "He gave me a proposition."

His brows creased into a scowl. "He? Your visitor was a man? And he propositioned you? Who was it? Ian?"

She threw him an agitated look and rolled her eyes. "Quit acting the jealous part. It wasn't Ian."

"Who then?"

"My visitor was Lord Thatcher."

His eyes widened. "Adam Newton? Earl of Thatcher?" Taking long strides, he crossed the room to her side. Heat from his breath whispered over her face.

She laughed lightly and nodded. "Yes, the one from the castle."

"How do you know him?"

"Umm—" She swallowed hard, quickly concocting a story. "I met him a few days ago while Allison and I were out riding in the country."

He casually folded his arms over his chest and leaned against the wall. "You don't say."

He didn't believe her, she could tell by his quizzical stare, but she continued, "Lord Thatcher has offered his help. He suggested you and I stay with him at the castle until you can straighten out your problem with the sheriff."

Neil snorted. "Why would Lord Thatcher offer his help? Why would the cold-hearted man be so generous—" He paused and his gaze hardened. "Unless it was to impress my wife?"

She rolled her eyes heavenward, then turned toward the fire. "Don't be a fool, Neil. Think how appropriate his offer is."

"So, then why would a beast like Lord Thatcher want us to come stay with him?"

Without thinking, she quickly spun around, her hair flying around her head and falling over a shoulder. "He's not a beast! If you knew him at all, you'd know he is really kindhearted and caring."

He pulled himself away from the wall and stood beside her. "Oh, my sweet, be careful how you speak of the man. Your husband might get the wrong impression of where your loyalties lie." His fingers curled around a lock of her damp hair and caressed it gently. "Do you want me to prove what a jealous husband I really am? Because, Mrs. Hamilton, you're the most beautiful woman I know and it's hard to stay sane around you. How can a man like me help but have jealous feelings when other men look at you, especially when you give them kind words but cannot do the same for your own husband?"

She tilted her head. "Perhaps they have earned those words and you have not."

"Ooh, so cruel." His fingers left her hair and caressed her cheek. "Where is that She-Devil I met the other night? That intoxicating woman wasn't mean with her words, but seductively charming instead."

"I fear, Mr. Hamilton, that woman departed when her identity was unveiled."

"Is there no way to get her back?"

The fire behind her suddenly became too hot, or was it the fire inside her, because his words were enticing. His suggestion wasn't totally unpleasant, but did she really want him to seduce her? But didn't she tell herself she'd keep her distance from him? Didn't she swear she wouldn't allow his charms to influence her again?

"Neil, please." She pushed his hand away. "We have gotten off the matter at hand." She tried to move past him, but his arms slipped around her waist and brought her body against his.

"No, I believe this is the matter at hand." His lips descended quickly, giving her no time to protest.

He pressed his mouth to her stiff lips. Through his tender caress, he coaxed her to relax. She fought him, but her struggles were for naught because his hands moved over her, assisting with the seduction. Gently and sensuously they roamed over her back. His fingers traced tiny circles up her spine, slowly, so slowly, weakening her resistance. Down further his hands slid until they cupped her buttocks.

A soft moan tore from her throat, and without being able to help it, she softened her lips beneath his. With a grunt of satisfaction, he wrapped his arms tightly around her. It wasn't long before she moved her arms upward to embrace his neck as her body melted against his.

Everything felt so wonderful, just like it had the other night at the mask ball. The intoxicating urgent kiss was exactly the same, and her body ached for the wonderful thing that she knew followed.

He cupped her breast and she moaned. Breaking the kiss, he breathed hot against her cheek.

"Charlotte? I want to make love to you." His lips moved across her cheek to her ear, nibbling slightly on the lobe, then down her neck.

Although her body's temperature rose dangerously high, confusion plagued her mind. Neil's passionate caress was the very thing her body craved, and even through the mist of chaos, his hands burned her body out of control.

His hand slid between their bodies and parted the robe as his mouth followed the path of the bare skin. Cool air touching her breasts woke her out of the cloudy haze filling her mind. Panic settled in her thoughts.

"Neil, no." She tried to pull away, but he continued in his efforts as he made his way toward her breasts. "Neil, please, don't do this."

He drew back and lifted his head. Passion was etched on his handsome face, and especially in his dark eyes, making him much more handsome than she thought possible.

"What am I doing to you except what you want?" His voice was husky, seductive.

Tears filled her eyes. "But I don't want this. It's too soon. I'm not ready."

"Yes you are." His thumb grazed her nipple and it tightened. "I can tell."

"No, Neil." She placed her hands on his chest and pushed him back, then clutched her robe together. "You don't understand. I don't even understand, but I know I'm not ready."

Sighing heavily, he ran his fingers through his hair. "Is it because you don't trust me?"

Charlotte couldn't control the hysterical laughter that left her throat. "Do you think I should trust you with my body and mind, especially my heart?" She shook her head. "Please forgive me if I don't just hand my heart to you on a platter for you to butcher openly. How many times do I have to keep reminding you that you left me two years ago?" Tears slid down her cheeks and her emotion broke. "How many times do I have to remind you that you were the one who didn't want to be my husband?" she sobbed.

"And how many times are you going to make me pay for my mistakes?" he snapped angrily.

She sniffed and wiped her eyes. "Until I can see you're truly sorry, but I don't think you'll ever be. You're nothing but a cold-hearted, inconsiderate man." She turned and ran to her bed, throwing herself on the blankets as her sobs echoed loudly through the room.

Neil didn't stay to comfort her. He left her room the same way he'd entered, quickly and unnoticed.

Chapter Nine

Charlotte stepped into the cobweb-laden rooms and sighed heavily as her slippers pushed through the half-inch layer of dust on the floor. When she thought about the work that would be needed to make the place livable, a shudder ran through her, but her strong will said she was up for the challenge.

The rooms Lord Thatcher had chosen pleased her. They were far enough away from his private chambers, but not too far from the library.

Lord Thatcher moved past her with an awkward limp and set a trunk down on the floor. "I'm sorry. I didn't have these rooms…ready for your…arrival." His breaths were labored.

She smiled. "They're just fine. I'll put on an apron, and between me and my servants, we'll have these rooms clean in no time."

"Oh, Mrs. Hamilton, you mustn't get your hands dirty."

She passed him a playful scowl. "Don't you think I can handle it? Besides, more helping hands will make the work move quicker. I need to keep busy."

He returned a smile and nodded.

"Now get out of my way and let me clean." She shooed him with her hands. "It's not every day you'll see me in this kind of mood."

His deep laughter echoed throughout the hall as his uneven footsteps moved away.

She instructed Neil's servants where to clean, then took up a broom herself and began sweeping. Her eyes watered and she sneezed, but stubbornly, she kept at the task until her rooms were livable.

During one of her breaks, she let herself think about Neil. She hadn't let him know she'd moved into the castle, but he'd find out one way or another. It'd been three days since their argument, and he hadn't returned.

The sheriff had stopped her momentarily as she tried to pass, but she bluntly told him she couldn't live with his men constantly under her feet while he made her feel like a prisoner in her own home.

When the sheriff asked where she was headed, she simply replied that she was going to stay with a friend and taking some servants with her. The servants packed most of Neil's belongings just in case Sheriff Franklin and his men wandered back inside the house once she was gone. She didn't trust those men with Neil's possessions.

She swiped her hand across her moist brow and looked at the sparkling floors. With a nod of satisfaction, she moved to her bedchamber to put her clothes away in the many armoires the room provided. She didn't worry about Neil's clothes. His servants would put his things away.

Leaning against the clean wall, she scanned the meager furnishings. Tomorrow she'd travel into town and purchase some necessary things for the room. A nice rug for the floor would be perfect for cold mornings, and a new washbasin and tub would make her baths more enjoyable.

Her feet dragged when she finally made her way to her bed that evening. Her maid had drawn a warm tub of water and helped her bathe before getting her ready for bed. As soon as her head hit the pillow, her exhausted mind gave into dreams.

****

The sweet fragrance of a rose drifted through Charlotte's senses, arousing her from a deep sleep, and the delicate softness swept against her cheek and lips. She fought to remain asleep, but the continuous stroke of the rose brought her to awareness.

She forced her heavy eyelids open, and then squinted from the brightness of the room as the sun's rays poured through the window's diamond paned glass. Through the streak of light, Neil leaned over her with a rose in his hand, moving it slowly across her face in a tender caress.

He smiled. "Good morning, my sweet."

Blinking a couple of times, she cleared the fuzziness from her eyes. Neil was certainly in a chipper mood. Had he forgotten about their last argument? She'd play along to see what he wanted.

"Good morning, Neil. I see you've found my room easy enough."

He chuckled and straightened. "Yes. Lord Thatcher escorted me. I have to say how surprised I am, though. He informed me you were the one to clean them."

She yawned and stretched, then winced when her stiff arms and back wouldn't cooperate. She struggled to sit. "Yes, I cleaned them, with help from your servants, of course."

"I think you did an amazing job putting everything together." He helped by placing more pillows behind her back.

It had been four days since they talked, and only one question hung heavy on her mind. "Have you figured out why you're being accused of thievery?"

"No, but I have a few suspects."

Disappointed, she sighed. "Who?"

"I know for certain somebody is setting me up, and a couple of people are top of my list."

"But nothing conclusive, right?"

He shook his head.

"Are you still disguising yourself as an old lady?"

"No. I've been masquerading as a businessman from out of town. I'll keep that role until the sheriff's men get suspicious."

Her gaze swept over his attire, plain cream-colored shirt, and coffee trousers. "But you are not disguised now."

"I thought it would be nice to be myself for a little while. Maybe you'll enjoy my company better that way."

She lifted her eyebrows. "Do you plan on spending time with me today?"

"Of course, my sweet. How else are we going to get to know each other? Although you might think differently, a month's time will really pass by quickly."

"Yes, I'm aware of that." She paused, and then asked, "What do you have planned?"

He toyed with the loose sleeve of her nightgown and when his finger touched her skin, a tingle ran up her arm. She quickly withdrew from his touch.

He placed his hand by her leg. "I'd like to escort you outside the castle for a walk and take in this very beautiful morning with you."

"Aren't you afraid of being discovered?"

"By whom?"

"Some of the servants."

His happy expression dropped and he stood. "I didn't stop to think about the servants turning me in."

She reached out and touched his shirt. "Maybe they won't. I think they're very loyal to you."

"But who can say for certain? And I don't want to take that chance." He shrugged. "Perhaps we should dismiss them."

"Can you afford to keep them around, Neil?"

"What do you mean?"

"I heard about your money situation. I heard you haven't been getting many clients for your business."

His gaze narrowed. "Who told you that?"

"Does it matter? Is this information true?" She knew his answer by the way his shoulders wilted.

"Some of it's true. I haven't been getting many new clients, but I'm not out of money."

"How long will it last?"

He lifted his gaze and stared into her eyes. "I don't know, my dear."

"Neil?" she asked, cautiously. "Is that the reason you wanted me back in your life? Did you know you were running out of money, so decided to bring me back so I could help?"

Anger crossed his face once again, but she didn't regret the question. The mere idea of him cuckolding her had plagued her for days.

"Do you really believe that? What do I have to do to make you trust me?"

She shrugged. "Just be honest with me for once."

"Honest with you? What are you talking about?"

Her temper teetered close to the edge of exploding, but she forced herself to remain calm. His answer was vital to her decision about staying with him, and she couldn't put off knowing any longer.

Straightening her shoulders, she met his angry expression. "Just tell me if you want me for my money or not."

Neil's heart hammered in anger and frustration as he glared at Charlotte. Her question shocked him, and his mind literally numbed. He couldn't decide whether to laugh or cry. How dare she even think that? The fact remained, she didn't know him, or she would know the question was totally absurd.

She lifted her stubborn chin higher and didn't cower beneath his scowl. "Just answer the question. And while I'm thinking about it, I'd like to know if the reason you decided you wanted me was because you knew this was going to happen, and by some slim chance, thought I would give you a good alibi?"

Once again, shock vibrated through his body,

and his mouth gaped open. This time, numbness didn't affect his tongue. "You really have an overactive imagination. I cannot believe you'd even think that of me. But let me tell you, I'm not the kind of man who thieves, or am I the kind who'll use a woman for her money. I've always taken care of myself. I've made my own living ever since I was a young man of age eighteen. And I'll continue to do so, thank you." He paused for a breath. "I also want you to know I'm not the kind of man who runs away from the law."

His breath came in heavy pants as he watched her expression change. The longer he stared into her eyes, the softer her face became. Would she finally believe his words?

She swung her legs off the side of the bed and stood. She wrapped her robe around herself before moving in front of him. Sighing, she raised her eyes to his. "Neil, please excuse my doubtful behavior."

His temper subdued.

She shrugged. "I cannot help myself. It's true, the reason I'm like this is because I don't know you." Lowering her gaze, she continued. "I hate to keep bringing this up, but if you had only stayed with me two years ago, things would be so different."

His hands gently grasped her shoulders and her eyes met his. "Charlotte? Can we forget the past and start over? I hate having all these doubts between us."

Uncertainty crossed her gray gaze. "I don't know, Neil. You really hurt me."

"You really hurt me, too."

Her brows drew together. "How?"

"Because you tried to control my life. You had to have me. Your father even threatened me."

She hung her head. "Yes, I was very selfish. I couldn't lose the opportunity to get away from my father." She glanced at him in desperation. "You were my only hope."

Her confession surprised him. "And now? Do you still feel the same?"

She backed away, releasing his grip. "I dare not answer that, Neil."

"I think I already know the answer, my sweet." He grinned. "You can get any man you choose. Of course, you're still married to me, so maybe you'll not accomplish that task as easily as you'd like."

She laughed.

He leaned against the bedpost. "Charlotte? Can we begin again? I'd really like you to get to know me. What do you say? Will you give me another chance?"

"Yes," she answered softly. "But will you do something for me?"

He grinned and moved to her, sliding his arms around her waist. "I'll do anything your lovely heart desires." He placed a small kiss on her exposed neck.

She giggled. "Neil, I'm being serious."

"So am I." He kissed her neck again, this time closer to her ear.

Pushing with the heels of her hands, she moved him a few inches away from her. "Neil, look at me."

He did and was amazed how beautifully her eyes sparkled. The gold flecks in her gray orbs looked like stars. "Yes, my love?"

He hadn't meant to use that endearment, but he saw the effect it had on her and was pleased.

She let out a small gasp, and her body relaxed into his embrace. "Neil, I...I..." She swallowed hard. "I'd like you to give me some time also. I promise I'll try really hard to turn my thoughts around and get to know you better."

The longer he stared into her eyes, the longer he had the urge to kiss her. Of course, ever since the night he had kissed the Devil-woman so passionately, he'd dreamed about kissing those heart-shaped, rose-petal lips again. She might not want it, and she might try to push him away, but he had to feel her lips on his.

He pulled her closer slowly, then his lips touched her tempting mouth. Her body stiffened, so he gently moved his lips across hers, pleading, begging, and yes, even seducing her.

She melted in his arms.

It was a long-awaited kiss, and when she willingly responded, excitement tore through him. He pulled her closer until her soft bosom pressed against his chest. Once he parted her lips, he dipped his tongue inside. When her velvet softness met his, a deep groan tore through his throat. She clung to him as their mouths tasted and enjoyed, and she pleasured him immensely. Her participation spurred him to a higher passion and made him turn the kiss urgent, and she responded to his wild eagerness.

Her warm body felt wonderful up against him, and holding her in his arms made him want to protect and comfort her—forever. It was heaven the way her lips moved across his, and yet it was pure torture when her tongue caressed with his.

He could kiss her like this all day, but she broke the kiss and turned her head.

"Neil? We have to stop." She breathed heavily.

"Why?"

"Because it's too soon. I don't want to rush things."

She was correct. He didn't expect her to jump right into his arms after all that had happened. Courting her was the best way to win her trust and her affection.

He sighed heavily as his face nuzzled her neck. "Yes, I know," he said reluctantly.

Gently, he stroked her back. She sighed and remained in his embrace until he finally broke contact and stepped away.

A blush covered her cheeks as she lowered her

gaze to the middle of his chest "Neil, I...I need to get dressed. Will you please leave so I can make myself presentable?"

He moved away from her and to the door. "You'll always be presentable to me, no matter what you're wearing."

He walked out the door grinning from ear to ear, his heart bursting with happiness once again. It pleased him that they were starting over, and he promised himself he wouldn't mess things up this time.

But staying in this castle bothered him more than he dared to admit. There were too many secrets here. He knew things about Lord Thatcher that she wouldn't like. She obviously thought highly of the beast, but he must protect her from the mystery. At all costs.

****

The large stone castle loomed dark, mysterious, and forlorn. Shadows whispered of secrets, of events best forgotten, and hinted of dangers unseen. But those shadows said nothing about the love and safety Charlotte needed most.

Looking back, it was a whirlwind of events that had led her here, and it was the mystery surrounding the castle and its beastly master, which had beguiled her the most.

As the morning sun peeked through the slit in the curtains and touched her face, she sighed. Charlotte took a deep breath, inhaling the sweet, fresh perfume of blossoming flowers and rich green leaves. Outside, little white cotton puffs of clouds dotted the bright blue sky. The sun's warmth spread throughout her body and made contact with her heart. Joy nearly caused her heart to leap right from her chest.

She and her wayward husband would start their life together anew and put their painful past behind them. Through their new discovery, they'd see if they really did have a future together.

His kisses already stirred desire deep within her. Could she forget he'd left her two years ago to seek out a different life? And could she admit it was her own selfishness that had forced him to leave her in the first place?

Charlotte's maid helped her slip into a short-sleeve blue day dress with a square neck and tight waist. Clara pulled back Charlotte's hair and tied it with a matching ribbon. Before a full-length mirror, she turned one way and then another, inspecting her attire to be assured all was in place. She brought the bulk of her hair forward and over her left shoulder. Her complexion was white and illusive pink. A shimmering gray-gold flecked her eyes and her long hair was a rich, glowing auburn.

She smiled. Thanks to the generosity of her new friend, Lord Thatcher, she and her husband had decided to take advantage of the seclusion the castle offered by getting reacquainted with each other.

Once she left her room, she called for O'Toole. "Would you please gather the others and take on the task of cleaning the remaining rooms?"

"Of course, Mistress."

Lighthearted, she practically skipped along the stone path to the back of the castle. As she turned the corner, the vista caused her to stop in her tracks. It was magnificent, from the rolling green lawns to the bed of water bordering the land. The scent of wildflowers filled the air, and she closed her eyes and breathed in the heavenly aroma.

When she opened her eyes, there was Neil, standing near the castle's far wall. He had his back to her and didn't seem to know she was there.

Casually, he leaned against the elderly stone wall, still dressed in the coffee trousers and beige shirt. The fabric stretched across his wide shoulders, yet tapered to his narrow waist. He turned slightly and she looked at him in silhouette. Regal nose and strong chin aimed upward as though he soaked up the morning sunshine, which glinted off his dark brown hair.

She watched him in silence for a long moment, drinking him in. It thrilled her to know all she had to do was snap her fingers and this man would be hers. The sexual magnetism that made him seem so self-confident urged her to be near him. But she fought the overwhelming need to let go of her insecurities and trust in her husband. She had to be certain. Her heart could not take another rejection.

Yet the question still remained. Did she really want to rekindle their relationship? Hopefully today, she'd discover for herself what she truly wanted, and if it was indeed his heart she hoped to gain.

She stepped out of the shadows and he spotted her. His wide smile and extended hand welcomed her. His gaze was as soft as a caress, and there became an instant tingling in the pit of her stomach. He was so incredibly good-looking and she reacted so strongly to him, to his touch, his smell...the very nearness of him. Doubts were dispersed at the tenderness of his long stare.

She wanted to love him, but she didn't want him to know. Not yet.

He placed a chaste kiss on her knuckles then hooked her fingers around his elbow.

They walked along before his eyes caught hers. "What is it?'

"Nothing."

"Tell me, Charlotte." He stopped and faced her.

"I have the feeling you still think of me as your troublesome child bride."

"How should I think of you?" His voice and eyes softened as he looked into her face.

"Think of me as a woman. How would you like it

if I thought of you as a boy worse as a rogue, or a thief?"

His eyes blazed, and he roughly gripped her shoulders. Before Charlotte knew what was happening, his arms encircled her waist, his head lowering. His mouth covered hers in a passionate kiss of exploration. The kiss was so erotic and sensual that her hands went to the heavy sinews of his back, pulling him closer as they deepened the kiss. Never before had she wanted to move from his arms, but then he thrust her from him.

He smiled. "Now, was that the kiss of a mere boy?" Without any further ado or seduction, he proceeded with their walk.

She kept in step along side him, her heart aching due to the jumble of emotions beneath her breast.

"All right," he began, "if we are going to begin fresh, let's do it the right way. I will no longer think of you as a child, and you will not think of me as your wayward husband...or rogue, as you so eloquently put it." He gave her a significant lift of his brows.

Charlotte let her mind relax as she gazed into his intoxicating blue eyes and listened to his sultry voice.

"So, what is it you'd like to know about me, my dear?" His eyes twinkled.

She smiled. How could she resist him? She could probably ask him anything and he would be truthful, but suddenly her mind went blank, and all she could do was stare at him and inhale his spicy scent.

"You're not going to believe this, but I can't seem to think of one question. Why don't you tell me anything you'd like."

He chuckled and covered her hand on his elbow. "I suppose I could tell you a little about my family."

For the next few hours, she listened to his

baritone voice as he satisfied her curiosity on most subject matters.

He'd told her about some of the cases he'd solved and what disguises he'd worn. Hearing devotion laced in his words wrenched her heart. Obviously, he loved his investigating business.

He led her around the castle, and although the landscape was beautiful, she kept her gaze on the interesting man beside her. Her husband.

Between a pair of tall cedars, he led her to a gurgling brook. She stood on the side watching the water tumble over the rocks. Then she noticed the picnic lunch spread out on a blanket. It surprised her that he'd gone through this much trouble just to please her, and her heart melted just a fraction more.

"Neil, where did you get all this food?"

"When Lord Thatcher left the kitchen, I took the opportunity to make us an afternoon meal."

She chuckled and shook her head. "You're incorrigible."

"Thank you, my dear."

She sat unbidden on the woolen blanket and straightened her skirts around her. He watched her, a glorious smile on his face. As he knelt before her, he plucked a grape from its stem. Neil had the fruit about eye level and waited until she peered upward at it. He lowered it, slowly to her mouth. She smiled, not recalling when she'd ever been this content.

"Have you found out anything about the false charges against you? Or who would want to do this to you?"

The smile faded as he rested back on his elbow. "Unfortunately, not yet. But I believe the sheriff realized I'd be the perfect scapegoat because I know so much about these people's lives, and especially, about their homes. I know where they keep their jewelry, and about their secret hideaways. I know the different ways to get into their homes without being seen, and where to hide when I'm in there."

He raked his fingers through his hair. "It's just not fair," he continued with a cold edge of irony in his deep voice. "They've got me trapped, and I can't find a way out." He met her stare as a deep sigh escaped him. "But Charlotte, I didn't steal from them. I swear on my mother's grave."

She willed herself to believe him. She had to believe him. "Do you think the sheriff is at the forefront of this travesty?"

His jaw tightened, his lips stretched in irritation. He nodded. "I would bet money on it."

"I want to help."

He touched her hand. "You cannot because I'm not certain who's setting me up. I don't want to put you in any danger. I'll not have you subjected to any peril, do you understand?"

She hung her head. "Yes. I just feel so helpless."

"Promise me you'll not interfere."

She hesitated. Really, she should promise, but if the chance presented itself, she'd gladly do all she could to get him out of this mess. "I promise."

His finger lifted her chin, and when she met his eyes, she saw uncertainty on his grin.

"I don't believe you, my sweet."

She smiled. "You're not being fair."

He laughed. "Oh, I think I am. Now, are you going to promise me?"

"Yes."

"Good." He stroked her cheek once, and dropped his hand.

He moved the conversation away from him and onto her. He urged her to relate stories from her life. She liked the way he hung on her every word.

She switched topics, once she ran out of things to say, and an awkward silence seemed to stretch between them. "I'm so very grateful Lord Thatcher let us stay here. Isn't he a kind man?"

He looked at her intently. "Charlotte, although I'm relieved Lord Thatcher is allowing me to hide here, I really think you need to go back to my townhouse. It's not proper for you to be staying with him. He's unmarried, you know. I don't like it."

She smiled to herself at the protective tone in his voice. "I know, but who is going to care? As far as anyone knows, I've gone back home. Ian and Allison won't say anything, I assure you."

His brows drew together in confusion. "Ian and Allison know where you are?"

"Of course. You don't think I'd come here without telling my friends, do you?"

Her heart hammered quickly. Did he know the truth about her and Ian? Did he know she'd lied about their relationship?

She didn't realize she was holding her breath as she watched his reaction, but soon the worry was erased from his forehead and his mouth relaxed.

"I just don't want people spreading rumors that aren't true," he said.

Breathing a heavy sigh, she smiled. "It's like I said, who in New York is going to care? Up until the other day, your friends didn't even know you had a wife."

He nodded. "You're correct. But..."

In a moment of silence, she saw him watching her through hooded eyes, and as the seconds ticked by, it made her uncomfortable. Did he know her thoughts? She shifted on the blanket, absently picking off crumbs on her dress.

"Charlotte, just promise me you won't get too deeply involved with Lord Thatcher. He's still a stranger to you."

Charlotte didn't understand the uneasiness her husband displayed. "Why? I don't feel that way when I'm with him. He has been the perfect gentleman.

He's very charming and helping."

A look crossed his face that resembled jealousy, but before she had a chance to analyze it, he stood.

"Just be wary, Charlotte. Always keep on guard. Don't ever turn your back on him."

"Neil." She jumped to her feet and grabbed his arm. "You're worrying me. Tell me why you feel this way."

"All I can tell you is I don't trust the man. There has to be some reason he'd been a recluse for all these years."

"Of course there is," she said quickly. "He doesn't want people pitying him because of his deformity."

"There has to be something more to it than that." Impatience seeped into his voice.

"Maybe if you just got to know him better. He really is a nice man," she quipped.

"He cannot stand me. He won't let me get close enough to him to become his friend."

"Why does he hate you?"

He shrugged. "I suppose he has his reasons."

"Do you know what they are?"

"No."

She sensed he held something from her, but his mood had changed and he wouldn't explain himself.

His hands tenderly cupped her face while he stared at her.

"Either you are a very jealous man, or you're very overprotective." She was pleased with their initial intimacy and the soft way he was looking into her eyes. Happily, she could drown in those eyes.

"I'm both." Slowly, he leaned forward and pressed his lips to hers.

Her heart pounded madly. Perhaps she could learn to love and trust him again. One thing was for certain, no man had ever affected her the way he did. Never had she found herself responding so quickly to another man's touch or kiss.

When he pulled away, his breathing was shallow and his face slightly flushed. He moved away and cleaned up the picnic items. He led her back to the castle, his guiding hand on her back keeping her beside him all the way.

Before reaching the castle, he stopped, pulled her into the shadows of a group of elms and looked around to make sure they were alone. "I'd better leave your side right here, just in case the servants are lurking about."

Sighing, she touched his sleeve. "I can't wait until this is over and you can come out of hiding."

He grinned teasingly. "Why, Mrs. Hamilton, do you miss me already?"

Her cheeks burned, so she slapped his shoulder playfully. "Quit reading more into my words than I intended." She tried to sound nonchalant but the tone of her voice lifted, betraying her true feelings.

He laughed then gathered her in his arms. "I, too, can't wait until I can take you out in public and show you to the world." His hold tightened. "But for now I rather enjoy our privacy."

Against her ribs, her heart thundered. His mouth descended and captured hers again, but instead of the gentle kiss she'd expected, he crushed his mouth to hers, sliding his tongue inside for a quick sweep while his hands caressed her back. She fell against him and pushed her hands up his chest, but before she could really enjoy the passionate moment, he tore himself away and stepped back.

"I'd better stop. I have to remember to keep things slow so you can learn to trust me."

Disappointment washed over her, surprising her. "Thank you."

"I'll see you later."

He turned to leave, but she stopped him. "Neil? Please take care."

"I will." He gave her a wink, then left.

With a heavy heart, she walked slowly back to the castle, her mind repeating everything that happened this afternoon. When she realized the time spent with her husband had been extremely pleasurable, a smile touched her lips. They didn't argue or bring up the hurtful past, and their steps toward making amends had started out well.

She entered the spacious old castle, her footsteps echoing as she walked from room to room. In just the small amount of time she'd been with Neil, the servants had been very busy. They had taken the boards off the windows and the sunshine streamed inside. It illuminated the clean marble floors. The spider-webbed corners were wiped away, and the walls displayed newly papered decor.

The creak of the door pulled her attention down the hall just as O'Toole exited from one of the rooms.

"O'Toole?"

"Yes, Mistress?"

"I wanted to praise you on doing such a splendid job with the cleaning."

He smiled and his face stained a dark pink. "Thank you."

"Has Lord Thatcher seen this room yet?"

"No, he has been busy cleaning another part of the castle."

"Where is he?"

"I believe he's on the third floor on the north end." He pointed his hand in the direction.

"Thank you. Keep up the good work," she cheered before leaving to go find Adam.

When she reached the third floor, she gasped. Just like the second, this floor had many spacious rooms, certainly created for a king and queen. These rooms weren't dirty. Adam must have been busy this afternoon.

A loud bang drew her attention to a room

farther down the hall. When she entered, she noticed it hadn't been cleaned as well as the others, and that some of the windows were still covered with boards. Her attention turned to the large presence standing at the top of a ladder. Lord Thatcher pulled off boards from a window, his arms straining with each movement.

Her gaze moved over his body as he labored. His old trousers were worn and a gaping hole peeked at her from his buttocks. She sighed inwardly, watching the rippled motion of his shoulders as he yanked on one of the boards. Not only did his pants fit him like a glove, but he also had the front of his shirt unbuttoned, and when he turned, she caught a glimpse of his robust frame.

She didn't turn away. Lord Thatcher was certainly a well-built man. Even though he wore the dark scarf over half of his face to hide his scar, it didn't take away from his masculinity. His profile was strong and rigid, and she found herself feeling strangely attracted to this mysterious man.

As the board came loose, he muttered a heavy sigh. Light flooded into the room even though the window was etched with years of soil. Excitement pounded in her heart, and she knew this was definitely not proper to be witnessing, but for some insane reason, she couldn't turn her eyes away.

He swiped his sleeve across his forehead, then paused when he saw her standing there. Her mouth turned dry and her tongue swelled, and she couldn't form the words to speak.

"Good afternoon, Mrs. Hamilton." He spoke, breaking the incredible silence.

Her heart fluttered again as her gaze moved down the front of his opened shirt. He was definitely a fine specimen of a man. She took in his tempting, attractive male physique as the rich outlines of his broad shoulders strained against the fabric of his shirt.

"Good afternoon, Lord Thatcher. You've been rather busy today."

"Yes. I couldn't leave these rooms looking haunted forever." He smiled at her, bringing an immediate softening to his features.

She took two more steps into the room. "I think you've done a remarkable job."

"Mr. Hamilton's servants have accomplished more than their share. They should be rewarded." He climbed down the ladder and picked up the towel lying across the back of a chair. With the corner of it, he dabbed his forehead.

"Yes, they have," she agreed. "I shall see that their pay is increased."

"Did you need something?"

She shrugged. "I was going to offer my help with assisting of the cleaning, but I see that has been taken care of already."

He shook his head. "You have done your share, and I won't ask for more." He rubbed the towel on his neck. "How was your morning? Did you enjoy your little outing with your husband?"

She tore her eyes from his chest and met his stare. "How did you know I was with Neil?"

He chuckled. "Where else would you be?" He tossed the towel back on the chair. "He came here last night looking for you and I told him which rooms were yours."

"Were you able to visit with him?"

"Yes, but don't make too much out of it. We're not friends, nor are we ever going to be."

"But Lord Thatcher, I think that whatever it is between you and Neil can be worked out—"

"No, it cannot," he cut her off sharply. "Please, Mrs. Hamilton," he continued in a gentler tone, "if you want to remain my friend, don't push me."

Hesitantly, she asked, "Will you at least tell me

why you dislike my husband so much?"

"I'll tell you, but now is not the right time."

She scowled.

He laughed. "You'll be patient, right?"

"Yes," she answered, grudgingly.

"Do you know, Mrs. Hamilton, you're a typical woman."

She creased her head in confusion. "What's that supposed to mean?"

"That means..." He paused, taking a step closer as his gloved knuckles brushed her cheek. "You care too much about other people's lives."

Tilting her head, she propped her hands on her hips. "Are you saying I'm sticking my nose where it doesn't belong?" She tried hard not to smile.

"Yes, and what a lovely nose it is. But all I'm saying is that you care too much, and because you do, you feel the need to fix things."

She smiled. "Well, I do care, but the main reason is because I know what it's like to be on the wrong side of Neil Hamilton. It's not an enjoyable situation."

His dark bushy brows lifted. "What's this? You've already experienced one of Hamilton's volatile mood swings?"

Laughing lightly, she stepped away. "Let's just say he wasn't a very nice man when I first met and married him. Yes, I've witnessed his erratic moods, like a summer storm. He is like a confounding, ever-changing mystery that I want to unravel."

Concern stretched across his face, and it comforted her to know he cared. "He didn't hurt you, did he?"

"Only emotionally." She paused, and decided to be open with him. "You see, two years ago, I practically forced Neil to marry me."

The anger left his face and was replaced with humor. "Why would you have to force any man to marry you?"

"Two years ago you'd not have said that. Womanhood came late for me and I wasn't very attractive in my youth. In fact, I looked like a twelve year old boy."

"You're jesting."

"No. Back then, the boys only looked at me as their playmate, yet I was almost eighteen. I couldn't find one man who'd even consider marrying me. So, when Neil entered my life and rescued me from kidnappers, I'm ashamed to say I decided to make him marry me. He was my only hope, and I clung to him. In the process, I threw my spoiled tactics in his face." She hesitated then added softly, "He married me, but only because I bade my father to pay off his debtors."

She ran her hand along back of the wooden chair frame and looked away. "Three days after our wedding, Neil came here to New York to pursue a case. I suppose his popularity and his homely wife gave him a reason to stay." She lifted her gaze and met his. "I haven't seen him in two years. Neil and I have only been together as husband and wife just a little over one week now."

He closed the space between them and cupped her face in his gloved hands, gazing deep into her eyes. His brows furrowed. "After being gone for two years, what made him decide he wanted you back?"

She laughed and withdrew from his heated touch. "I actually came to seek him out for an annulment, but before I did that, I wanted to give him a taste of what he gave up. So one night at a masquerade ball, I lured him into a private room. He stirred in me passions I'd never known existed. It was then that Neil first laid eyes on his wife, the same wife he had left two years ago." She took a deep breath. "The following day he made a bargain with me. He wanted us to spend some time together, so I promised to stay with him for a whole month. If afterwards I still felt as though we didn't suit, he'd agree to an annulment."

He touched her cheek again, his stroke bringing tingles to her skin. "And it has been a little over one week of your bargain, right?"

"Yes."

"I hope you don't mind if I ask how things are going?"

A blush warmed her cheeks. "It was unsteady at first, but we've come to an understanding. We have decided to start at the beginning and get to know each other and give our marriage another chance."

He nodded. "I see." His gloved fingers trailed to her chin.

She dropped her gaze to the front of his shirt, and her eyes stayed on his moist skin. His masculine scent drifted through her senses, and the heat from his body poured from his leather covered hand to her skin. The strange feelings of arousal made her slightly uncomfortable, but she couldn't move. She didn't know if it was because of the way he looked at her with so much tenderness, or if it was because she could still see his exposed muscular chest. But whatever it was, her insides quaked with desire.

She had to conquer her involuntary reactions to that gentle affectionate look of his and his closeness; so male, so bracing. Her mind clouded with confusion and she stepped away. "Well, now that I've bored you completely with my story," she said in a quiet voice that seemed to come from a long way off, "I think I should take my maid and go down to the kitchen to see what we can prepare for supper tonight since you don't have a cook."

He laughed deeply. "I'll make something."

"No. I'll take my maid. I need to learn to help out around here. I'm not a charity case, so I don't need you treating me like one."

He bowed slightly. "Then if you feel the need to learn to cook, go right ahead."

"Thank you, Lord Thatcher. I'll let you know when the meal is ready." She smiled widely.

"Please, call me Adam."

"And I give you permission to call me Charlotte."

They shared a smile before she turned and scurried out of the room, trying hard to ignore the strange sensations her body had just experienced. Whatever it was that caused her to feel this way, it had better leave because she couldn't have these feelings for Adam Thatcher, especially if she and Neil were mending their lives.

Chapter Ten

Charlotte clenched her hands in the folds of her skirts as she paced her bedchambers, feeling like a volcano ready to explode. An entire week passed since she had arrived at the castle and her nerves were growing frazzled. She hated sneaking around just to spend time with her husband, but Neil's suspicion for his servants grew, and he was determined not to let anyone see him.

Although Adam kept her entertained by taking her on long walks around the castle and letting her go horseback riding, Neil's predicament drove her insane. If he didn't have a lead soon, she seriously thought about packing and returning home.

The early afternoon's gentle breeze came through the open window and beckoned her closer. She stood with her head uplifted, letting the sun warm her skin and the slight breeze tease the soft wisps of auburn hair around her face. As she took a deep breath of fresh air, a movement below caught her attention. Adam stood talking to a trio of farmhands. She couldn't help but notice the way they stared openly at Adam's scar, and it upset her to see people treat him like a beast when she knew he was a sweet, caring man.

The servants had been working in the yard for a few days, and in the short amount of time, the grounds had come to life. An assortment of flowers were planted, weeds pulled, and lawns manicured. It didn't resemble the pitiful land she'd seen a little over a week ago.

But although it did her heart good to gaze upon

its beauty, her insides twisted in turmoil. She couldn't sit still and watch her life whither away just because somebody had framed her husband. Even if it went against the promise she had made to Neil about getting involved, she needed to so something.

Without letting Adam know about the plans forming in her head, she donned her bonnet and shawl and hurried out to the stable to fetch a buggy. As she waited for the groom to prepare the vehicle, O'Toole ran to her side and begged her not to leave without an escort. She quickly assured him everything would be all right, but his constant pushing made her suspicious. Of course, lately she'd been suspicious of everybody. She guaranteed O'Toole her trip to town would be properly supervised when she met up with Allison and Ian.

The ride into town was enjoyable. It gave her time to think about how she could help her husband get himself out of this calamity. Searching through his office was first on her agenda. Perhaps she'd quiz his secretary and a few other people Neil might have been to see.

Entering Neil's office, she walked with an air of self-assurance. His secretary sat behind his small desk, but rose when he saw her.

"Hello, Mrs. Hamilton," he greeted with a pleasant smile.

She returned the smile. "How are you today, Mr. Stout?"

"I'm fine. And yourself?"

"Splendid."

"What do you need, Mrs. Hamilton?"

"Well, if it doesn't bother you too much, I'd like to look through my husband's office."

His brows pulled together. "Whatever for?"

"I'm not certain." She untied the bow at her throat and lifted off her bonnet. "I'd like to try and help him prove his innocence, you understand, and I just want to see if there's anything in his office that might be helpful

"You don't think he's guilty?"

Her gaze clashed with his. "Of course not. Do you?"

He shrugged. "According to the sheriff, the evidence against him is dismal."

"No, it's not." Her tone hardened, and she retorted tartly, "In fact, there is no real evidence against my husband, Mr. Stout. All Sheriff Franklin has on my husband is that he's helped these poor people who've been robbed. Neil Hamilton is the only thing that ties all them together."

Ewan hung his head and shifted his feet.

"If you'll excuse me, I'd like to get started," she said with a dismissive air.

After searching for two hours, exhaustion whirled through Charlotte's body like a wild storm. It would have been worth her time if she'd found anything helpful, but her efforts turned up empty. During all this time, only one thing really disturbed her. The first time she'd snooped through her husband's office, she'd found files and notes about Lord Thatcher and the castle, but this afternoon, there wasn't one trace of any of it. It seemed strange to her because she didn't see why the sheriff would take them. Perhaps Neil had them.

According to what she'd found over two weeks ago, Lord Thatcher's castle might have been Neil's last case. But then, she couldn't be sure. Perhaps it was just something Neil had been working on in his spare time.

She sighed deeply and gazed one last time around her. There was nowhere else to look, so she moved to leave, but before reaching the door, it swung open and in stomped Sheriff Franklin. From his sudden surprise, she jumped, but then annoyance settled in her chest.

"Hello again, Mrs. Hamilton. Didn't think I would see you here."

"And why not?" her voice rose in irritation. "This is, after all, still my husband's office."

"Yes, but what are you doing here?"

She laughed haughtily. "I should be asking you the same thing. What are you doing? Looking for incriminating evidence perhaps?"

A dark scowl appeared on his stern face, and she knew her words hit a bad chord.

He took a step further into the room. "Actually, I was passing by and happened to drop in on Mr. Stout for a visit. He told me you were here."

The hairs on the back of her neck stood on end from the way he looked on her, like a wolf eyeing his prey. The sickening feeling crept over her entire body, the longer he stared. She needed to leave—immediately.

"Yes, I'm here, but now I'm leaving. So, if you'll please excuse me." She tried to push past him, but he closed the door and blocked her path. She glared at the man. It wasn't his authority that frightened her, but his sudden and unexpected appearance that gave her cause to worry. He wasn't exactly a mean looking man, but his actions proved he enjoyed bullying people into doing his will.

Jeffrey Franklin was a bulky man, medium height. Light brown hair topped his nearly baldhead, and his dark brown eyes combed over her attire, sending a frightful chill down her spine.

Sheriff Franklin folded his arms across his sagging middle. "I need to speak with you in greater detail before you leave."

"Well," she snapped, "please get on with it, sheriff. I don't have all day. I'm a very busy woman."

His bushy eyebrows arched.

She wished she could slap that stupid superior look off his face, but she didn't want to get into any trouble with the law, and she was quite certain he'd do anything to get her behind bars. Sighing heavily, she plopped her hands on her hips, trying not to bend to his authority.

"What is it?"

"Please, call me Jeffrey."

"I'd rather not."

He stepped closer, and his hand brushed her cheek softly so she withdrew. "But Charlotte, my dear, we should be calling each other by our first names, especially since we'll be working so closely together to find your husband."

She pushed past him. "Whatever are you talking about? I would never work with a man like you. It would be different if we were on the same side, but as it is, you seem to think my husband is the criminal and I happen to believe him innocent. Now let me pass or I shall scream, you brute!"

His large strides brought him toward her, preying on her like a tiger on the kill, but she dodged his every move. She slipped behind the large desk and kept it between them. A flicker of apprehension coursed through her. She needed to stay calm and in control or lest she betray herself and Neil.

"You have the tongue of a viper, Charlotte. How can you believe he's so innocent?" A dark, congested expression settled on his sinister features.

"You don't have enough evidence against him to prove otherwise," she remarked, pleased at how nonchalant she sounded when her heart was beating a mad tune of panic.

"But Charlotte, my dear," he said, quickly stepping around the table.

She circled the other way.

"I heard a little rumor that you don't know you husband well at all. Isn't it fair to assume his accusers are the more adept judges of his character?"

"It's not fair to assume anything of that nature."

Sidestepping him, she once again slipped away, but the impossible man didn't give up. He lunged across the side of the desk and seized her roughly by the arm.

"Unhand me this very second!" Fear gave way to anger and she lifted her chin, meeting his icy stare straight on.

He cackled a victorious laugh when he stood beside her. "Or what, my dear? Are you going to scream?" He laughed wickedly, his tone low and sinister. "If you're thinking Ewan Stout will come to your rescue, think again. I sent him away."

"You are no certainly no gentleman."

"Of course not." He snickered again. "However, the ladies seem to like that particular trait in me."

His beady eyes narrowed on her face and slithered down her body, making her feel repulsed.

"What ladies? I don't believe you've ever in your life been close to a real lady."

She struggled against his tight grip, but he was much too strong. Her fear escalated by the second. What kind of sick game was he playing with her?

He sneered. "Come here, my little hell-cat. I'm going to teach you to respect authority, the same lesson Hamilton needs to learn. Through you, I'll hurt him as much as he's hurt me."

Surprise and horror siphoned the blood from her face. She choked back a frightened cry of outrage. With a viselike grip, he pulled her hard against his body, bending his head as his disgusting mouth hovered above hers. She turned her face to avoid the sickening contact. Her struggles didn't faze the man. Her small frame couldn't compare to his strength.

He pressed his open mouth to hers, and his slobbery lips sent a wave of nausea to her stomach. She tried moving away, but his mouth stayed over hers no matter which way she turned. Up against the wall he pushed her until his hips pressed next to hers, making her feel his growing arousal.

Anger surged through her, and she pulled a hand free and clawed at his face, but quick as lightning, he captured her wrists and imprisoned them behind her back. With his other hand, he ran it over the bodice of her dress, grabbing, feeling, hurting, as he clumsily groped her breasts. A frightful sob tore from her, but nothing would stop this madman.

Painfully, he yanked her to Neil's desk and pushed her down, his fingers searching frantically for the buttons on the bodice of her blouse. As each button came loose, her bosom slowly came into view. She took the chance to scream, but he placed his mouth over hers again to silence the noise.

Tears streamed down her face into her hair as his hands ripped at her clothes. He shred her bodice, buttons breaking away from the material. There wasn't one thing she could do to stop him. The muscles in her arms screamed out in protest as she continued to struggle to free herself, but his weight kept her in place.

"If you violate me, I'll personally seek you out and kill you!" she cried.

His mocking laugh was scornful. "I don't think so, my dear Charlotte," he hissed. "If you even harm one hair on my head, I'll see you hanged along with your husband, and you know I'll do it."

She let out another cry of anguish.

Miraculously, his weight suddenly lifted off her and he was thrown against the wall. A strong voice thundered through the room. "And, if you touch Mrs. Hamilton again, I'll surely kill you, and love doing it too...painfully and very, very slowly." Adam's voice came out low and dangerous like a growl.

She swung her head to the large presence limping toward the sheriff who now jumped to his feet and feasted his eyes on Lord Thatcher.

Charlotte whimpered with relief. His anger was evident in his fierce expression. At this moment, his tight jaw, pursed lips, and dark scowl made him look like the beast everyone thought he was. She quickly pulled her bodice together to cover her breasts.

Adam grabbed the other man's lapels and yanked him closer. The sheriff stared wide-eyed at the vicious brute before him. The man of the law swallowed. She knew Adam could kill him with his bare hands if he chose.

Jeffrey Franklin pulled himself upright and lifted his chin. "If you kill me, you will hang, too. Ewan Stout knows I'm here."

Adam let out an evil laugh. "Then I suppose I'll have to kill Mr. Stout, too."

Color left the sheriff's face. "If you kill me...it'll look bad for Neil Hamilton because we're...in his office," he stammered.

Charlotte's heart dropped. At this moment, she wanted Adam to kill the sheriff, but not if it meant getting Neil in trouble, or Adam hanged for murder.

Lines of worry etched across Adam's face. Would he give in—or kill?

"You're better off dead, but you're not worth my efforts." Adam's tone was edged with steel. "Besides, I don't want my friend or his wife hurt anymore by the likes of you. I will, however, warn you, sheriff. If you ever so much as look at Mrs. Hamilton again, I'll tear you limb from limb, slowly and very painfully. You'll beg for a quick death. Do you understand?"

Sheriff Franklin nodded, then groaned and looked down at his pants as wetness darkened the material at his groin. "I—I—I'll not speak to her again."

"You'll not even look at her," Adam warned again in a louder voice.

"No, I'll not even look at her," he answered obediently, hanging his head.

Adam gave him a vicious shake before dropping him to the floor in a heap. The insipid sheriff stumbled quickly to his feet and left the building.

When Adam turned back to Charlotte, tremors of relief swept through her body. Her clumsy hands tried ineffectively to cover her torn bodice. In two large awkward steps, Adam was in front of her, gathering her in his strong arms.

Her sobs gushed forward and she cried into her protector's chest. "I thought he...he...that he would..."

"Shhh, Charlotte. Please don't fret. He'll never touch you again, I promise." He stroked her hair softly.

"How...did...you...know I was here?" She tilted up her head to look at him.

"One of Neil's loyal servants was worried about you and told me of your plans." His gentle smile turned into a scowl. "Of course, I didn't think the man whom I'd be protecting you from would be a man of the law."

She sniffed. "Neither did I."

Adam reached into his over jacket and pulled out a handkerchief and gently dabbed her eyes, then pressed it in her hand. He shook off his own overcoat before draping it around her shoulders. He gathered her in his arms where she clung to him until her body regained control and the shakes disappeared. His hold comforted and relaxed her.

"Thank you."

"No need to thank me. I did what any man would have done for a woman who needed to hide her bosom."

"No, Adam, I didn't mean that." She struggled with her emotions, which were on the brink of crumbling. "I just don't know what would have happened if you didn't come." Tears spilled from her eyes. "Yes, I do know what would have happened."

"Shhh." His hands cupped her face as his thumbs wiped the wetness from her cheeks. "It's over now. Please, don't cry."

She circled her arms around his waist and pressed her body against his. His nearness was incredibly reassuring, and cozy. She didn't want to move. It was improper to show him this kind of affection, but she refused to let this wondrous feeling end. The comforting soon turned into something entirely different, and her bosom tingled. Precedence dictated she withdraw, but she waited for him to make the first move. The moment never happened.

Quickly, the heat of his body merged with hers and excited her. His hot hands drew small circles on her back, his steamy breath against her neck. Her nipples hardened, and she couldn't believe her body would respond so urgently to his mere touch.

"Charlotte?" he whispered huskily as his lips moved closer to her ear. "We should really get you back to the castle now."

"Yes…"

Still he didn't pull away, but this incredible moment had to be broken. She pulled back, but only slightly. Raising her gaze, she looked into his shadowed eyes, dark with desire. The knowledge stirred a roaring fire deep within her that she couldn't extinguish. When his gaze dipped down to partake of her exposed chest, her body's temperature soared.

She studied every inch of his scarred face, coming to rest on his mouth and the black mustache above his lip. His tongue slowly darted out, adding moisture, and she copied the movement on her own lips, feeling the urge to kiss him. Fierce rhythms from her heart beat loudly throughout her body, warning her she was a married woman and this wasn't proper, but the tingles in her body urged her to do it anyway.

Feeling the need to reward him for rescuing her, she followed her body's influence and slowly lifted her head to press her mouth to his inviting lips. Lightning bolts erupted inside her, making her want to touch him, but when she touched the side of his face where the scar was located, he jumped back and broke the kiss, and the exquisite feeling that accompanied it.

She stared into his wide eyes as their deep breaths mingled. She swallowed her guilty feelings when he lowered his gaze and rose.

He cleared his throat. "Please forgive me, but I couldn't seem to refrain myself." Huskiness laced his speech. "I suppose I'm no better than the sheriff."

Shame washed over her, clenching her chest. "No, Adam. You're one hundred times better than that man. The kiss we shared was done in kindness, not forced as was his."

Adam avoided her gaze, focusing on her torn bodice. Her bosom tingled again.

"But it wasn't right. You're a married woman, and it shouldn't have happened." He shook his head. "Let's get you out of here before Neil's secretary returns. I'm afraid I might severely hurt him for allowing the sheriff into the room alone with you, knowing full well what the bastard intended."

Charlotte quickly moved off the desk, still keeping the jacket securely around her, hiding her ripped bodice from his heated stare. It was hard to believe what had just happened between them, but she couldn't deny the curious sensations her body had experienced.

Today's astonishing thrill left her confused. She needed to do some serious thinking about her own husband and these new feelings she had for Lord Thatcher.

Perhaps she and Neil were not meant to be husband and wife after all…

Chapter Eleven

Charlotte sank into the bubble-filled tub and moaned softly, letting the hot water relax her tense muscles. Like dancing fingers across her skin, the steam healed her. When she let herself think about what that son-of-a-bitch had done, she could still feel his slobbering mouth upon her flesh. Her skin crawled with disgust.

Instead, she tried to focus on the way Adam had comforted her, something she shouldn't let control her mind. Somehow, she had become attracted to Adam, an attraction that went far beyond appearance. Her feelings for him had nothing to do with reason. Although his body was more muscular and alluring than she'd first thought, it was actually his sweet and caring nature that lured her. She was able to look past his scar and see deep inside to the man he truly was. And she liked what she saw.

She held the sponge up and allowed the water to drip across her arm and trickle between her breasts. Charlotte closed her eyes and thought about the two men in her life. First, there was Neil. Strong, devilishly handsome, and determined, but plagued by problems in both his business and his private life. And Adam, also strong and muscular, not ugly, but gentle and caring. If it weren't for Neil, would she fall for Adam?

She climbed out of the tub and toweled herself dry, then dressed in her shift. The sheer ice blue matching robe with billowy sleeves was comfortable enough for her to just lounge around her room. The weather had turned warmer this afternoon, and she welcomed it.

With her brush, she stroked her long auburn locks, the bristles on her scalp relaxing her. As she peered out the window down at the yard, her mind returned to Adam once again. He'd apologized for kissing her, which was incredibly sweet, but then not a word had been spoken between them on the way back to the castle. By Adam's furrowed brow, she wondered if guilt ate away at his conscious.

Why didn't she feel any remorse for kissing him? She should. After all, Neil was her husband. They were gradually putting their marriage in order. Yet, her relationship with Adam had been growing stronger lately.

A sound from the corner of the room pulled her away from her thoughts, and she swung her head in that direction. She stared in dismay, for someone was in the room! Was it the sheriff coming to torment her again?

A lean frame emerged from the shadows, and she gasped with surprise.

"Your loveliness is such a vision for these lonely eyes of mine," Neil told her as he walked to her, his stare boldly moving over her body. From his heated expression, she suddenly realized that standing in front of the window as she had, she'd been in total silhouette. The blood rushed to her face.

"Neil!" she gasped, stepping out of the light. "Do you always have to sneak up on me?"

"Well, yes. I can't just knock on your door. You know I'm trying to keep myself out of sight. That is why I use the hidden passageways through the castle."

She arched a brow. "Hidden passageways?"

"Yes. I'll have to show them to you sometime, my sweet. I'm quite certain you'll enjoy yourself." He stopped in front of her and leaned over, kissing her cheek. "How are you today, my sweet?"

"How am I today?" Her voice rose as she pushed him away. "You really want to know?" She threw her brush. It crashed on her dressing table, knocking over her powder. Charlotte planted her hands on her hips and took two steps backward. "I've had the worst experience of my life...and it was all your fault!"

Amusement flickered in the eyes meeting hers. "My fault?" His very tone aroused and infuriated her.

"Yes. I went into town to your office, trying to find anything that might help convince the authorities of your innocence. Just as I was leaving, the sheriff arrived, and because I couldn't succumb to his advances, he took it upon himself to...to..." Her voice broke. "To attack me!"

"What?" His voice escalated in furious anger. "He touched you?"

Tears quickly gathered in her eyes, her voice barely above a whisper. "Yes. He ripped my dress and forced his disgusting lips and hands on me. I tried to fight him, but he was too strong." She covered her face with her hands and sobbed at the burning memory.

He wrapped his arms tightly around her and she leaned her head against his powerful chest. "What happened?" Anger tightened his voice.

She tilted back her head and looked up into his face. "Adam saved me." Her voice was soft.

His brows drew together. "Adam? Do you mean Lord Thatcher?"

"Yes. He saved me from being violated."

Pain etched itself in the lines of his expression. "Oh, my darling, I'm sorry." He pulled her to him again. "I'm so very sorry I wasn't there to save you."

Charlotte didn't cry as she had when Adam comforted her. She sniffled. "I didn't know whether I should trust your servants. O'Toole tried to go with me into town, and I refused his help. Thankfully, he went to Adam. I think we can trust O'Toole after this."

"Oh, yes, my darling. We'll trust him, but where was Ewan Stout while all this was happening?"

The strong steady beat of his heart lulled her, and gave her peace. Finally, she lifted her head and gazed into his eyes. "I don't know. He wasn't there. The sheriff said he sent him away."

His hand stroked the side of her face lovingly. "Can you ever forgive me for not being there when you needed me the most?"

Wiping her eyes, she turned her back on him. "I suppose, though I wish you had been there instead of Adam…but don't look so worried. I can take care of myself."

"I know, and you've done that masterfully. But damn it, I should have been there to protect my own wife!" He rubbed his thumbs across her shoulders.

"No, Neil. We need to clear you from these false crimes before you can be seen in public."

"No." He moved closer to her until the buttons on his shirt touched the back of her robe. "Let's leave this God forsaken place and go back to South Carolina. We'll escape these charges against me and start a new life somewhere else together, my love."

"No, Neil." She turned. His arms slipped around her shoulders, and she rested her hands on his chest. "You're not the kind of man who runs from his problems, and I wouldn't let you. You need to stay and see this thing through to the end. I don't want to live my life in fear that you might get hung for a crime you never committed. I don't want to live every day glancing over my shoulder either."

Sighing heavily, he nodded. "You're right." His lips brushed across her forehead. "But, my darling, I don't want you going into town unless somebody is with you. Do you now see how dangerous the sheriff is? I cannot trust him with the fate of my own life."

"Yes." She laid her hand gently along the side of his face. "I'll not go into town by myself again. And, I'm sorry for blaming you. It wasn't your fault that I was in your office at the same time the sheriff came."

"Yes it was," he said sadly.

"No, Neil. It was my fault."

"But you were trying to help me—" He stopped when his voice caught.

"But if I had listened to you when you told me to stay here, it wouldn't have happened."

"I should kill him for doing that to you."

"No. Then there will really be a reason to hang you."

He sighed again, pulling her close to his body as he kissed the side of her face. "Thank you for caring about me. I really don't deserve it."

She drew back and looked up into his blue eyes, then chuckled. "No, you don't."

He smiled. "You didn't have to agree."

"I needed to do something to keep you from kissing me."

One of his eyebrows arched. "Was I going to kiss you?"

"You know perfectly well you were."

"And you wouldn't have liked it?" he teased.

A blush warmed her cheeks. "That's not the point."

He chuckled deeply. "Oh, Charlotte, how can I keep myself from being near you when you are this breathtakingly lovely? And how can I keep my lips from yours when they are so lusciously inviting?" His lips began descending to hers. "And how, my love, can I keep my heart intact when it belongs to you?"

He'd always seduced her with his words, and this time was no different. She was drawn to him, innocent and uncaring about the outcome, because once his lips touched hers, she was lost in his hungry and exciting kiss. Wildly, their tongues met as she clung to his shirt, fearing if she broke their embrace, the thrill would die.

His strong hands moved up and tangled in her hair as he met her demanding kisses. She thought this was never going to happen, but it was real, and he was real, kissing her and exciting her just as much as he'd done that night of the masquerade ball.

His hands floated down her neck, slipping inside her robe, the tips of his fingers brushing her shoulders as gently as a butterfly. Down, down, they swept across he skin, and drifted to her heaving breasts. His thumbs ran across her nipples, circling and arousing, and they hardened.

His mouth left hers and moved down her throat. He touched his tongue to certain areas on her neck, but never lingered in one particular spot. As his lips moved further, his hands untied the robe.

Hasty fingers parted the sheer fabric. He touched his mouth to her breast, his tongue wetting the tip. She moaned, then his voice followed and she buried her fingers through his thick hair and held his face to her bosom.

Wonderful, sensitive tingles poured through her body warming her, heating her to a boil. She didn't know how it happened or why, but this was exactly what she needed at this particular moment. Neil knew how to excite her, pleasure her beyond imagination. She let herself go; allowing his seduction to carry her skyward...but then her mind conjured up an image that made her pause.

Adam's face held a sad expression it made her catch her breath. As suddenly as it had come, the image changed, and he was the one kissing her with such passion.

Her mind screamed for her to stop. What was

she doing? Why was she allowing Neil to make love to her when not more than thirty minutes ago she was thinking about Adam, and dreaming about him kissing her the way she wanted a man overcome with love to kiss?

Having this attention from Neil was what she wanted. Wasn't it? Her heart argued with her head, but it was her body that won out.

Neil's warm and seeking hands excited her, yet the thoughts of Adam left her very confused. She didn't like feeling this way. What she and Neil were doing was right, because they were, after all, still married, but it didn't feel right in her heart. Until her heart and her body could share the same signals, she couldn't let Neil make love to her.

"No, Neil. I cannot do this." Breathlessly, she pulled away. He removed his hands from underneath her robe. He reached out, but she stepped away.

"Why? What's wrong?" His voice was deep and still laced with passion.

"I...I can't do this yet. It's too soon."

"But I can tell your body is ready. Don't you remember the passion we shared between us that night at the Mask?"

How could she forget? She still dreamed about it at night. Taking quick steps, she moved to her bed. She grabbed a pillow to her bosom and lay down, curling her legs up to her stomach. "Neil, there's no mistake that my body responds to your touch, but my mind and heart are still very confused about many things."

Neil took in a few labored breaths, trying to gain control. His obvious desire strained against the fabric of his trousers, and the imprint of it against her stomach made her heart leap. But she couldn't continue. Her confusion was still too great.

With a deep sigh, he sat beside her on the bed

and softly stroked her thigh. “What’s it that you’re confused about, darling?”

She shrugged. His touch sent heat up her thighs.

“Is it another man?”

Her eyes widened and her heart quickened. “Another man?” she asked quickly. “What makes you think it’s another man?”

“Well, since Ian was the reason you came to find me seeking an annulment, I just wondered if...well if you still held feelings for him.”

The rhythm of her heart slowed considerably. “Neil, I know I led you to believe Ian and I were going to become lovers, but the truth is, he’s not the reason I sought an annulment.”

“He isn’t?” His luminous eyes widened in astonishment.

“No.” She sat up, still keeping the pillow clutched to her bosom. “To be honest, Ian is in love with Allison, not me.”

“Then why did you tell me differently?”

She shrugged. “I didn’t want you to pity me. I didn’t want to show you how pathetic I was. I also wanted to make you jealous.”

He studied her expression, then brought his hand up and cupped her face. “I’m sorry I was such an ass.” She laughed, which made him laugh. “I suppose your plan worked.” His thumb stroked her cheek tenderly. “It’s now my turn to confess something to you.”

“What’s that?”

“I knew about Allison and Ian.”

“You knew?”

He dropped his hand. “I didn’t really know about them until after you had moved into my townhouse, but I noticed them together in town one day and could tell they were very much attracted to each other. After that, I put the pieces together.”

She sighed. “Are you angry with me?”

“Why should I be angry?”

“Because I lied.”

He chuckled. “It worked, didn’t it?”

She smiled. “Yes, I suppose, but that doesn’t make it right.”

Leaning closer to her, he circled her in his arms. “You don’t need to suppose, my darling. I grow more and more attracted to you as each day passes. It’s as I told you before, my heart belongs to you and no other. I want you as my wife, Charlotte, and I’ll never give you reason to doubt or mistrust me again.”

Her smile disappeared and she wanted to cry. She had waited so long to hear him say that to her, and now he had, and she was the one who couldn’t return the words because of her scrambled mind.

He crushed his lips to hers. A spurt of hungry desire spiraled through her, and the degree to which her body responded stunned her. They were kissing with so much unreleased passion that she grew aroused. Again. She struggled against him, but his kiss left her weak. It was a kiss for her weary soul to melt into, to surrender to.

He hesitated, then pressed his lips to hers once more, smothering her with a demanding mastery. She felt breathless. Instinctively, her body arched toward him and he pressed her tightly against his silky shirt.

Why did she lose all self-control whenever he was near? Her emotions whirled and then skidded. No! What was she doing? Yet, her treacherous body strongly responded to his nearness. She needed to think and to give her impetuous heart a chance to beat normally again.

She withdrew. “Thank you.” Her hand moved up to caress his face. “You have no idea how much I’ve longed to hear those words from you, but...” She shrugged. "But I need more time to unscramble my mind."

His hand covered hers and moved it up to his lips as he tenderly kissed the palm of her hand. "I'll give you more time, darling."

She nodded. "Thank you for understanding."

****

She had thanked him for understanding, yet she couldn't understand it herself. She'd waited so long to hear Neil say such kind and sweet words to her, so why couldn't she respond the same way? Had she really hardened her heart toward him? Was it too difficult to forgive him for leaving her two years ago? Or were her feelings for Adam stronger than she first realized?

Leaning back in her chaise, she pushed her fingers through her long hair, sweeping it away from her face. With a heavy sigh, she realized something must be done about her dilemma, and soon.

Her maid stepped into the room and smiled. "Are you up for a visitor today?"

Charlotte really didn't want one. She'd planned on staying cooped up in her rooms, but the older woman's cheerful disposition sparked her interest. "Who's calling?"

"Your friend, Mrs. Archibald."

Charlotte smiled wide and she jumped to her feet. "Quickly, Clara. Help me dress."

The maid hurried and dressed Charlotte in her burgundy day dress with bell shaped sleeves and heart shaped bodice. The slender skirt dragged behind a small train, making her feel very elegant.

She did nothing fancy with her hair, just brushed it until it shone, then pulled back the sides, tying it with a burgundy ribbon on top her head, letting the curls cascade down her back.

When she hurried downstairs to the parlor, Allison was sitting by herself. Charlotte's first instinct was to question about Ian's absence, but then she wondered why Adam hadn't kept her friend company.

"Allison!" Happily, she rushed to her friend and hugged her. "I'm so pleased you're here. I've certainly missed you."

"I've also missed you," Allison replied.

"I would have come to see you today if you hadn't come first." She turned toward the chairs. "Let's sit."

Allison's wide eyes scanned the room. "I can't believe the remarkable changes in this place."

Charlotte laughed. "Yes, we've certainly been busy, and Neil's servants have been so helpful." After they were seated, she patted her friend's hand. "So, what have you been doing?"

The smile left Allison's face. "I've come to say goodbye."

"Goodbye? You cannot leave now."

"Charlotte, honey, I can't stay here forever. I'm getting rather bored, and I feel it's time I go back home."

Sadness clenched Charlotte's heart and tears sprang to her eyes. "But what will I do without you?"

Allison laughed. "I think you'll be just fine. In fact, you've been doing just fine without me for more than a week."

"But I don't want you to leave. Can't you and Ian stay just a little while longer?"

Allison hung her head as she looked at the hands resting in her lap. "I can't speak for Ian, but I'll not be able to stay any longer. I'm sorry."

Charlotte scrunched her forehead. "What's wrong, Allison?"

"I believe Ian has already left to return home."

"What happened between the two of you?"

Laughing lightly, Allison lifted her gaze, showing watery eyes. "Can you believe he thought I was getting too serious? He doesn't want a commitment and he thought I was pushing him into marriage."

"Were you?"

"I might have, I don't know. I'm in love with him, but to marry again..." She paused and shrugged. "I don't know how I feel about that."

"I'm sorry." Charlotte squeezed her friend's hand. "Are you all right?"

"I'll be fine."

"Would you like to go shopping? That has always cured our unhappiness in the past."

Allison smiled. "No. I'm on my way home right now. I just dropped by to say goodbye and to wish you luck with Neil."

"Would you like to stay for tea? I'm certain Lord Thatcher would like to visit with you before you leave."

Allison shook her head. "He's already visited with me. He told me I was more than welcome to stay in his castle, but I declined. I'm homesick and wish to return to South Carolina."

"Oh," Charlotte mumbled softly. "I'll miss you terribly."

"Are you still planning on ending your marriage when the month is over?"

Laughing softly, Charlotte shook her head. "I don't know what I want any longer. I've been so confused lately that I just don't know what to feel."

"What's causing you such turmoil?" Allison asked.

She hesitated then whispered, "The other day Lord Thatcher kissed me."

Allison gasped and clung to Charlotte's hands. "Continue."

"He'd saved me from the sheriff's advances, and..." She took a deep breath. "We were caught up in the moment. He was there comforting...I was in his arms...it just happened." She smiled. "And, I liked it."

"Oh, Charlotte, no. What about Neil?"

"I also shared a nice moment with Neil. He told me I held his heart. He promised he'd never cause me to doubt him again." She shook her head. "I just don't know what to do. I'm so confused. I have feelings for both of them."

Allison's expression turned to humor as a twinkle shone in her friend's eyes.

Charlotte cocked her head. "This is not humorous, Allison!"

"I know, but I can't hold it in. For two years you did nothing but make yourself beautiful so your husband wouldn't be able to resist you, and now you finally have him, you're not sure you want him?"

"Yes, it does seem rather surprising, doesn't it?"

"How does Lord Thatcher feel about you?"

Charlotte shrugged. "I believe he's attracted to me. He wouldn't have kissed me otherwise. He hasn't declared any intentions toward me other than friendship."

"I see. But isn't it true Neil told you he lived like a hermit? Well, maybe he's just using you, taking advantage of your time of confusion. Maybe he's after your money."

"Allison, no. Adam wouldn't—" But she wasn't certain. How well did she really know him?

"I didn't think Ian would give up so easily, either." Allison shrugged. "Do you think perhaps you have feelings for him only out of pity?"

"Pity?" Charlotte shrieked. "I think not! I've gotten to know the real man, and there is nothing to pity. He's a kind and decent human being, not to mention his loving and sweet qualities. Believe me when I say I think he's a very handsome man."

Allison smiled. "I'm glad you think that. But you're right. You do have a problem." She patted

Charlotte's hands. "Do let me know which man you choose."

Charlotte nodded. "I'll write you."

Allison leaned over and gave her a hug. "I really have to go now. Take care and don't get into any more trouble."

"Don't worry so much."

Charlotte walked out of the parlor with Allison and as she turned the corner, she saw Adam standing not too far from the door. Charlotte's heart accelerated. Had he overheard the conversation? She almost hoped he hadn't, but then he looked at her differently with warmth and tenderness in his eyes. Or was that just her imagination?

Charlotte watched Adam closely as they waited by the carriage and wished Allison a safe journey home. They stood side by side, waving goodbye as the carriage pulled away.

He turned to Charlotte, a soft smile bracketing his mouth. "Are you all right?"

Charlotte shrugged. "I think so."

"Does a picnic sound enjoyable this afternoon?" Adam asked.

She smiled wider, her heart pounding in her chest. "Would you be my escort?"

"Certainly."

"Then I think a picnic would be a wonderful idea."

"I have a basket already prepared. Would you like to leave right now, or do you need to change first?"

"I might like to get a shawl. What do you think?"

His focus moved from her face down over her chest, making her bosom burn with pleasure. "It's warm today."

"Then I should be fine." She stepped to him, hooking her hand through his elbow.

He escorted her out to the waiting buggy, and

then turned to fetch the basket, but O'Toole had brought it out, along with a blanket. After thanking the butler, Adam climbed in the buggy beside her.

"Where are we going?" she wondered.

"There's a spot on my estate that's just perfect for a picnic. I don't believe you have been there, yet. A gurgling brook and large oak trees will be our companions."

"Sounds lovely."

Adam urged the horses onward as they began their journey. During the short ride, he kept the conversation polite and proper. Charlotte wanted to ask him about the kiss; wanted to know if he had enjoyed it, too. She also wondered if he'd overheard the conversation she had with Allison, but she didn't dare ask. She watched him out of the corner of her eye, wondering why he was so quiet as she regarded him with somber curiosity.

The shaded grove was absolutely beautiful, with a light patch of lavender and yellow wild flowers growing near the green grass where they spread their picnic. Tall trees canopied their little spot, and a clear gurgling spring trickled a few feet away. Everything was perfect.

Adam laid the blanket next to the oak tree, then set out the picnic. Charlotte quickly moved next to him to help. The aroma from the roast beef caused her stomach to rumble, and the juicy apples made her mouth water.

"Adam, this smells wonderful. Did you make it yourself?"

"Of course, my dear, since I've not hired a cook as of yet."

She smiled. It made her happy to think he'd take the time to do this for her.

"Mrs. Archibald's departure was rather sudden, was it not?" he asked.

She swallowed down the bite of biscuit before

answering. "Yes. I thought she was going to stay until my month with Neil was over."

Adam gave her a quizzical look. "Does that mean you don't plan on staying as Neil's wife?"

She laughed lightly. "To tell you the truth, Adam, I don't know what I plan on doing. Not now, anyhow."

"Why?"

She shrugged. "Because I'm confused." She shyly met his gaze. "I really don't know why I'm confessing my personal feelings to you."

"I was out of line for asking."

"Oh, no. I think the reason I say so much is because you're so easy to talk to. I've never known a man like you."

He smiled. "I've never known a woman like you."

She looked back down at her half empty plate and realized she wasn't hungry. Setting her plate aside, she gazed back at him. "Adam?"

"Yes?"

"Can we talk about the kiss we shared the other day?"

He quickly looked away. "No."

His gloved hand lay on the blanket between them. Gently, she placed her hand over his. "Please? I'd really like to get it out in the open."

Slowly, he turned and gazed deeply into her eyes. "I don't think I'll be able to say no to you, especially when you look at me like that."

"Then will you talk with me about the kiss?"

He blew out a heavy sigh. "What do you want me to say? It happened and it shouldn't have."

Now that the moment was upon her, she really didn't know what to say. Would he admit his feelings about the other day?

Laughing lightly, she shrugged. "Why did you kiss me, then?"

He peered down at their joined hands. "Would

you hate me if I said I didn't kiss you just to comfort you?"

Her heart pounded faster. "It would be hard for me to hate you."

"You were so very beautiful, even with your tears. You looked at me as if I was a real man, and God help me, I couldn't help myself."

"But Adam, you are a real man."

"Don't talk like that, Charlotte." His voice was soft, but husky. "You're still another man's wife, and I shouldn't have taken advantage of you."

"You didn't, I assure you. I'm very grateful you saved me. And...I welcomed your kiss."

His eyes widened. "Why?"

"I think our relationship has progressed nicely, and we've become very close friends of late. I think the kiss was meant to happen."

He pulled his hand away from hers. They sat in companionable silence for several moments. She tried watching the stream babble over the rocks, but her gaze returned to him.

His dark eyes softened. "You must know what kind of emotions are going through me. You're a hard woman to resist, and sometimes I have a devil of a time controlling myself around you." He raised his hand and grazed his fingertips across her shoulder. "Do you realize how much I want to touch and kiss you like a man does to a beautiful woman?"

"How much?"

Their eyes met, and invisible sparks happened between them.

He withdrew his hand. "I mustn't, and neither should you."

"Do you know it's because of my feelings for you that I'm confused about staying with Neil?"

"Don't say such things."

"You're both so different, and I believe it's the differences that attracts me."

He swallowed hard, running his tongue around his lips. "Please stop this insanity right now. My defenses are weakening."

Bringing his hand up to her mouth, she kissed his gloved fingertips softly, then turned and kissed his palm. Adam slowly moved toward her. He placed his lips on hers and kissed her so very gently. She slid her hand up to his neck and touched him.

He moved his lips across her mouth for only a few moments before she tilted her head and opened for his tongue to enter. He did not hesitate. Velvet hot wetness entered her mouth and danced slowly back and forth with hers. He lowered her gently to the ground and leaned the length of his body alongside hers.

"Adam," she mumbled against his lips. "Take off your gloves. I want to feel your hands on me."

"No." He withdrew and stood. "You may be ready, but I'm not. I shouldn't have even done this to you, considering what you are to me—"

Confusion clouded her mind. "Please explain."

Turning away from her, he shook his head. "I've said too much."

"Adam, please. I don't understand." She stood next to him.

Sighing heavily, he turned toward her. His hand stroked her cheek. "I suppose since your husband hasn't told you, then I must be the one." He paused, briefly. "Your husband's family and the Thatchers are related. The Hamiltons and the Thatchers are cousins."

Her eyes widened in shock. "Cousins?"

"Yes."

She studied the side of his face that was not scarred, and could finally see the similarities. Both men had high-defined cheekbones and sharp angular noses. "I cannot believe I didn't see it before."

"Neil didn't want you to see it. In fact, I was

reluctant to tell you."

"Why?"

"Because our families hate each other."

"Is that why it was hard for Neil to agree to living out here while in hiding?"

"Yes."

"Why should it make a difference?"

The hard lines in his face relaxed and he smiled. "Charlotte?" He cupped her face with his hands. "Don't you know? Because of you..." He shook his head. "You're married to my cousin, and even though the thought of having you for myself thrills me beyond anything, the fact remains that you're still married to Neil."

"But, if after the month is over and I don't wish to be married to him, he promised he'd grant me the annulment."

"Is that what you wish? Do you really want to resolve the marriage to a strong and vital man like Neil? Do you really want to give up going into society functions with him on your arm? If you chose me, you'll not have any of that. You know the sort of life I'm forced to live."

"But I don't see how—"

"Yes, I know," he cut her off. "You can see past the scar, but other people will not. They'll not even take the time."

"I really don't want to think of other people."

"Charlotte, you cannot put off the future any longer, because if you chose me, I'll want you as my wife and nothing less. I don't want to fall in love with you and have you break my heart when you go back to him because you've realized the life I give you is not the life Neil can give you."

"You're not judging me fairly." Tears welled up in her eyes because she knew deep down in her heart he spoke the truth.

"Please, do this one thing for me. Give this

matter some serious thought. Think about the both of us; what each of us can give you, and what we cannot."

She nodded. "I'll do that, I promise."

Smiling, he took her loosely in his embrace as he stared down into her face. "Now that lunch is out of the way, would you like to go on a walk? Let's put aside our feelings of passion for now and merely enjoy the rest of the day."

She stroked his neatly groomed beard. "I'd love to."

Chapter Twelve

Neil sat quietly on the edge of the bed and watched Charlotte's angelic expression as she continued in her early morning slumber. Gently sweeping the delicate petals of the rose he held over the creamy skin on her face, he tried to waken her. He had plans for them today, and he hoped her enthusiasm would match his.

He worried she was developing feelings for the beast, yet he had to be patient and wait for her decision. It scared him to think she'd not want to be his wife after the month was over. He couldn't have that. Not now that he'd fallen madly in love with her.

As he continued his stroking, she stirred. He leaned closer, awaiting the moment she would open her intoxicating eyes and look at him. They fluttered open. He grinned, watching her come awake. At last, she smiled and his heart raced.

"Good morning, beautiful," he whispered.

"Good morning yourself."

"Are you up for some chasing around today with an old, haggardly looking woman? Or would you rather be with a bent and crooked old man?"

She laughed lightly. "I can't be with the real you?"

He merely grinned. "It will be me, silly. I'll be disguised."

"What will we be doing?"

"I'd like your help."

She snapped up to a sitting position, her face aglow with enthusiasm. "Really?"

"Yes."

"Oh, Neil, this is wonderful!"

"You need to get dressed right away."

Pushing him off the side of the bed, she climbed out. "I'll be ready in one hour."

"Don't rush yourself." He chuckled, leaving the room.

Running his fingers through his hair, he took a deep sigh and shook himself more alert. He'd been up for twenty-four hours straight and was ready to rest, but this needed taking care of first. Of course, a strong coffee would help wake him, too, he thought as he walked toward the kitchen.

During the night, he'd sneaked into the sheriff's office and peered through the locked files, looking for clues to whoever had been helping the man-of-the-law to frame him. An overwhelming feeling of renewal swept over Neil, which made him more determined to find the real thief. It hurt to think the people he'd trusted and befriended at one time would now stab him in the back. Who could be doing this? Hadn't he served New York well in the last two years? Yet somebody was out there putting distrust into these people's minds. Could this have something to do with Charlotte? But he quickly banished the thought.

He wouldn't be a bit surprised if it was the sheriff himself, but he didn't know why Jeffrey Franklin would have such a grudge to settle. Granted, Franklin wasn't a pillar of the society, but Neil hadn't done anything to make the man do something this vicious.

When he thought about Charlotte's enthusiasm this morning, he grinned. He planned to take her with him to his client's houses and let her question them. Hopefully, she'd get answers to questions that he could not. Also, he'd be able to keep an eye on her. Not that he thought there was any danger of the sheriff attempting anything so foolish again. Neil's mind wandered toward Adam. If anything were to happen to Charlotte, Neil would be able to protect her—not Adam!

With his cup of coffee in hand, he exhaled deeply and sank into the soft chair. Slowly, he sipped the drink, savoring the taste and the warmth that spread deep within him.

The month he'd promised her was quickly slipping by. Would she still want to leave when her time was up? His only hope was she'd fall in love with him.

He wanted her so badly, and he couldn't wait until she finally gave in and let him make love to her. She'd almost relented a couple of times, but for some reason she always pulled away. He needed to get her so aroused she wouldn't want to stop. He had to make her fall in love with him. He intended for her to feel the same love that was spreading throughout his heart, because every time his gaze met hers, his heart turned over in response.

It wasn't her beauty that had him mesmerized, but it was her personality. He enjoyed being with her, discussing things, and seeing the way her eyes lit up when she laughed. He cherished the fact that she was on his thoughts as he drifted off to sleep every night, and when he arose in the morning. He wanted to please her...to show her the man he really was.

Neil waited for exactly one hour then he wandered upstairs toward her room. Just as he reached her door, she flung it opened and rushed out, knocking into him.

He grabbed her shoulders to steady her. "Whoa, slow down, my love."

She laughed. "Sorry. I'm ready now." Then her attention swept over his face and dipped down to his clothes. "But you're not."

“I know. I thought you might like to see how I get into disguise.”

Her eyes widened. “Oh, yes.”

He took hold of her hand and led her to his room. “Have a seat and watch.” He motioned to the small chair beside his dressing table.

She sat, straight back with her hands folded in her lap. He kept one eye on her while he selected his outfit. She looked so lovely wearing a blue day dress. The round bodice enhanced her bosom, and he couldn’t keep his attention from wandering there.

“Before I start caking my face with make-up,” he explained, pulling her to her feet, “I want to do something first.” Then, before she had time to ask, he took her face in his hands and kissed her. He wanted it to be tender and slow, but just as always, the urge to seduce her with wild abandonment came over him.

Charlotte gasped from the suddenness, but responded quickly. She wrapped her arms around his neck and met his probing tongue. She liked the way his hard chest fit with her soft one. She also liked Neil’s way of kissing. It had always excited her, and she realized at this moment just how much it really got her juices flowing. Her mind whirled, and her body cried out for more, but before she could beg him to do more, he stopped and stepped back.

She opened her eyes to find him gazing tenderly at her.

“Thank you,” he said.

“For what?” Her voice was deep and sedated.

“For not pulling away.” He placed a tiny kiss on her cheek before turning to his dressing table.

Charlotte sat back in the chair, hoping her trembling legs wouldn’t give her away. His kisses had always left her weak. Before she’d been upset, but now she enjoyed the way he made her feel.

What form was he going to take today? She

amused herself, guessing as he worked.

"Neil?"

"Yes, my darling."

"Where do you get that...goopy matter you're putting on your face? I don't think I have ever seen it before."

He turned and grinned at her. "I don't think you would believe me if I told you."

"Try me."

"I made this myself."

She gaped in amazement. "Really?"

"Yes. I've always been fascinated with disguises. When I was young, I used to blend different formulas in hopes of finding something that worked the way I wanted. It took me five years to do it."

"Unbelievable."

"I told you that you wouldn't believe."

She laughed lightly. "It's not that. I just think it's remarkable you have such strange talents."

"So, you think I'm strange, do you?"

"Only in the good sort of way."

Neil turned back to his mirror. "When I was younger, I would fix my face to look menacing so I could frighten my sisters. When I created this mixture, I was able to make myself not only scary, but look ill as well. I could transform myself to look like a woman, an old man, and all other different kinds of people. I even made my arm look like it was cut and bleeding once." He laughed. "My sister almost made me bleed for real when she found out I was only teasing." He smiled at the memory.

"Can you change my appearance, too?" she asked.

"No."

"Why not?"

He turned away from the mirror and gazed upon her. "Because I love the way you look. You're the most beautiful woman I've ever seen, and anyone who'd want to change you should be strung on the highest gallows."

Charlotte's cheeks burned from his flattering remark. "Thank you. But I just want to know what it feels like to pretend to be someone else."

He laughed. "It's a pain in my backside."

"Thank you for being so blunt," she retorted flippantly.

He laughed harder. "I would apologize to you for being so open with my obscenities, but you forget, I know you, Mrs. Hamilton."

It took a few minutes, but a grin soon touched her mouth. "So you do."

While getting ready, he explained why he needed her help. He turned back to the mirror, and a short time later, he was ready. Before her stood a haggard, looking old man, peering intently at her.

She nodded in approval. Wrinkles marred Neil's once handsome face. Crow's feet around his eyes made them look tired and aged. A gray wig topped his head, hiding any hint of the dark hair she liked to run her fingers through. Even his face didn't hold the healthy color of his natural bronzed skin, but almost a sickly gray instead.

He held out his elbow. "Shall we go, my sweet?"

Neil led her outside where O'Toole waited beside a two-seater carriage. He even walked like an old man, stooped and slow.

Inside the conveyance, she asked, "What do you want me to ask these people?"

"Be friendly and gain their confidence. Be honest and tell them who you are. Let them know how upset you are about the accusations made against me. Ask them exactly what items were stolen, and when. Find out why they suspect me of doing it."

Without meaning to, she laughed. "I'm sorry, Neil, but it's so funny to hear your voice come from that face. Your disguise is so clever, I can hardly see my husband in there."

"You think this is humorous?" he questioned.

"No." She tried to sober her expression. "I'm sorry. Please continue."

He chuckled and shook his head. "Just be sweet to them and pour on your charm."

"Will they let me in their homes? And will they be pleasant?"

"I don't know, but I'm hoping they will."

Charlotte turned her focus to the road. "I definitely hope so. I don't enjoy heavy confrontations, but I'll do it if I have to."

Within half an hour, they came upon the home of Lord and Lady Stringham who Neil explained had moved here from London three years ago. Charlotte wrung her hands. She didn't want to mess things up. Moreover, she wanted to do it right so that he'd soon be free from these false charges.

"I'll park the carriage slightly out of sight. I'll wait here. I'll look more like your servant that way," he told her.

"It's too bad you didn't dress more respectably," she commented.

"Why?"

"Because then you could pass for Neil's father. You could come inside with me and help me through this."

A scowl appeared on his withered face. Suddenly he laughed. "I can't believe I didn't think of that." Still chuckling, he climbed out of the carriage, then turned and helped her down. "Good luck." He winked.

Keeping her chin held high and her back straight, she made her way to the front door. The family's wealth was evident. The fancy double doors with the decorative knockers, and the large stained glass windows were almost as lovely as a few of her father's homes.

She announced herself to the butler as Mrs. Charlotte Hamilton. As Neil predicted, she was shown into the drawing room where she waited only a few minutes before the lady of the house greeted her. Lady Stringham floated gracefully into the room wearing a beautiful silver dress that shone in the morning sunlight. Sparkling jewelry hung on her neck, wrists, and ears. The striking woman held out her hand to greet Charlotte, her expression pleasant. It relieved her that Lady Stringham hadn't instructed the servants to throw her out—yet.

"Your name is Mrs. Hamilton?" the lady asked.

"Yes."

"Are you, by chance, any relation to Mr. Neil Hamilton?"

Charlotte nodded, keeping an amiable smile on her face. "Yes. He's my husband."

A look of surprise and then annoyance crossed the woman's regal face. "What is your purpose here, Mrs. Hamilton?" She motioned for them to sit.

Charlotte's insides shook nervously, and she hoped it wasn't apparent in her outward appearance. She sat, straightening her skirts around her.

"Lady Stringham, a grave injustice has been made. My husband hasn't done the crime for which he is being accused."

Three lines appeared across Lady Stringham's forehead. "What makes you so confident?"

"May I be blunt with you?"

"Certainly."

Charlotte looked deep into the other woman's eyes. "Because, quite simply, I'm a very wealthy woman, an heiress to a great fortune. There's no reason my husband needs to steal from anyone."

"I can see your point, but I and my husband believe your husband to be guilty."

"Please tell me what makes you think he's

guilty."

"He knew of a secret door into our quarters. He used this passageway to spy on one of our servants who was stealing from us at one time he was in our employ. This door was also used by the thief, so it's only common sense."

Charlotte studied the other woman, then asked, "Did you actually see Neil steal from you?"

"Of course not. It was early in the morning. We were all in bed. Even my servants."

"Are you certain nobody else knows about this secret door?"

"I'm positive."

"What makes you so sure that's the entrance the man used?"

"Because the door was left slightly ajar."

Charlotte tried to think of some logical explanation, but nothing intelligent came to mind. "Did my husband do a good job when he worked for you?"

Lady Stringham nodded. "Oh, yes. My husband was quite pleased."

"Did you consider it money well spent?"

"But of course. Your husband is one of the best."

"Did you know my husband used to work for the mayor of New York?"

"Yes. It's common knowledge."

"Do you know if the mayor was impressed with my husband?"

"Of course. His recommendation was the reason Mr. Hamilton's business flourished so quickly."

"Don't you find it strange my husband didn't steal from him when he had the chance? When my husband worked for the mayor, he was practically penniless."

Lady Stringham kept her lips pursed for the longest time. Unease began to settle in Charlotte's limbs, but she managed not to fidget. She sat quietly, letting the other woman ponder her information.

"If what you say is correct," Lady Stringham finally spoke, "then the fact still remains…the thief knew of the secret door."

"When did you first suspect Neil?"

Lady Stringham remained quiet for a few minutes, looking to be in mental deliberation, then her eyes widened. "We informed Sheriff Franklin as soon as we discovered the theft, and he realized that at that time, your husband must be the culprit."

Charlotte tried not to shiver with disgust from mere mention of the man's name. "What did he say?"

"He brought to our attention that your husband was the only one to know the way our house is set up. And of course, about the secret door."

She arched her brows. "How did he know about the secret door?"

Lady Stringham shrugged. "I think my husband mentioned it."

Charlotte nodded and stood. "Thank you for talking with me, Lady Stringham. I hope my visit was not an inconvenience."

"It was nice to meet you, Mrs. Hamilton. I hope your husband is not the thief. You seem like an exceptional woman, and during the time your husband worked for us, we liked him immensely."

"Thank you. I'm going to do all I can to prove his innocence." She struggled to maintain an even, conciliatory tone.

Charlotte kept silent during their ride to the second residence on Neil's list. Neil had asked her a few questions, but all she told him was she had learned nothing new, which of course, was true. But her mind worked a million miles a second. What she had told Lady Stringham made Charlotte really wonder about him. Would Neil steal from his clients when he was making good money? Did he have some need for cash that she wasn't aware of? Since Neil, in reality, didn't have access to her money, had he truly helped himself to his client's things? Or was the sheriff clever enough to be setting Neil up? But there were so many things to think about and trying to think of them was giving her a headache.

The visit with Mr. and Mrs. Peterson wasn't quite so friendly as with Lady Stringham. Mr. Peterson was obviously angry and acted imposed upon. He asked to be excused before he said something that might cause an uproar.

Mrs. Peterson didn't bother to invite Charlotte to sit. She watched Charlotte with jaded eyes. Charlotte wondered if the lady feared she might attempt to steal something also. Mrs. Peterson said her husband gave Neil a key to one of the side doors never used by them or by their servants. This, of course, was the way the thief came into their home. Several large Oriental vases were stolen and artifacts from India. Priceless items that could not be replaced.

Charlotte asked the same questions about the sheriff and Neil's situation, but Mrs. Peterson didn't respond. She was adamant about Neil being the thief just as Lady Stringham had been. She vowed to pursue the case until her priceless belongings were returned.

"Mrs. Peterson, you've been most gracious this afternoon, and I appreciate your time."

The older woman nodded stiffly.

Charlotte swallowed, moistening her dry throat. "One more question, if you will...when did you come to suspect my husband?"

For the first time since their visit, Charlotte witnessed the older woman's facial features relax as she remained silent, apparently, deep in thought. Just like Lady Stringham, Mrs. Peterson's eyes widened. She lifted her chin once again. "It was when the sheriff was here asking us questions right after the robbery. It was he who indicated that it must have been Mr. Hamilton."

Charlotte nodded. "What did he say?"

"He stressed how Mr. Hamilton was the only person to have that key to the side door."

Charlotte cocked her head to the side. "Has Sheriff Franklin ever been in your home?"

The older woman shook her head.

"Don't you find that rather strange? I mean, how would the sheriff know about the side door?"

Mrs. Peterson gave her a scowl. "I think our conversation has ended."

Charlotte nodded. "You've been most gracious, Mrs. Peterson."

It relieved Charlotte to know the other woman didn't have her servants physically show her out. When she left the house, her hopes were lower than before. This time, Neil didn't ask any questions when he helped her inside the carriage. She slumped back in the seat as he grabbed the reins and urged the horses forward.

He glanced at her with a frown on his disguised face. "Do you think we should go back home now?" he asked.

"I am rather tired."

"Can you manage just one more house?"

She nodded and massaged the back of her neck.

When they drove up to the next place, and Charlotte was shown into the parlor by a servant, she knew immediately this was some man's mistress. The gaudy red and gold carpets and drapes, and the naked statues in the parlor were dead giveaways. It made Charlotte wonder if Neil had ever been involved with Miss Jacqueline Fonteneau in the biblical sense.

Miss Fonteneau was a striking woman, and much younger than Charlotte had expected. The woman's personality was as bouncy as the red ringlets framing her painted face. As Charlotte talked, she studied Miss Founteneau's expression. The woman was completely at ease. When Charlotte mentioned Neil's name, the woman gave no adverse reaction at all. All she wanted, she said, was to find out who had taken her jewelry. The expensive jewels had been gifts, but Miss Fonteneau didn't mention who'd given them to her.

Charlotte repeated the same questions to Miss Fonteneau, but the woman acted as if she had trouble focusing on the topic. The hesitation drove Charlotte absolutely mad. She knew getting angry wouldn't accomplish anything so she simply clasped her hands tightly in her lap.

"I was shocked when Jeffrey first suggested it might be Neil," Miss Fonteneau told Charlotte. "Neil was so very friendly. He was also so very good, um, at his job, I mean."

Charlotte tried to maintain a steady expression. What gave the gaudy woman the right to use Neil's given name? Obviously, Miss Fonteneau wanted Charlotte to know that she and Neil had been intimate.

Charlotte pasted on a fake smile. "I see...what else can you tell me?" She kept her voice steady.

"Of course, he came recommended very highly," said Miss Fonteneau.

Annoyance and jealousy began to consume Charlotte. She took a deep breath for control, and then asked coldly, "Why did the sheriff suggest my husband, Miss Fonteneau?"

"Please, Mrs. Hamilton, call me Jacqueline. Since your husband is a very good friend of mine, I feel as if we are friends also."

Charlotte really didn't want to, but she should discern a little more information before she exploded in rage. "So, Jacqueline, it was the sheriff who suggested my husband had stolen from you?"

"Yes. When Jeffrey first told me, I laughed. I couldn't believe Neil would do something so underhanded."

Why did the sheriff dislike her husband so much? And why did Jacqueline call the sheriff by his first name, almost as if she was on familiar terms with him?

"Is there anything else you remember about your conversation with him?"

Jacqueline chewed lightly on her fingernail, then finally shook her head. "No. Nothing more."

"Well, if you remember anything, please let me know." Charlotte stood. "I really believe Neil is innocent and I want to help him clear his name."

"I'd really like to help. As I said before, your husband was a friend of mine, and he was so very good," she purred, making Charlotte's stomach twist in disgusting knots. "His secretary is also a funny, charming man," Jacqueline added.

Confusion clouded Charlotte's mind. "Do you mean Mr. Ewan Stout?"

"Yes. Neil and Ewan visited me here once a week. Not at the same time, of course."

"I didn't know Mr. Stout helped out my husband with his cases."

"Oh, he usually doesn't, but only in my case," Jacqueline paused, her smile widening.

Charlotte's mind worked faster now. Everything made a little more sense, and because of that, she felt exhilarated again.

"I must go now. Thank you for your help, Jacqueline. Please let me know if you remember anything else."

"I will. Please come back again. You're a very sweet woman. No wonder Neil married you."

Charlotte practically ran out to the carriage, almost knocking Neil over in the process. "Hurry.

Let's leave. I have a theory to try out on you. We'll discuss it when we get home."

Neil waited patiently to continue the conversation with Charlotte, and when they finally reached the house, he told Charlotte he'd meet her in her room, just in case there were curious and deceiving eyes lurking about in the shadows around the house. Hurrying through the secret passageways of the old castle, he arrived in his room and quickly disposed of his disguise. After dressing in his own attire, he crept into Charlotte's room.

Charlotte sat in her heavily cushioned chair beside the fire. Her lovely smile took away all the worry he'd been agonizing over these past few minutes. He sat in the chair next to her.

"Neil," she began, "did you and Miss Fonteneau ever have intimate relations?"

It was as if a bucket of icy water dumped over his body, and he jumped out of his chair. After catching his breath, he realized what a mistake it was to take her to meet Jacqueline. He hesitated in his answer. "What does that have to do with anything?"

She sighed and gave him her pity look. "I think it has a lot to do with this case."

Running his long fingers through his hair, he sighed. "Charlotte, this is very uncomfortable for me to talk about."

"Neil." She reached out and touched his arm. "It's all right. If I hadn't been so ashamed of being a virgin, I'd have probably had secret affairs also. We were two different people back then. I'll understand if you and Jacqueline were intimate."

His heart softened from the gentle expression on her face. Kneeling beside her chair he took her hands in his. "I didn't have an affair with her, although I had been tempted a few times. We were friends, and I wanted to keep our relationship on that level. She tried many times to seduce me, but I never gave in. I promise. Besides, she was another man's mistress."

Charlotte nodded. "I suspected her immoral lifestyle when I first walked into her home and met her. But it wasn't until the very end of our conversation when I realized who pays for her way of life."

"Did she tell you?"

"No, but she gave it away easy enough. Sheriff Franklin is the man warming her bed and paying her way."

Shock entered Neil's body again. "Are you jesting?"

"While we talked, she called you by your given name as if the two of you had been intimate. She also called the sheriff by his given name." She paused for only a moment. "Did you know that your secretary, Mr. Stout, goes to see her also?"

Neil lifted to his full height from the jolt of surprise. "Ewan? Was she...um, pleasuring him too?"

Charlotte laughed. "I'm almost certain of it."

He walked to his chair and sat. "So, why is this so important to my case?"

"I believe the sheriff somehow found out you were seeing her, and he and Mr. Stout concocted this scheme to set you up. Mr. Stout, being your secretary, has access to your files. He could have discovered Lady Stringham has a secret passageway in her house. He could have taken the Peterson's key. And, Mr. Stout knowing the relationship between he and Miss Fonteneau, we can also assume he knew the layout of her house intimately."

She placed her hand on his knee. "Everyone told me the sheriff suggested your name to them as a suspect—that it wasn't their idea." She squeezed his knee. "Neil, the day he tried to force himself on me, he said, 'I'm going to hurt you just as much as your husband has hurt me.' Doesn't that sound like a threat?"

Neil rubbed his forehead as he pondered the startling information. Everything Charlotte said fit together, and to think that his wife figured all of this out by just talking to three people. She was better at solving mysteries than he thought. Suddenly, his love and respect for her grew to enormous proportions.

He rose, pulling her up with him, wrapping her in his arms. "All right, how do we prove it?"

She shrugged. "That's something I haven't figured out yet." Her face took on a pensive look.

"So, the plan is to get the sheriff to confess."

"No," she corrected, "the plan is to find out if Mr. Stout is the sheriff's scapegoat and see where he's hidden the evidence."

Neil's insides were wrung out. This woman overwhelmed and surprised him, first with her extreme beauty and now with her supreme logic. What was she going to surprise him with next? "How are we going to do that?"

"I'm still working on it. I must get him to trust me somehow. That's the only way. I know," she added excitedly, "we can ask Lord Thatcher to help us."

Jealousy hit Neil again, bringing a tightening pain to his chest. "No. I don't want to bother him with our problems. Besides, he has helped us out enough by letting us stay here in his castle."

"You're correct," she said sadly, dropping her gaze.

"Charlotte, if I arrange it with Lord Thatcher, would you dine with me tonight, in my room? We'll dismiss the staff and have a quiet evening, just the two of us."

Charlotte started at her husband as he waited for her response, and despite his closed expression, she sensed his vulnerability. She knew what was on his mind. She stifled the smile that attempted to squeeze between her lips. They'd been through this so many times before. The question was, did she, in spite of everything, still want him to seduce her? Lately, it had been so hard to choose between him and Adam. If Neil had stayed the same selfish, cold-hearted man she'd married, she'd have had no problem deciding between the two men. But Neil had changed over the past week.

Every day she was with him, he acted different, growing on her in a very comfortable way, actually becoming the man she'd always wanted. She was attracted to each man, but for completely different reasons. Although she was beginning to like Neil more, she didn't dislike Adam any less and the admission was dredged from a place between logic and reason.

But, the fact remained Neil was her husband. Eventually, she'd have to give in to his lusty desires—and her own. She'd promised him that she would act like his wife for an entire month, and she hadn't really done it. The pain he'd caused her two years ago still hung in her heart like a heavy fog. But thankfully, his kindness had softened her soul more than she'd realized.

"Dinner would be nice," she answered softly.

Neil kissed her forehead then backed away. "Why don't you rest now? I'll go ask Lord Thatcher if he'll make us a special dinner."

Nodding, she moved to her bed and sat on the edge. "Then I'll see you tonight."

"I miss you already." He winked, then turned and left through the secret spot on her wall.

Chapter Thirteen

Charlotte awoke from her nap, yawning and stretching. She quickly rang for her maid. Excitement bubbled inside her now, and the unexpected feeling made her giddy like a schoolgirl. She was actually looking forward to seeing Neil again—and hoping he'd continue with his seduction.

For tonight's dinner, she picked out one of her more sensual gowns. A velvet green sensation with black lace decorating the low neckline and off-the-shoulder sleeves. Perfect for her mood, teasing, yet not overly so.

Leaving her hair down, she slipped a diamond-studded band along her forehead to keep the long mass off her face. She rubbed her favorite aroma on her wrists and neck, then dabbed a little shine to her lips before leaving the room.

In hopes of finding Neil, she wandered to the kitchen, but once she entered, the startling realization hit her. Subconsciously, she'd been seeking Adam.

The moment she spotted him slaving over the hot stove, her heart picked up rhythm. She cleared her throat. Adam looked up at her and smiled.

"Good evening." Adam's deep, scratchy voice sent sensual tingles down her spine, just as it had always done.

"Good evening." She moved toward the stove. "I thought I would see if you needed any help with dinner."

His eyes widened in surprise. "You would like to help me?"

"Yes. If you don't mind and if I'll not be in the way."

"Charlotte, you're never in my way. Come."

She liked the way his dark gaze swept over her dress. His eyes were bluer tonight and she wondered if it was because his face was caked with sweat due to the hot stove. But it just wasn't the color of his orbs that set her heart pounding, it was the way his gaze moved over her with so much emotion. She listened to Adam explain what he was making. He showed her the fancy ways that kitchen servants prepared them, and Charlotte was surprised to see how easy he made it seem.

"Strange, but I never once thought about what the kitchen staff goes through every time they prepare a meal. Now I'll be more patient with them when an entrée is late."

Adam watched her in silence for a few more minutes. "So, I suppose your absentee husband is coming around to scratch. I bet he has a perfect seduction planned for you tonight."

She lowered her eyes. "I wouldn't know."

"How is the fugitive anyway?"

She snapped her attention to him. "Adam, he is not a fugitive."

"What else would you call him? He's on the run from the law. That makes him an outlaw."

She frowned. "But Adam, he's innocent."

"Do you know for certain?"

She hesitated before answering. "I can feel he's not guilty. Besides, I think we have figured out who's setting him up. Now we just need to trap the real thief and make him show Neil where he has hidden the stolen items."

"Who do you suspect?"

Before she could reply, O'Toole stepped into the kitchen. "Excuse me, Mistress, but Mr. Hamilton is wondering where you are. Shall I tell him you're with Lord Thatcher?"

"Is he in his room?"

"Yes."

"Please tell him I'll be there shortly."

O'Toole nodded then left.

Adam looked down at her, his smile gone. "Don't let me keep you any longer."

The pain was evident in Adam's frown and his sad eyes. She didn't want him to feel as if she was going to allow Neil to seduce her, but she couldn't come right out and tell Adam it was none of his business either. But she didn't want him worrying.

She laid her hand on his arm. "Adam, I haven't come to a decision yet."

He nodded. "Have an enjoyable time with your husband, my dear."

She dearly wanted to fling her arms around him and kiss his lips, but held back. "Good night, Adam, and I will see you tomorrow." Her pulsing blood warned her not to stand too close to him.

She stood in place for a few minutes, waiting for him to do something, say something, but he didn't, so she turned and left.

****

The room flickered in the light from a dozen candles, and Neil's spicy scent surrounded Charlotte as she stepped into his chambers. The lace-covered table was set for two with crystal goblets, china and utensils.

O'Toole nodded a greeting to Charlotte then busied himself, finishing the last minute touches by lighting the two candles on the table.

She glanced around the room searching for her husband. "O'Toole? Where's Mr. Hamilton?"

"The master left for a moment. Said he had a surprise for you. He'll be here shortly."

"I see," she said.

"Will you have some sherry, Mistress?"

"No, thank you."

"Then, if you'll excuse me, I'll finish helping Lord Thatcher in the kitchen." He bowed and left the room.

She pushed aside one of the curtains. The silver moon cast tiny triangles of light onto the floor. A little further, she opened the window and raised her head, sniffing the cool breeze. Fresh cut grass tickled her nose, and she smiled. Neil's servants had been working hard on Adam's grounds, and it thrilled her to think they'd be so generous.

A faint light caught her eye, and then disappeared. The fine hairs of her neck snapped to attention. Someone was below, looking up...watching her.

She stepped away from the window. Who was spying on her? But more importantly, why? When she looked back, the dark figure was gone.

The longer she waited for Neil, the more anxious she became. She shivered with anticipation and closed the window.

Charlotte paced the room as her mind drifted through the events of the day. They'd accomplished a lot, but still, things were up in the air. When she thought about his disguise this afternoon, she grinned. He'd acted just like a servant. Yet when they were alone in the carriage, he was as attentive as she'd wanted. His casual touches, the tender concern in his voice melted her heart. Gradually, he was turning into the husband she'd always wanted. The same kind Adam might make.

She must make a decision. Neil or Adam.

But she realized her body had already chosen Neil. Each time he tried to seduce her, it became harder and harder to refuse his advances.

"You are breathtakingly beautiful tonight," Neil whispered from behind her, breaking into her thoughts.

She swung around and faced him, surprised she hadn't heard him enter the room. She drew her brows together when realizing she'd been facing the door waiting for him.

"How did you get in here? You couldn't have come through the door because I've been standing right here."

He chuckled, his gaze boldly moving over her body, pausing on the roundness of her breasts. Her heart hammered quickly.

"Remember when I'd mentioned the hidden passageways in the castle?"

She nodded.

"There are more secret doors in Lord Thatcher's castle than you can possibly imagine."

She gasped. "Indeed? Will you take me through them?"

"Of course, but let's wait until morning. I'd hate to have you step on a small furry creature."

She shuddered. "Good idea."

He looked so incredibly handsome tonight. The deep forest green vest over his white silk shirt accented his face, aglow with desire. His black trouser and over-jacket seemed to glisten in the candlelight.

Her mouth turned dry and she swallowed hard. Flowing through her fast, her body's juices picked up speed. She wished he didn't have this kind of affect on her, but watching his gaze boldly scan her face, hair, then bodice, made her heart pound with excitement.

He took a step toward her and held out a bouquet of flowers.

She grinned. "They look freshly picked."

He chuckled. "They are." He handed the long stemmed rainbow assortment to her. "These are for you, my sweet."

She took them and buried her nose in the soft

petals. "They smell heavenly. Thank you."

"Are you ready to eat?" He motioned to the table. "It looks as if O'Toole is ready to serve us now." Neil offered his elbow, walked her to the table, and seated her.

"I hope I didn't make you wait long," he whispered near her ear.

Her skin prickled with sensitive shivers. "No. But where were you?"

"Outside."

She laughed. "Doing what? Picking flowers?"

"You'll see." He grinned.

"So tell me," she said, placing the flowers on the table beside her and lifting her napkin, "how did you find out about Lord Thatcher's secret passageways?"

"I actually stumbled across them accidentally. Since I've been doing a lot of studying on these older style castles, I read in one of the books that some have secret passageways." He shrugged. "Because of my curious nature, I searched them out until I found them. One day while in my search, I happened upon one passageway, which led me to look for others."

"Where does it lead?" she asked before taking a sip of her drink, keeping her gaze riveted to his.

"They all lead to the same place, really, but start outside the back of the castle. I will show you tomorrow. You'll be amazed."

"I'm amazed already," she said.

"Whoever designed this castle was very brilliant. I still haven't found out about the original owner."

"Wouldn't it be one of Adam's ancestors?"

"Possibly, but I don't think it is. Like I said, I've been doing some looking around into old documents and such, and I have no reason to believe Lord Thatcher's relatives owned this. Didn't he tell you this castle was given to him by the mayor of New York not too long ago?"

"No." She paused for a moment, collecting her

courage to tell him what she knew. "Neil? I think I should tell you something."

"What's that, my darling?"

"I know about you and Adam."

Neil stopped the drink from reaching his mouth. "Exactly what do you know about me and Adam?"

"He told me you two are related."

He sat the drink on the table. "He did, did he? I'm surprised he would confess such a thing. He loathes me, you know."

She chuckled. "He makes it sound as if you loathe him."

"Perhaps I loathe his title and lands."

Her lovely forehead creased in question. "Do you?"

"I'd rather not talk about it."

She reached across the table and touched his hand. "But I'd like to talk about it. You're so secretive about your cousin. Can't you just tell me?"

He shrugged. "I just recently found out about the ties between the Thatchers and the Hamiltons. I tried to speak with Lord Thatcher about our ancestors, but he adamantly refused to admit we were even related. I'm just one of his penniless American relatives he'd rather not think about."

"Oh, no, Neil. Adam is not like that. After all, he let us stay here."

He cocked his brow. "You think too highly of the beast."

"Neil," she replied sternly. "I'd appreciate it if you wouldn't refer to him as a beast. He's not anything of the sort. He's a kind and gentle man who really cares about people."

She noticed his uneasy expression as he kept his eyes on her. Had she upset him by defending Adam?

She tilted her head. "Why, Mr. Hamilton, I do believe you're jealous of Adam."

Neil sipped his drink slowly, and then placed it

on the table. "I have no reason to be jealous of him…do I?"

"But you are, aren't you, Neil?" she teased.

Neil's dark eyes became hooded, and his eyebrows arched. "You're talking nonsense, Charlotte…" But he looked away.

She smiled to herself

They were silent while O'Toole served the meal, and she was glad to be able to dive right into it. Her nerves had made her hungry—or was it that she just needed something to do with her hands and mouth?

"Charlotte?" Neil asked. "Have you seen Ian lately?"

Her head snapped up and met his eyes. "No. Have you?"

"Yes. He told me what happened with Allison."

She frowned. "Did he seem heartbroken?"

"Not entirely. I think Ian respects Allison very much, but he's just not ready to marry. He's still a free spirited young man and it'll take a very special woman to keep him still."

"That's sad. Allison would have made him a good wife."

"He would have made Allison a good husband, but he needs to sow his oats, so-to-speak."

"So, what kind of oats is Ian sowing now? Has he gone back home?"

"He's staying at his cousin's place in New York for a little longer. Ian told me he will probably return home in another month."

During the rest of the meal, Neil kept the subject of the conversation on his case. Charlotte told him since Ewan Stout wasn't likely to confess, she would just have to figure out another way to solve this ridiculous charge against her husband.

Charlotte put down her napkin and leaned back in her chair. Neil stood and took her hand, leading her from the table to the large hearth. The low burning fire was perfect, she thought, very relaxing and yet stimulating enough for a night of passion. Obviously, this is what Neil had in mind. But would she let him accomplish his goal? She shivered and wrapped her arms around her waist.

"I do have to admit," she said after a lengthy pause, "that these old castles are extremely drafty. Thank heavens they hold such deep hearths."

"I think the reason they are drafty is because of the secret doors in most of the rooms."

She turned toward him. "So, which door did you come through this evening?"

"There's a door behind that small bookcase near the window." He pointed in the direction.

Charlotte squinted into the shadows. "It's so hard to believe you've been sneaking around this castle and I haven't even realized it."

Her thoughts turned dark suddenly when she realized Neil could have been spying on her and Adam. Many times, they had been alone together here inside as well as outside of the castle. Could Neil have possibly been spying on her and Adam the afternoon at their picnic or perhaps he witnessed their kiss? It made her apprehensive to think such a thing, but it was possible. But if Neil had, wouldn't he have said something about it? She eyed him warily.

"I need to sneak around, remember?" he answered her question with a steady voice. "There are still a few of my servants I don't trust totally. O'Toole is helping me out by keeping an eye on them, though."

"Thank heavens for O'Toole." Now she found herself wondering if O'Toole had been spying on her. Oh! She hated having these suspicions.

"Neil, what are we going to do about Ewan Stout?" She quickly changed the topic.

"You know," he said, moving closer, then taking

her in his arms, "I think we'll worry about him tomorrow. We should think about other things right now."

Her heart pounded fiercely. The heat from his body slowly blended with hers, and the fire from behind warmed her. Of course, it didn't help she'd always enjoyed being in his arms. She felt so comforted and protected, and yes, God help her, she even felt the passion.

"Neil," she whispered brokenly, staring at his mouth, but that was all she could think to say right now. He was heating her up and his eyes were laced with desire.

"Charlotte?" Neil's voice was deep and husky. "Do you know how much I enjoyed being with you this afternoon? You're such a brilliant woman, and so very fascinating. I didn't think it could happen, but I've fallen even deeper in love with you."

Tingles shot all through her body at the mention of the word love. She'd longed to hear that come from his mouth, and even though she'd just heard it, she didn't believe.

"What did you say?" The rhythm of her pounding heart made it difficult for her to breathe.

A smile touched his lips as he stared into her eyes. "I said, my darling, that I've fallen deeply in love with you." He swept his fingers lightly across her cheek. "Remember when we went to the opera with Ian and Allison?" She nodded. "When I took you outside, you told me I wanted you only because of your appearance. You were correct. I've never cared about spending quality time with a woman and trying to get to know her, but I took the time with you. I cannot believe how much I've learned about myself."

"And what is that?" She was melting, but luckily, he held her in his strong embrace.

"When I'm with you, I'm a complete man.

Whenever we are apart, I'm lost. Every day I wake up and cannot wait to see you, to be near you. You're always on my mind, interrupting my thoughts to where I can't concentrate. Why do you think I cannot solve my own case? It's not because I'm confused about my feelings for you, but because I know without a doubt that I'm deeply in love."

Speechless, she stared into his eyes. She still thought they were the most spectacular eyes she'd ever seen. In fact, even now she realized she'd always thought he was a very handsome man. With only a few words, he could hypnotize her. "Why...why are you telling me this?"

His grin widened. "Don't you want me to confess my feelings?"

The answer was yes, but was she ready to hear it? Could she accept it as truth? "I suppose I just never thought I'd hear you say that to me."

"Charlotte, my love, I know I'm getting ahead of myself on this, but well...have you decided about our marriage? Have you decided whether or not to leave me or to stay? Because I'll do anything I can to keep you. I don't know what I'll do if you decide to leave me. I love you so much."

Without waiting for her answer, he brought his mouth down and placed it on hers. Pulling her tightly against him, he kissed her tenderly, but then more urgently as she responded with passionate kisses of her own.

She clung to him as her tongue danced with his. His hands moved over her back, caressing from her neck down to her buttocks, squeezing as he pulled her against his rising desire. Once her body touched his, she moaned and he ground his hips into hers.

For the first time since they had kissed so passionately at the masquerade ball, Charlotte touched him. Her heart hammered out of control as she caressed his neck and down his hard chest, then up over his wide shoulders.

Her bosom burst with so much tender emotion it surprised her. It wasn't lust this time, but an emotion she'd never experienced before. Was it love? Was it possible she actually loved him? The more time she spent with him, the more she liked him, and the feelings of hurt she once experienced because of his rejection slowly disappeared. She could actually feel his emotion with each kiss given, and with his caresses, she could feel the warm sensations of his love.

"Charlotte?" Neil broke the kiss as his lips traveled over her face in soft sweeping motions. "Let me make love to you."

She thought those were the sweetest words she'd ever heard. He actually considered her feelings. The thought made her heart burst again with that strange emotion.

"Oh, Neil." She sighed and her head fell back as his lips moved down her neck. "You know how confused I've been."

"No, you're not confused," he mumbled against her skin.

"Then tell me why I feel this way?"

He pulled back slightly, looking into her face. "What are you feeling, my love? Are you feeling excitement? Is your body tingling in a heated sensation when I touch and kiss you? Is your heart ready to burst whenever you look into my eyes or hear my voice?"

His hands were on her body, moving slowly over her skin. His fingertips caressed her, the sensation subtly enticing, inviting. A sweet warmth flooded through her body, seeping into every pore, every fiber of her being burned with desire.

"Tell me you don't love me…want me," he said softly.

She remained stubbornly silent while his fingers

traveled up her arms to tease her languidly. Then she closed her eyes, knowing in her heart that she was going to surrender.

She opened her eyes and nodded slowly.

"I feel the very same way about you, darling. It's love. I've admitted it, so why can't you?" His large fingers moved up to her hair and tangled inside her thick locks as he held her face to his. Tenderly, his lips brushed her lips. "You were made for me, just as I was made for you. We are perfect together, can't you see? Tell me please, that your heart belongs to me and only me."

She didn't know how to respond, but even if she did, she wouldn't have been able to speak. His mouth was upon hers, sapping every last bit of strength she had left. But she didn't care. This time she responded to his demanding kisses, returning them with equal fervor.

Neil lifted her in his arms and carried her to his bed. The sheets had been turned down and red rose petals lay sprinkled across the bed. The whole room smelled spectacular. There was a low fire in the hearth making everything perfect...more than perfect.

He laid her gently on the bed. She gathered a handful of rose petals from the silk sheets and let them flutter between her fingers. A grin touched her mouth. "What have you done here, Neil?"

He shrugged out of his over-jacket and neck cloth before laying himself on the bed next to her. Taking her in his arms, he brought her body to the full length of his. "I've thought about this moment for a long time."

The flame from the fireplace was the only light in the room, but it was reflected in his smoldering eyes. He had this seduction planned and was confident she'd bend to his will. Instead of upsetting her, it thrilled her to know he cared about her and about what she thought.

She stroked the side of his face. “Thank you.”

He threaded his fingers through her hair and brought his mouth down upon hers, starting the wild and hungry surge of emotion all over again. She clung to him with the desperation of someone who was starving.

His hands traveled all over her, caressing, feeling, and arousing. Charlotte returned his touch, amazed with his masculinity. She reveled in the way his muscles rippled and moved beneath her fingers.

Neil leaned up and finished removing his shirt. She watched him reveal his chest, darkly tanned. A light patch of hair rested in the middle, and she reached out and touched the softness, then ran her fingertips across his nipples. They quickly hardened.

“I love the way you touch me,” he whispered, huskily.

She smiled. “Then you know exactly how I feel when you touch me.”

He kissed her again, but focused mainly on undoing the buttons on her gown. She watched him undress her, and within minutes, he’d taken off her dress and slips, leaving her in her chemise and pantaloons, but she felt no fear or embarrassment. His hands swept over her breasts, making her points harden with excitement. How could she deny the pleasurable look laced in his expression?

“Are you certain this time?” His hands squeezed her, making her sigh heavily.

“Oh, yes, Neil. Please.”

He climbed off the bed and finished removing his trousers, then crawled next to her.

“Neil, you’re magnificent.”

A deep groan tore from him when he gathered her back in his arms and met her mouth. The kiss became wild again, and his hands wouldn’t stop moving over her body. He took away the last layers of her clothes and soon his mouth followed the trail his hands had gone. Flames of desire danced over her skin when his tongue touched certain places on her.

While his hands worshiped her body, his mouth devoured her breasts, and her body quickly filled with a different kind of fire. She wiggled underneath him.

"Oh, Neil," she cried out, "please take me now."

He did as she requested, lifting himself above her, breast to breast, hip to hip as she opened her legs for him. When he slipped inside, a slight pain speared through her, but through his kissing, he relaxed her once again, and she welcomed him eagerly into her body.

Her heavy gasp matched his. She circled her arms around his body, meeting the rhythm of the building passionate ride. Tears of joy and sexual release filled her eyes as she cried out his name, clinging to him, not wanting him to leave her body—ever. Neil's groan of release sounded just as pleasurable.

Slowly, the beating of her heart returned to normal. He remained on top, kissing her mouth until exhaustion poured over her, and then he rolled on his side, bringing her with him.

For the next few minutes, there was no sound, but the gentle whoosh of their breathing. This, as unbelievable as it seemed, had been worth the wait. The pleasure he gave her was beyond compare. Making love with him had been the most wonderful experience of her life, yet she felt as if she just betrayed Adam, and it tore at her heart.

She peered up at him. Through closed eyes, he smiled. "I love you, Charlotte."

Her heart twisted with that strange feeling again. "Neil, I—" she began, but was interrupted when a loud knock came upon the door.

Groaning in irritation, Neil moved off the bed, retrieved his robe, and hurried toward the bedchamber's door. "Who is it?" he snapped.

"Master, it is I, O'Toole."

Charlotte gathered the sheets high to her neck as Neil opened the door and let the trusty servant in.

"What is it?" asked Neil.

"Someone downstairs demands to speak with Mrs. Hamilton."

Neil glanced over at her then back to the servant. "Why can't Lord Thatcher keep the visitor company?"

"I cannot find the lord. He has disappeared."

Neil scowled. "Who's waiting to see my wife?"

"It's Sheriff Franklin."

Chapter Fourteen

After O'Toole left, Charlotte scrambled out of bed, searching frantically for her clothes. "What in the name of…" She gritted her teeth and took a deep breath. "Why is he here?" She glanced at her husband as she slipped on her undergarments. "If he catches you—"

Neil rushed to her and took her in his arms. He won't." He kissed her nose. "I'll hide in the castle's passageways. He won't find me."

Panic clutched her heart. "I don't want to face the sheriff alone."

"I'll search for Lord Thatcher. Meanwhile, O'Toole has a pistol. He knows how to use it, and he will give his life protecting you."

Tears stung her eyes. "Oh, Neil. I can't let him do that."

"Shhh." He kissed her lips, then pulled away and proceeded to dress. "I don't think anything is going to happen. The sheriff isn't going to bring any harm to you while he's in Lord Thatcher's home. He's here on business."

She nodded and pulled her gown over her head, slipping her arms through. Neil came behind her and fastened the row of buttons. He kissed her neck before stepping away.

"Be strong. Don't let him take control."

She nodded. "I won't. But Neil...please be safe."

He reached the hidden door, turned and smiled. "I will. I have something to live for, and that's my beautiful wife. There is no way I'll let the sheriff take that from me."

Charlotte wiped the wetness from her eyes and tried to make herself presentable. Once satisfied, she calmed her breathing and walked slowly out of the room and down the stairs.

As she neared the drawing room, the sheriff's voice and those of his men boomed through the room and echoed down the hallway. O'Toole stood near the doorway, his narrowed gaze on them. Although she wished Neil or Adam were here with her, the servant's presence eased her fears slightly.

"Sheriff?" Charlotte spoke in a stern voice as she entered. "What's the purpose of this late night visit? Aren't you aware how ill-mannered it is to drop by unexpectedly like this?"

He quickly stood, and his gaze swept over her. Disgust rolled in her stomach as bile rose to her throat. She had to believe he wouldn't hurt her in the castle as Neil had promised.

A mischievous grin pulled on the corners of his mouth. "Mrs. Hamilton, I assure you I wouldn't have done such a thing if I didn't feel this visit was necessary."

"So, why did you come?" she asked.

"I have reason to believe your husband is hiding in this castle."

A gasp stole from her throat before she could stop it, and her hand flew to her throat. When the sheriff's eyes widened, she quickly tried to gain control of the situation, so she chuckled. "Oh, Sheriff. How foolish can you be? Don't you think I'd know if my own husband were here? Although it's a large castle, I think I'd have run across him at some point."

Jeffrey Franklin balled his hands into fists and kept them at his sides. "As it is, Mrs. Hamilton, I have reason to believe Mr. Hamilton is hiding here, so if you'll let me and my men pass, we will search this castle. And you cannot stop us," he quickly reminded as she stepped forward. "This isn't your residence. You're only a guest here, remember?"

Before she had a chance to protest, he pushed her aside, and strode past her. A large dark figure appeared in the doorway, making the sheriff stop in his tracks.

"This may not be Mrs. Hamilton's place of residence," Lord Thatcher's scratchy voiced boomed through the room, "but she is as much a ruler here as I. Since Mrs. Hamilton is my cousin's wife, she has just as much right to tell you what to do."

Charlotte breathed a sigh of relief. Adam had come to her rescue once again. Although she wished it had been her husband, Neil would have definitely been in danger.

The steely dark look in Adam's eyes made her think he would kill the sheriff with his bare hands. Thankfully, he remained composed, yet overbearing as he limped toward the sheriff.

Jeffrey Franklin cleared his throat. "Lord Thatcher, I'm certain you're a man who upholds the law, and so if you will, we need to search the premises. We have reason to believe Neil Hamilton is hiding here."

The two men eyed each other in silent combat. Adam's expression blazed with fury and hate, his mouth forming a thin white line. It seemed Charlotte could hear their gazes clashing with the sound of swords. One could cut the tension in the room with a knife.

Adam kept quiet for a few minutes, and then nodded. "If you feel there's a fugitive in my house, then feel free to do your job, but I'll have Mrs. Hamilton's servants watching you very carefully to make certain you don't touch anything of hers."

Adam stood tall like a cobra arching his back and making himself appear bigger, venomous and dangerous, never taking his eyes off the older man's, which grew small and burned with a strong, mean fire. Then the sheriff looked away, and to Charlotte's delight, Adam became the winner in this battle of wills.

After the sheriff and his men walked out of the room, Charlotte ran to Adam and tugged on his arm. "Adam? They cannot search the house," she whispered. "Neil is still here!"

"Shhh." His gloved finger touched her lips gently. "Everything is being taken care of."

"But—"

"Trust me, Charlotte," he whispered.

"What if they find the room where Neil and I had dinner? There are two plates, two glasses...everything will indicate to the sheriff that I didn't have dinner alone. Plus we dined in Neil's chambers." She didn't dare mention the bed they'd made love on, and the rose petals sprinkled everywhere.

Slipping his arm around her waist, he pulled her beside him as they left the room. A sly smile played on his lips. "Come, Mrs. Hamilton. Let's see what the sheriff is up to, shall we?"

Charlotte tried to appear calm and collected, but her insides jumped crazily. What if the sheriff found something that indicated Neil was staying here? Would they arrest her and take her to jail too? They couldn't do that...or could they?

Neither Adam nor Neil would be able to protect her in jail from the sheriff's clammy, pawing hands. Her limbs shook the closer the sheriff and his men came to Neil's room, but when the men entered, there was no evidence of the dinner. The fire was almost out, making it look as if the room had not been occupied for several hours. When the sheriff walked into the same room where she and Neil had just finished making love, she was shocked to see there was no evidence of that either. The bed was made and there wasn't a trace of the rose petals—not even the smell lingered in the air. Nothing in the room gave substantiation that anyone had been in there. Even when Sheriff Franklin had opened the closet doors of Neil's bedchamber, there was not one stitch of clothing. Charlotte tried to act normal, although she was probably just as perplexed as the man of the law.

The sheriff angrily marched out of the room and into Charlotte's bedchambers. A few moments later, Charlotte and Adam entered. Once again, Charlotte was shocked. Placed in the middle of her sitting room was the dinner table where she and Neil had shared a meal, but instead of being two place settings, there was only one.

Sheriff Franklin turned to her. "Do you normally dine alone and in your room?"

She lifted her chin stubbornly. "Is that a crime?"

"No. I just assumed...um, well," he stuttered.

His anger was evident by his pursed lips. Charlotte stopped the laugh she wanted to release. When he turned on his heel and went into her private room, she quickly followed. He stood in the middle of the floor, staring at her bed. When his expression relaxed, she bunched her hands by her side, feeling the urgent need to claw at his face. A wicked grin sneaked across his mouth before he licked his lips. Tremors of disgust ran over her, and she couldn't wait to get him out of this castle.

"Sheriff?" Adam asked. "Have you satisfied your curiosity yet?"

The sheriff turned around with a flustered look on his face. "I'm finished. I would, however, like to search the grounds, too."

"Be my guest," Adam replied with a grand gesture of his hand.

Charlotte sighed heavily. Out of relief, she relaxed against Adam's solid form. "I can't believe..."

She looked up at him. "How did you know? How did you know Neil would cover up everything?"

Adam smiled down at her. "You seem to forget, I know your husband almost better than you do. Besides, O'Toole and the other servants are keeping an eye on things also."

She smiled. "I'll never doubt you again." She glanced around the room, then at him again. "Do you know where Neil is right now?"

"He's probably in one of the tunnels. Charlotte, why don't you ready yourself for bed? I'll see the sheriff out. You look very exhausted from this whole ordeal." His gloved fingers caressed her cheek.

"Thank you. I do feel very tired right now, but I don't think I'll get much rest worrying about Neil."

"I wouldn't stress too much. He's a professional, remember?"

She laughed lightly. "How could I forget?"

Leaning down, he brushed his lips across her forehead. "Good night, Charlotte. Rest yourself and I will see you in the morning." He left the room, closing the door behind her, limping his way down the hall.

As Charlotte's maid helped her undress, she couldn't stop thinking about how much her feelings had changed since Neil had made love to her tonight. Earlier this evening, she was convinced she wasn't going to let Neil touch her because she thought she was falling in love with Adam. Now everything was different, but yet it wasn't different at all. Although she had stronger feelings for her husband, she still held the same tender emotions for Adam. None of this made any sense, but yet it was how she felt. Ignoring the problem was impossible. But, could she continue to make love to Neil and harbor such strong feelings for Adam at the same time?

After bathing, she put on her nightgown and robe and excused her maid. Charlotte wandered into the room where the table was set and took her glass of wine. She sipped, and moved toward the small fire, picking up the bottle as she left. As she sipped her drink, she thought over her problem again. She needed to make a decision. She could not keep stringing the men along. She needed to choose…Adam or Neil.

Charlotte filled her glass again and drank. She moved to one of the chairs and sat, cradling the bottle in her other hand. There was really no choice at all. She was married to Neil and so would continue to be his wife. She knew it would hurt Adam, but it was the only way. But if she picked Adam over Neil, things would be much more difficult. She'd have to obtain a divorce, and marry Adam. Nothing but a hassle. Staying with Neil was the safest and easiest. And, if Neil made her nights as exciting as the one they had just shared, she was certain living as his wife would be wonderful.

Staring into the fire, her body relaxed and her eyes drooped, but she didn't care. It was nice not to think for a while. But just as she closed her eyes, a soft knock came upon her door and she jumped to her feet. Her heart pounded with fear.

She hurried to the door. When she saw Adam standing in the corridor, surprise overwhelmed her.

"What's wrong?" she panicked.

"May I come in?"

Stepping aside, she let him enter, then shut the door. "Has something happened?"

"No. I just wanted to tell you the sheriff and his men are gone."

She sighed. "Oh, thank heavens. Have you seen Neil?"

"O'Toole told me your husband is following the sheriff."

Disappointment washed over her. "I suppose that would be a wise thing to do, wouldn't it?"

"Yes."

Adam's gaze moved over her attire, darkening in the familiar expression she'd seen on him lately. She knew her blue silk robe clung to her curves, so she folded her arm across her chest. The forgotten empty bottle in her hand clunked to the floor.

He laughed softly and bent to pick it up. "Have you taken to drinking alone?"

She giggled girlishly and took it out of his hand. "No. I was very thirsty." She moved to the table and set the bottle down. "I would offer you a taste, but it looks as if the bottle is empty."

He moved behind her, circling his arms around her waist and pulling her back against his chest. "I don't need anything to drink, my dear. I enjoy drinking in your beauty and tasting your sweet lips."

She trembled from his words, but mainly from his nearness. She'd just decided to choose Neil, yet why couldn't her body stop responding to Adam's touch? He kissed her ear and she relaxed against him.

"Charlotte?" he whispered huskily. "I've thought about you all evening." He kissed the base of her ear, then her neck. "I've never been a jealous man before, but tonight I could have killed for you."

The quick rhythm of her heart pounded. She wanted to stop him, really, she did, but her body didn't cooperate when her mind told her to step away from him.

"Charlotte?" He kissed her ear again. "I shouldn't be doing this."

His mouth moved down her neck as his hand tugged the tie holding her robe together. It opened and his hands tenderly cupped her breasts. She moaned and arched.

"Charlotte? Tell me how you feel about me. Tell me what you're thinking?"

"Adam...we must not do this," she told him in a

strained voice.

“I know. I cannot stop.”

“What if Neil returns?”

He sighed and rested his chin on the top of her head. “You’re correct.” The huskiness lingered in his tone. “I will stop, but trust me when I say this isn’t the end. We will continue this later.” Before he pulled away, he made certain she was able to stand by herself. He gazed lovingly down at her as his fingers caressed her cheek, then he turned and left her room.

Tears stung her eyes, and she realized she couldn’t say no to him either.

****

Daylight crept in the bedchamber and awakened Charlotte’s senses. She felt as if a blade sliced through the middle of her head. She couldn’t have consumed that much liquor last night, could she? Wine wasn’t that potent, was it? But how would she know? She’d never done anything like this before. She couldn’t remember going to bed, she seemed to have blacked out.

Luckily, her maid let her sleep in this morning. Charlotte wasn’t certain what time it was, but was sure it had to be the middle of the day.

Painfully, her heavy eyelids opened and she sensed someone was in the room with her, sitting on her bed. A flicker of trepidation coursed through her. She bolted upright in bed. She turned her head toward the familiar presence of her husband.

He smiled down at her and chuckled. “I didn’t know you were a drunk.”

“Shhh,” she whispered as her hands flew to her throbbing head.

Neil leaned over, placing pillows behind her. “I had O’Toole make a special drink for you.” She glared at him through half closed lids as he handed her a cup of liquid. “It will help the headache and upset stomach, I promise."

How she dared to partake the awful tasting drink, she wasn't sure, but she forced the vile liquid down her throat and held back the urge to regurgitate.

"What I would like to know," he continued, "is what possessed you to consume the whole bottle?"

After she finished the last drop in the mug, she answered, "I was waiting up for you, you imbecile. I was worried about you."

He laughed again. "I wanted to come back so badly last night, but couldn't. Didn't O'Toole tell you I was following the sheriff?"

"Yes, it was mentioned, but I waited for you nonetheless, and unfortunately, my worry kept me drinking that horrible drink."

"From now on, I'll make certain liquor is no where in sight when I'm not around."

Charlotte watched him through squinted eyelids, and his comment made her smile. "I have been mistaken. You are the one who is horrible, not the wine." She enjoyed their playful banter.

"Ah, but I still love you," he said, then leaned over and gently kissed her lips.

Suddenly, another kiss was deeply embedded in her mind, and she thought the alcohol must have still been in her system, because she was certain it felt as if Adam had kissed her. Adam had always been gentle, whereas Neil was wild. She mentally shook the thought from her head when Neil pulled away.

"Do you want to know what I discovered last night?"

She sat up a little more. "Yes, of course."

"Well, I am certain Ewan is working with the sheriff. Jeffrey Franklin went to Ewan's place directly from here last night. I don't know what was discussed, but Ewan looked just as upset as the sheriff."

"I wish there was a way we could trap them."

"There is."

"We should get started on it right away, whatever it is." She pulled back the covers to climb out of bed, but was stopped when Neil's body moved to lay over hers, pushing her back across the sheets.

"Later, I have other things on my mind right now," he said, eyeing her seductively.

She would have agreed, but without warning, her stomach lurched. "Neil, you'd better move before I do something that will be quite embarrassing!"

He quickly jumped off of her and helped her out of bed. She ran to the bathing chamber to empty her stomach. Taking a wet cloth, she dabbed her head and neck and returned to her bedchamber. Neil's worried face made her heart melt. It was very obvious he loved her.

"Give me an hour and I will be presentable, I promise."

"All right, but just one hour. I don't think I could last very much longer without seeing you." He winked.

A smile touched her lips as she watched him leave.

****

This afternoon was a perfect day for shopping in town. Charlotte needed to be away from the two men in her life, so she took her maid and went into the city. As she wandered from one shop to the other, she tried to come to a decision about Adam and Neil. By the early evening, she'd ordered several new gowns, which she purchased with matching shoes and bonnets, and she had eaten a meal. Thanks to O'Toole's drink, the food stayed down. But she'd yet to make a decision about the men she was in love with.

As Charlotte walked out of one of the shops, she

bumped into a woman she hadn't thought she would see so soon. Charlotte's packages tumbled to the cobblestones.

"Oh, good heavens, Mrs. Hamilton," Jacqueline Fonteneau gasped. "I'm truly sorry." She bent to help her pick up the packages. "I suppose I wasn't paying attention to where I was going."

"I'm all right, Miss Fonteneau. Please do not give the matter another thought." Charlotte smiled. "How are you?"

After every last package had been picked up and handed over to the maid to put in the carriage, Jacqueline straightened. "I'm doing wonderfully. But how about you? Have you heard any more about that handsome husband of yours?"

Charlotte blushed. It was a little difficult and rather embarrassing to be discussing Neil with the woman who'd tried to seduce him while he was married. "I haven't, I'm sorry to say. I pray something will happen one way or the other. I'm tired of worrying."

"Yes, I can understand what you're feeling." Miss Fonteneau tapped Charlotte's arm. "Would you like to have some tea with me?"

Charlotte really didn't want to, but the look on the other woman's face told Charlotte she had something she wanted to discuss. "Tea would be nice, Miss Fonteneau."

"Please, call me Jacqueline."

Charlotte nodded. "Jacqueline."

The two women entered the nearest food establishment, and after receiving their tea, Jacqueline cleared her throat. "I had a visit from Ewan the other day."

The teacup was halfway up to Charlotte's lips when she stopped and stared across the table. "Really?"

"It seems as if Ewie has taken over Neil's

business."

"He told you that?"

"Yes."

Charlotte set the cup down. "Can he do that?"

Jacqueline smiled slyly. "Not to worry. It won't work out. It's quite obvious the main reason Neil was so well liked was because he was so incredibly handsome and charming. Most of his cases involved women, married or not. The women spread around gossip that Neil was the best, and the men soon heard about him, but of course, they thought it was because of his detective work."

Charlotte really did not want to hear about Neil's other liaisons. He'd promised her he hadn't had affairs during their marriage, and she wanted desperately to believe. "But Jacqueline, Neil is a good detective."

"Oh, yes, of course, but not at first…I mean, that was not what originally got him the jobs."

"But you were speaking about Mr. Stout?" Charlotte quickly went on. "Why don't you think he'll be able to take over Neil's business?"

Jacqueline giggled again. "Well, you've met Ewie, right?"

Charlotte nodded.

"Then you know. He's a mousy sort of man. Not one that would attract a woman's eye, if you know what I mean."

"I understand." Charlotte took a sip of her tea, then set it back down on the table. "What did he tell you?"

"Well, we really didn't do that much talking." She giggled. "But his business must be doing all right. He gave me this." Jacqueline stretched her arm across the table and showed Charlotte an expensive bracelet.

Charlotte hitched a breath. "Oh, my. This is certainly worth a lot of money."

"That's what I'd thought."

"Those diamonds and rubies are definitely real."

When Charlotte reached for her teacup again, someone knocked into her chair, and a cane bumped against her leg. She looked up to scowl at the clumsy oaf, but his hand fell to her shoulder to steady himself. It irritated her to think this elderly man would be so openly rude, but just as she was about to personally remove his hand, she noticed the familiar large fingers. As recognition struck, she glanced into the man's wrinkled face. The face was the same one that had gone with her and portrayed a servant when she had visited those clients of Neil's, except for this time, he wasn't wearing servants clothing, but fancy attire instead. He gave a wink and then straightened himself.

Charlotte smiled widely. "Uncle Edward," she exclaimed, jumping up to give him a hug. He was still looking at her strangely, so she continued. "It's your niece, Charlotte Ashton Hamilton, your brother's only child."

"Oh, my goodness. It is you." He laughed. "It's hard to see clearly without my spectacles."

"Why aren't you wearing them?"

"I've misplaced them, my dear." His hands patted the pockets of his jacket, then his waistcoat until he found the object he was looking for. "Oh, here they are," he said, putting them on. "How are you, my dear Charlotte?"

"I'm fine, Uncle Edward. Would you like to join my friend and I?"

Neil glanced at the other woman. "Oh, yes." He sat as a serving girl brought him a cup of tea, then he looked from his cup to the other woman at the table. "So, are you two lovely ladies enjoying your day?"

Jacqueline smiled at the older man. "Yes, very much."

"Uncle Edward?" Charlotte spoke quickly. "Miss Fonteneau just showed me her beautiful diamond and ruby bracelet. If my memory serves me correctly, didn't you used to work in a jewelry shop?"

"I did."

"Well, my friend is not certain if the diamonds were real. Do you think you could look at them and see?"

Jacqueline stretched her arm forth as she showed the older man her bracelet.

Charlotte watched as Neil studied the piece of jewelry, then after a few seconds, he looked up. "Yes, Charlotte you are correct. The diamonds and rubies are real."

Jacqueline squealed with delight. "I didn't think Ewie liked me that much."

"Now that you know he does, what are you going to do about it?" Charlotte wondered.

Jacqueline shrugged. "I have no idea, but I'll discover my true feelings after he has given me more pieces of jewelry, I think." She picked up her purse and stood. "I hate to be cutting this short, but I have a million things to do before dusk. It was a pleasure meeting you, Uncle Edward." She looked over at Charlotte. "It was nice to see you again. Come by sometime when we can chat more."

"I will."

After Jacqueline left the shop, Neil leaned over, taking Charlotte's hand in a tender caress. "Charlotte, my darling," he whispered, "that bracelet was one of the items stolen from Mr. and Mrs. Peterson."

Her eyes widened in surprise. "Are you certain?"

"I helped recover that piece of jewelry while working for them not too long ago."

"Oh, my," she gasped. "And Ewan Stout gave it to her?"

"Which means Ewan is definitely involved.

Possibly he still has some of the stolen items."

"How can we find out?"

"We'll have to sneak into his house."

Charlotte's mind worked quickly. "Or, maybe I could become friends with him."

"Don't you dare!" His voice rose. "Have you any idea what Jacqueline does with him to make him her friend?"

Blushing slightly, she nodded.

"But the fact is, you are not going to become that close to Ewan."

"You need not worry about that."

"Well, I hate to inform you, but that's the only way he's going to give you jewelry."

Charlotte sighed heavily in defeat. "So, what shall we do now?"

"I don't know just yet. Let me think on it for a little while. I'll come up with something."

She touched his arm softly. "Let me know if I can help."

His blue eyes darkened with desire. "I know how you can help, but it has nothing to do with Ewan Stout." His deep voice simmered with barely checked passion as he gazed upon her.

Laughing lightly, she slapped his arm playfully. "Uncle Edward, such an inappropriate idea."

"In fact, I've been meaning to ask, when can we have a repeat of last night?"

Her heart tripped and she caught her breath in her throat. "We shouldn't be talking about this right now."

"Then let's talk about it in the carriage on the ride home."

"I don't think I'll be able to make love with an old man," she whispered softly, but smiled at him in jest.

"Then I shall take off my disguise."

"Then you'll be seen when we reach the castle."

He sighed and shook his head. “Why do you always have to make sense?”

“Just my nature, I suppose.”

Taking her hand, he stood and brought her up with him. “Come, my dear Charlotte, and I’ll walk you out to your carriage. I’ll let you ride home alone, but,” he lowered his voice, “I’ll be waiting for you in your room when you arrive at the castle.”

Chapter Fifteen

Charlotte stepped into her bedchamber and closed the door. Neil emerged from the shadows and circled her in his embrace. She wrapped her arms around his neck.

"The ride home was too long," he whispered, his mouth hovering above hers. "My body has been sorely strained from the wait."

"Then do something about it," she said before she touched her lips to his in a sweet kiss, which soon filled with fire when Neil's mouth responded. His arms tightened, pulling her against him with such ferocity she thought she'd break in two. All conscious thoughts stopped and she suddenly became a creature of delightful sensations, enjoying the heat of desire coursing through her.

He broke the kiss only briefly as he picked her up and placed her gently on the bed. She eagerly reached for him. The only light was the shimmering silver orb glowing through the half-opened window.

Neil threw off his shirt, his muscles bunching together when he reached for her and drew her against his hard chest. Timidly, Charlotte ran her fingers through the springy soft hair on his chest, growing a bit bolder when he groaned.

Her mind dissolved of every thought but him when his expert hands peeled away her dress. His warm mouth moved across her shoulders to find the sensitive tip of one of her breasts. Charlotte moaned and a familiar churning began in her loins, pulsating between her thighs.

He shifted his attention to her breast, fondling

them with expertise. Her hands stroked his broad back, her flesh very much aware of the powerful man pleasing her.

His lips trailed across her nakedness to kiss her breasts, her navel, and down the flat plane of her abdomen. His hands roamed intimately over her breasts, and her breath released in a long-awaited surrender moan of ecstasy.

His slow, drugging kisses and caresses brought her body to great heights of pleasure. His ardor was surprising, touching and restrained as though he was worshipping every part of her body. When his fingers delved between her legs, into her moist heat, she panted and lifted her hips to him.

Charlotte's mind screamed for him to go on—to never stop! She had never known such a gathering of violent and infinitely delicious feelings. Her body writhed, unable to discover what to do with the building force spiraling within her. She felt as if she'd been thrown into an attack of white heat, so scalding that she only knew something wonderful was destined to happen. Quickly, her body exploded in a tempest of sparks, so fantastic and intense in feeling that she cried out Neil's name over and over again.

When her body was fully satisfied, she realized Neil had moved up beside her and held her close. She buried her face in the hair on his chest, her face burning with embarrassment and she was glad of the darkness.

Neil kissed the top of her head. "I told you, I'm a man of my word. When I tell you I will please you, I follow through."

She lifted her face and met his stare. "You pleased me beyond anything I could imagine." Her voice was soft and far away.

He pulled away and stood, quickly undressing.

The feel of his hot naked body against hers

made her moan again. Pulling him closer against her with her legs, she reveled in their complete joining. All she could feel was the heat of him as he took her to a new level of passion, and her cries of ecstasy tumbled from her mouth. Her body melted against his and the world was filled with only him.

An instant later, Neil grew still and moaned aloud with pleasure.

Neil's lips caressed the top of her head resting against his chest. "You know," he said, stroking the side of her face, tenderly pushing back the hair that had fallen into her eyes. "It's so satisfying to make love to you when love is the emotion behind it."

"Oh, Neil," she sighed dreamily, sleepily, "you really are sweeping me off my feet, aren't you?"

"That's what I'm shooting for, my love." He moved off her, pulling her next to him.

She smiled and cuddled closer, pressing her face back to his hard chest. The light strokes of his hand on her back began to ease her mind and relax her body. This felt nice, very nice, and she anticipated their next coupling. Neil had been so very tender, yet the wildness in his lovemaking thrilled her beyond all expectations. Being his wife would certainly be eventful.

Her heart dropped a notch, for they first had to clear him from these false charges and clear his good name. But how? Instead of letting her mind slip into rest, she stewed about all the ways they could prove his innocence. Somehow they had to catch Ewan in the act, and for some reason, Jacqueline's name kept popping into her head. Jacqueline Fonteneau was the only way to get to Ewan.

Suddenly, an idea struck her.

"I have it," she exclaimed, sitting up straight in bed.

"What do you have, my love?" Neil pulled her back down and into his arms.

She leaned up on her elbow and gazed down into his sleepy eyes. "How much do you trust Jacqueline?"

His forehead creased. "Why in the hell are you thinking about her at a time like this?"

She quietly laughed at his shocked, and quite disturbed, expression. "I wasn't really thinking about her. I was trying to think of a way to get you cleared of these ridiculous crimes, and Jacqueline crept into my mind."

"And why is that?"

"Well, I don't believe she's clever enough to be in on the theft with Mr. Stout and the sheriff."

He laughed. "Sweetheart, Jacqueline cannot be considered clever in any aspect of the word. She's as dim-witted as they come."

"So, does that mean you don't trust her?"

"I don't know. If she's the sheriff's mistress, then I'm not certain we can trust her." He paused. "Why?"

"Because, I was just wondering if she would be able to get into Mr. Stout's house to see if the stolen items were in there."

"It's a good idea, but like I said, I don't think we should trust her with my life. Mainly because of Jeffrey Franklin."

She leaned over him, wrapping her arms around his neck, crushing her breasts to his chest. "There has to be a way. I'm certain there's some reason she keeps going back to him. She would have cheated on him with you, and now with Mr. Stout, so why doesn't she just move to another man? There's got to be a reason, and I'm going to chum up with her tomorrow and find out what it is."

His eyes widened. "Oh, no, you're not!"

A grin spread across her face. "I bet I can convince you otherwise."

His hold tightened around her as his hands spanned over her derriere, pulling her up against his surprisingly growing arousal. "And how are you going to convince me, my love?"

"Any way I can," she answered huskily before kissing him. He accepted and answered back with hunger in his kiss. She loved his demanding response, showing her through his actions just how much he enjoyed this.

Soon, his wandering hands excited her, and her body flowed as hot as before as they began to make love again. The different feeling overwhelmed her, and as she moved her hips with his rhythm, her emotions whirled around her, causing her chest to ache. Dare she admit aloud she loved him, too?

****

Charlotte sat patiently in the drawing room and waited for her guest to arrive. Early this morning she sent a note over to Jacqueline Fonteneau, inviting her to tea here at the castle. O'Toole informed Charlotte that Miss Fonteneau had quickly accepted. Of course, Charlotte wondered if Jacqueline was more eager to see the castle or Lord Thatcher than anything else.

Charlotte planned to have a heart-to-heart talk with the woman whose reputation was deplorable. Charlotte chuckled. If she were back home right now, she'd be banned from associating with high society. Those uppity women condemned women like Jacqueline, but who could blame them? Maybe if Charlotte could help Neil through this mess and put away the sheriff and Mr. Stout in the process, perhaps Jacqueline would change her immoral ways?

From down the hall, voices carried into the room. Her guest had arrived. Charlotte rose and waited for O'Toole to show Jacqueline in. Instantly, Charlotte's attention was drawn to Jacqueline's brilliant pink dress, pink parasol, and frilly pink bonnet perched atop her red head. The poor woman looked like a walking flower bush and probably had trouble swatting off the bees on her way over. No matter how silly Jacqueline looked in pink, her red hair and delicate skin radiated her beauty.

Charlotte smiled. "Thank you for coming."

"The pleasure is all mine." Her gaze flew around the room. "I can't believe the grandeur of this place. I thought it would be spooky with cobwebs and boarded up windows." She giggled. "But it's nicer than anything I've ever seen."

"You should have seen it when I first arrived. I was afraid to even step foot in this room." She flipped her hand through the air. "Enough about the castle. Would you care to join me for tea?"

Jacqueline nodded and took a seat while Charlotte poured.

"I must confess," Charlotte began, "I had a purpose in asking you here today. Although I'm fond of small talk, I need to be forthright and ask you a personal question."

"What do you need to know?"

Charlotte set her own teacup down on the end table in front of her. "Are you having a...relationship with the sheriff?"

Jacqueline's face paled slightly. "What makes you think that?"

"I've got a quick wit about me and I figured it out by the way you talked so personally about him. I know how you felt about my husband, and I think you and Mr. Stout are lovers. I'm not blind or dense."

Jacqueline's gaze dropped to her lap. "You are correct. Unfortunately, Jeffrey thinks he has claim over me."

Jacqueline's voice trembled, and Charlotte became suspicious. "Are you saying you're trapped in this relationship?"

Jacqueline lifted her gaze and met Charlotte's. "I suppose that's what I am. Trapped."

"Would it be too personal to ask why?"

"All I will say is Jeffrey knows something about my past. For his silence, I agreed to be his mistress."

"What does the sheriff think about you and Mr. Stout?"

Jacqueline laughed. "He doesn't know."

"Did the sheriff know how you felt about Neil?"

"Yes. He discovered Neil leaving my house one afternoon. Nothing had happened between us, mind you, but Jeffrey didn't know that, and he didn't believe me when I tried to tell him what an honorable man Neil was. Jeffrey was going to let out my secret, but I talked him into beating me, instead."

Charlotte gasped. "No, Jacqueline! He flogs you, too?"

"Only when I don't please him, which is really not that often."

"Are you worried he will find out about Mr. Stout?"

Jacqueline chuckled again. "No. Why would Jeffrey suspect me of spending time with him? If you remember right, Ewie isn't the kind of man who has a lot of women admirers."

"But they are good friends, are they not?" Charlotte asked perplexed.

"I wouldn't say they're good friends. I think Jeffrey is blackmailing Ewie too."

Charlotte widened her eyes as shock vibrated through her. "Are you jesting?"

"I don't have proof, but I can sense Ewie doesn't have good feelings for Jeffrey. Every time they talk, Ewie gets very angry."

Charlotte paused for a moment while her mind spun in circles. She still couldn't come up with any link between Ewan and the sheriff and Neil besides Jacqueline. "Did Mr. Stout know about your feelings for Neil?"

She shrugged. "I don't know. Ewie knew Neil was helping me, so..." She paused and scowled. "I loathe Jeffrey Franklin and would do anything to get out from under his thumb." Jacqueline's eyes lit up like midnight stars. "Why all the questions? Do you have a plan?"

Charlotte patted Jacqueline's arm. "Not quite, but we have an idea and might need your assistance. Would you be willing to help?"

Jacqueline's smile was genuine. "Certainly."

"Unfortunately, I think we may end up with Mr. Stout in the snare, too."

"My Ewie? Why?"

"That bracelet you showed me yesterday was a piece stolen from none other than Mrs. Peterson a few weeks ago."

Jacqueline gasped, her hand flying to her throat. "Stolen?"

"Yes."

Jacqueline sighed. "I wondered how he could afford something as expensive as that."

Charlotte squeezed Jacqueline's hands. "Thank you for agreeing to help." She sat up straighter as she and Jacqueline began making plans.

****

"It won't work," Adam told Charlotte that night over dinner.

"What do you mean it won't work? All Jacqueline has to do is get into Mr. Stout's house and look around. Neil can take over after that," Charlotte said.

Adam shook his head as he gazed at the beautiful woman across from him. He worried about her interfering in her husband's case. He certainly didn't want her harmed, and he'd kill anyone who touched her, especially the sheriff.

"My dear, Charlotte. Miss Fonteneau isn't an actress. She can't act innocent. I don't think Mr.

Stout will detect anything, but the sheriff will no doubt become suspicious."

Charlotte sighed heavily and sipped her wine. "I think she's going to surprise you. She's very angry that they lied to her. Besides, all she has to do is look through Mr. Stout's house. She has already told me, she plans on giving him some sleeping powder for his tea."

"But Charlotte, you seem to forget one piece of vital information." He paused for exaggerated affect. "She's his mistress."

"What difference does that make?" she asked.

"I don't think Jacqueline will have an easy time getting into Ewan's house."

"She'll find a way."

He shook his head. "Mr. Stout isn't a stupid man. He'll surely see through her."

"She's willing to take that chance."

Adam pushed himself away from the table and stood. "Charlotte, would you like to go for a walk? The moon is full tonight and we won't stray far."

Her head snapped up when she met his gaze. "I'd love to. Maybe the cool air will clear our heads and give us more ideas."

Taking her hand in his gloved one, he led her from the dining room and outside the castle. They walked in silence. He didn't know how to talk her out of this ridiculous plan she'd concocted. He feared for her life.

Adam glanced down at Charlotte and realized she was frantically eyeing the back of the castle. Her squinted eyes wouldn't stray from the wall.

"Charlotte, my dear? Is something amiss?"

She jumped from the sudden noise, then turned and looked at him with a sweet smile on her face. "Well, um...yes, sort of."

He stopped. "What? Is it something I need to worry about?"

"No. I was just…just looking...well, I was hoping to find—"

His chuckle came out deep and scratchy, interrupting her. "Charlotte, quit stuttering and tell me."

Stopping in her tracks, she turned toward him. "Neil told me about the secret passageways in the castle." She pointed to the stone wall. "He told me they all come together at a point and exit out one of these walls. I just wondered, well...I hoped you would show it to me."

His gloved hand cupped her face tenderly. "Charlotte, there's no need for you to be nervous. I'll show you anything your lovely heart desires. As a matter of fact, I'd consider it a privilege to take you through the tunnels."

He linked her arm back through his elbow and led her to the secret opening toward the outside wall where two walls connected. They finally reached the spot where the secret tunnel opened up, and stopped.

Charlotte stood, staring right at the rock wall, and he could tell she couldn't see the opening. "This is it?"

"Yes."

"But where?" she asked.

He smiled. "Walk up to the wall and stop."

She snapped her head around to him, giving him a skeptical look.

"Go ahead," he urged.

Charlotte did what she was told. The night shadows surrounded her, making it impossible for her to see the opening, so he gave her a little help. "Look to your left."

She looked. "Adam, I—" She reached her hand out in front of her and felt for the wall, but nothing was there. She gasped.

"You found it, my dear."

Her hand stayed out in front of her as she slowly walked into the passageway. "I can't believe this. It looks as if I'm walking into a wall. This is incredible!"

Once inside the passageway, blackness surrounded her like a thick cape. A cold draft swept over her, chilling her spine. Not even the moon from outside shone through. She stopped as soon as she lost light.

Adam came behind her, his hands gently touching her back, reassuring her, but it was impossible to steady her erratic pulse.

"So, now we are in the secret passageway," she stated, hearing the slight echo through the cave. The smell of mustiness hung thick through the air, and she sneezed.

"There's a candle somewhere around here," he said, groping along the wall next to him. "Ah, here it is."

Charlotte heard the scratch of a match and smelled the smoke as he lit the candle. She was relieved when a light came to the tunnel, but she wished there was more light. But from what she could see, the dirt ground and slimy stone walls were not that impressive.

"Here, hold this and I'll light another." Adam handed over the first candle.

A few seconds later, he had a lit candle in his hand. "Keep close to me and you'll be all right. These passageways can be a little tricky, but I know my way."

Her free hand clung tightly to the arm he held out for her. She was very excited about finally being in here, excited he trusted her enough to show her this ever so secret spot. With Adam beside her as they walked, peacefulness settled in her chest.

There really wasn't much to see. It was exactly as Neil had told her it would be: dark, long, and mysterious. They walked a long time it seemed. Then Adam stopped. Four passageways stretched out before her.

"As you can see," Adam said, "there are many tunnels. Which part of the castle do you want to end up in?"

Holding her candle higher, she looked at the different paths.

"Surprise me."

"All right."

He took hold of her hand and moved farther down the tunnel to his right. Charlotte stayed close to Adam's side. The vast tunnels jutted this way and that like a labyrinth of uncertainties. She peered into the darkness of each one.

"And where does this one go?" she asked.

"To the library."

They walked further into the impeding darkness, and another path broke off. "Where does this one go?" she asked again, noticing they were now walking at an uphill climb.

Her companion regarded her with amusement. "You'll get to know them as well as I do before too long."

"Adam? How can you possibly remember your way around?"

"I admit, I became lost on occasion, but you learn to memorize them." He laughed. "When I found out about these secret passageways within the walls of the castle, I thought it was the most ridiculous thing in the world, but they have been quite helpful many times."

"Yes, especially when New York has such an unlawful sheriff," she replied, quite jadedly.

"Well said, my dear."

The candlelight flickered on his face and cast ghostly shadows on the walls. Her heartbeat sped. Their eyes locked in silence as she tried to read the meaning behind his long, intense gaze.

Then he resumed their ascent, deeper into the bowels of the great fortress. He led and she followed quietly behind.

Finally, after what seemed like they'd been walking forever, they came to a stop. In front of them was a closed door.

"Here we are," he said.

"Where are we?"

"You'll see in a moment. Now close your eyes."

She arched her eyebrow. "It is a surprise?"

"Yes, I suppose it is."

"All right, I'll close my eyes, but don't lead me into any walls," she joked.

He laughed and pulled her closer to his side as he opened the door. After they stepped in, he let go of her. The warmth of the room surrounded her.

"You can open your eyes now."

When her lids fluttered open, they were standing in a bedchamber. She blinked, feeling lightheaded and momentarily blinded by the strong light. It was the grandest bedchamber she'd ever beheld. The enormous bed drew her immediate attention, decorated in dark blue and brown silk. It was large enough for royalty. The solid oak and large canopy were its crowning glory. Many pillows and blankets covered the mattress.

She stepped further into the room and gasped over the sight of the beautiful Persian rugs, Chippendale chairs and wooden cabinets, paintings and statues that probably came from Rome. Three very large windows surrounded the room, and the heavy hanging curtains looked very antique as if they had come right along with the castle. Candles were lit upon the mantel and about the tables, casting a romantic glow about the room.

Everything in this room was romantic only because of the grandiose size and the decoration, but this was, indeed, a man's room. Was this Adam's bedchamber? It certainly smelled like him.

"Well, what do you think?" he asked.

"I think it's the most astounding room I've ever seen." She turned toward him. "Did the King himself stay here?"

He chuckled. "No. This was the bedchamber of the very first master. The first lord did most of the woodwork. Over the years, the pieces were either added or refurbished. The curtains are original, though."

"I thought so." She paused, then asked, "So, who sleeps here now?"

He smiled and gave her a conspiratorial wink. "The present lord of the castle."

She responded with a quick smile, thinking he looked so good with that serene expression. Lately when she gazed upon him, she hardly realized there was a scar that dominated half of his face, and she rarely noticed the scarf around his hair. Sometimes she didn't even realize he kept black leather gloves on his hands. She didn't even hear his raspy voice any longer, or see his prominent limp.

"Adam? Why did you bring me to your room?" she asked in a small voice.

He moved closer until he stood in front of her. "For two reasons. The first is because I figured you'd want to see this room. I know how you like reading a good mystery, and I happen to think this room was taken right out of a page in one of your favorite books."

She nodded.

"And the second reason," he said in a low, husky voice, circling his arms around her waist and pulling her slowly to him, "is because this is the only room in the castle where Neil won't be."

He looked at her and the double meaning of his words and long gaze was very obvious. Charlotte couldn't stop her heart from accelerating. It always did whenever she was close to Adam. He was really a romantic man. She wished her husband were more like that. Adam had always been so very tender and gentle. She didn't think Neil would ever be that way. Yet the wildness in Neil was exciting, too, just as the gentleness in Adam made her heart beat out of control...like now.

"I know you're worried Neil might see us. Well, he won't."

His compelling eyes rendered her frozen and vulnerable. He wanted to seduce her, even if it was wrong, but being held so closely in his strong arms made her mind and body weak. She didn't know if she had the strength to stop him. Her feelings were confusing. She was falling in love with Neil, so why did Adam's presence also thrill her? She found it hard to remain sensible or coherent when she was this close to him.

"Adam—" She took a deep breath, trying to control the fast gushes of air coming out of her throat. "This is wrong."

"I know." His hand moved up and softly caressed the side of her face, slowly moving down to her neck. "But I need to know right now how you feel about me. I desperately need your affection." His lips touched hers for a brief, tender kiss. "I cannot wait, Charlotte." He kissed her longer this time, but then stopped. He looked deeply into her eyes. "What have you decided about your marriage?"

Heartrending tenderness filled his gaze. She hesitated, torn by such conflicting emotions.

As his gloved hand was sending warmth through her face and neck, his lips were spreading it through the rest of her body with his sweet kiss. She held onto his shirt for support, afraid he might let her go and she'd fall to the floor because of her weakened knees. Her mind slipped into pleasure, leaving her no room to think logically.

He kissed her again. “I want you so much.” He breathed against her lips. He deepened the kiss when his tongue entered her mouth, sweeping gently through, exciting and enticing.

She answered him with her tongue. Although she should fight for control, the more he kissed and the longer her body pressed against his hardness, the weaker she became. If she didn’t do something soon, she’d end up in his bed. Was that something she really wanted? Was she willing to risk her marriage now that it was going so well?

Charlotte’s resolve weakened. She needed Neil desperately to rescue her from this confounding dilemma, before she did something rash and emotional. She was in over her head. Charlotte couldn’t think clearly, whenever she was near Adam. Why did he affect her so?

As her body considered yielding, she was startled because she was excited and aroused, and the embers always between her and Adam caught fire. Even as Charlotte struggled with indecision, something just as insatiable that had come over him betrayed her and made her respond to his kisses and caresses. Her deep desire and hunger for him overrode everything else. Their bodies molded together, all her soft curves flattened against his hard muscles. He was breathing very hard.

Charlotte’s heart jolted and her pulse skittered. Suddenly, Neil’s handsome face flashed before her. He’d be crushed! What was she doing letting Adam hold her and kiss her? She had to stop this. Now!

Suddenly, there was a knock at the door. Charlotte flew out of Adam’s arms and panicked. “Adam, I can’t be seen here,” she whispered.

“Go back through the secret doorway and stay there.” He led her to the bookcase, pulled on a book that opened the secret wall. Before closing it, he leaned over and gave her another kiss. “Stay right here.” Then he backed out of the tunnel and closed the wall.

Charlotte’s body trembled, and she wrapped her arms around her middle as her heart beat wildly. To think she’d almost been caught in another man’s arms—in his bedchamber, no less! She couldn’t let this happen again. There had to be some way to keep Adam from touching and kissing her into oblivion. She just had to think of a way to stop herself from wanting to make love with him.

On the other side of the door, a rumble of voices was heard. She stepped closer to the door and leaned her ear against the cold wood. It was easy to recognize Adam’s raspy voice, but when the person spoke, recognition hit, and her heart dropped to her feet. Neil! He was the person who’d interrupted a very intimate moment.

Guilt washed over her. Tears sprang to her eyes as she concentrated on the voices behind the wall. Although she couldn’t hear everything, she knew they were talking about her. From the way it sounded, Neil was worried because he couldn’t find her and Adam tried to reassure him.

The worry laced in Neil’s voice made her heart break, and another wave of shame poured upon her. What had she done? Neil didn’t deserve her treachery.

There was silence, and Charlotte guessed that Neil had left. Soon the wall opened and light poured into the tunnel. Adam stood before her looking as guilty as she felt.

“Neil is looking for you. It worried him when he couldn’t find you.”

She nodded and took a shaky breath. “Adam, I must go.”

“Yes…I know…”

They stood in silence for a few awkward

moments, then Charlotte made the move toward the door, but Adam stopped her and took hold of her hand. "Charlotte, forgive me. Please don't think I was pushing you into doing something against your will."

Hanging her head, she sighed heavily. "It wasn't your fault, Adam. It's mine."

"How is it yours?"

She sneaked a peak at him and grinned sheepishly. "I can't stop myself from wanting to be kissed by you. I know it's wrong, but once I'm in your arms, I'm powerless to stop you."

"Do you want me to stop?"

She sighed again and lowered her gaze in confusion mixed with shame. "The fact is we shouldn't have even begun. I am married."

He nodded. "I know." His tone was apologetic. "But I can't seem to keep my hands off you. I know it's wrong. Regardless of what I think of my cousin, it's wrong. I'll try harder to keep myself from touching you. You are just so beautiful and…so damn lovely. What mere mortal could resist your charms?" A melancholy frown flitted across his features.

She smiled. "Then I will keep myself from tempting you."

A smile tugged at the corners of his frown. "Oh, my dear, you'll never be able to accomplish that, no matter how hard you try." He leaned over and kissed her again, but this time on the cheek. "Come. Let's get you back to your husband."

"You're a good man, Adam"

"I wouldn't go quite that far." His left eyebrow lifted a fraction. "Now, let's go before I do something immoral, and ruin your high opinion of me." But he smiled as he said it.

Chapter Sixteen

Neil stared at his food as he sat at the table. His fork, seemingly unbidden, moved his mashed potatoes in small circles. His eyes never left the plate. His chin rested in his cupped hand and, foregoing his manners, he leaned his elbows on the table. A feeling of doom had seeped deep into his bones and it twisted his stomach.

Time was running out. No matter how the case ended, it would probably signal the end of his marriage. Blackmailing her into staying with him was wrong, but just as he was powerless to resist her charms, he was also powerless to keep her with him if she chose to leave.

In the past hour, Charlotte had been distant and uncommonly silent. This bothered him more than he could handle. He'd convinced himself she was making plans for her return to home. She'd yet to confess her love for him or tell to whom her heart truly belonged. This could only mean one thing.

He lifted his gaze and looked across the table at her. She, too, picked at her food. His heart dropped. She looked absolutely miserable, just as he felt.

It was nerve-wracking eating his meal without conversing, yet Neil knew it was his fault. He shouldn't have played this game. The end of his married life loomed near, and he didn't like the heavy ache in his chest when he thought about losing Charlotte.

The worried creased on her forehead, and the way she avoided looking at him let him know she had something on her mind. But he waited until she was ready to break her news to him.

Finally, she wiped her mouth with her linen napkin and cleared her throat. "I spoke with Jacqueline this afternoon, and you'll not believe the idea she has for getting into Mr. Stout's house."

Although this bit of information disturbed him, Neil breathed a sigh of relief when she didn't speak the words he'd feared. He shook his head and looked down at his plate. "What does she have planned?"

"She has figured a way to get both of us into Mr. Stout's house, plus have you look through the sheriff's house at the same time. Neither the sheriff or Mr. Stout will suspect a thing."

Neil met her stare. Guilt laced her smile, twisting his gut. He could read people well. He'd been studying people's expressions for most of his life. This fact made him positive she wasn't in love with him. His heart ached at the realization.

"How?" he answered, without much feeling.

"She and Mr. Stout are giving a party at his house. Naturally, they'll invite the sheriff and his men. While they're there, she'll give them a drug called Opium. Jacqueline assures me they'll not remember a thing."

Neil's lips tugged into a grin. "Opium, huh?"

"That's what she called it."

"Well, they'll certainly be in dreamland."

"Anyway, while they're sleeping away the effects of the substance, Jacqueline and I will search through Mr. Stout's house. And you'll be across town searching the sheriff's cottage."

"You're overlooking one small detail, my love."

"What's that?"

He leaned back in his chair and folded his arms. "The sheriff's men are watching his place constantly. I've tried to get into his home while he's away, but one of his men remains lurking around."

A sly look crossed her pretty face. "I haven't

overlooked that at all."

Neil raised his eyebrows. "Please, tell then. How does Jacqueline figure to keep them all busy and drugged at the same time?"

Her lips twitched. "You know her better than anyone. I'm certain you can speculate."

Neil sat in silence while his mind scrambled to find an answer to Charlotte's question. He leaned forward and rested his arms on the table once again, looking straight into her beautiful face. "If I know Miss Fonteneau at all, I'm sure it has something to do with her considerable charms."

Charlotte laughed. "You're correct."

"I see…"

"Actually, she calls it a private gala."

His eyes opened wide in shock. "She's going to seduce *all* of them?"

She didn't have to answer him. The scarlet color quickly covering her face told him what he needed to know.

He laughed louder and shook his head. "But I can't believe Jacqueline would use her feminine wiles to seduce those men and then drug them. I'll have to hand it to the wayward woman, because she thought of such a brilliant folly! I wondered there for a while if she had a brain at all..." He paused, watching the color slowly disappear from Charlotte's face. "I suppose she'll supply the Opium?"

"Yes. She told me she knew of someone who could supply that sort of thing."

"So, where do you come into all this?"

Charlotte bit her lips in hesitation, but he read her well. Shock mixed with his temper shot to surface.

"Oh no, she's not!" he shouted. "She is not going to have you there as well, pretending to seduce these men!"

"You're forgetting one thing," she replied. "The

men will be drugged and so there'll not be any foreplay at all, except of course, in their dreams." She smiled slyly.

"But, won't the sheriff think it's strange to have Mrs. Hamilton suddenly accepting his advances?"

"I'll not go as Mrs. Hamilton." She shrugged. "Jacqueline thought this one up, but I'll go as one of her friends. You can disguise me to look like one of those girls. A rouged lady of ill repute..." She sat still while he studied her, but he could see she nervously wrung her hands. "Neil, if it'll make you feel any better, you can come along in your own disguise with me until the men are under the influence."

He gave a hard laugh. "Sweetheart, I'm one of the best at disguise, but even I can't pass as a harlot."

She chuckled. "I wasn't thinking of that. I was thinking about being our footman or something along those lines."

He nodded, carefully weighing the plan, wishing he'd thought of it. "All right. That's what I'll do."

"Promise?" Her tight expression relaxed, a full smile touching her mouth.

He moved out of his chair and came around the table, kneeling by her side. Taking her hands in his, he said, "I'll do anything to make you smile and to make your eyes light up like stars."

Charlotte couldn't believe he'd agreed, but he'd been so charming lately, and his words were certainly melting her heart. Without replying, she kept her gaze on his, communicating with her eyes just what his comment meant to her.

"I'll even dress as a concubine if I have to," he added.

She laughed.

"Why are you doing this? Why are you willing to dress up like a soiled dove just to help me?" he whispered as he gazed into her eyes.

She shrugged. "Because I'm tired of it all. I want these false charges against you dropped. I want a normal life again. I want...a normal marriage."

"Does that mean you want to be my wife? Have you finally decided it's me you want?" Excitement crept into his voice as his eyes searched hers.

It was hard to believe, but that was exactly what she was saying. She really did want to be his wife, if only Adam wouldn't send her heart pounding with desire like just her husband could do.

"Yes, Neil. That's exactly what I am saying."

A joyous look crossed his face, and she'd never seen him so expressive. He threw his arms around her, pulling her close in a tight hug.

"Oh, Charlotte! My sweet darling, you've made me the happiest man alive." He pulled back slightly. "In fact, if I could marry you all over again, I would."

She couldn't stop the tears of happiness from filling her eyes. "You have no idea how long I've waited to hear you say that."

She leaned in and kissed him. Just as always, the kiss was exciting and wild, and this time she actually felt the love growing within her heart. The capricious feeling brought out a giggle from her chest.

Neil pulled back and gave her a strange look. "What was that about? Do you find the way I kiss comical?"

She smiled. "No, it wasn't that."

"Then what is it?"

"I just couldn't help it. I'm so happy," she cried, feeling as though she was wrapped in a silken cocoon of euphoria.

His hands stroked her face and neck. "What makes you so certain I'm the man for you, my darling?"

"Because I've realized just how much I love you."

"You...love me?" His voice broke.

"Yes. I don't think I've ever loved you as much as I do right now."

"Oh, Charlotte," he groaned, wrapping his arms around her, crushing her body next to his while his mouth hungrily took over.

Neil picked her up and carried her into his bedchambers. Not another word was spoken as they began their glorious lovemaking. It meant more to Charlotte this time, and with each touch of his hands, each touch of his hot tongue, and the nibble of his expert lips, it thrilled her beyond anything she'd ever imagined. His kisses were more loving, and when he finally made love to her, he did it with so much more emotion that she felt just as restless, hungry, and passionate for him as he did for her. Charlotte participated fully this time, helping to guide him with her hands as her legs wound around his waist and kept him inside her.

Their lovemaking went slower, and the need to please him overwhelmed her. She stroked his firm buttocks as she leaned up and kissed him. She enjoyed kissing his chest, his neck. He placed his mouth over hers while his body imprisoned hers in a web of growing ecstasy. Her climax was wonderful, and after it was over, she felt satisfied and whole. She'd made the right choice in loving him. And her body and mind heartily agreed.

****

The day of the party quickly came upon Charlotte, and she felt exhilarated, yet frightened. Could she pull it off? Would Jacqueline be able to put the drug into the men's drinks before anything happened? Would Neil find the jewels, which would release him from these false crimes?

Neil appeared much more in control. He helped her look through her closest to find the outfit she'd wear. After sorting through two closets, he pulled out a dress, then shook his head and chuckled.

"As much as I detest having the sheriff and Ewan ogle your chest like you were going to give them a sample, I think this is the only dress that will pass for your disguise."

When she noticed it was the dress she'd bought on impulse the day after the masquerade ball, she groaned. "I suppose if it's the only dress that will pass."

"Unfortunately, it is." He held up the garment. "Will you allow me to assist you?"

She grinned and untied her dressing robe, letting it slide down her body to the floor. Her heart picked up rhythm when Neil's gaze roamed over her chemise and bloomers. He licked his lips then stepped toward her, lifting the dress and pulling it down over her body. As he adjusted the garment in place, his hands wandered to her breasts, pausing briefly to caress her now pointy tips. He dipped his head and kissed the top of each soft mound, teasing her with his wild, passionate kisses. With a sigh, she held onto his arms to keep her melting legs from dissolving beneath her.

When he pulled away, regret stabbed at her. She sighed and finished doing up the buttons. He then took her hand and led her into his rooms, to the small corner where he kept his disguises. He opened a large case full of wigs and pulled out a long black one. The tresses were pitch as night with long tendrils of curls.

"Have a seat, my love." He pointed to the chair.

She did, and once she was seated, he began his work, fitting the wig over her head until all of her hair had disappeared. He took a comb and fluffed up the black hair, making it wave all over her head and down her shoulders, seductively. He deftly attached a pair of diamond-studded combs at each side. She tiled her head toward the mirror, watching the stones catch the light.

He then took out some colored powders and began painting her eyes, cheeks, and lips. When he turned her toward the mirror, she couldn't believe the difference. She was the prettiest harlot she'd ever seen.

"They're never going to believe this is me," she exclaimed.

"That's the whole idea."

"I look too high priced to be seen with the likes of those who will be at the party," she teased.

Neil's laughter filled the room. "Oh, my darling, you're going to be just fine. Just remember, though, I don't want you acting the part. You can talk seductive, but do not let any of those men touch," he warned. "I won't allow it."

She studied him in the mirror with a scowl. "You're the only man I want touching my body." She leaned back and looked at her reflection pensively. A grin crept onto her face as she realized she'd finally banished Adam from her mind and heart. She was free to give her heart and soul to Neil now…for her heart did indeed belong to him.

He moved behind her and pulled her up against his body. "I'm glad you feel the way I do."

Laughing, she pulled away. "Come, let's get you ready now."

She moved to his make-up case and rummaged through the disguises. "What are you going to go as today?"

"I don't know. Help me decide."

She couldn't believe the selection of facial hair and wigs. She picked up a gray wig and placed it on his head.

"How about the one you wore when you were the old man who rescued me two years ago?" she suggested.

He nodded. "I'm surprised you remembered."

She picked up another wig, curly and blond. "Oh Neil…how could I forget?" Their eyes locked and a sigh escaped her lips. "Oh, and this was what you wore when you were the haggardly old woman." She laughed. "Now that's an image I'll never forget."

He laughed with her. She picked up another wig, grayer than the first. "Do you want to be an old man today?"

He chuckled. "I'm going to have to be. Any younger man who is a footman to someone as beautiful as you is going to have to be immune to your body, and I'm definitely not that."

She picked up some matching sideburns and held them to the sides of his face. "Yes, I think these will work just fine. So, how do you put these things on?"

"See this jar? It has a sticky substance that will help keep the hair to my face." He took a small spatula and dipped it into the jelly. With great patience, he placed the film on his skin where the sideburns would go, then carefully placed the facial hair in place.

She pulled her attention away from him and back to his crate of disguises, wondering what else he should wear. Her fingers brushed against a black mustache that looked more used than the others, so she picked it up. Although the mustache wasn't the same shade as his wig and sideburns, she turned and stuck it over the top of his upper lip for fun.

"Here, put this one on." She chuckled.

After a few moments at looking at his reflection through the mirror, he joined in her laughter. She smiled at him as she admired his tempting mouth. Suddenly, she received the strangest feeling, almost as if she had seen this particular mustache before. In her mind, a picture formed of Adam. His mustache was like this one. In fact, Neil's lips were—

With shaky hands, she turned quickly and put the mustache back in the crate. Numbness spread through her body the longer Adam's image remained in her mind. It wasn't his face that she thought about, but the lips. She closed her eyes and tried to fight away the feelings of deceit consuming her very soul.

It couldn't be! But Neil was the master of all disguises. When he'd been the old man who saved her from kidnappers, the only thing that gave away his character was his lean fingers. And Adam always wore gloves...to hide his hands. Why? Because they were scarred? And even when he had played the part of the old haggardly woman, his eyes were the only thing that looked familiar. But what about Lord Adam Thatcher? She thought there was a resemblance in their eyes, but Adam had explained that it was because they were related.

Now she doubted Adam's story. She doubted Neil's story, too. Who could she believe? There was only one way to tell.

Fighting for control over her twisting emotions, she turned back toward Neil and watched him put on the gray mustache. The more she stared at his lips, the more unease washed over her. Those lips were just like Adam's. The realization struck her in the stomach like a fist, and she released a long sigh.

"If you keep looking at my mouth the way you're doing," Neil said, bringing her out of her jumble of confusing thoughts, "I'm going to think you want to be kissed good and hard."

Her gaze flew to his eyes. "I do," she blurted out.

His eyes widened, but he drew her into his embrace and lowered his head. She pressed her mouth to his, moving her lips over his softly and seductively, which made him groan. He tried to turn the kiss wild, but she wouldn't let him. She kept the kiss gentle until he responded the same way. She didn't have to open her eyes to know who was kissing her right now…even the tender caress of his hands were Adam's!

Once she was satisfied, she pulled away, and looked into his eyes. Why hadn't she caught on before now? But then, the question was, why did Neil have to play the part of Adam at all? Her eyes narrowed suspiciously on his ruggedly handsome face.

Neil grinned. "What was that all about?" he asked as he stepped back to the mirror.

"I just wanted to see how it felt when I kissed you wearing a mustache," she said slowly, trying to read his expression.

He laughed. "And how did it feel, my love?"

"It felt like Adam," she said, unable to contain herself any longer.

His head jerked around quickly, his eyes met hers, then quickly diverted elsewhere. As she studied his reaction, her first thought was she'd been mistaken, but the way he glanced at everything but her, said it all.

"So...do you go by Neil...or do you prefer to be called Adam?" she asked sarcastically.

Coldness rushed through Neil's body, and his heart sank. But at least the truth was out. He didn't want to deny it, yet he didn't want to lose her. Lying was not the answer this time.

"Can I explain?" he asked in a voice filled with despair. Tears filled her eyes and he reached out to her. "Please, let me explain."

"No." She slapped his hands away and turned and ran out of his room. He chased after her. Her tiny feet echoed his large steps behind her. He caught her beneath the flickering lamplight, his fingers gouged deeply into her arms as she struggled to get away.

"Please, Charlotte! Let me explain," he pleaded.

"No," she cried, yanking her arms out of his grasp.

She wouldn't look at him, and he feared she would never forgive him.

He caught her again before she could turn to run, and pressed her body against his, pinning her arms to her sides. "Charlotte, you need to know the truth. I won't let you leave until you've heard it all."

"You...you...lied to me!" She sobbed.

His heart tore in pieces as he watched sorrow leak from her eyes. "I know, but I did it for a reason."

"No reason can be good enough for hurting the woman you proclaim to love!" She twisted in his arms to free herself of his tight embrace.

He sighed heavily and loosened his hold. Thankfully, she didn't turn and run this time. "I really wanted to tell you, but I had to know if you could love me," he began quietly. "At first, I started the charade because you were bored and needed a good mystery to solve. Before you had walked back into my life, I began to write a novel. The notes you read in my office were those from my manuscript."

Her tear-stained eyes lifted and met his.

"Then, problems with the sheriff arose and I needed somewhere to stay, and yet still be myself. When you met Adam and actually liked him, well, I knew I couldn't tell you at that time because I so desperately had to know how you felt about me. It was important the servants thought of me as Adam. At that time, I didn't trust anybody."

He reached up and wiped a streak of tears from her cheek. She withdrew, her eyes narrowing in anger.

"You couldn't even trust me?" She glared at him with burning, reproachful eyes.

"As Adam," he went on slowly, "I became your friend, but I couldn't hold back my desire for you.

That's why Adam fell in love with you and tried to seduce you. Then I noticed you were more at ease with Adam than you were with me. Never in my wildest dreams did I think you'd desire a man like him, and when you did, I definitely couldn't tell you the truth."

"Why did you think you couldn't tell me?"

"Because I feared when you discovered the truth, you might hate me." He paused, searching her eyes and pleading with his own for her forgiveness and understanding. Then he asked, "Do you hate me for not telling you?"

She lowered her gaze and his heart dropped. She did hate him, he could sense it, and the pain tore viciously at his gut. But he had to make her see...make her understand. He couldn't lose her, not now, not after everything they'd been through together. It couldn't end like this. He wouldn't let it.

"I don't know how I feel right now," she whispered with emotion. "I do know that because you've withheld the truth from me, you've hurt me all over again. You could have told me, Neil."

"Oh, Charlotte, my love." He tightened his arms around her, but she pushed him away.

"Please, don't touch me," she snapped. "You have to get ready for the party. I'll be downstairs waiting."

She fled down the hallway, and he didn't stop her this time. His whole world had shattered into a million pieces. He never wanted things to end like this. He was going to tell her after she confessed her love, but their lovemaking kept his mind side-tracked. It was too late, now. How could he make amends with her at this point in time? Well, no matter how difficult it seemed, he had to try. He must make her realize she loved him. He also needed to make her see she was an understanding and forgiving woman. It would take time. He, of course, would have to hold her and kiss her, making her see how she melted in his arms—and then everything would be all right.

It just had to.

Chapter Seventeen

Charlotte sat in one corner of the coach and stared blankly out the window, slightly bouncing to the rhythm of the vehicle. Jacqueline sat beside her. Opposite them, Neil's attention rested only on Charlotte, but she refused to look his way. He'd tried many times to apologize since this afternoon, but she informed him she needed time to think. His treachery had left a gaping hole in her heart, and she felt as if she'd been used—like she'd been the victim of a cruel joke.

Now she understood why she had craved Adam's touch as well as Neil's. They were the same man. Yet, she'd suffered through guilt because of having these feelings. And to think if Neil had confessed the truth, she wouldn't have suffered.

The ride to Ewan Stout's estate was almost unbearable, but Charlotte held her silence for the duration of the journey.

The coach stopped in front of Ewan's little two-level house, and many fancy carriages parked along the street. Neil climbed out first and helped the ladies down. Charlotte let Jacqueline go ahead of her, and when it was her turn, she hesitantly placed her hand in his. Shooting waves of pleasure filled her body from the warmth of his skin, and she cursed the effect his caress had always created. After her feet touched the ground, she tried to slip her hand from his, but he held tight and turned her to face him. He waited until she grudgingly met his stare.

"Please forgive me," he whispered. "It's killing

me to see you this way. I love you."

It tore at her heart to see such painful emotion written on his face, but it made her that much angrier. She yanked her hand away and marched toward Jacqueline without giving him any kind of verbal response.

Jacqueline and Neil huddled together near the coach as he quickly explained what he wanted her to do, how he wanted her to act, and especially what she should *not* say. Jacqueline kept casting glances her way, but Charlotte didn't join in the conversation. She wrapped herself tightly in her own self-pity.

When Mr. Stout opened the door of the house, Charlotte put on a mask of cordiality and entered her new role, wondering why she continued this farce as she walked into the house with Jacqueline. If Neil had lied to her about Adam, maybe he had lied about the theft. But deep in her heart, she knew Neil had not committed the crime. Besides, the sooner they found the real thief, the sooner Charlotte could go back home and get far, far away from Adam and Neil.

As she passed by a window, she saw Neil peeking in. Mostly, he watched her. She willed him to keep his mind on their objective. His presence, although hidden from the others, made her feel comforted.

"Welcome ladies," Ewan greeted Charlotte and Jacqueline warmly.

Charlotte buried her feelings deep inside and returned Mr. Stout's greeting as Jacqueline introduced her as Jennifer.

"Good evening, gentlemen." She made her voice purr. Her gaze moved around the room. The sheriff waited with an eager, incongruous expression. He was dressed outlandishly, wearing brighter clothes than she'd seen him in before. As always, he held a superior expression on his face. But where were his men? Could she be so fortunate he'd not invited them? But she must keep her guard up just in case they showed up.

Ewan and Jeffrey Franklin watched the two scantily clad women with hungry eyes.

Jacqueline pulled her arm. "Come, Jennifer. These men look thirsty. Let's fix them some drinks."

Thank heavens for Jacqueline. At least she knew what to do. Charlotte mentally focused on her task. As she poured the drinks, Jacqueline discretely slipped the powder into the glasses. The hairs on the back of Charlotte's neck rose, and she felt as if she were being watched closely.

She peeked over her shoulder and was immediately accosted by the sheriff's look of desire. The leery grin on his face, the gleam in his glazed brown eyes let her know exactly what he wanted. She realized the drinks Jacqueline made were not his first of the evening. Her stomach twisted and her skin crawled. Turning back to watch Jacqueline, she still felt those eyes burning into the tender skin of her back. She felt as though she stood before him naked, then realized she nearly was. The dress she wore revealed more than was acceptable in normal company.

"Jacqueline?" she whispered. "The sheriff is watching me. I have to take his mind off what we're doing or he might see you pouring Opium into everyone's drinks."

Jacqueline froze. "What are you going to do?"

Charlotte sighed heavily. "The only thing I can do, I suppose. I'll have to keep him company while you finish this by yourself," Charlotte said in a hushed voice.

"Are you going to be all right?"

"I certainly hope so. If he starts pawing at me, I might be tempted to punch him in the face."

"Keep your temper hidden, Charlotte. Once the men drink this, it won't take long before it starts to work," Jacqueline replied in the same quiet tones.

Taking a breath of courage, Charlotte casually left Jacqueline's side and sashayed over to the only man in the room who watched her. Ewan threw a sidelong glance her way, but withdrew when the sheriff passed him a warning glare. She strutted across the room toward him, keeping in mind her role for the evening.

"Good evening," she greeted, allowing a note of promise to enter her voice while batting her eyes seductively.

Jeffrey grinned, his eyes darkening with lust. "You're not from around here, are you?" He didn't wait for her to answer. "I would have known if you lived in my jurisdiction."

"No, I'm not from around here."

"How long are you staying in New York?"

She shrugged. "I don't know. It depends on the offers I receive."

"What kind of offers are you looking for?"

She grinned. "That all depends. Anything that would tempt me to stay."

He dropped onto a lounge in one of Ewan's loveseats and patted his knees. "Why don't you sit and rest a spell?"

She would rather regurgitate all over him, but instead she tampered the smile as she lowered to his lap. Right away, his hands wrapped around her waist, holding her body much too close for her comfort. She also didn't like the way he kept studying her face. It was if he suspected who she really was.

"So, what's your name?" she asked.

"Sheriff Jeffrey Franklin," he boasted. His breath was foul, and she longed to turn away.

"Could I be that fortunate to be sitting on the

lap of a man so powerful?" she purred with false charm.

"Darling, if I get my way, which I'm sure I will, you'll be doing more than just sitting on my lap tonight."

From underneath her skirts, the hard pressure of his arousal leapt to attention. Her stomach churned. "Then I'll be a fortunate girl, won't I?"

The longer he continued to study her face, the more uncomfortable she became.

"Jennifer? Do you have a sister, by chance?"

She gave him a quizzical look. "Why do you ask?"

"Because I know a woman who resembles you quite a bit."

Her heart dropped. "Really? Who is she?"

"She's new in town, also, so I'm sure you won't know her unless she's your sister. Her name is Charlotte Hamilton."

Charlotte hoped her expression hadn't changed, because the rhythm of her heart had. She laughed. "Sorry, I don't have a sister," she replied quickly, trying to sound nonchalant.

One of his hands moved from around her waist and rested on her knee. "That's all right with me. Mrs. Hamilton is as cold as ice, and I know you're not that way, so I'm most fortunate you're here and she's not."

She forced herself to run her fingers through his unclean hair without shivering with disgust. "Yes, you're the privileged one, aren't you?"

His eyes kept dropping to her lips, and she prayed she didn't have to fight off his kisses. Her mind scrambled for something else to say—something to keep him from putting his mouth over hers. Thankfully, Jacqueline chose just that moment to bring his drink.

"Here's your drink, Jeffrey." Jacqueline smiled,

then left to deliver the other drink to Ewan.

The sheriff didn't bother to do more than nod. He downed most of the drink in one gulp. Charlotte breathed a sigh of relief.

"Would you care for another?" Charlotte purred.

"No. I'd rather drink from your cup of passion."

"Well, then, my handsome man," she said, slipping off his lap, "if you want me that badly, I'll have to go get myself ready."

"I hope you don't plan on giving yourself to others. I'm the kind of man who doesn't share easily."

"Tonight I'm all yours."

"You're so good, aren't you? Do you know how excited I'm getting right now, and we're just talking?" He rubbed the bulge in his trousers.

She laughed huskily, still feeling the imprint of his excitement on her back side and wanting desperately to fiercely scrub the feeling away. "I can't tell you how happy that makes me," she cooed.

"Come here, my little sex kitten." He lunged for her, but she backed away, swaying her hips as much as she could, batting her eyes and giving him the most heated expression she could, hoping and praying the drug Jacqueline gave the men would work quickly, very quickly.

****

"I can't believe there's nothing here," Charlotte shouted in fury as she marched out of the last room, closing the door behind her. Jacqueline came running out to meet her in the hallway. They had spent an hour looking in every room of Ewan's house, but their search had turned up nothing. "It's got to be somewhere!" Charlotte cried in frustration.

"Charlotte, we've turned this place upside down. There's nothing here. Ewan's going to be livid when he sees the place."

Charlotte chuckled nervously. "Let's hope he

merely thinks the party got out of hand."

"Do you think it's possible you were wrong about Ewan?" asked Jacqueline.

Charlotte sighed. It was beginning to look that way, but she wasn't willing to give up quite so soon. She'd never been a quitter and wasn't about to be one now. Hopefully Neil was having better luck. Although she was still very angry with him, she sincerely wished he'd found what she and Jacqueline hadn't.

"I really do like Ewie," Jacqueline continued in a hopeful tone.

"If he didn't steal the bracelet," Charlotte said, more to herself than to her companion, "then where did he get it? It was definitely the bracelet stolen from Mrs. Peterson's house."

"Do you want me to just ask him?"

"Not yet. Let's wait and see what Neil finds."

"Let's return downstairs and see how they are doing."

Charlotte shuddered with dread. "Do I have to? Seeing that filthy sheriff without clothing is something I'd rather not see."

Jacqueline laughed. "Then I'll go first."

Charlotte followed Jacqueline down the hallway. Charlotte sucked in a breath as she stepped into the room and bumped into Jacqueline, who had stopped. Just as she opened her mouth to apologize, a man's voice overrode her thoughts. The hairs on the back of her neck rose. Fright took on a whole new meaning.

"What in the 'ell is goin' on?" The voice boomed through the room.

Charlotte's first reaction was to turn and flee. Instead, she stepped up boldly beside Jacqueline. Although he wasn't a fancy dressed man, he wasn't a miscreant either. His clothes were rugged and fit his large frame perfectly. Deep scars marred his ugly face, one by his left eye and two by his cheek and mouth. Even so, it was his expression that caused her breath to catch in her throat. Green eyes, dark as midnight, pierced the six feet that separated them. The gaze held a mixture of emotions, none of which were pleasant.

But there was something even more frightening than his eyes. Something about that man was familiar to her. She frowned as she tried to search her memory for where she might have met him before.

"What's goin' on 'ere?" the man repeated when he saw Jacqueline and Charlotte standing in the doorway.

"Um...we're having a...simple soiree," Jacqueline stuttered.

"I can tell," he replied ignorantly.

The man's mouth took on a pleasant twist, making Charlotte's blood run cold. She held herself strongly erect. "I don't believe I know you. Did someone, perchance, invite you here tonight, sir?"

"'ell no!"

"Then please, tell us who are you and why you're here?" Charlotte asked again.

His dark penetrating gaze never left hers for an instant.

"I'm 'ere to see the sheriff."

"He's, ah, rather indisposed at the moment—"

"You don't need to tell me somethin' I can obviously see for m'self," the man shouted. "But what I'd like to know is why doesn't 'e wake up when I try and shake 'im? All 'e does is look at me and smile like 'e's gone daft."

Charlotte's heart pounded in her ears, and she frantically tried to think of an intelligent answer. She forced a pleasant smile. "Haven't you ever seen a man who's been completely satisfied by woman and drink?"

The angry scowl didn't diminish. All of

Charlotte's nervousness slipped back to physically grip her. She glanced helplessly at Jacqueline.

Jacqueline tried to explain further. "He's had an awful lot to drink," she added softly.

The man's arm flashed out. When he yanked Charlotte roughly toward him, she cried out.

"I know this man personally and 'e never gets this drunk. What did you do to 'im?"

She swallowed the lump of fear lodged in her throat. "How do you know the sheriff?"

"'e's my brother."

Charlotte could have swooned, and from the way Jacqueline sagged against her, she knew Jacqueline was close to doing it, too.

"Please, sir." Charlotte tried peeling his fingers from her arm. "I don't know what else to tell you. I don't know why your brother is acting this way, except he has had quite a lot to drink."

The man peered suspiciously again around the room. "Why aren't you actin' the same way? And why is your friend normal? Everyone 'ere is like my brother, except for the two of you."

With sinking fear, Charlotte knew she was in trouble. There was no explanation. "Jacqueline and I haven't had that much to drink. We have been too busy upstairs getting the bedrooms ready."

He studied her face for a few seconds, then leaned forward. "Woman, you're lyin'," he shouted. She reeled back from his odorous breath. He shook her roughly. "Now tell me what's wrong with my brother!"

Suddenly, the sheriff muttered. Charlotte couldn't understand what he said, but she nearly gasped in surprise.

"Benji? Is that you?" Jeffrey grumbled.

She glanced toward him. His torso was naked. Thankfully, his trousers were still on. He held his hands to both sides of his head. A look of utter confusion was plastered on his face.

The man released Charlotte's arm and moved over to his brother. "Jeffrey? What's wrong with ya?" He shook his brother's shoulders.

The sheriff laughed deeply. "What do you mean? Nuthin's wrong. I'm hav'n the time of me life." His gaze moved to Charlotte. "See that woman? Ain't she sweet?" He laughed again. "She also knows how to please me."

Benji let go of his brother and marched back to Charlotte, roughly taking her wrist. "You drugged 'im, didn't you?"

"What?" She tried to appear shocked by his accusation. "We've already told you. We were upstairs getting the rooms ready. Besides, why would either of us want to drug your brother? To get him to do things to me, he might normally not do?" Charlotte's fake laugh was high-pitched. "If that's the case, you obviously don't know him very well—"

Benji's expression turned from anger to confusion. Charlotte finally saw the similarities in the two brothers.

"I don't know why," Benji said, his eyes narrowing first on Charlotte, then resting on Jacqueline. "But you're lyin'. Just as certain as I'm standin' 'ere, I know you're lyin'. My brother says you pleased 'im, yet you've been upstairs gettin' the rooms ready. Besides that, ya don't even look as if you've been tumbled at all." His eyes swept over their attire from head to toe. "In fact, you look almost too perfect." His gaze moved back up to Charlotte's hair and he studied it curiously. Then, his hand moved up and quickly snatched off the wig.

She cried out in surprise and horror.

Benji's bark of laughter made her cringe. "You're in disguise!"

Where is Neil? Her heart beat erratically. Wasn't he watching what was going on from outside? He wouldn't have left yet, would he? Of course, he would, she sadly mused.

"We'd been upstairs for more than an hour." She steadied her voice when she answered, "Most women in my profession wear costumes. It's more fun, more mysterious."

The man glanced over her shoulder, then quickly scanned the room. "Where did the other woman go?"

Charlotte finally realized Jacqueline wasn't standing beside her any longer. A wave of relief swept over her. Jacqueline would go for help. Jacqueline would find Neil, but just as Charlotte's thoughts brought her a measure of relief, the front door flew open. A second man, much larger than Benji, strolled inside. He held a struggling Jacqueline under one arm.

Jacqueline kicked and screamed. She tried to bite the man's arm, but he merely laughed and flipped her under his other arm in one fluid movement.

"Lookie what I found running away from the house," he announced with an air of self-congratulation.

It was then that Charlotte finally recognized the two men. They were the same men who'd kidnapped her two years ago! The sheriff had already called his brother Benji, and she was willing to bet the other man's name was Henry.

Did they recognize her? She knew she'd changed a great deal—more than most people change in two years. But a wave of insecurity hit her. The fright she'd experienced two years ago closed in around her like a shroud, and she knew she was in grave danger. What were the odds that she would see these two blackguards again? And where was Neil? He'd been there to rescue her the first time, but she feared her luck wasn't going to be that good this time.

"There you are," Benji hissed at Jacqueline.

"What is going on here?" the other man barked.

"Well, it looks as if these two women 'ave drugged my brother and that other fellow, and it seems as if we 'ave an impostor among us."

The larger man with the pocked face moved to Charlotte and stared deeply into her eyes. "You know, I would think so. She don't look like no whore I've ever seen before. A little too fancy, don't ya think?" His sinister voice chilled her.

"That's what I thought, too, 'enry."

She gasped. Henry! The room had grown quiet and it felt as the walls were closing in on her. Panic like she'd never known before welled up in her throat and flooded up her eyes.

"So, what are you gonna do with her?" Henry asked.

Benji glanced at the sheriff who still reposed in front of the settee, a look of total satisfaction on his ugly face. "I think we'll 'ave to sober my brother up first, then we'll go from there. I'm certain 'e'll know what to do about these women."

Sheer black fright swept through Charlotte and her knees started to buckle. Her mind raced, trying desperately to find a way out of this dilemma. She glanced over at the doors, but both men were blocking the only exit in the room.

"What should we do with them while we wait?"

"I think we should tie them up. I don't want to 'old them the whole time."

Benji dragged Charlotte over to a chair and forced her down, then roughly wound disposed socking and pantaloons around her wrists and ankles. She gave the man a hostile glare through her struggles.

Jacqueline fought with them also, but the larger man struck her across the face and she quit. A trickle of blood ran down her lip. Jacqueline stared at the floor and let them bind her hands and feet.

Seconds ticked off a half hour as Charlotte watched Benji and Henry force coffee down the sheriff's throat, coaxing him sober. They'd dragged him outside for fresh air a time or two, then returned to pour more coffee down him. Finally, Jeffrey showed signs of normalcy, and once he was coherent enough and able to see what was going on, his temper exploded. The men quickly explained to him that they had been drugged and duped.

"What the hell were you thinking, harlot?" he yelled at Jacqueline, and then backhanded her across the face. Her head swung to the side in a violent motion. Tears filled the woman's eyes. Her gaze lowered to look at the large red poppy on the rug. She didn't speak, or even so much as replied. Several times, he shook her, brutally slapping her face. Blood trickled from her nose, and the left side of her face was bruised and swollen.

Charlotte flinched each time he struck her, thinking how brave Jacqueline was. *How strong will I be when it's my turn?* Icy fear twisted around her heart. *Neil! Where are you?*

Then, it was her turn. The three men surrounded her chair. "I have many questions for you, the first of which is, why all this deliberate pretense?" The sheriff's hands waved to take in the house, her costume.

"I…I…was just…bored," she said in a choked, frightened voice.

"So, the rumors must be true. Hamilton is impotent." A self-satisfied grin spread across his face. Charlotte wished she could pound that smile away. She struggled against her bonds, but they were too tight. She took a breath and spat in his face. Her frightened mood veered sharply to anger. She flashed him a cold look of disdain, and raised her chin defiantly to meet his icy stare.

She didn't waste energy trying to tell him the truth about Neil's sexual exploits. She didn't want to upset the sheriff too much. Obviously, the man was envious of Neil in all aspects of his life.

He didn't bother to wipe the saliva off, just stood with his evil smile. Charlotte knew retaliation would be rapid in coming, but she wasn't going to bow down to him no matter what he did to her. Her pride returned in full dress parade, for she would not let herself be put down by this brute.

Jeffrey folded his arms across his beefy chest and glanced at Jacqueline. He shook his head.

"I'm a little disappointed in you, my dove. After all I've done for you, this is how you repay me?"

"Yes, sheriff," Charlotte spoke, knowing he was probably going to kill her, and not willing to die without having her say. "Let's look at everything you've given her, shall we? Not only have you given her a bad reputation, you've given her reason to hate you more than anyone on this earth."

She didn't believe it could happen, but his gaze became even more inflamed. Inwardly, Charlotte cringed, but she was determined not to let her fears show.

"Yes, Charlotte, my dear. I suppose you could say I've given her reason to hate me, but I have also taken very good care of her."

"Maybe she doesn't want your kind of care."

He laughed, his gaze wandering over Charlotte's dress, lingering mostly on the exposed skin at her chest. She wished she could cover her bodice.

"Maybe you don't know her as well as you think," he sneered. "And what about you, my precious beauty?" He moved closer. "What have I ever done to you?"

"Don't tell me your memory is that short."

Confusion crossed his brow for only a moment,

then his face relaxed as a smile spread across his face. "Oh, do you mean that time in your husband's office? You can't still be upset over that."

She glared at him. "What do you think? You forced yourself on me, you beast! If it hadn't been for Lord Thatcher, you'd have violated me."

"Oh, I don't think so, Charlotte. In fact, I'm quite certain you would have enjoyed my style of lovemaking—"

"And, after being with my husband, I'm quite certain I wouldn't. You don't measure up to Neil Hamilton, and you never will."

Charlotte didn't realize her mistake in saying those words aloud until after she had spoken them, and it wasn't the sheriff who worried her. At that moment, she received looks from the other two men, and she noticed that they finally recognized her.

It was Henry who laughed first. "Oh, my God!" he exclaimed. "I don't believe my luck. Benji? Do you know who this girlie is? It's that same ragamuffin we kidnapped two years ago!"

"Nooo. Can't be the same one. She don't look nuthin' like that girl."

The sheriff glared at his brother. "What are you two imbeciles rambling on about?"

"Jeffrey, this girl right 'ere is the one we kidnapped two years ago. Remember, we could 'ave been rich off 'er. Everythin' was messed up when we trusted that rickety old man to help." Benji's fists clenched and he took a pair of steps toward her.

Jeffrey's eyes widened and he nodded. "Yes, and that's the reason you hate Neil Hamilton so much, right? He was the old man you thought was going to help you."

"Yer correct," Henry said as he walked to Charlotte. "And we also promised revenge when we met up with him again." His hand came out as he touched her face, his knuckles caressing the side of her cheek. "But is this beauty really that 'lil rag doll?" He studied her face closely. "I don't believe someone could change that much in two years."

Jeffrey nodded. "Her father's name is Ashton. Didn't you say he was William Ashton?"

"Yup, that's the bloody bastard!"

Jeffrey looked at Charlotte and grinned. "Well, well, well, my lovely Charlotte." He rubbed his hands together. "This makes things so much more interesting. Looks like my brother and his friend like you as much as I like your husband."

She maintained her glare when she looked at him. "With all this hate going around, I'm in with the right company, aren't I?"

He laughed. "You're certainly a feisty one."

"This is the girl, 'enry," Benji said. "Don't you remember 'ow stubborn and ornery she was back then?"

"Yes, but what are we to do with her now?"

Jeffrey grinned. "Maybe you could demand another ransom from her father." His lips twisted into a cynical smile. "This time, you might be able to get two of them...get a second one from her husband." His eyes darkened dangerously as he rubbed his chin thoughtfully.

"No. 'er father's dead now."

"Then get the bloody ransom from her damn husband!" Jeffrey yelled.

"But didn't you say Hamilton was in 'iding?"

"Yes, but don't you see?" Jeffrey moved closer to Charlotte as he cupped her face. His foul breath fanned her face. "This is the one thing that will bring the coward out of hiding and we'll be able to hang him for his thievery."

"Neil is not a thief." She spat out the words.

He laughed, looking at her with a sardonic expression that sent her temper soaring. Then he quickly bent his head and placed his lips over hers for a kiss. She struggled, but he held her face to his until he was done. Before he pulled away, she bit him. When he yelped and jerked back, she spat at him.

He hauled his hand back as though to strike her, but stopped, looking as if he had decided against it. His poised hand dropped to his side. His expression changed and he laughed. "I can't wait to tame you, my dear."

"Do you think it will work, brother?" Benji asked. "Do you think it will bring Neil out of 'iding?"

"It's the only thing we have going for us right now. We might as well try."

Charlotte said a silent prayer, hoping Neil was at the sheriff's house waiting for them. He'd save her as he'd always done. She hoped.

Chapter Eighteen

Neil found some of the stolen jewels, enough to prove he wasn't the thief. Good fortune was certainly on his side. But now he needed someone else to see and witness the stolen items kept in the sheriff's townhouse down in the cellar.

Neil needed to contact his friend who worked with the mayor. The man owed Neil a favor, and he was the only one who would help him out of this mess. If there was anyone who could free him from these false charges, it would be Ian's cousin, William Stanhope. Now that Neil had the proof, the rest would be simple.

He carefully made certain to put things back the way they were. He checked his makeup and wig in the hall mirror and headed into town. The first thing on his mind was to send a message to William Stanhope, and hopefully, Neil's freedom wouldn't be more than days away. It was so close he could taste it, but he mustn't get too excited. Not yet. Not until everything was completed.

The weather turned cool and windy tonight, so wearing a hooded cloak wouldn't look too conspicuous. He went straight to his office, and quickly penned a note to Stanhope. After putting his own seal on it, he carried it outside, and to the nearest delivery person.

After everything was done, he headed back to Ewan's house. The women would be finished with their search by now and they were probably waiting for his return. He hoped everything had gone well. The plan was infallible. Charlotte and Jacqueline had worked out every detail.

But as Neil approached the house, he knew something was amiss. It wasn't so much that the lights were all on, nor was it the lack of movement behind the drapes, but something else he couldn't quite put his finger on.

He tiptoed closer, keeping among the shadows of the hickory trees. No movement. No sound either. That's it! There was no sound. The place was dead quiet. Yet, what did he expect to hear? Ewan and the sheriff were all in dreamland.

Neil cautiously opened the front door. Everything seemed as it should, but Ewan was the only person in the room. He stepped past the sleeping man on the floor and walked upstairs, checking in every room. No sign of his wife, Jacqueline or the sheriff.

Panic tightened his chest and he ran back down the stairs. He kneeled by Ewan's side and shook him. "Ewan, wake up."

His secretary groggily opened one eye, smiled, then slumped back into dreamland. Neil slapped his friend's face, but still didn't get a response.

Irritation rushed through him. Somebody had to know something!

He took a deep breath and convinced himself there was a good explanation for all of this. The women probably went back to the castle.

Neil left the house, climbed atop the coach and urged the team forward, pushing them as fast as they could run. After he arrived at the castle, he ran into O'Toole, who was the first servant he saw.

He paused to catch his breath. "Is Charlotte home yet?"

"No, Master. She left with you earlier and hasn't returned."

Neil swore under his breath, the ache in his gut growing. His hand clutched his side and he tried to slow his breathing. "Quickly, get the servants together and search the castle anyway!"

"What's wrong?"

"She's missing."

"Sir? Before you leave, an urgent message was delivered for you."

Neil didn't have time for this nonsense, and was going to refuse the missive his servant held out, but then doubt snuck in through his worried mind. What if this was a letter from Charlotte informing him she was leaving?

Neil took the letter from his servant and opened it.

We have your wife. And just like two years ago when you robbed us of our money, we demand one hundred thousand pounds in twenty-four hours. Your time starts at eight this evening, so we encourage you not to waste a minute. Your wife's life is at stake, and be assured, this time we'll kill her. We're also going to lead you on a little scavenger hunt. We want to have a little fun at your expense, just like you had with us two years ago. We also want to test your skills to see if they are any good. By eight on Tuesday evening, if we haven't received any word from you, we'll kill your wife...after we've taken our pleasures out on her.

In a frightened rage, he crumbled the paper in his hands. What in the hell had he gotten her into? If it were not for him, she would be back home right now, safe with Allison. Why had he insisted on her staying?

His gut wretched with apprehension…he had to find her! But how? He already guessed by the note that these were the same blackhearts who had kidnapped her two years ago, but what were they doing in New York? And how did they find her? The only thing he could presume was that they were somehow linked with Jeffrey Franklin.

Was Ewan part of this? No. Especially when the man was still passed out at his home and the sheriff was missing.

Neil looked at O'Toole, standing still, wringing his hands against his middle. "She's been kidnapped."

His servant hitched a breath as color seeped from the older man's cheeks. "Oh, no. What can we do?"

"Nothing yet. I need to find out where the sheriff has her first. If I need your assistance, I'll let you know."

He turned and dashed out the door. As he untied one of the horses and mounted, Neil prayed she was safe and the sheriff hadn't touched her improperly. He'd kill the man with his bare hands.

Oh Charlotte, my love…I'm coming! Hold on. Hold on.

When he reached Ewan's house, he stopped his horse and jumped down. Instead of knocking on the front door, he threw it open and entered. "Stout?" Neil yelled. "Stout? Where are you? Answer me, damn it!" He didn't hear an answer, so he sprinted up the stairs in a panic, his heart beating so hard he thought it would break a rib.

Just as he reached the top floor, Ewan trudged out of his bedchamber, wearing a black robe. The man's thin brown hair looked like it hadn't been combed in a week, and a growth of stubble covered the lower half of his face. Ewan rubbed his red, tired eyes, blinking them into focus.

Once he recognized him, he gasped. "Hamilton? What do you want? And please, lower your voice," he complained, holding his head in his hands.

Neil took Ewan by the elbow and led him downstairs into the kitchen to prepare the coffee.

"Am I seeing right? Is it really you?" Ewan asked.

"Yes."

"But...but...I thought you were in hiding."

"I am, so don't tell anyone you saw me."

Neil placed the kettle on the stove. Not too long ago, they'd done this together as friends, each helping the other when they had drunk too much.

"So, Ewan, how was your night?" Neil asked.

"Aw," he groaned as his head pounded. "I don't want to talk about it."

"Well, that is too bad, because I do." Neil sat at the table by him. "What happened to the sheriff during your little party?"

Confusion crossed Ewan's brow when he looked back at Neil. "How did you know the sheriff was here?"

"Because the party was mainly for that imbecile. Jacqueline and my wife planned everything. I won't go into it right now, but I need to know if you have seen Jeffrey Franklin." He tried to keep the impatience from seeping into his voice.

"What makes you think I know?" Ewan's eyebrows shot up in surprise.

"Because he was here, in this house, when I dropped off Charlotte and Jacqueline. When I came to pick them up, they were gone. All three of them."

Ewan shook his head, holding it in his hands as if it were going to fall apart.

"Think really hard, Ewan. This is a matter of life and death."

"Whose death?" He looked up expectedly.

"Charlotte's and possibly Jacqueline's."

Ewan's eyes widened. "Jacqueline?"

"I believe the sheriff has kidnapped them."

Ewan's hands massaged his forehead as he squeezed his eyes closed. "I thought it was a dream."

"Tell me all you can remember," Neil urged.

Ewan opened his eyes, staring into thin air for a long moment. "I vaguely recall a man trying to awake the sheriff. I also believe this same man was yelling at that new girl who Jacqueline brought."

"That was Charlotte in disguise."

Ewan's eyebrows lifted. "It almost seemed as if they were upset at her for some reason." He paused. "I remember them tying her to a chair."

"Think. Was there anything else?"

"I can't remember. I don't think I even remember them leaving," Ewan said.

"Damn it!" Neil slammed his fist on the table.

Ewan jumped, then moaned as he held his head again. "Wait…I think I do remember something else."

Leaning forward, Neil grasped his friend's arm. "What?"

"I think the sheriff's brother came. I remember seeing him…"

"His brother?"

"Yes, his younger brother, Benji."

Neil pulled away from the table. "Thank you, Ewan. You don't know how much you've helped me."

"Neil? Are you going to get Jacqueline back, too?"

"I'll get them back. They're holding Charlotte for ransom." He moved to leave, then turned back to Ewan. "By the way, where did you get that bracelet? You know, the one you gave Jacqueline?"

His face turned a deep red. "I—I—I stole it from the sheriff. He has so many pieces of fine jewelry, I didn't think he would miss one."

"Do you know where the sheriff got it?"

He shrugged. "No. I figured since he's blackmailing me and Jacqueline, he's probably getting money and jewelry the same way."

Neil grabbed the collar of Ewan's robe roughly, jerking him out of the chair. "Ewan, did you tell the sheriff about some of my clients? Did you divulge information about their secret rooms and where they kept their jewels? Did you?"

Once again, Ewan held his head as if it would explode. "Please…I need a drink...a strong one."

Neil let go of the man, shoving him away. He quickly hurried to his liquor cabinet and poured him a whiskey.

Ewan gulped it back, then choked as tears filled his eyes.

"Ewan, please. I need to know."

Ewan nodded. "He tried to get me to confess. I wouldn't, but he knew things about me...things I didn't want others to know." He sank into his chair, lowering his head, and covering his hand over his eyes. "I'm sorry, Neil, but I had no other choice. He threatened to tell everyone." His voice tightened.

"Ewan, I have connections with the mayor. Will you tell him what you just told me?"

"Will it get Franklin arrested?"

Neil nodded. "He'll get his comeuppance, I assure you." He patted his friend's shoulder. "I must leave so I can rescue the woman I love."

"Neil? Thank you. You're a good friend." Ewan's squeaky voice stopped him.

Neil nodded, and walked to the door, then he heard Ewan call out again. "I think the sheriff might have taken the women to his cottage in the country."

"He has a cottage?"

"Follow the road leading north out of New York. It's about three miles northwest."

"Then, that's where I'll go." He hurried out the door and mounted his horse.

****

"Your plan won't work," Charlotte told Henry as he paced the floor in front of her.

So far, Henry had been ignoring her angry outbursts. Since the sheriff had brought them here, she'd been taunting both Henry and Benji. She detected that Henry was the meaner of the two, and she'd overheard the sheriff instruct them not to lay a hand on her. So she felt safe enough to continue her insults.

Henry walked past her again and she snickered. "Neil will see past your tiny little brain and fool you once again. He did it before when you first tried to kidnap me. And he'll do it again. You spineless fool!"

When he spun around and moved toward her, she realized this time she'd gone too far. She trembled and an oddly primitive warning sounded in her brain.

Henry grasped her shoulders roughly and jerked her once. "Then Neil will have a dead wife, won't he?"

"Henry," Jeffrey said calmly as he descended the stairs to the cellar where she was tied to a chair. "Please handle my woman a little better than that."

Charlotte shivered and her stomach churned.

Looking over his shoulder, Henry gave him a quizzical stare. "Yer woman? When did that happen?"

Jeffrey laughed. "From the very first moment I laid eyes on that lovely creature. She's like a spirited filly that just needs to be reminded who really holds the reigns." He moved to Charlotte, and caressed her cheek softly. "Say the word, my beauty, and I'll not let this beast lay a hand on you."

"Go to hell!" she snapped.

He shook his head. "Tsk, tsk, Charlotte. Those are not the right words, but I'll give you another chance."

She decided to hold her tongue. She didn't want to ruin her chances of having the sheriff's help when she needed it, but she also didn't want to give him the wrong impression, either. She tilted her head beguilingly, the way women often did to charm men. She flirtatiously batted her eyelashes, lowered, and then raised them demurely, looking through them at him. She smiled sweetly, turning her shoulders.

She felt like a complete idiot, but what other choice did she have? None!

The sheriff laughed and shook his head.

It was rather unnerving, waiting, praying, and hoping against hope to be rescued, but that was all she could do in her position. She had to pray Benji would deliver her ransom note before the sheriff gave up restraining himself. She also hoped Neil was as good at investigating as she'd been told. He just had to find her at the sheriff's country cottage. She deeply hoped Neil knew the man of the law had two residences.

Benji came stumbling through the cellar door, bringing in the wind as he entered. He turned and latched it tight, holding the piece of wood as if the horrendous wind would blow more leaves and dust into the house. After he accomplished his task, he walked into the room and smiled. "Mr. 'amilton should be reading 'is note any time now."

"Where did you deliver it?" Jeffrey asked.

"To the castle. That's where you told me to."

"Why the castle?" asked Henry. "I thought ye said Neil wasn't there."

Jeffrey bestowed upon Charlotte a wicked grin. "That's what Lord Thatcher and Mrs. Hamilton told me, but I think differently. If I know Neil the way I think I do, then he wouldn't stay very far away from his lovely wife."

"So, how long should we give him to show up?"

"Not more than twenty-four hours."

"And if he doesn't respond?" asked Henry.

"Then we'll kill her," Jeffrey answered with a shrug. "But not until after I have had my way with her."

Charlotte panicked. She'd rather die than let him touch her. With a silent plea, she prayed Neil would come rescue her. He just had to come.

But he could not get caught. She wondered if these men knew of his many disguises. She certainly hoped not. Her salvation depended on it.

****

Lord Thatcher needed to make another performance. That was the only way to save Charlotte. If Neil was spotted, he'd be arrested.

Neil gathered the hooded cape around him as he descended the carriage. Ahead of him stood the sheriff's cottage.

Taking deep breaths, Neil tried to calm his anger. He was Lord Thatcher now, not Neil.

He reached the door and rapped hard. Within a minute the heavy oak opened, the sheriff peering into the near-dawn morning as he held a lamp. Recognition must have struck the imbecile, because he gasped, his eyes widening.

"Lord Thatcher?" Jeffrey swallowed hard. "What do I owe the pleasure of your company this early in the morning?"

"I have an urgent matter which needs discussing. May I come in?"

"By all means." Jeffrey stepped away, opening the door wider. "Would you like some tea?"

"No." Once Neil was inside, he removed his cloak, showing the sheriff his gruesome scarred face. "I'm here to pay the ransom for Mrs. Hamilton."

Jeffrey lifted his brows. "What ransom?"

Neil swept quickly upon the insipid man, trying to intimidate him with his large frame. "You know damn well what I'm talking about, so I suggest you get to it. I have the money to pay for Mrs. Hamilton's ransom, so if you will please get her for me, I'd be most obliged."

Jeffrey remained standing where he stood. His expression wavered between fright and confusion.

"Well now, Lord Thatcher, I don't believe I can do that," he said, stepping away. "If you're as smart as I think you are, coming here to find the lady when the ransom note clearly said nothing of her whereabouts, then I'm certain you can also figure out I'm a desperate man. And you must be aware of the animosity between Neil and myself. So, I really must insist that Neil deliver the ransom."

Neil clenched his fists, reminding himself this was not the time to pummel the sheriff. "Hamilton isn't coming. He's far away and smarter than you think. He knows you'll ambush him as soon as he approaches your property."

Jeffrey scowled. "I cannot turn the lady over, my lord."

Neil moved like a panther, swift and effortlessly. He took Jeffrey's lapels in his fists and lifted him off the floor. The man of the law gasped and tried to kick out, but Neil ignored his protests.

"I said, get her—immediately!" he growled.

Through Jeffrey's frightened face, another emotion crossed his features, and he lifted his brows.

"I think we can work something out." His voice took on a conspiratorial tone as he tried to peel Neil's hands from his shirt. "I think if we can act like gentlemen, then we'll be able to come to some sort of compromise."

"A compromise?"

"Well, it occurs to me you are in love with the woman."

Neil hardened his expression. He didn't say anything, but Jeffrey probably guessed the answer.

He chuckled. "Now my lord, we might be able to help each other out. You want Mrs. Hamilton, and I want her husband. If you help me get her husband, she'll be free for you to have for yourself."

"What makes you think I can get Mr. Hamilton?"

"I have a strong feeling Neil is hiding in your castle."

"Why would you think that? You and your men searched it thoroughly and left empty-handed."

"True, but I still think he's there."

"Why?"

"Because, Lord Thatcher, if you had a wife as sensual and lovely as Mrs. Charlotte Hamilton, would you be away from her side for very long?" He paused, shaking his head. "I think not, my lord."

"And are you willing to risk a woman's life on that theory?" Neil snapped. "Shame on you, Sheriff. I thought you were smarter than that."

Jeffrey lifted an eyebrow. "Can you prove differently? Has Mrs. Hamilton been in your company twenty-four hours a day so that you could honestly say that Neil has not been with her?"

Neil scowled. "No, I cannot honestly say I've kept watch on Mrs. Hamilton twenty-four hours a day, but from what she has confided with me, she hasn't seen her husband since you accused him of thievery."

"Then she's lying," Jeffrey stated. "The woman is obviously seeing her husband."

"How are you so certain?"

He shrugged. "Why else would she proclaim he's innocent and that he's going to rescue her if she doesn't know where he is?"

Neil's heart softened, yet emotion tightened his chest. Charlotte waited for him to rescue her. Could he fulfill her wish? "I don't see how Mr. Hamilton could possibly know where she is, because I was the one who received the ransom note."

Jeffrey laughed. "You don't know the man as well as you think. Hamilton is clever and full of surprises. Are you not aware of his investigating talents?"

"Yes."

"Well, that proves right there he'll come for his wife. Trust my words, Lord Thatcher, he'll be here soon."

With a nod, Neil turned and limped to the nearest chair, sitting down on the expensive piece of antique furniture. "Then I suppose I'll just wait right until the time comes."

Anger creased the lines on Jeffrey's face. "I have a better idea. Why don't you return home and tell your servants to spread the story of Mrs. Hamilton's kidnapping? That way, Hamilton will eventually hear."

Neil grinned haughtily. "That has already been done. Don't you think the servants knew when I did? They were Mr. Hamilton's servants before coming to my castle."

"Well, Lord Thatcher, you're welcome to wait." Jeffrey's eyes narrowed and his mouth pulled into a thin line. "If you're quite certain Hamilton will get the ransom note, then feel free to stay."

"I will, Sheriff, but while I'm waiting, I'd like to see Mrs. Hamilton—just to make certain she's unharmed, mind you."

For a split second, panic crossed Jeffrey's features. "Um...well, my lord, I really don't think that's necessary."

Neil tightened his hand over the golden handle of his cane as he glared at him. "Now, Sheriff, you wouldn't want to get me upset, would you? Need I remind you what happens when you make me angry?"

They stared at each other coldly, each man assessing the other. Neil's heart beat anxiously, hoping the man of the law would follow with his cowardly ways as Neil had been used to.

The sheriff's Adam's apple dipped in his throat and he straightened his shoulders. "No, milord. You need not remind me. I'll get Mrs. Hamilton."

Turning on his heels, he marched out of the room. Neil sighed with relief, yet he worried if his anger would make its debut once he saw Charlotte. If the sheriff or his men have touched one hair on her head...

Neil breathed deeply, trying to control his emotions. He couldn't come out of character yet. Although he could take on the sheriff, he knew he'd not be able to fight the man's bullies lurking around the cottage. Which means he'd have to act quickly, and not let the sheriff out of his sight.

Just as Jeffrey reached the stairs to go down into the cellar, Neil hurried upon him, making his limp distinct as he neared. "On second thought, Sheriff, why don't I just follow you?"

A low curse rattled from the sheriff, and triumph flowed through Neil. But he hadn't won yet.

Jeffrey led Neil down a flight of stairs to the cold, dark, musty cellar. The hallway in which they walked was not lit very well, but the room ahead had enough light to help them see their path. Although Neil couldn't see as well as he'd like, a woman's loud voice directed his footsteps. He grinned. Even in the face of danger, Charlotte was very spirited.

"I can see why my father discovered you and your friend stealing from him," she snipped. "The two of you are nothing but a couple of bumbling oafs!"

"Listen, 'lil lady. I've had just about enough of yer squawkin'," one of the men shouted. "If you don't stop yer bitching, I just might have to hurt ya."

She laughed harshly. "You cannot lay a hand on me and you know it. The sheriff has you and your friend wrapped around his little finger." She snickered. "And I can't believe you haven't seen that yet. I also can't believe you still trust him. Look around you and see what he has taken, blaming my husband, of course, but has he even offered to share any of this wealth with you? In fact, I'm willing to bet after you get my ransom money from my husband, the sheriff will take it from you and kill you both."

Neil gritted his teeth. Charlotte didn't know the sheriff was so nearby and could hear. He knew his wife and how her vicious words could cut a man.

Jeffrey quickly rushed ahead of Neil and moved to Charlotte. Neil held his breath, hoping the man wouldn't lay a hand on her.

"Charlotte," Jeffrey said, red-faced. "Henry may not be able to lay a finger on you, but I still can, and if you don't keep that luscious mouth of yours closed, I'm going to do it for you. Do you understand? And you'll not like the way I keep you from talking, either."

Charlotte threw him a glare. "I'm most certain I'll not like it, especially if you have any part in it."

Neil couldn't help but chuckle aloud from her stubbornness. Everyone's attention flew toward him. Charlotte's eyes widened and she gasped.

"Why, Sheriff," Neil began, continuing in his beastly voice. "I don't believe you have won over this young lady. Perhaps she knows you too well to feel anything but pity."

That comment brought a chuckle out of Henry and Benji. Jeffrey glared at them, so they quickly shut up.

"That's enough," the sheriff yelled. "I won't have my name slandered in my own home."

"You're right, of course," Neil said in a sarcastic tone. "I'll try not to do that again."

While he spoke, Neil's eyes remained fixed on his wife. She didn't appear to have been injured, nor violated. He wondered what could have happened to prevent the sheriff from touching her as Jeffrey had threatened to do.

Her face relaxed when she looked upon Neil, but her eyes watered when she smiled. "My lord, what are you doing here?"

Keeping in character, he limped to her. He examined her face and body as much as he could, checking to see if there were any marks of any kind. Thankfully, there were none. "I've come to pay your ransom, but the sheriff won't take it."

Right away, Benji huffed. "You won't take it? Why not?"

"Shut up," Jeffrey hissed.

Charlotte glanced at the sheriff and scowled. "Yes, why won't you take the money?"

"Because I want your husband, that's why. He's going to hang. I'll see to that personally." He turned to Lord Thatcher. "Now that you know I haven't harmed her, are you satisfied? Will you return home?"

"I'm satisfied. In fact, I believe you and your friends are worse off than I first realized. I'm certain I don't know how you have put up with her complaining this long."

Franklin laughed as Neil turned to walk out of the room with him.

"You're right," Jeffrey said. "It's been hard. She has a sharp tongue, that's for certain. But all you have to do is look at her, and she stirs your loins. I don't think I have to tell you that."

Neil glanced over his shoulder to look at her again. Tears were in her eyes and her brows were drawn with worry. Just looking into her lovely face made his heart melt.

He had to rescue her. But finding a way without showing his true identity was going to be a great effort. And if he wasn't careful, they would both end up in more danger…or dead.

Chapter Nineteen

Neil paced the floor, using Lord Thatcher's cane for support as he remained in his disguise. Seconds ticked by, minutes, and hours, and he couldn't stand the wait. Jeffrey Franklin sat in his chair, appearing patient as he sipped his tea, calm and collected like a damn woman.

Neil didn't know what would happen next, and the uncertainty of the situation made his heart burn with terror. Would they harm Charlotte? Would he be able to stop them before they did? Could he rescue her as he'd done before without complications? With a sinking feeling, he doubted his own ability. Too many players stopped him this time.

Footsteps clomped up the stairs from the cellar. Neil stopped and turned toward the hallway, waiting to see who came. Henry marched into the parlor, his face set hard in a scowl when he looked at the sheriff.

"She's demanding to see Lord Thatcher again," Henry barked.

Jeffrey sighed heavily in irritation. "Can't you clumsy oafs control her? I'm certain you've dealt with women like her in your miserable lives before."

"No, we haven't. Not anything like this tornado. She's got a wicked tongue," Henry mumbled.

Jeffrey glanced at Neil then back to Henry. "Why does she want to see him?"

"Don't know. She won't say."

Neil spoke, making his voice deep and raspy like Adam's. "Perhaps she's bored with your company."

"No matter," Jeffrey quickly cut in. "Tell the

woman she cannot see Lord Thatcher."

"I'll go see what she wants," Neil said, ignoring the other man's instructions. "I'm certain she just wants to be reassured I'm still here."

Jeffrey scowled openly, letting his irritation show through his distasteful grunt of annoyance. "All right, you can go, Lord Thatcher, but just for a moment." He rose from his chair and followed behind Neil as he hurried down the stairs.

Neil entered the room. Charlotte's mouth was pulled with worry. He walked to her and bent to her level, peering into her eyes. "How are you holding up, my dear?"

Charlotte eyes misted. "I...I..." She motioned with her head for him to come closer.

He bent further and she whispered in his ear what she needed. A smile spread across his face as he straightened. "It appears," he directed his comment to Jeffrey, "that you and your men haven't considered the needs of a woman." By their drawn expression, Neil could see the men were still mystified, so he said succinctly, "She needs to use the privy."

Henry and Benji chuckled. Jeffrey rolled his eyes heavenward. Charlotte passed him a scarlet-faced scowl.

"Then, I suppose we'd better let her go relieve herself." Jeffrey untied her arms.

"Thank you," Charlotte snapped, rubbing her wrists. "Do you mind if Lord Thatcher takes me? I'd rather have a gentleman escort me instead of farm animals like you and your friends."

Jeffrey nodded. "That's acceptable, but we'll be watching closely."

Charlotte hurried into the privy, not saying a word. Neil stood guard, relieved the other three men were farther away.

"When are you going to get me out of here?" she

whispered through the wooden door.

"Patience, my dear. I'm biding my time until a friend of mine arrives. He works for the mayor and will be able to clear me from these false charges."

"When will that be?"

"I don't know. Soon, I hope."

"What am I to do during that time?"

"Keep irritating Henry and Benji. That will keep your mind busy." He paused, then asked, "Where's Jacqueline?"

"I don't know. The sheriff took me downstairs without her." There was a brief pause. "Neil?" she whispered.

"Yes?"

"I'm...sorry."

His heart lightened, and he wished he could take her in his arms. "For what, my sweet?"

"For...well, for yesterday. I have a quick temper and I allowed it to explode before thinking things over."

Neil closed his eyes, keeping his blissful emotions inside for now. "Do you know I never meant to hurt you?"

"Yes."

He sighed heavily with relief and looked at the door. "Charlotte?" he asked, touching the wood, imagining he touched her instead.

"Yes?"

"I love you."

"I love you, too, Neil." She stepped out and gazed at him. Her eyes were moist. "How can I make up to you what I've put you through?"

He chuckled. "The same way I will make it up to you."

From the corner of his eyes, Neil spotted Jeffrey walking their way. He took a step away from Charlotte and turned toward the sheriff, getting back in his Lord Thatcher character.

"Are you ready, Mrs. Hamilton?" the sheriff asked. "We don't want to be out here for very long."

She glared at him. "Why? Are you afraid Neil will come rescue me and you won't be able to do a thing about it?"

Jeffrey grabbed her by the arm and pulled her back into the house. Neil kept in step behind them, hiding his fists in the folds of his cape.

Once inside, Jeffrey pushed her toward Henry. "Take her downstairs, and tie her up," he snapped.

"'ow much longer do we 'ave to wait?" Benji asked, a whine in his voice.

Jeffrey glanced at Lord Thatcher, then back to his brother, sighing heavily. "Let's give him four more hours, but that's all." He turned and marched into the parlor.

Charlotte took one more look at Neil before they dragged her downstairs. Her eyes stung with the tears she refused to shed. Not now. She had to be strong. But the wait nearly killed her. She wanted to be back in her husband's arms, making up for everything that had happened lately.

"You're a feisty wench," Benji barked when he pushed her in the chair. Henry knelt behind her and tied her hands with rope.

When the band tightened, she cried out. "Do they have to be so tight? My hands will go numb."

"Too bad yer mouth don't go numb," Henry replied, getting a laugh from Benji.

She threw a glare over her shoulder, aimed at the larger man. But somehow, she needed to get one of them on her side. Out of the two, Benji looked the most submissive. Hopefully, she could use her womanly charms and persuade the sheriff's brother to help her. Of course, she'd have to be nice to them, which might be harder than she realized.

"I want Benji to tie my hands."

"Why?" Henry asked, rising from his position

and walking in front of her.

"Because he's gentler. Two years ago, he was always nicer to me, too."

She noticed Benji's smile widen. "You remembered?"

"I remember a lot of things."

"Well, too damn bad," Henry snapped. "This isn't one of your little tea parties, you know. You're our prisoner, and you'll be treated like one."

Lifting her chin, she ignored the bulky man beside her and put her attention on Benji. "Would you mind answering a question for me?"

Benji nodded.

"How long have you been working alongside your brother, Jeffrey?"

"Several years now."

She shook her head. "I just don't understand why you would want to be in business with somebody like him."

Benji moved in closer, wearing a scowl. "Just what's that supposed to mean, lady?"

His ugly face frightened her, but she knew he was not allowed to lay a hand on her, thanks to the sheriff, so she decided to let her razor-sharp tongue loose. "He's an imbecile. He's possibly the worst man to do business with. I'm amazed you even trust the lout."

Benji's eyes darkened. "'e's my brother."

"Then why is he not as honest and devoted to you as you are with him?"

Benji shook his head in confusion. "Huh?"

"He's a very greedy man. Granted, I haven't known him for very long, but I've realized this particular trait in him, nonetheless." She hesitated for a brief moment so they'd absorb what she was saying. "I just cannot understand why you would want him to be your partner if it's obvious he'll go behind your back and deceive you."

"You know nothing, lady!" Benji yelled.

"Hasn't he deceived you before? Look at those items right over there." She pointed with her head to the small room on her left, which held items the sheriff had taken from Neil's clients. "Has your brother even told you about taking those things? Has he even shared any of them with you?"

Slowly the two dimwits moved to the stash and looked through the items.

"Do you see all that jewelry?" she asked. "Has he even offered any to you?"

"'e would've told us sooner or later," Benji defended.

"No, he wouldn't. Do you know how long he has had these things? Do you think you'd know anything about it if he hadn't made you bring me down here?"

Benji shook his head, still denying.

But Charlotte wouldn't give up. "At least a month, right? Has he spoken to you during that time?"

He nodded.

"And, did he mention to you he had all this jewelry worth so much money?"

"No," he said a little softer. "But that doesn't matter. Besides, he finally told us."

"Not until after I had mentioned something first. And when the topic was finally brought up, he tried to change the subject quickly, hoping you'd soon forget."

Benji shook his head. "But now we know. 'e'll share."

"So, you're not afraid he'll take the ransom money and keep it himself?"

"Listen, lady, my brother will share the ransom money, and 'specially this newly acquired treasure."

"What if he doesn't?"

"My brother knows what 'e's doing. We follow him because 'e's more educated. 'e is never wrong with 'is ideas."

"Except, of course, for this time."

Henry stepped forward, his massive arms crossed over his chest. "Now, what are ye yapping about?"

The wheels in her mind turned like crazy, trying to find some way for these two men to doubt their so-called leader. "Well, the sheriff thought he had this whole thing planned, and so far, it's not turning out the way he wanted. Look how long you've been with him, and you're not rich yet. But, on the other hand, the sheriff is very wealthy. He owns a townhouse and this cottage. Isn't it obvious he's using the two of you, yet he's not paying up?"

She could tell she hit a nerve with them, because their expressions looked actually clear, as if a light had come on inside their tiny little brains. Maybe, they would see the sheriff as she saw him.

Benji shrugged. "Well...perhaps 'e's getting paid better than we thought."

"Benji," Henry warned to keep quiet, but the other man continued.

"Jeffrey means well, but I'm sure 'e's been too busy—"

"Benji, the woman doesn't need to know."

"But we 'ave always been a team," Benji continued. "Jeffrey 'as always led us...although most of the time it 'as turned out badly."

"Benji. That's enough," Henry snapped. "Can't ye see what she's doing? She's trying to make us doubt him. She wants us on her side." His gaze switched from Benji to Charlotte. "But it ain't gonna work. I can see through that brave mask yer wearing, and yer scared to death, so don't try and trick us. We're actually smarter than ya seem to think."

Charlotte sighed in defeat. Now what could she do?

****

While Jeffrey hurried outside, Neil rushed through the small cottage, looking for Jacqueline. There wasn't a trace of her anywhere. Would the sheriff have just let her go? Perhaps she escaped and was finding help right now. Neil wished that were the case, but he didn't want to depend on Jacqueline. The woman was very weak and dependent on the sheriff for everything. It had something to do with her past, but Neil didn't want to get involved. Not now.

Hurrying back down the stairs, he quickly entered the parlor before the sheriff returned. Neil had come back just in time. Not more than two minutes later, Jeffrey walked through the front door.

"Well, Lord Thatcher," he said as he entered the room. "It looks as if you were right. Mr. Hamilton must not care about his wife, or else he would've been here by now."

"Then, will you let me pay for her ransom?"

"But what are we going to do about Neil? If I hand Charlotte to you, that doesn't accomplish anything. You'll have the lovely lady, of course, but I'll have nothing."

"So what are your plans?" Neil's voice turned harsh as panic rose in his throat.

"I think we can come to some sort of bargain." He paused, then glanced back at him. "Let's go down and see how Charlotte is faring, shall we?"

Neil could read people well, and by the cocky expression on Jeffrey's face and the way he talked to him, Neil detected things weren't right. The man acted too nonchalant. How could the sheriff be so calm when it was obvious his plans were not going well? Alarm rose in Neil's head, and he prayed he'd know what to do when the time came.

Neil followed Jeffrey down the stairs, still keeping in Adam's character. The cane he used definitely helped with his disguise.

The warnings pounding through his brain grew stronger. The longer he watched the sheriff, the more he suspected something would happen soon. He needed to warn Charlotte, but how? Fortunately, Jeffrey gave him that chance when he left him by Charlotte and took his men to the corner of the room.

Charlotte's eyes were wide with wonder. "What's going on?" she whispered.

"Listen to me, darling," he spoke softly. "I don't know exactly what's happening, but I feel as if the sheriff knows something. Don't ask me how, but I get the impression he knows who I am."

"That can't be right. You've done a fabulous acting job so far, and he's played right into your hands."

He shrugged. "But, he's been different since he came in from outside. I don't like it." He touched her knee. "Just be ready for anything."

She nodded.

Neil's gaze softened the longer he stared into her eyes. He smiled. "Not to worry, my love. Your knight will save you."

Charlotte's eyes filled with tears again. "I know he will. I've never given up on him."

They didn't have much time to talk. Jeffrey and the other two were back. Neil stood and moved aside, letting the sheriff stand in front of his wife.

"Well, Charlotte, my dear, it looks as if your husband has not come for you. It has been twenty-four hours, and still Neil has yet to appear." He paused as his hand rubbed over his unshaven chin. "What I find interesting is that you're still proclaiming he'll rescue you."

"He'll be here," she growled.

He laughed. "See, there you go again. How many times do you have to be kicked down by that man to realize he's thoroughly unworthy of you? First, he leaves you after only three days of marriage, not even planning on returning. And then you have to come all the way here to seek out an annulment."

Charlotte crinkled her forehead.

Neil wondered how the sheriff knew this bit of information.

Charlotte kept quiet, although she shot daggers at the sheriff with her eyes. It was only a shame the man could not seem to feel them.

Kneeling on one knee, Jeffrey eyed her. "The only conclusion I can come to is that he doesn't care about you. All your husband cares about is his own freedom. He must know coming here will get him caught." He brought his hand up to her face, his knuckles gently caressing her cheek. "But that's his loss and our gain."

"I don't think you're giving him enough time. Are you even certain he received the message?" she asked.

"Oh, yes. I'm quite certain. Although you keep telling me he wasn't hiding out at the castle, I think he was."

"What if you're wrong?"

Jeffrey laughed. "My dear, I'm never wrong."

Charlotte grinned. "That's not what I've heard about you. In fact, I've been led to believe you're nothing but a greedy bastard who doesn't even care about others. All you care about is yourself, and in doing so, you make a mess out of other people's lives, especially your brother's."

"But of course." His wandering hand moved to her hair, caressing a long lock between his fingers. "Why should I care about others? They never cared about me. I'm the only one I can rely on."

Benji cleared his throat softly. "And your brother."

Jeffrey rolled his eyes and threw a glare over his

shoulder at his brother. "Yes, of course." His gaze moved back to Charlotte. "My dear, I get the impression you're stalling, but your time is up. And so is Neil's."

"So, what are you going to do, Sheriff?" Neil finally spoke. He'd been gritting his teeth so hard—he knew he'd kill the bastard soon!

Jeffrey continued looking at Charlotte. "Before I do anything, I want to do something that's been on my mind since meeting the very lovely Charlotte Hamilton."

Anger pulsed through Neil's head. That man was touching *his* wife! Yet could he stop him without revealing his true character?

Jeffrey's hand moved from her hair to her neck, then slowly slid down the skin the dress. Unfortunately, the dress she wore displayed a lot of skin, making it easy to touch her.

"I thought I'd get out of you what I missed on that day in your husband's office."

Charlotte's gaze flew to Neil, and he swallowed hard. "Sheriff, I don't think you'll get it this time either," he spoke in harsh tones. "If you remember correctly, I was the one who stopped you before, and I'll be the one keeping you from doing it again." He made a move toward Charlotte, but was stopped when Henry and Benji grasped his arms.

Jeffrey laughed. "I don't think so. You see, I didn't have my two gorillas with me before. I also have quite a few men outside, just waiting for my command, and they'll come to my aide. So, I'm afraid there's nobody going to stop me this time." His hand moved down, cupping one of her breasts.

"Get your slimy hands off me," she screamed, struggling as much as she could. Her arms were tied tightly behind her to the chair. Her head thrashed about side-to-side, trying to avoid his mouth.

Neil knew Benji and Henry were not as strong

as he was, but in order to overpower them, he would have to relinquish his disguise. He couldn't stand back and watch Jeffrey attack his wife.

The sheriff's face moved to her breasts and he kissed the exposed part of her bosom. Neil could stand no more. The man had to die!

"Maybe when I'm done," Jeffrey mumbled against Charlotte's skin, "the others can have their turn."

"Over my dead body," she cried.

"And over mine!" Neil yanked himself away from Jeffrey's henchmen and barreled headfirst into him, knocking him away from Charlotte. Neil picked up the sheriff by the back of the shirt and threw him across the room. Jeffrey thumped against the far wall.

Neil wrapped his arms around Charlotte, protecting her from harm. A sob tore from her throat. Suddenly, laughter came from Jeffrey, and Neil glanced over his shoulder to see what the man could find so humorous at this moment.

Just as he focused on the sheriff, Charlotte yelled, "Look behind you!"

Henry stepped forward, a pistol in his hand, pointed directly at Neil.

Jeffrey lifted off the ground, brushed his clothes, then walked to Charlotte. "Well, it seems you were right after all, Mrs. Hamilton. Your husband did arrive, just as you had promised." He gave Neil an evil grin. "And, it appears I have caught my man."

Charlotte stiffened. "What do you mean?"

Jeffrey moved next to Neil, grabbed the cane away and dropped it by his feet. Jeffrey reached to Neil's face and ripped off the scar, and with his other hand, took off the wig. "Behold, Neil Hamilton!"

Neil didn't move. Although he'd been caught, he wasn't ready to surrender. Henry's aim steadied as he pointed the weapon at Neil's heart.

Neil glared at Jeffrey. "What gave it away?" he asked. "Something must have given it away for you. You're not intelligent enough to figure it out by yourself."

"I have to confess, it was one of my men outside who discovered you. He'd overheard you and Charlotte talking at the privy, and figured it out when she called you Neil."

Hanging her head, Charlotte sobbed. She pressed her face against Neil's shoulder.

Jeffrey motioned his hand to Henry. The big ox's strong fingers grabbed Neil by the collar and yanked him away from Charlotte. She cried out. Neil reached for his wife, but when Henry clicked the pistol, Neil knew he'd better follow orders...for now.

Benji grabbed Neil's other hand, and both men pulled him away from Charlotte. Tears streamed down her face. His heart broke with each drop running off her chin.

"It doesn't matter now," Jeffrey continued as he walked to Charlotte. He lifted her head and bent for a quick kiss. When he pulled away, Charlotte spat at him.

He laughed. "It doesn't matter what you say or do, you still make my loins turn to fire." He turned back to Neil. "I now have the man I plan on ridding the world of, and my greatest decision will be whether I'm going to kill him in front of his wife, or do it alone with nobody to see." He rubbed his chin thoughtfully.

He looked from Charlotte to Neil, then back to Charlotte. "Maybe I'll kill him in front of you, but before I do that, I'll take my pleasures out on you while your husband watches, unable to do a thing about it." He laughed deeply. "Oh, yes. This is going to be such fun, don't you think, Benji?"

Benji grinned. "Can me and 'enry 'ave our turn with the lady after you're done?"

Jeffrey glared at him. “Of course not, idiot. I plan on taking my pleasures out on her until she’s dead.” He looked back at Charlotte. “It’s up to you now, my dear. Your fate lies in your hands.”

Chapter Twenty

The sun descended, leaving the sky dark with night. Only a few stars twinkled against deep velvet from out the window. Several lamps lit the room Jeffrey Franklin had forced Charlotte and Neil into. When she tripped on the hem of her dress, she stumbled, but Neil caught her and protectively held her in his arms. Agony clutched her heart. This may be the last time she would be in her husband's embrace. She loved this man more than life itself, yet she may lose him this very night.

Jeffrey walked in behind them, a superior expression on his face. Henry and Benji stepped in behind him, both cocky with ignorance.

"What's your plan now?" Neil snapped.

Charlotte wished the fire in his glare would somehow injure Jeffrey and his men.

The sheriff's laugh sent chills up her spine. She didn't want to hear what waited in their future.

"First off, Hamilton, you will kindly step away from your wife."

Neil scowled, and the set of his jaw hardened. "And, if I refuse?"

Jeffrey glanced over at Henry who pointed the pistol at Neil. "Then, I'll have Henry kill you."

Neil held firm, his arms tightening around her. "Do it then, for I'll not leave my wife to the likes of you."

Jeffrey growled. "Then, you'll die holding your wife." He shook his head. "You won't be much help to her after that."

Charlotte's throat tightened from the mere

thought. She looked up at Neil as tears stung her eyes. "Do what he says. Please."

Neil's forehead creased. His eyes moistened as he shook his head. "I promised I wouldn't let them touch you."

"You have no other choice. I don't want them to kill you," she whispered with a cracked voice.

She didn't see Benji and Henry move until they were behind Neil. Henry yanked on Neil's arm.

"Are ye gonna come nice an easy like, or do we need to use force?"

Neil mouthed to her the words she'd come to cherish. *I love you.* A tear slid down her cheek. He stepped away. The loss of his protection was like her soul being ripped out of her body, and she wrapped her arms around her waist, sobbing. Yet, it was the only way.

When Henry and Benji took Neil's arms in a viselike grip, she feared the worst. Jeffrey slowly walked to her, his gaze boldly sliding up and down the length of her body. Sickening waves sluiced over her, and her stomach lurched. If she'd had food in it, she would have emptied now.

Jeffrey rubbed his chin as if in deep thought. The longer he remained silent, the more frightened she became.

"Charlotte, my dear. The first thing I'd like you to do is take off your dress."

"No!" Neil struggled against Henry and Benji, but they held him tight.

"And, if you don't," Jeffrey continued, "I'll have Henry shoot your husband in the leg. For every time you don't obey, your husband will be shot."

She released a fearful sob, unable to stay strong. With a nod, she unlatched the buttons. Her hands shook uncontrollably, but soon the gown fell in a heap at her feet.

The evil man's eyes turned darker and more

lustful. "Good girl. Now take off your chemise."

She didn't dare look at Neil. From the corner of her eyes, his struggles were evident as he tried to free himself from Jeffrey's men. She kept her attention on the evil man as she untied her chemise and let it drop on top of her dress. Jeffrey licked his lips nosily. The urge to gag was strong, but she swallowed.

"Next, your petticoats."

She removed those, now standing only in her camisole and drawers.

Jeffrey stepped closer to Charlotte and touched her bare shoulder. "You're so beautiful. Just as I remembered." His finger traced an invisible line on her skin. "I could've had you in your husband's office that time. You would've liked it."

She glared into his eyes, hoping he'd be able to see how much hatred she held for him. "Don't flatter yourself. After having a man like Neil, nobody would be able to please me."

He tilted back his head and roared with laughter. "That's not what I hear. In fact, Jacqueline says I'm the best lover she's ever had."

"She lied to you so you wouldn't beat her. Besides, I happen to know she's taken another lover."

"Charlotte, no," Neil shouted.

She knew he didn't want her to make Jeffrey angry, but right now, she merely stalled for time.

Jeffrey's hands stilled for a moment as he met Charlotte's glare. "She has, has she?"

"Yes."

"You're lying."

She grinned. "Are you certain? I've become good friends with her of late."

Grabbing her shoulders, he roughly shook her. "Who is it? Tell me, bitch."

"Ewan Stout," she answered smugly. "She

prefers his mousy little body over yours."

"Impossible. Ewan is nothing but a lily livered pansy. He's just an inexperienced virgin. Why would she pick someone like him over someone like me?"

She laughed harshly. "You really have to ask? Isn't it obvious?"

He scowled and backhanded her across the face. Her head snapped to the side, her ears ringing, but she was still able to hear Neil cry out. She focused bleary eyes on him.

Neil's left arm flew from Benji's grasp, and he knocked the gun from Henry's hands. Quick as lightning, Neil spun around and kicked Benji in the knee, buckling him to the ground. Neil turned once again to Henry and punched him in the face with his elbow. Henry howled and stepped back, his hands protectively covering his nose.

Neil lunged at Jeffrey and tackled him to the ground. Neil's body imprisoned the sheriff's, but her husband still wouldn't relent. Neil pulled back his fist and let it fly through the air, only stopping when it connected with the man's jaw. The loud crack echoed in the room.

Jeffrey fought, his fists flying in front of him, but he couldn't keep up with Neil's punches. Out of the corner of her eyes, Charlotte saw Henry move toward the gun on the floor. She threw herself toward it, but before she could grab it, Jeffrey's hand enclosed around her ankle. She tripped and fell into a table. She stretched for the pistol, kicking at Jeffrey's hand at the same time.

Neil shouted her name. He yanked her away from Jeffrey and protectively wrapped his arms around her once again.

Over his shoulder, Jeffrey picked up the gun. She could have had it. It was in her reach. Now what would they do?

The sheriff regained his balance and stood. He

raised his hand.

"Neil, watch out," Charlotte cried.

But it was too late. Jeffrey brought the butt of the pistol up to Neil's head. Her husband's expression turned to one of confusion before his eyes rolled back in his head and his body crumbled to the floor.

Charlotte screamed. "Neil. Don't leave me."

Jeffrey turned to his brother. "Benji, you worthless son of a bitch. Why did you let him get away? Can't the two of you take care of one man by yourselves? Do I always have to save your good-for-nothing hides?"

Benji scowled. "That man knows the right places to 'it to make a man crumble." He rubbed his knees.

"Stand up, you gutless coward." Jeffrey's gaze switched to Henry. "And you, you worthless fool. Get hold of Hamilton and do not let him go. I want him to watch me make love to his wife, and I don't care how much he struggles, you two imbeciles better hold him. Do you understand?"

Charlotte tightened her grasp on Neil's unconscious form, shaking him, hoping he'd awaken.

"He'll come to, my dear, and when he does he's gonna watch me put my hands all over your naked body," Jeffrey snickered.

"You're nothing but a heartless bastard! Leave us alone and go scurry off to live your miserable life with the rest of the gutter rats," she hissed.

"You're going to pay for every single insult you've ever flung at me, my dear."

Growling, Jeffrey moved to her, bent and grabbed her arm. Neil's hand reached out and seized Jeffrey's. Charlotte gasped.

Neil wrapped his large, strong fingers around the sheriff's neck and squeezed. The weapon flew from Jeffrey's hand and he squirmed like a caged rabbit, clawing at Neil's fingers, gasping for breath.

A trickle of blood ran down Neil's head from his wound and dropped on Jeffrey, but it didn't stop her husband's angry strength.

"I'll kill you before you touch my wife again," Neil rasped.

Charlotte spied the gun still on the floor. She dove for it, but so did the other two men. Benji was quicker. Kneeling, he aimed point blank at Neil. Benji's hands shook violently and Charlotte threw herself at Benji's legs.

"No, Benji!" she cried.

"Let go of 'im!" Benji shouted at Neil. But Neil made no move to do what was ordered.

Jeffrey's gasps were getting tighter, his face turning bluer.

Benji's gaze moved to Charlotte. "Tell your husband to take his hands off my brother or I'll shoot him." He scowled. "I mean it."

She nodded and scooted next to Neil. "Neil?" she said softly, touching his shoulder. "Benji has the gun. Do as he says or he'll kill you."

"Then, let him kill me," he snapped, "because I'll not let go. I'll not leave the sheriff alive to harm you."

Charlotte glanced back at Benji, silently pleading with her eyes not to shoot Neil.

Benji growled. "Fine, if you don't let go of my brother, I'll kill your wife." Moving his aim, he pointed it toward Charlotte.

Neil finally looked at Benji. Immediately, he let go and turned to her, taking her in his arms, blocking her from Benji.

Jeffrey lay on the floor, gasping for air. He stroked his throat, massaging the red finger marks Neil had left.

"Give me that pistol," Henry hissed as he moved to grab the weapon.

Benji shook his head. "I can hold it."

"Son...of...a...bitch," Jeffrey rasped, still on the floor. "Kill him! Kill...Hamilton! Kill him...now!"

Benji took aim.

Charlotte's tears streaked down her face as she pleaded with him. "Benji. Please don't."

Benji's hesitation made Jeffrey growl. "Kill him, you worthless piece of trash. Kill him, I say." The sheriff's voice squeaked out in agony. "Can't you do anything right in your miserable life?"

"No, please don't," Charlotte whispered softly, her gaze never leaving Benji.

"Give me the gun and I'll do it," Henry snapped.

Benji shook his head. "No. I'll do it. If there's going to be a killing today, I'll be the one who'll pull the trigger."

When Benji's shaky hand subsided, she let out a cry and buried her head in Neil's neck. The gun boomed in the room, but Charlotte's scream was louder. It only took a few seconds for the smoke to clear, and Charlotte realized her husband hadn't moved.

Had Benji missed? She lifted her head and gazed into Neil's eyes.

He shook his head. "I'm all right."

Their faces went immediately to Jeffrey. The fleshy burned smell came from him. A bloody hole pierced his chest. Red pooled in the wound then spread in a widening arc in the fabric of his shirt. His eyes were wide with surprise. Confusion etched his brow, then turned to fear when he peered down at his chest. His shaky hands touched his blood-soaked shirt. He looked up and Benji and shook his head.

"Why...why did you shoot me?"

Heavy footsteps drew Charlotte's attention to the stairs.

Five men rushed into the room, Ian Fauxley in the lead. All held pistols alert and erect. Ian's gun still had smoke rising from it. Charlotte glanced at Benji, who stood holding a bleeding shoulder. The weapon in his hand still smoked, also.

Ian knelt beside them and touched Neil's shoulder. "Are you all right?"

"Ian? What just happened?" Neil asked. "Benji shot me, yet I'm all right."

Ian shook his head. "Benji didn't shoot you. He aimed his gun toward you, but before pulling the trigger, he changed his aim to the sheriff. Of course, I didn't know he was going to shoot his brother or else I wouldn't have shot him myself."

Neil's eyes widened. When Charlotte realized all would be made right now, a gush of fresh tears fell from her eyes. She buried her face in Neil's neck and sobbed. Ian's hand stroked her back.

"You're safe now," Ian assured. "There's nothing to fear any longer."

Chapter Twenty-One

The wind whistled around the castle. It tore through the trees and crashed against the double-paned windows. Neil tightened the blanket around himself and his wife and cuddled her closer while they lounged on the long sofa. The roaring fire kept them toasty warm, but he refused to release her.

The events from the past twenty-four hours kept replaying in his mind, and he knew Charlotte would never forget what happened, either. The sheriff had died from the bullet through his heart. Benji lost a lot of blood from his gunshot wound, but he'd live. Both Benji and Henry were arrested.

Charlotte sighed loudly and rubbed her face against his shirt. "This feels so good."

"I agree."

"I never want to leave."

"You won't."

"Neil?"

"Yes, my love."

"We should really do something special for Jacqueline. If she hadn't escaped and ran to Ewan, Ian wouldn't have found us."

"Yes, I can't believe Ian's cousin never received my letter for help. It certainly explains why it took so long for the mayor's men to arrive."

"We were very fortunate."

"I agree. We have many people to thank for saving our lives." He kissed the top of her head. "I love you," he said for the millionth time since they'd been home.

"I love you."

"Darling? What do you think of returning to South Carolina?"

She turned slightly in his arms and looked into his eyes. "Where did that question come from?"

"It has been on my mind quite a bit lately."

"What will you do with the castle if we return?"

He shrugged. "I don't know. What do you think I should I do with it?"

"You could give it back to the mayor."

"No, this castle was his way of showing his appreciation for my work and my friendship."

"What if you just rent it out while we are away? We can visit once a year if we like."

Silence lasted only a few moments before he nodded. "I suppose I could do that. To whom could I rent it?"

Her smile widened. "What about Ewan and Jacqueline? They need to start a new life, and this would help them out considerably."

"True. I never though of that. But you're right. I will do that for them."

He kissed her again, but this time, she turned her head and met his lips before they moved away. He kissed her this way for several minutes, enjoying the burst of happiness inside his chest.

She broke the kiss and stared up at him. "Neil? I think it's time to talk about our marriage."

He lifted his eyebrows and a grin touched his mouth. "What would you like to discuss, my darling?"

"Well, you know the annulment papers are still in my room."

Neil's heart dropped for only a second, then he realized the lift of her mouth explained her humor. He shrugged. "I suppose I could sign them if you don't think we're suited, although we have consummated our marriage—a few times already."

Her gray eyes twinkled. "And what if I'm with

child?"

Neil shook his head. "Then we'll have to stay married, won't we? For the sake of the baby, of course."

She laughed and held him tight. "I've been doing some serious thinking. I'd like to stay married to you, but only on a couple of conditions."

"And what conditions are they, my love?"

"You have to promise me to give me at least one child every two years."

His grin widened. "That can be accomplished, but you know, we'll have to practice for a while."

"I can handle that."

"Is that all, my love?"

She shook her head. "And I want you to always be the man I fell in love with."

"What about your Lord Thatcher?"

Charlotte shrugged. "You did have a lot of good qualities when you were him, but I'm not talking about that man. I was thinking more on the lines of that sensual, charming French man I met at the masked ball...just as long as he doesn't get tired of me when my belly is round with child."

Neil threw back his head and laughed. He kissed her on the nose and smiled. "Oh, my love, I gave my heart to you that night without knowing it."

She rested her head against his chest and sighed deeply in satisfaction. "Have I thanked you yet for saving my life?"

He chuckled. "You were the one who saved me. If you hadn't pleaded with Benji, I'm certain I'd be dead."

"I definitely did some fast talking while I was tied up," she said. "I tried to make those two dimwits see the sheriff wasn't going to share his wealth with them. I think it worked. I believe that was the reason Benji got fed up with his brother."

"No. I think it was looking into your intoxicating

eyes. You know, those eyes of yours make men do things they wouldn't usually do."

She smiled. "Good. Then I know I have a little power over you when I need it."

He laughed heartily. "You'll always have power over me, my love."

Charlotte moved out of his arms and stood. "I think I'm ready for bed."

"You are?"

"Yes," she said in a silky voice. "Now I want you to take me to your room and make mad passionate love to me."

"Which room?"

Her smile widened. "The lord of the manor's room, of course."

A word about the author...

Phyllis Campbell is an award-winning, multi-published, and best-selling author with Champagne Books, The Wild Rose Press, and Vintage Publishing. Most of her reviewers have given her the title of "Queen Of Sexual Tension." Married with kids (and three grandchildren), Phyllis has lived in Utah all of her life and enjoys family activities when she's not writing her next sensual story.

Visit Phyllis at www.phyllismariecampbell.com.

Other Historical Roses to enjoy from The Wild Rose Press

from Vintage Rose (historical 1900s):
DON'T CALL ME DARLIN' by Fleeta Cunningham: In Texas, 1957, Carole the librarian faces censorship. Will the County Judge who's dating her protect or accuse her?
SOURDOUGH RED by Pinkie Paranya: At the end of the Klondike gold rush, Jen and her younger brother search for her twin, lost and threatened in Alaskan wilderness.

from Cactus Rose (historical Western):
OUTLAW IN PETTICOATS by Paty Jager. Maeve had her heart crushed; it won't happen again. Zeke has wanted Maeve since he first set eyes on her...
SECRETS IN THE SHADOWS by Sheridon Smythe. Lovely widow Lacy had taken in two young children—and the rambunctious little angels wasted no time getting her into trouble with Shadow City's new sheriff...

from American Rose (historical U.S.A.):
EXPEDITION OF LOVE by Jo Barrett. An up-and-coming scientist in the world of paleontology collides heart first with an unconventional suffragette who has no desire to marry. Can they resolve their differences?
WHERE THE HEART IS by Sheridon Smythe. Orphan Natalie Polk steps into the shoes of the errant orphanage house mother. The new owner not only accepts her as capable of running the home but falls in love with her, with obstacles galore. How can they have a future?

from English Tea Rose (non-American):
HIGHLAND MOONLIGHT by Teresa Reasor. Seduced by the warrior to whom she is betrothed, Lady Mary flees to sanctuary. But she is forced to wed him, to save him from the executioner. Was her dream as elusive as Highland Moonlight?
THE RESURRECTION OF LADY SOMERSET by Nicola Beaumont. An age-old mystery, a risky assignment, a marriage devised to suppress a secret... Lark has been hidden most of her life. With the death of her mentor comes the command to marry the new Lord Somerset. Without this marriage, the estate falls to his wastrel brother. Can either suitor satisfy the lady?

LaVergne, TN USA
09 November 2010
203984LV00008B/2/P